THE
DEVIL'S
ASSASSIN

Paul Fraser Collard's love of military history started at an early age. A childhood spent watching films like *Waterloo* and *Zulu* whilst reading Sharpe, Flashman and the occasional *Commando* comic, gave him a desire to know more about the men who fought in the great wars of the nineteenth and twentieth centuries. At school, Paul was determined to become an officer in the British Army and he succeeded in winning an Army Scholarship. However, he chose to give up his boyhood ambition and instead went into the finance industry. Paul Fraser Collard stills works in the City, and lives with his wife and three children in Kent.

To find out more, follow Paul on Twitter @pfcollard or go to his website: www.paulfrasercollard.com.

Praise for Paul Fraser Collard:

'Sharpe fans will be delighted to welcome a swashbuckling new hero to follow . . . Marvellous fun' *Peterborough Telegraph*

'It felt accurate, it felt real, it felt alive . . . The battles had me hooked, riveted to the page, there were times when I was almost as breathless as the exhausted soldiers' *Parmenion Books*

'A confident, rich and exciting novel that gave me all the ingredients I would want for a historical adventure of the highest order' *For Winter Nig*

By Paul Fraser Collard

The Scarlet Thief
The Maharajah's General
The Devil's Assassin
The Lone Warrior

Digital Short Stories

Jack Lark: Rogue
Jack Lark: Recruit
Jack Lark: Redcoat

Paul Fraser Collard

THE
DEVIL'S
ASSASSIN

headline

The right of Paul Fraser Collard to be identified as the Author of
the Work has been asserted by him in accordance with the
Copyright, Designs and Patents Act 1988.

First published in Great Britain in 2015 by
HEADLINE PUBLISHING GROUP

First published in paperback in 2015 by
HEADLINE PUBLISHING GROUP

1

Cataloguing in Publication Data is available from the British Library

ISBN 978 1 4722 3675 3

Typeset in Sabon by Avon DataSet Ltd, Bidford-on-Avon, Warwickshire

Printed and bound in Great Britain by Clays Ltd, St Ives plc

Headline's policy is to use papers that are natural, renewable and
recyclable products and made from wood grown in well-managed
forests and other controlled sources. The logging and manufacturing
processes are expected to conform to the environmental regulations
of the country of origin.

HEADLINE PUBLISHING GROUP
An Hachette UK Company
Carmelite House
50 Victoria Embankment
London EC4Y 0DZ

www.headline.co.uk
www.hachette.co.uk

To Dan, Mandy, Kayla and Harry

Glossary

———————————

bahadur	hero, warrior
britzka	long, spacious horse-drawn carriage with four wheels, with a folding top over the rear seat
charpoy	camp bed, usually made of a wooden frame and knotted ropes
Chillianwala	Battle of Chillianwala, 13 January 1849
chummery	officers living together sharing living expenses
dacoit	bandit/thief
daffadar	native cavalry rank equivalent to sergeant
dakhbash	Persian rank equivalent to corporal
dekho	look (Hindi)
doli	covered litter, sedan chair
firangi	derogatory term for a European
fuadji	Persian infantry battalion
ghats	steps to a river
griffin	nickname for an officer newly arrived in India
hookah	instrument for smoking tobacco where the smoke is passed through a water basin before inhalation

Jack Sheppard	infamous eighteenth-century thief
jawan	slang for a native soldier serving in the East India Company
jewab	answer
kick up a shine	make a fuss
kot-daffadar	native cavalry rank equivalent to troop sergeant major
kurta	long shirt
mofussil	country station or district away from the chief stations of the region, 'up country'
munshi	language teacher
pagdi	turban, cloth or scarf wrapped around a hat
pankha-wala	servant operating a large cooling fan
pannie	London slang for burglary
picquet	soldiers placed forward of a position to warn against an enemy advance
popakh	conical hat made of ram's wool worn by the Persian army
pagdi	turban, cloth or scarf wrapped around a hat
sahib	master, lord, sir
sarbaz	regular Persian soldiers
serrefile	line of supernumerary and non-commissioned officers placed in the rear of a squadron or troop of cavalry
shigram	rural Indian carriage usually drawn by two bullocks
talwar	curved native sword, similar to 1796 light cavalry sabre
Thuggee	cult based on the worship of the goddess Kali
thug	a member of the cult of Thuggee
tiffin	light meal or snack served at lunchtime
vedette	a mounted picquet
vekil	Persian army rank equivalent to sergeant

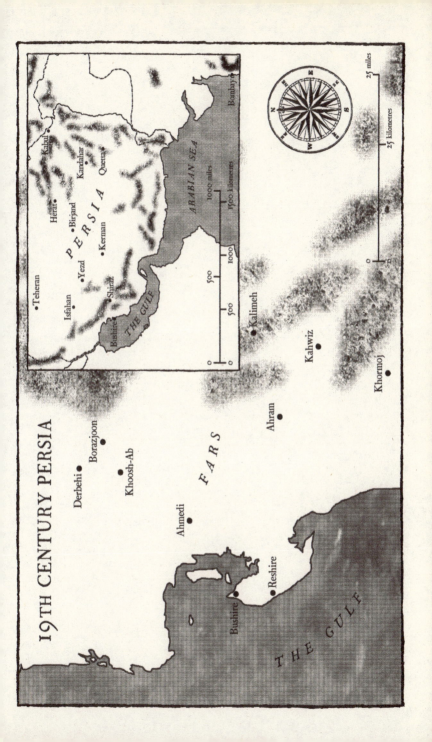

19TH CENTURY PERSIA

FARS

Derbehi•
Borazjoon•
Khoosh-Ab•
Ahmedi•
Ahram•
Kalimeh•
Kahwiz•
Khormoj•
Bushire•
Reshire•

THE GULF

25 miles

25 kilometres

PERSIA

Kabul•
Kandahar•
Quetta•
Herat•
Birjand•
Yezd•
Kerman•
Teheran•
Isfahan•
Shiraz•
Bushire•

THE GULF

ARABIAN SEA

Bombay•

1000 miles
1500 kilometres

1000
500
500

0
0

Chapter One

The valley was the perfect place for an ambush. The rider scanned the steep sides with concern, his hard grey eyes roving over the heavy boulders that littered the slopes, wary in the face of the imagined danger. He saw the places where men could hide, the positions where he would disperse his soldiers if he were not the one riding through the narrow, gloomy defile.

A small avalanche of stones caught his attention. Each fast-moving boulder kicked up a puff of dust, the thin, dry soil easily disturbed after so many months without rain. There was nothing to hold a man in his grave, the arid, friable surface reduced to so much sand.

The rider moved his hand carefully, unbuckling the holster on his right hip. He reached inside and wrapped his fingers around the hilt of his revolver, the metal hot to his touch. He felt the gun's weight, its solidity reassuring. It was ready to fire, the five barrels loaded with care that morning, each one sealed with a thin layer of grease to prevent a misfire. The rider had learnt never to leave anything to chance. He could never be sure when the dacoits who roamed the high ground and preyed on the unwary and the unready would try to take the lone traveller who rode the barren lands. So he prepared for battle each day, priming his weapons and hardening his soul.

His eyes were never still as they roamed over the hidden crevices, his senses reaching out, searching for danger. He stopped his horse and listened. At first he heard nothing, the lonely quiet of the high ground pressing around him. He was thinking of slipping from the saddle and putting his ear to the ground to listen for movement when he heard the rumble. It sounded distant, like an early-morning express train far in the distance. His sable mount twitched its ears, sensing its master's unease, its right foreleg pawing nervously at the soil as it was ordered to wait.

The rumble increased, the noise building steadily. The rider tightened his grip on the reins, shortening them and bunching them together so he could hold them in his left hand, his right clasped firmly around the hilt of his revolver.

He sensed movement to his left and tugged hard at the reins, pulling on the heavy metal bit forced into his horse's mouth. He jabbed star-shaped spurs into the animal's sides, forcing it into motion so quickly that its hooves scrabbled at the stony soil. As it lurched away, he saw the source of the movement . The heavy boulders kicked soil high into the air as they picked up speed and thundered down the sharp sides of the valley. They gathered momentum as they hurtled towards the solitary rider, careering down the slope, knocking other lesser stones from their precarious perch so that they created an avalanche that roared downwards in a wild melee of dust and stone.

The screams of the thugs echoed around the cramped confines of the valley as they unleashed their ambush. Ever since William Bentinck had taken over as governor of Bengal in 1830, the British authorities had brutally suppressed the followers of the cult of Thuggee. These worshippers of the goddess Kali had been the target of a concerted campaign to eradicate them, until only a few scattered bands remained, their brutal ritualistic killings a threat only to those foolish enough to travel the wild and lonely roads far from the influence of the British.

The rider reined his horse hard round, blinking away the dust that rolled over him. The inhuman shrieks of the ambush rang in his ears, drowning out even the heavy thump of his heart. The familiar icy rush of fear flushed through him before settling deep in his gut. There it twisted, churning his insides like a beast fighting to be freed, but imprisoned, held captive by the barriers he had constructed to contain it.

The first thug leapt over the fallen boulders, screaming like a banshee as he charged the rider, the naked steel of his talwar catching the sun as he flashed it overhead, readying the first blow.

The rider lifted his right hand. The fear was controlled, the bitter calm of experience overriding the terror of the ambush. The thug was close enough for the rider to see the animal snarl of hatred on the man's face, the bared teeth as he howled his wild war cry, the bearded face beneath the stained pagdi twisted with rage.

The revolver coughed as the rider pulled the trigger. The bullet thudded into the thug's face, smacking him backwards as if his feet had been pulled away sharply by an invisible rope. His corpse hit the ground like a rag doll, the contents of his skull spread wide, staining the dusty soil red.

The other ambushers did not hesitate. The rider had time to see the dirt on their faded robes, the tears and the rents in the worn fabric. The next face filled the simple sight on his revolver, the same visceral expression of hatred looming into view for no more than a single heartbeat before he pulled the trigger once more.

The man was punched to the ground, the revolver's heavy

bullet tearing through flesh and bone with ease. The second would-be killer crumpled, his pathetic, twisted corpse left lying no more than a yard away from the first.

The two remaining bandits rushed the rider. He got off a third, wild shot as they came close, but the deadly missile cracked past the ear of the nearest thug to score a thick sliver of stone from one of the boulders that had been meant to crush the rider into oblivion.

The rider gouged his spurs cruelly into his horse's sides, forcing it to lurch forward. He rode at the surviving bandits, charging his enemy. They closed at a terrifying speed, coming together in a sudden blur of movement. The bandits had no time to slow their wild attack and the rider was past them before they could react. The treacherous ground gave way under their boots as they tried to turn to face him. One slipped, his curse the last sound he would ever utter.

The rider had forced his mount into a tight turn the moment he had burst through the pair of bandits. He let the still-smoking revolver fall from his hand and drew his sword. It was a fabulous weapon, the kind found in tales of valiant knights and beautiful damsels. Writing flowed down the length of the steel blade, the swirling script etched deep into the metal. The golden hilt wrapped snugly around the hand of the man wielding the sword, its dark red sharkskin grip mottled and stained from use.

It was the blade of a prince and it cut through the fallen bandit's neck, slicing through the gristle to leave his head half severed, the blood darkening his filthy robes.

The last bandit threw his talwar across his body in a wild parry as the glorious sword whispered through the air, keening for his flesh. The rider twisted his wrist as he brought the weapon scything backwards, aiming the next blow even as the bandit attempted to recover from his first desperate parry, the fabulous sword moving quicker than the eye could follow.

The attacks followed swiftly, one after the other. The rider sat his horse as though the two were one single, monstrous beast, his skill instinctive. His pace never once faltered, forcing the last thug to scramble clumsily up the side of the valley in a desperate attempt to keep the steel from beating aside his defence.

The bandit screamed, his terror given voice as he slipped and fell, his notched and pitted talwar knocked from his hand by the relentless salvo of blows that came at him. The rider remained silent, even in the moment of victory. The thug scrabbled on the ground, trying to escape his fate. He had time to look once into the rider's merciless eyes before the tip of the beautiful sword pierced his heart, the rider forced to lean far forward in the saddle as he drove the steel deep into his enemy's flesh.

The rider twisted his sword, releasing the blade from the body of his fallen foe, then carefully manoeuvred his horse backwards, leaning from the saddle as he scanned the valley, looking for any threat that he had missed. A lone vulture met his gaze. The wizened old bird flapped its wings lazily as it landed on one of the boulders that had been meant to kill the white-faced rider. For a moment, man and bird stared at one another, the last two living creatures in the narrow valley contemplating the sudden arrival of death in such a remote place.

The rider slipped from the saddle. He wiped the sleeve of his coat across his face, smearing away the river of sweat that had run down to sting his eyes. The wool was heavy, the fabric poorly woven. The garment was not tailored to fit and it bunched uncomfortably over the rider's shoulders. The red cloth showed the ravages of weeks in the saddle, but its pedigree was still recognisable. It was a uniform made famous the world over by the men who sheltered beneath its folds. It was the red coat of a British soldier.

The rider retrieved his revolver, a wry grimace appearing on his lean face as he inspected the metal and saw the deep scratch that the impact with the stony soil had scored into its side. He paid no heed to the four corpses that littered the ground. He was long accustomed to death.

He walked quickly back to his horse, anxious to be away. He murmured quietly to calm the beast, the first sounds he had uttered since the four wandering thugs had launched their sudden ambush; then, with a single bound, he hurled himself into the saddle and turned his tired mount to face the path that had been partially blocked by the fallen boulders.

He let the horse pick its own way through the rubble, turning his back on the men who had sought his death, leaving them to the vulture and the other animals that would relish a feast of fresh flesh.

Another band of dacoits was no more.

He reached into the saddlebag that contained the ammunition for his revolver. He frowned as he saw how few cartridges were left. His days wandering the lonely paths were coming to an end. He would have to face a return to civilisation, to the people he had rejected for so long.

He gathered his horse's reins in one hand and urged it to pick up the pace. It would take him many days to reach his destination, but he was in no hurry. He had not set out to be alone for so long, but still he did not feel the need to find company. The days had dragged into weeks, the weeks into months, but he would not rush to find the future as once he had.

He would let it find him.

Chapter Two

--◆◆◆--

Bombay, October 1856

The British officer was sprawled in the leather club armchair, a week old copy of the *Times* laid carelessly in his lap. Three bottles of Bass beer sat on the drum table beside him, their precious contents long gone. The officer slept fitfully, despite the effects of the food and drink he had consumed. He was not alone in the guests' lounge. It was the time for rest, for slumbering through the hottest hours of the day, when all sensible fellows retired to the cool of the lounge or slunk away to their beds to await the fresher air of evening. The better echelons of Bombay society had only just returned to the city, and they slipped into a coma of indolence after tiffin, hibernating until evening arrived and the coaches came to collect them for a turn around the Esplanade or, for the more energetic, a drive to the splendour of the Malabar Hills or the harsh beauty of the black rocks at the Breach.

'Excuse me, sahib?'

The proprietor of the Hotel Splendid stood at a respectful

distance, contemplating the British lieutenant as he fidgeted in his sleep, the starched collar of his shirt bent and distorted as his head twisted from side to side. Abdul El-Amir was painfully aware that he had paid for the starch in the officer's collar, just as he had paid for the bottles of beer that had helped induce the afternoon's siesta. The lieutenant's bill had been unpaid for the last fortnight, a state of affairs that had inspired Abdul to rise from his own afternoon rest to disturb his guest's peaceful nap.

'Sahib!' Abdul was a slight man. He rarely ate, preferring to obtain his sustenance from the hookah that was never far from his side. Yet it was a rash man who took his lack of bulk for weakness. He might be a Muslim in a Hindu world but his connections with the local gang of dacoits made him a formidable adversary, even for a sahib. Abdul El-Amir was not a man to be crossed.

The British officer jerked at the abrupt summons, his breath snorting in his nose as he awoke.

'I am so sorry to disturb you, sahib, please forgive me.' Abdul bowed low at the waist, though his simpering smile did not reach his eyes.

The lieutenant rallied quickly, wiping a shirt cuff across his mouth and running his fingers over the thin layer of dark hair that had been cut unfashionably short. He sported several days' growth of stubble but was otherwise hair-free, something of an oddity amongst the fabulous beards, moustaches, whiskers and mutton chops favoured by most of the British officers who passed through Abdul's hotel on their way in or out of Bombay.

'What can I do for you, Abdul?' The British officer addressed the proprietor in the calm tone of a man well used to being in control. He gathered up the remains of the *Times*, carefully folding it before placing it underneath one of the empty bottles on the table at his side.

Abdul reached inside his cream robes. Like most locals he wore a long, flowing kurta devoid of all decoration. His sole concession to fashion was a fabulous scarlet waistcoat covered with the images of a thousand flowers, each picked out in exquisite detail, the fine thread and bright colours an indication of the garment's value.

'There is the small matter of your bill, sahib. I fear there has been some mistake as it does not appear to have been settled as I requested last week.'

The officer reached behind him to pull his scarlet coat on to his shoulders, the single crown that denoted his rank catching the light. The cuffs of the red shell jacket were green and the sphinx on the collar revealed that the officer served in the 24th Regiment of Foot. The sphinx was the legacy of a battle fought in Egypt against Napoleon back in 1802. It was an honour worn with pride by all who joined the regiment, a symbol of the men who had died in its name. A symbol the man dressed in the uniform of one of its lieutenants had no right to wear.

'How remiss of me. Here, leave it with me and I will see to it.' The officer reached for the offending document.

Abdul hesitated, pulling the sheet of paper away from the questing fingers.

'In cash?'

For the first time the lieutenant's annoyance showed. His hard eyes fixed on the proprietor. 'I will arrange for a transfer of funds. Cox and Cox will be only too pleased to assist with the transaction.'

'I would prefer cash. In the circumstances.' The smile was gone now. With a nonchalance born of long experience, Abdul turned and beckoned to one of his men.

'So be it.' The officer made no show of having noticed the heavyset enforcer Abdul had summoned to join the conversation. The man must have stood close to seven feet tall and was built like a brick outhouse. The threat was clear.

'And today, sahib, not tomorrow or the day after.' Abdul offered the bill, bowing at the waist as he held it towards the seated officer.

There was no trace of fear on the lieutenant's face, even with the bulk of the enforcer looming large over his chair. Instead he sighed, as if disappointed by the display. 'I understand.'

The hotel's owner sneered at the mild response, his thin moustache twitching. 'Thank you, sahib.'

He turned and waved his bodyguard away before leaving the British officer to his afternoon at leisure. He was not concerned that his unabashed approach risked losing him a guest. His hotel was always full, the lack of accommodation in Bombay forcing a steady stream of white-faced firangi to stay in his establishment before they went up country. Abdul made sure that the place appealed to a certain class of officer. His was one of the few guest houses in the city that could boast a bath for every half-dozen guests, and he kept the best British beer chilled and ready. For the more discerning guest there was even a ready supply of clean, beautiful women, available at any hour of the day or night. Abdul might be a violent thug at heart, but he knew what his particular type of customer valued most of all.

Jack Lark sat in his darkened room. He savoured the solitude, enjoying the peace that only came when he was alone. It had been a struggle to become accustomed to being around so many people after so long spent with no one but his horse for company, and part of him craved a return to the airy quiet of the high ground. A life alone was so much easier than one where others encroached to prod and poke into his affairs.

With a sigh he began gathering together his few belongings,

packing them into his worn leather knapsack. He kept back his one good uniform. The dress of a lieutenant in the 24th Regiment of Foot ensured he was not often troubled on the turbulent streets of Bombay, except, of course, by the hundreds of hawkers and stallholders desperate to have him part with the coins they believed he carried. The other officers and civilian officials would leave him be, allowing him a freedom of movement he could never hope to enjoy if he wore the simple red coat of an ordinary soldier.

He had spent two weeks in the dubious surroundings of the Hotel Splendid. He had chosen his accommodation with care, locating a place that asked few questions of its clientele. His first steps back into society were cautious ones, and the anonymity of a place like the Hotel Splendid suited him very well.

He bundled the worn red coat of a private soldier into a ball, stuffing it to the very bottom of his knapsack, hiding it away until he next left the confines of polite society and ventured back to the wild lands. He laid his few shirts and a spare pair of breeches on top of a blue uniform coat that was creased and rumpled from being hidden for so long, and added four freshly purchased boxes of ammunition for his handgun, ensuring that he had easy access to this most important of all his possessions. He had learnt that the bullion of his epaulettes could only be trusted so far. Sometimes there was nothing better than a fully loaded five-shot Dean and Adams revolver to ensure his safety.

Packed and ready to leave, he sat back heavily on the cast-iron bed, taking a few moments' rest before he moved on. The room was hot and stuffy despite the large window that was kept open every hour of the day and night. A thin grass screen known as a tattie covered the opening. Every few hours, one of the hotel's servants came to douse the tightly woven grasses in water. It cooled the room for a while, adding a delicate fragrance to the sweaty atmosphere before the heat outside baked it dry once again.

Jack had wandered his way towards Bombay thinking to find some anonymity in the bustling hub of the British Empire's presence in India. He had many pressing needs, the most important of which was money. Only with a full pocket book could he begin to rejoin the world he had walked away from. Until he could find a way to raise some rhino, he would have to live on his wits, finding the necessities of life where and when he could.

Wherever he went, he brought his past with him, a burden much heavier than the single knapsack that carried all he possessed. Bitter memories lurked in the depths of his mind, festering in the darkness. He had learnt to control his thoughts, forcing them away from the recollection of the life he had lived. He had not always been alone; he had once been an ordinary redcoat, planning for a future with the woman he loved. When that had been snatched from him, he had been left alone without hope and without a future. So he had stolen a new life, taking the identity and the papers of his deceased commander. He became the officer he had always dreamt of being, securing the station in life denied him due to his low birth and the lack of the one commodity that society judged the most important when selecting those granted the power of an officer's rank: money.

As an officer, he had thrived, leading his stolen company into battle in the Crimea. In the terrifying encounter at the Alma river, he had discovered the ability to fight and to set the example that men needed if they were to function when their lives were on the line. Where some found an aptitude for working with wood or for shaping iron, the art of killing had become his trade.

He had come to India in search of a new life, but so far he

had found nothing but war, his skills on the battlefield needed once again as the British authorities strove to oust the Maharajah of Sawadh from his kingdom. When diplomacy had given way to violence, Jack was once again forced to fight for his country, his duty tethering him to the British army no matter what his heart desired.

Now he was alone once again, bereft of ties to family or regiment. He had assumed the name of a dead lieutenant, a man he was reasonably certain no one would know in the eclectic society of Bombay, where he hoped to start again, far away from his past. For the spark of ambition still flared deep inside his battered and troubled soul. He was determined to prove, to a world that neither knew nor cared, that the product of London's vilest rookeries could achieve so much more than polite society allowed. It was the one honest thing he had left, and he clung to it like a recently converted soul clung to their new faith.

'Sahib! How may I help you?' Abdul sat up abruptly. He had been dozing; the hookah pipe was dangling from the corner of his mouth. He put it to one side and straightened in his chair, making a mental note to berate his hapless clerk, who had forgotten the strict instruction that the hotel's owner should not be disturbed.

Jack smiled. 'I have come to settle my account.'

Abdul simpered, the thought of money assuaging his anger. 'That is most gracious of you, sahib. I am so sorry for having brought the matter to your attention, but we all have bills to pay.' He spread his arms in apology, conveniently forgetting the implied threat he had delivered alongside the bill. 'You have the cash?'

'Of course, but I thought you might like to take part in a little financial transaction in lieu of the debt.'

Abdul's eyes narrowed. 'What sort of transaction do you have in mind?'

'I have a certain object that I wish to sell. I had thought to ask for your assistance in the matter.'

'What kind of object?' Abdul's accent became thicker. He could not hide the spark of avarice that the British officer's request had kindled.

Jack slipped a hand into a pocket. With his eyes fixed on the hotel owner, he flicked a single fat ruby on to the mahogany desk. He saw the swift lick of the lips as Abdul sized up the jewel, the flicker in the man's soft brown eyes as he contemplated its value. Jack knew he would be cheated. He did not expect to get more than a fraction of the ruby's true worth. But he was penniless and he needed some ready cash. He was not in a position to sell the gem openly; not even the uniform of a British officer was sufficient protection against the barrage of questions a legitimate dealer would ask. Jack was a charlatan and a fraud. He had to deal where and when he could. If that meant supping with the devil, then all he could do was pass the port.

'It is a difficult thing you ask.' Abdul sat back in his chair as if trying to distance himself from the precious jewel that had appeared so miraculously. 'I cannot sell such an object.'

Jack recognised the tone. The first stage of the barter had begun. 'I'm sure a man with your contacts can find a buyer. Even for a trifle such as this.'

Abdul leant forward. His hand reached for the gem, but he hesitated before he could touch it, as if he had become suddenly nervous. 'Where did you come by such an interesting item?'

'It was a gift.'

'A gift? You have some generous friends, sahib.'

'And you have an enquiring mind. Be careful it does not get you into trouble.'

Abdul sniffed at the threat. 'Do you have more?'

'No.' Jack's reply was firm.

'I may be able to do something.' Abdul smiled with all the warmth of a cobra. 'It is, as you say, just a little thing.'

'There's a good fellow.' Jack gave no impression of caring whether the sale of the stone would be easy or hard. His expression was neutral.

Abdul reached out and smothered the gem with his hand, snatching it away and hiding it in the depths of his robe with the speed of a striking scorpion.

Jack turned, and was about to walk away when he stopped, as if struck by a sudden thought.

'You wouldn't think of cheating me, would you, Abdul?' He asked the question gently, as if making an innocent enquiry about something as inconsequential as the weather.

Abdul scoffed at the idea with a short cackle of laughter. 'Of course not, sahib. But it would be unfair for me not to take some sort of commission, no?' It was hard for the hotel's proprietor to keep the glee out of his voice.

'How much?'

'Fifty per cent.'

It was Jack's turn to laugh. 'That's not a commission. That's robbery.'

All trace of laughter was gone. Abdul's face was hard. 'Non-negotiable.' He stumbled over the longer word, but there was no doubt he meant what he said.

Jack looked at his boots. He knew he had no choice, yet he wanted Abdul to know what would happen if he cheated him too badly.

The steel whispered from its leather scabbard. The beautifully decorated blade hummed as it slipped through the air, moving quicker than the eye could track. The razor-sharp tip stopped no more than half an inch from Abdul's throat.

'Do not cross me, Abdul El-Amir.' Jack's voice was like

stone. The tip of the blade pressed forward, caressing the soft flesh at the base of the hotel owner's throat. 'I am not a man to be taken lightly.'

Abdul smiled sickly, trying to ignore the threat of death that hovered so close to his skin that he could feel the heat radiating from the blade. 'Of course, sahib. How can you doubt me?'

Jack held the blade still. He knew his display meant little, but it was good to feel the coarse sharkskin under his fingertips, the power of the sword resonating in his soul. He reversed the blade, thrusting it back into the scabbard at his side. He hoped Abdul had not looked at the weapon too closely. The golden hilt was decorated with half a dozen other precious stones, each as beautiful and as valuable as the ruby that had now disappeared into the hotel owner's clothing. A single setting was empty, its precious contents prised free to buy Jack some time.

Chapter Three

Jack sniffed once before he buried his face in the collar of his uniform. He wished that he had thought to bring a fresh handkerchief to cover his mouth and nose and prevent the God-awful stench from making him want to retch. It was not a long walk to the esplanade, but he already regretted not jumping in a doli. He might slowly be getting used to being around so many people, but he had yet to become accustomed to the fetid air that lay over the city like an ever-present fog.

Bombay stank, no matter what the season. The stench of its bazaars had become quite famous; it was claimed that no other place on the face of the earth could rival its olfactory horrors. Visitors would recoil in disgust, and even those familiar with the filth and squalor of Calcutta would be shocked by what they discovered in the reeking streets of Bombay. Such vileness forced the white-faced ladies and gentlemen to hide away in the enclaves catering to their needs, and to escape to the cooler hills around the city whenever they could, deserting Bombay for months at a time.

Jack had learnt quickly that good water was scarcer than good wine. When forced to stay in town, the British enjoyed only such drinks as they could rely on. Hodgson's Pale Ale, Tennent's and Allsopp's beer were favoured over anything local, and the importers of European goods were able to generate enormous profits supplying the tastes of the Westerners. French wine and champagne were by far the most profitable, their high price making them the exclusive tipple of only the highest echelons of Bombay's close-knit and clique-riddled society.

But despite its horrors, Bombay was seeing improvements all the time. As more and more newcomers came to India via the overland route from Cairo to Suez, so the city's importance grew. The Bombay Golf Club had just been formed, and the ice ships that made the long journey from Boston now arrived every few days to keep the clubs and hotels supplied with the precious substance that made life in the broiling city bearable. The Byculla Club boasted a growing membership, even though its pedigree was barely twenty-five years old, the fashionable crowd seeking it out as a haven of culture and taste amidst Bombay's wild bedlam.

It was only now, in the cooler months of October and November, that Bombay came truly alive, the misery of the monsoon months quickly receding into memory. The esplanade was replete with pavilions set up to entertain the returning crowds, and the new horticultural gardens bustled with visitors seeking a refreshing venue for their evening promenade. The streets echoed to the sound of iron-clad hooves as carriages made the nightly journey from the ghats on the northern boundary of the city to the fabulous Hindu temple perched on the pedestal of black rock not far from the Breach, where foaming surf broke upon the black rocks of the shore.

Bombay thrived on its growing importance. The popularity of the overland route across Egypt was allowing it to overtake even Calcutta as the favoured point of entry to the wilds of the Indian interior. The city might have been filthy, yet nowhere else could boast such vibrancy. To be in Bombay was to be at the heart of a great adventure.

Jack slowed his pace as he approached his destination. The pavilion was full of noise and people, the sound of their revelry echoing along the esplanade. He had overheard a group of fellow guests at the hotel discussing this particular event and it had seemed too good an opportunity to miss, even though it would inevitably require conversation, something he preferred to avoid. Yet he had to eat, and with the price of his ruby still to be agreed, he did not think it wise to try to extract another meal from the hotel.

'Good evening, sir, are you bride or groom?' The major-domo greeted the tall, well-dressed officer with a slight bow. The breeze had picked up, sweeping in across the esplanade and into the huge pavilion erected to house the three hundred and fifty guests attending the wedding feast being held in honour of the marriage of the Governor's niece. The awning had been positioned with care and the wide openings in the thick canvas allowed much of the precious draught to enter the pungent interior of the pavilion.

Jack paused before answering, hiding his rapid scrutiny of the happy throng under the calm manner of an officer forced to deal with a trivial request.

'Groom.'

'Thank you, sir.' The man tasked with controlling access to the pavilion smiled as if applauding the choice. 'If you could give me your name, please?' He turned and selected one of two lists waiting for him on a table positioned near the entrance.

'Fenris. Arthur Fenris.'

'Thank you, sir.' The official began to run his thumb down the list of names.

In the background, the garrison band of the Bombay Sappers and Miners struck up the lively two-four time of a polka. Many of the younger guests cried out with delight at the change in tempo and charged the wooden dance floor. The celebration was already several hours old, and ranks of empty French wine bottles stood like a silent battalion on the huge sideboards ranged along one side of the pavilion, testament to the amount of alcohol already consumed.

'I must apologise, sir.' A bead of sweat ran down the major-domo's face. It had been a long afternoon and he was tiring of his role in the proceedings. He had been looking forward to sneaking away from his post and enjoying one of the half-empty bottles of wine dotted liberally around the room. 'Did you say "Ferris"?'

'I did not. The name is Fenris, not Ferris. There shouldn't be a problem. Alfie invited me personally.'

The official anxiously wiped away the sweat from his forehead. He had no idea who Alfie might be. There were so many young gentlemen attached to the Governor's new relation that he had quite lost track.

'Very good, sir.' He took one look at the officer's lean, hard physique and the calm stare that met his appraisal, and decided to retreat gracefully. 'Please go ahead, sir. Enjoy the evening. I hope . . .'

The words died on the official's lips. The British officer had already left him and was striding purposefully into the heaving throng.

'The name is Knightly. Once of Hampshire, but now stuck in this festering sore of an arse pit.' The man introducing himself slurred his words. He took a huge swig of brandy, rolling the liquid around his mouth before swallowing. He grimaced as the fiery liquid burnt his throat. 'God, I hate this muck.'

Jack grinned at the show. He took a more circumspect sip of his own drink. 'Then have something else.'

Knightly snorted. 'I don't like any of it.' He waved an arm to encompass the phalanx of empty bottles and stained glasses that smothered the table where they sat. 'I should've joined the bloody temperance movement.'

Jack caught the empty champagne bottle knocked flying by Knightly's wild gesture. He had been brought up surrounded by drunks. His mother's gin palace in Whitechapel was a thousand of leagues below this beautifully decorated wedding pavilion. He had seen all manner of men, and women, drunk on the filthy gin he had helped his mother water down. Drunkenness was a great leveller, its effect the same regardless of the rank, sex or position of whoever threw the bitter liquid down their neck. He had carried them all out on to the street, the stench of their debauchery thick in his nostrils, the stink the same no matter if it were a lord or a lad from the rookery. Yet despite all he had seen, he had never hesitated when the wine was being poured or the bottles of beer were being handed out.

He beckoned over one of the dozens of servants dotted around the room.

'Sahib?'

'Arrack. My friend would like to try some.'

The servant bowed low and nodded before scurrying off towards the entrance at the back of the pavilion that led to the separate awning dedicated to preparing the evening's feast.

Jack sat back in his chair, stretching out his long legs. He had made himself at home, eating his fill of the remains of the wedding feast before turning his attention to the legions of wine bottles. It was not the first time he had bluffed his way into such an event. With Bombay full of officers passing through, either travelling up country into the mofussil or on their way to board one the steamships heading for England, there were myriad opportunities for anyone with the gumption and the guile to make the most of them. So long as a man spoke correctly, possessed passable manners and carried himself with the right attitude, there were few limits to how far he could take himself.

Knightly belched. 'I always hoped to become a ten-bottle-a-day man. My father . . .' he paused as he tried and failed to hide a fart, 'now he could drink claret like you or I drink water.'

'I don't drink the water here as a rule, and neither should you if you fancy living for more than a month.' Jack offered the advice as he welcomed back the waiter, who had brought a suspicious-looking wineskin to the table. 'You won't like this either, but I've found I've a taste for it.' He emptied the champagne from two cut crystal glasses by simply tossing it on to the floor before pouring a healthy measure of the dark liquid for them both. 'Bottoms up.'

Knightly peered at his glass with caution. 'Is it safe to drink?'

'Safer than the bloody water.'

The younger man continued to stare at the arrack. He was a handsome fellow who wore the uniform of a lieutenant with the black facings of the 64th Foot. Jack knew nothing more about him and had little inclination to find out anything else. He had found Knightly slumped at the table well into his cups. Jack usually preferred to drink alone, taking his fill and slipping away before the party crowd thinned out too much. Yet for a reason he could not truly fathom, he had taken the seat next to the young lieutenant, seeking the company of a stranger to temporarily ward off the loneliness that dogged his every step.

'Have we not got any more champagne?' Knightly pouted as he contemplated the evil-smelling liquid that had been presented to him.

'I thought you said you didn't like champagne. Now drink up, there's a good fellow.'

Knightly licked his lips nervously before finally lifting the glass to his mouth and taking a tentative sip. 'Good Lord.' The young officer winced as the liquid ripped through his palate like a cannonload of canister.

Jack laughed at the reaction. 'The natives swear by it.'

Knightly took a second, less hesitant mouthful. 'I cannot see why.'

'Neither can they. This stuff makes them go blind.'

Knightly ignored the comment, holding his nose and downing the rest of his glass. He winced, closing his eyes and shaking his head like a gundog irritated by a persistent fly. When he had recovered, he wiped the tears from his cheeks and looked at Jack through bloodshot eyes. 'You see to know an awful lot about his place. Have you been here long?'

'Long enough. You?'

'Three weeks, four days and a few damn hours.' Knightly smiled sadly at the revelation. 'It's not quite what I expected.'

Jack snorted. 'So you're a griffin?'

'A what?'

'A griffin. It's what newcomers are called. You shouldn't worry. It takes a while to get accustomed to being out here.'

'It is nothing at all like home.'

Jack tried to hide his grimace. He had a notion that Knightly's home was a mansion in the country, with maybe a fine town house in London or Bath. Life was different in the rookeries. Boys like Jack were lucky to reach the age of thirty. He had only escaped such a dour fate by joining one of the recruiting parties that came to his mother's gin palace as the British army scoured the dregs of London's society for any lad likely to be able to handle a musket.

'Sadly, it's just like home.' He looked around the room as he spoke. The sweaty faces were exactly what he expected to see. There were the keen-eyed young officers carousing and dancing with any female under the age of forty. The matrons sitting in their cliques, gossiping behind fast-moving fans. The senior officers and Company officials, their bulbous chins constrained by starched collars, gathered in sombre groups, their heavy beards and moustaches slick with sweat or stained with fallen food and wine. He had seen it all before. From the officers' mess back in England to the gathering of polite society in the cantonment in the Maharajah's kingdom on the very edge of the Empire, the faces were the same.

Knightly helped himself to some more of the arrack. 'Goodness me, it's Mrs Draper.' He slunk lower in his chair, making a desultory attempt to hide.

Jack looked up as an elegant lady glided past. From the clutch of fat pearls around her neck and the princely diamond in her tiny fascinator, it was clear she was the wife of a wealthy man. She was a handsome lady too, with long legs and a narrow waist. Jack found himself staring. Her blond hair was cut shorter than was fashionable, something he did not think he had seen before. She might not have possessed the naïve prettiness of a young girl, but she was certainly striking.

'Who is she?' He asked the question casually.

'She is the wife of Colonel Draper.'

'And he is . . . ?'

'My colonel. And if she is here, then so must he be. Oh God.'

Jack grinned at his new friend's obvious discomfort. 'Should you not be here then?'

'I should've left a week ago. The battalion is up at Karachi. I am supposed to be with them.'

'Why aren't you?' Jack could not help but censure the young officer. He had spent time posing as a captain. He knew what it was to have to command subordinate officers like Knightly.

'It was a damn long voyage. I needed some time to recover.'

'You call this recovering?' Jack's reply was tetchy. The redcoats deserved the best officers. They endured dreadful hardships that often culminated in being dispatched into the catastrophic maelstrom of battle. They were expected to weather everything the enemy threw at them before they were unleashed to kill, with their bare hands if necessary. To have to do so under the command of callow officers who had not the first notion of how to lead them was a disgrace.

Knightly went grey, though not at Jack's biting reply. 'I think I'm going to be sick.'

He looked so abjectly pathetic that Jack forgot his anger. 'Come on. Let's get you some fresh air.'

He lifted the young lieutenant to his feet and half dragged, half carried him outside. On the way, he caught a glimpse of a frosty glare on Mrs Draper's face. He offered a rueful smile and was rewarded with a downturn of her lips as she took in the sorry state of one of her husband's officers, her mouth puckering as if she had suddenly tasted something sour. But he also noticed the sly appraisal she gave him. She was a cool-looking piece, but Jack saw the narrowing of her eyes as she studied his form. He repaid the look in kind. Mrs Draper was an undeniably attractive woman, with an hourglass figure that captured his attention. He had been on his own for a long time, but he was still surprised by the sudden desire he felt fire within him. The colonel was a lucky man. In his choice of wife, if not the quality of his junior officers.

Chapter Four

—❖—

Jack lay on his bed underneath three sheets and a blanket. The heat of the day had given way to the cooler air of the night. A few months before, he would have been sleeping naked under a linen sheet liberally doused in cold water. Now, with the rainy season past, the nights quickly grew cold and he was glad of the extra blanket.

He lay in the darkness thinking of Sarah Draper. His lust was like an itch that he could not reach. It scratched at his mind, keeping him awake despite the copious amounts of champagne and arrack he had consumed.

A floorboard outside his room creaked, interrupting his thoughts. There was nothing unusual in the noise; it interrupted his rest whenever one of the guests enjoying the late-night charms of the Hotel Splendid walked past. He listened for the next creak as the guest carried on down the narrow corridor that ran outside the three rooms on Jack's side of the hotel.

He heard nothing.

He came fully awake. He slid his hand under his pillow, wrapping his fingers around the reassuring solidity of his revolver. Every instinct screamed out in danger and he slipped from the bed, careful to keep it between him and the door. The draught from the window was cold on his skin, his naked body tingling as he felt the first twist of fear in his gut.

The room was dark, but enough light filtered through the grass tattie at the window to let him see the door handle start to turn slowly. He lifted the revolver, aiming it at the crack that was steadily widening between the door and its frame. As he opened his mouth to challenge the unwelcome visitor, a figure burst into the room. Jack caught a glimpse of bared steel before the talwar slashed down at the bed, the heavy blade slicing deep into the mattress.

There was no need for any further proof of his attacker's intent. Jack lifted his arm and pulled the trigger, aiming the barrel squarely at the shadowy figure who had burst in to murder him in his bed.

The revolver misfired.

His attacker saw the flash as the firing cap went off but failed to ignite the main charge in the first chamber. His eyes immediately picked Jack out in the gloom.

Jack caught a glimpse of surprise and anger on the man's face before he leapt across the bed, the sharp talwar slashing at Jack's head. He ducked away from the blow and threw himself under the bed just as the assassin's blade slashed down for a second time. He saw a set of fingers grasping the edge of the door as he scrambled back to his feet, so he lashed out, kicking it shut, hearing the yelp of pain as he crushed a second would-be assassin's fingers beneath the heavy wood. He had time to snap the bolt across the door before the first attacker's blade slammed into the frame, missing his head by no more than an inch. He twisted away, ducking low as he threw himself past the man who had come to kill him. He had left his own sword on a scarred and battered wooden chest under the window, and he dived forward, his only thought to retrieve his blade.

His hand wrapped around the scabbard and he rolled hard to the right, narrowly missing a fast-moving thrust aimed at his naked back.

He felt the madness of battle surge through him, the urge to fight, to hack at the enemy forcing all other thoughts from his mind. His own talwar whispered from the scabbard. He let the madness have its head, releasing the wildness that had kept him alive on the vicious battlefields of the Crimea and the frontier.

In the darkness of the room it was hard to see his attacker as more than a fleeting shadow. Jack released a flurry of blows, cutting hard then following up with a quick thrust, parrying the counters before slamming his talwar forward once again. He let the attacks flow, his sword keening as it cut through the air, the powerful salvo forcing the assassin backwards.

Jack went after him. There was little room for finesse, so he battered his talwar at his enemy, hacking at the shadowy form. The assassin parried the attacks but the onslaught was relentless. Blow followed blow until one drove the attacker's sword wide. Jack saw the opening and punched his own sword forward, a shriek of incoherent rage bursting from his lips. He felt the blade slide into the man's guts and he pushed hard, driving the talwar deep. The man's scream was piercing as Jack twisted the sword. The assassin fell to the ground, his hands trying to pull his torn stomach together.

The door was kicked open and another figure burst into the room.

Jack stepped backwards, away from his new attacker. The body of the dying assassin fell between the two men and blocked a controlled thrust aimed at Jack's naked stomach. The second attacker grunted in annoyance before launching another blow. Jack let the blade come at him, then slashed his sword downward, slicing at his opponent's arm. The blow was weak, the angle of the attack spoiled by the dying man, who flapped and writhed in agony at their feet. But the steel of Jack's talwar was sharp and it sliced into his enemy's forearm, gouging a thick crevice in the flesh.

'You bastard!' Jack twisted quickly, narrowly avoiding a counterattack. The oath came to his mouth unbidden, the rage of the fight coursing through him. 'Come on!' He punched his blade forward, his wrist already braced for the inevitable parry. When it came, he rotated his talwar, flinging the sword backwards, slicing the sharpened rear tip at his attacker's eyes.

The man backed away, as Jack knew he would. As soon as he saw the first movement, he threw himself forward, careless of stamping on the ruined body of his first victim. He leapt at his attacker, punching the golden hilt of his sword into the man's face.

He felt the vicious impact, the crack of breaking bone loud over the pant of exertion that exploded from his own lips. The power of the assault drove the assassin backwards and sent him staggering out of the small room. Jack went after him, battering his sword forward again, smacking it into the centre of his enemy's face. The second blow knocked the assassin to the ground. As he fell, Jack snapped his knee forward, driving it into the man's bloodied face.

The assassin crashed down, all senses gone, bludgeoned by the salvo of blows. Jack felt nothing as he reversed his blade before stabbing downwards, driving the point into the man's heart.

He felt the rush of blood on his bare feet as he turned back into the room, careful not to slip in the puddle that pooled around him. The first attacker lay still, his eyes open and staring, his hands still pressed into the bloody remains of his stomach.

It took Jack less than half a minute to retrieve his fallen revolver and to stuff the uniform he had worn the previous night into his knapsack. Careless of his nakedness, he left the scene of death behind him, taking the stairs two at a time as he made for the narrow alley that snaked around the mismatched buildings of the hotel.

In the alley he paused, his chest heaving with exertion, the cold pricking at his bare skin. Only then did he curse himself for having revealed his wealth. He had taken the risk willingly, his need for money overriding his caution. Now he knew it had been both naïve and foolish, and he swore aloud, his frustration building as he realised that his chance of getting the cash he needed was gone. He spat out a wad of phlegm before delving into his knapsack and retrieving his lieutenant's uniform.

He would have to throw caution to the wind and leave the shadows behind. He had no other option. It was time for Arthur Fenris to fully rejoin polite society.

Jack smiled as he thought of Lieutenant Knightly. The man clearly needed a friendly guardian. He remembered the rooms he had seen when he had carried the young officer home. Knightly had rented a fine suite at Hope Hall, a family-run hotel in the Mazagon area of Bombay. There was plenty of space, more than enough for a pair of young lieutenants to form a chummery as they both enjoyed their last few days in Bombay.

It was time to pay his new friend a visit.

Chapter Five

———————

'Arthur! Meet the girl I'm going to marry!'

Knightly staggered to where Jack sat in a salon just off the ballroom. It was hot in the club, but the anteroom was something of an oasis. The pankha-walas stationed around the room pulled diligently at the huge sail attached to the ceiling, producing a welcome breeze, whilst a dozen waiters stood around like so many bronze statues, ready to deliver a fresh drink at the crook of a patron's little finger. The Byculla Club knew how to throw a party, and Jack had been happy enough to accompany Knightly to the evening's entertainment. It certainly made a change not to gatecrash an event, and for once he would try to enjoy himself rather than just seek sustenance.

Jack looked up and scrutinised the dishevelled girl buried beneath Knightly's arm. She was a winsome piece with pale gold hair arrayed in tight ringlets. He searched her eyes for some sparkle of mischief, but saw nothing but a pair of glazed hazel irises that peered back in dull myopic happiness.

By rights Jack should have loathed Knightly. His new acquaintance displayed every characteristic that Jack despised in the officer class. He thought nothing of languishing in Bombay when he should have been on his way to join his regiment, spending the days sleeping and the evenings cavorting around town. He came from wealth, so never doubted that his future was assured, his progress through the ranks guaranteed by a family who enjoyed both income and influence. He knew little of the men under his command, of what drove a man to accept the harsh conditions of a lifetime serving the Queen. Of battle he knew even less, and when Jack had talked gently of what it was really like, Knightly seemed to think of it as little more than a game of rugby, where one side beat the other before it was time for handshakes all round and a jolly good tea.

Yet despite his background, there was something in his rakish charm that was simply impossible to dislike. He was like a playful puppy. No matter how many times he was kicked, he simply got back on his feet and wanted to play again. Despite himself, Jack found himself liking the confident young officer.

'What's your name, love?' He addressed the young girl in an attempt to find a redeeming spark behind the dull appearance.

'Dorothy, Dorothy Squires.'

'Dorothy.' Jack pronounced the name carefully. He gave the girl a smile, but she was too busy staring up at her new beau to notice.

'Isn't she just the most beautiful creature you ever laid your eyes on?' Knightly struggled with his words and Jack could see from the grin slapped across his face that he was already three sheets to the wind.

'May I be the first to wish you both much happiness.' Jack managed a smiled for the happy couple before returning his attention to his brandy and soda.

He heard them move off and was quite content to be alone.

He just hoped Knightly did not try to bring the mousy Miss Squires back to the suite of rooms they now shared. He did not think he was ready to hear the sounds of his new friend's nocturnal revelry.

'Lieutenant Knightly appears to be enjoying himself.'

Jack turned and saw that a tall man wearing the uniform of a lieutenant colonel with the black cuffs and collar of the 64th Foot was addressing him.

'He should be with his men, sir.' Jack rose to his feet quickly, immediately respectful in the presence of a senior officer. Lieutenant colonels were not renowned for their patience.

'Don't I damn well know it.' The colonel plonked himself down heavily in the club chair next to Jack's and waved for Jack to join him. 'Sit down, old chap.' The senior officer sighed as he settled into his chair. 'I will have a word with young Mr Knightly tomorrow and remind him of his duty, have no fear on that account.'

There were few other guests in the anteroom. Most were congregated in the large ballroom where the dancing and gossiping was taking place. The anteroom was a haven of relative tranquillity amidst the high excitement of the ball, and it seemed Jack was not alone in seeking some solitude from the noisy bedlam of the dance floor.

'Draper, 64th Foot.'

'Fenris, 24th.' Jack shook the proffered hand. It was his first formal introduction. His heart beat a little faster and he wished he had not consumed so many pegs. This was the price of returning to society, and he needed to be on his mettle. He had known who the officer was the moment he had first been addressed, his badges of rank and the details of his uniform revealing his identity in a single glance. He just hoped Knightly was still capable of recognising his own commanding officer and was sensible enough to steer clear.

'The Warwickshire lads, eh? A fine regiment indeed. A good friend of mine served with your lot. Got caught out at Chillianwala.'

'Before my time, sir.'

'I thought as much. You're alive, for one thing. That damn shindig near killed the whole battalion.'

Jack watched Draper as he signalled to a waiting servant to bring him a drink. He judged the colonel to be in his mid forties. There were traces of grey in the black of his hair, with a wispy cloud gathered together on one side of his heavy beard. He was a tall man and he had the purposeful physique of a boxer, with wide shoulders and no sign of the paunch or double chins that affected so many senior officers.

'So, young man, are you on furlough?' Draper turned his attention back to Jack.

Jack felt his anxiety build as he faced the question. The bulk of the 24th Foot were serving up in the Punjab, but it would not have been unusual for a junior officer to be in Bombay, on his way either to or back from leave. Of course, neither applied to Jack.

'I am on furlough, sir, or at least I am at the end of it. My colonel gave me shooting leave. I have only a week or so left before I must return to my battalion.'

'Damned pity! You youngsters need to be let off the leash once in a while. Peacetime soldiering can take its toll on the young. Although things are never quite as peaceful as they seem, of course. I hear some of your boys got themselves into a fight up in the Bundelkhand whilst you were away.'

Jack did his best not to sit bolt upright. He had been in the thick of the fighting that had seen a single company of the 24th drawn into a desperate battle for survival when they were attacked by the local maharajah and his men.

'I heard as much myself, sir. I believe it was Captain

Kingsley's company. They gave a good account of themselves, I am told.'

'Kingsley?' Draper considered the name. 'I have not met him. I know Blachford. He's a good friend of mine.'

Jack's instincts for danger flared. Blachford was one of the senior officers in the regiment he had chosen as his own. It was time to beat a hasty retreat.

'Well, sir, if you will excuse me.' He made to leave, but his exit was blocked by the arrival of another red-coated officer.

'Good evening, James, I'm glad I'm not the only one wasting my evening at this tiresome affair.' The man pulled over a third club chair before taking a seat opposite Jack.

'Don't I know it.' Draper turned and summoned the closest waiter to take the new arrival's order. 'But Sarah said we must come, so here we are.'

'You are a good soldier, James. You do as your general orders!'

Both men barked with laughter at the remark. Jack did his best to smile gamely despite the icy flush running through his veins. There was to be no easy escape. This time he could not fight his way clear.

'Fenris, this is Major Ballard. Works in the brain-tub. Ballard, this is Lieutenant Fenris of Blachford's mob. Poor fellow is enjoying the last few days of his furlough, although quite why he would choose to waste his time at such an infernal affair as this is beyond me.'

Ballard smiled at the introduction before offering his hand. 'Pleased to meet you, Fenris.'

Jack met Ballard's gaze as coolly as he could as they shook hands. The smile on the major's face did not meet the icy eyes that narrowed slightly as they looked Jack over. Ballard's handshake was cold and his slim fingers glided smoothly out of Jack's grip. He was clearly not a fighting officer, his soft, cool hands bereft of the dry coarseness of someone who fought for a living.

'May I ask what the brain-tub might be, sir?' Jack did his best to feign interest as he tried to find a way out of the uncomfortable encounter. The effect of the drinks he had consumed was slowing his thoughts, and it was taking an effort of willpower to fight through the fug of alcohol.

'I work for General Stalker. For my sins, I am in command of his intelligence department.'

'Ballard has his fingers in so many pies that it is a wonder he is not as fat as a cow in calf.' Draper had clearly enjoyed a number of drinks himself that evening, and he chortled with delight at his own comment.

Certainly no one could have called Major Ballard fat. He was slim to the point of looking malnourished, with the same pinched face as so many of the army's redcoats, although theirs was normally the product of grinding poverty rather than an aesthetic choice. His thin moustache was neatly clipped and his cheeks were immaculately shaven. It was clear he took great care with his appearance.

'It is not quite like that. So, Fenris, when are you to return to the 24th?'

'I'm to be back with the regiment by the beginning of November, sir.' Jack picked what he considered a likely date, answering the question with as much confidence as he could muster. He would rather be facing the Maharajah's famous lancers than the twin peril of two senior officers who would both know people who should be familiar to a lieutenant in the 24th Foot.

'We were just discussing the affair up in Sawadh.' Draper returned the conversation to the last area Jack wanted discussed. 'Although I expect you know more about that than I do, Ballard.'

'The 24th did well.' Ballard watched Jack closely as he spoke. 'I have the full dispatch on my desk. Written by a Captain Kingsley. A friend of yours?' He arched a neatly plucked eyebrow in Jack's direction as he posed the question.

Jack kept his face neutral. 'No, sir. I believe he is newly arrived in the country. He went straight to the cantonment at Bhundapur, where his company was on detached duty. I serve with the rest of the regiment up in the Punjab.'

'Well, if his account is to be believed, he did the 24th a great service. Sounds like he beat the Maharajah's army all by himself.'

It was hard for Jack not to snort in derision. Kingsley was a useless popinjay whom he had been forced to knock to the ground to save the man's company from destruction. Kingsley had spent the rest of the battle hiding with the sick and the wounded; Jack doubted he had even seen the Maharajah's men, let alone fought any of them. The only success the British captain could claim was to have been the single white officer to survive the affair. Jack was not surprised to discover he had cast himself in the role of hero of the hour.

The thought of the bitter fighting made him shiver, despite his best attempts to guard his emotions. He looked into Ballard's eyes. He had the feeling the intelligence officer was reading his very soul.

'He had a fine company with him.' He felt the calm he sometimes experienced in battle, the fear corralled and caged in the depths of his gut. 'The men would've fought hard.'

Ballard's eyes narrowed, as if assessing every word. 'Which is your company, Lieutenant?'

'Number three company.' Jack gave the answer smoothly. The real Lieutenant Fenris had been in Kingsley's company. He had tried to murder Jack in the aftermath of the battle and had died for his efforts, killed by another British officer. The memory chilled Jack and it took an effort of will to meet Ballard's gaze.

'There are a number of items in Captain's Kingsley's account that have me perplexed.' Ballard sat back in his chair. His eyes left Jack's for the first time as he summoned another round of drinks for the three officers. 'I have only read the report briefly, but I am sure he lists you amongst the fallen.'

Jack kept his face calm. 'You must be confused, sir. There is a Lieutenant Ferris who serves in Kingsley's command. It must've been him, poor fellow.' His expression was grave, as if registering the sombre news of a fellow subaltern's death for the first time. He delivered the bluff smoothly, doing his best to betray no sign that he was lying through his teeth.

Ballard smiled. It was like watching a wolf trying to look friendly. 'You must be correct, of course. I have only had the opportunity to read the report very briefly. It is rather out of my remit, after all. However, I do recall one other interesting item.' He sat back and ran his forefinger along his moustache. 'Kingsley goes to great lengths to describe the actions of a deserter, a man called Lark or something of that ilk. A charlatan by all accounts.'

The major seemed about to continue when there was a crash behind them. The three officers turned to see Lieutenant Knightly lying face down on the floor. Dorothy Squire stood beside him, her hand covering her mouth in shock.

'Excuse me, gentlemen. I must see to my friend.' Jack leapt to his feet, using Knightly's dramatic collapse to cover his escape. His heart pounded as he made his way to the fallen lieutenant's side, hoping that somehow Ballard had not seen the reaction his casual remark had caused.

It was clear that the intelligence officer was close to discovering the truth about Jack's identity. He felt a frisson of fear. He knew it was time to move on, to find somewhere he could begin his life anew. Bombay was no longer a safe haven for an impostor.

Chapter Six

'Oh God.' Lieutenant Knightly contemplated the puddle of vomit on the ground between his legs. He was sitting in an alleyway a hundred yards from the main entrance to the Byculla Club. The two officers had not gone far, but Jack was relieved to have put some distance between himself and the uncompromising scrutiny of Major Ballard.

'Sorry, Arthur.'

Jack barely heard Knightly's mumbled apology. His mind was fully engaged on escaping Bombay. He knew he would have to leave the city that very night. He did not know where he would go, but that did not concern him. He had drifted for months. To do so again held no fears. He would see what life held for him elsewhere, either far away in Calcutta or even in Madras. He would learn from his mistakes.

'You must regret ever befriending me.' Knightly had lapsed into melancholy. 'I'm a complete wastrel.'

Jack was barely listening. He had one pressing concern: he was penniless. He had been getting by on Knightly's charity, the young officer accepting the story of a botched money draft without a murmur. Before he quit Bombay he would need to secure some funds. His thoughts turned to Abdul El-Amir and the Hotel Splendid. To the ruby he had abandoned when he fled the assassins. Its loss grated. And Abdul had tried to have him murdered. He owed the hotel owner a visit.

'You must be sick of the sight of me.' Knightly raised his hands to support the weight of his head. '*I'm* sick of the sight of me.'

Jack wondered where Abdul kept his valuables. He was certain it had to be in the office where the hotel's owner hid from his guests. He was no expert burglar, but he could think of half a dozen ways he could sneak into the hotel unnoticed. Once inside, he would make his way to the office and see if he could retrieve the ruby. If he managed to find other valuables, or even some ready money, he would feel no qualms in taking them too. It would be a fitting revenge.

'You're not even listening to me,' Knightly accused in a voice laced with self-pity.

'What's that?' Jack looked down at the pathetic sight. Vomit had splattered the riding boots Knightly insisted on wearing even though he rarely rode in the cramped confines of the city, and he stank, the sour stench of vomit catching in Jack's throat.

'I sicken you. I can see it in your eyes.' Knightly was wallowing in his misery. 'I need a bloody drink.'

'No. You need to stop pissing around and go to your battalion,' Jack growled, his patience wearing thin.

Knightly recoiled at the fierce words. 'You sound like my father.'

'Then stop behaving like a damn child.' Jack's veneer was cracking. 'You're an officer. You should start acting like one.'

Knightly fixed Jack with a look of abject misery before he bent his head and heaved what remained in his guts on to the ground. When he looked up again, his face was red and blotchy, thick strands of saliva gumming his mouth. 'Help me, Arthur. Please don't scold me,' he groaned.

Jack was spared answering the pitiful plea as a couple walked past the end of the alleyway. His heart fell when they stopped and peered into the darkness, the sight of the two British officers attracting their attention.

'You there! That man there.' The booming voice of Colonel Draper echoed down the confines of the alley. 'Make yourself known.' The colonel's hand went to the hilt of his sword.

'It is Lieutenant Fenris, sir. Lieutenant Knightly has been taken ill.'

Jack saw the senior officer hesitate, clearly torn between the need to protect his spouse from the sight of a drunken officer and his duty to address the needs of one of his subalterns. After a moment's delay, Draper led his wife into the alley. Even in the gloom, Jack could see the disgust etched on her face. He watched her closely as they approached, and smiled as her nose twitched in distaste.

'Lieutenant Knightly, this is badly done. Badly done indeed.' Draper patted his wife's arm to reassure her as he addressed his errant lieutenant.

Knightly lifted his head and saw his colonel looming over him. 'Dear Lord.'

'Dear Lord indeed.' Draper was clearly fighting to control his temper. Jack was certain that only the presence of his wife was preventing a violent tongue-lashing from being brought down on the head of the hapless lieutenant. 'You will report to me in the morning, Mr Knightly. I am going to say my goodbyes to the battalion before I take up a staff appointment here in Bombay, and I insist that you join me so that I can deliver you safely to Major Sterling, who will be commanding the regiment during my absence. If you fail to do so, I shall order you to be immediately cashiered and your commission to be sold. Is that clear?'

Knightly's head moved in an approximation of a nod.

Whilst the colonel addressed himself to dealing with Knightly, Jack was carefully inspecting Draper's wife. Sarah Draper was clearly several years younger than her husband. She was far prettier than he had first thought, with slim, elegant features that had been delicately emphasised by a subtle application of make-up. Her nose was a little crooked, but it only served to emphasise the perfect symmetry of the rest of her face. Yet it was her mouth that entranced him most. Her lips were thin but shaped like those of a porcelain doll. They were perfect, and he imagined what it would be like to kiss her.

As he studied her, he saw her returning his scrutiny. Her eyes were dark blue, and Jack saw the sparkle of life deep within them. He matched her calm appraisal, feeling the flicker of desire deep within. They stared at one another for several long moments before Jack forced himself to tear his eyes away, lest Draper discover him staring at his wife.

'Mr Fenris, I would be grateful if you would escort Mr Knightly to his accommodation.'

'Certainly, sir.' Jack's voice was husky. He glanced back at Sarah Draper and saw her mocking smile. She had recognised his desire.

'I am obliged to you.' Draper's voice was clipped and he showed no sign of being aware of Jack's reaction to his wife. 'I shall write to your colonel and commend your sensible actions. I only wish my own lieutenant could conduct himself with similar decorum.'

Jack did his best to hide his amusement at the remark. He wondered what the 24th's colonel would make of a letter praising an officer who had vanished several months earlier. Out of the corner of his eye he noted the impish grin that had appeared on Sarah Draper's face as she listened to her husband's pompous gratitude. He was clearly not alone in finding entertainment in the late-night encounter. He risked a final glance in her direction and felt a warm flush as he saw that she was staring straight at him. For the first time, the icy facade slipped and she smiled before looking away, fixing her gaze on her husband and dipping her head demurely.

Jack stood silent, watching as Draper escorted his wife back down the alley. He stared for a long time at the tight behind moving under the folds of the soft blue dress, wondering if he was reading too much into the silent exchanges. Then with a sigh he forced the matter from his mind and reluctantly turned his attention towards the vomit-smeared lieutenant he had befriended. But even as he heaved Knightly to his feet, his mind savoured the image of the colonel's wife. He would dearly like to meet Sarah Draper under other, more intimate circumstances.

Tucking his arm around the bedraggled Knightly, he began the long walk back to their hotel, forcing the lustful thoughts from his mind. For better or worse, his time in Bombay was done. As tantalising as Sarah Draper might be, he knew it was nothing more than a passing fancy, one he would have to ignore if he were to ensure his own safety. He could not afford to stay in the city in the hope of seeing her again, not now that he sensed Ballard had scented his trail of lies. There was one last act he wanted to perform, Then it would be time to quit Bombay and try his luck elsewhere.

The Hotel Splendid was still in the quiet hours before dawn. The trellis was old, and it creaked as Jack gingerly placed his full weight on its lowest spur. A thousand insects erupted from the dense foliage of the ancient jasmine that had made the rickety structure its home, and he paused, letting the cloud disperse, his mouth and eyes screwed tight shut lest they offer an attractive oasis to any of the multitude of flying creatures.

When the crowd of insects had passed, he took in a last deep breath before trusting his luck once again on the aged wood that reached up to the single window high above him. He had spent the day preparing for the expedition as best he could. Knightly had wisely obeyed his colonel and was now finally on his way to join his regiment, so at least Jack had been able to get ready without having to explain himself to his friend. Knightly had very kindly paid for his rooms for another few days, allowing Jack to stay on a little longer if he so wished. But Jack intended to be on his way long before he was forced to leave the comfortable suite. There was just time to secure his own funds and restore his independence before he disappeared.

His lieutenant's uniform was not perhaps the most common dress for a burglar, but Jack wanted the security of his officer's rank should he be discovered in or around the hotel. He had left his revolver behind, trusting to the talwar hanging at his hip and a stout cudgel that he had bought that day in the bazaar. He did not expect to have to fight, but he could not have considered risking the escapade without his sword. He would have felt more naked without the sharpened blade than he had facing the would-be assassins wearing nothing at all.

The spars of the trellis creaked alarmingly as he scaled the wall. The scent of the jasmine was making his eyes water, the pungent aroma catching at the back of this throat. The heady smell tickled his nostrils and he felt the beginnings of a sneeze. He stopped climbing and tried to stifle the sensation. The situation suddenly felt absurd, and he had to control the urge to laugh out loud, the sheer folly of the midnight escapade catching up with him. He had imagined his career as an impostor ending in so many ways. Being caught sneezing halfway up a trellis whilst trying to burgle a fourth-rate hotel had not been one of them.

A sharp splinter scratched at his hand and concentrated his

mind on his task. He decided it was time to gamble, and ignoring the ominous cracks as his weight snapped some of the bars of the old wood, he tried to move faster, reaching up as far as he could, ignoring the burning in his arms as he hauled himself up the wall.

Handhold by handhold he clawed his way up to the single window that overlooked the alleyway. When he reached the stone lintel, he hauled himself up the last few feet, his hands taking a firm grip on the cold stone, and with a final effort heaved his backside on to the ledge, where he sat sucking at the cut on his palm and calming his ragged breathing. The alleyway beneath him looked no more than a few feet away, and he could barely credit the effort he had expended to climb such a short distance. The weeks in Bombay had softened him.

Carefully he pushed back the simple grass screen that was all that covered the opening. The landing inside was dark, but enough moonlight was filtering through other grass-screened windows to let him see. All was quiet. He slid himself inside, taking care to land gently on the tiled floor. He made sure to shut the tattie, ignoring the temptation to wipe away the sticky red handprint he had left on the stone ledge. There was no time to dally.

He walked swiftly through the sleeping hotel. He had no need to be silent: there were always people walking around the hotel, even in the depths of the night, and it was unlikely that any of the night servants would challenge someone they would naturally assume was a guest.

He took the stairs two at a time, his boots loud on the whitewashed stone. The inner depths of the hotel were cool after the exertion of his climb, but he was still forced to wipe away the thick band of sweat that covered his face. He wondered again at the sanity of his decision to add burglary to his list of crimes. He had known a few thieves in his time – his first orderly had been a regular Jack Sheppard – but he had never expected to be forced into the role himself.

A servant bustled past carrying a bucket that stank of fresh piss. Jack simply ignored his presence and kept walking, careful not to even glance at the young boy, who scurried on as quickly as he could, his attention focused on not spilling any of the noxious liquid he carried rather than on the guest wandering the hotel in the small hours of the night.

It did not take long to reach Abdul's private sanctum. Jack remembered that there was a small anteroom outside the office itself. He paused, taking a moment to compose his thoughts and to steel his mind as he prepared to force his way inside, then tried the handle of the outer door.

It was locked. Had he been a proper burglar, he would have known how to pick the lock, a basic requirement for any practitioner of the pannie. It was the sensible course of action, the need to remain quiet of more importance now that he was out of the areas where the hotel's guests would be expected to reside. He turned the handle a few more times in the vague hope that somehow the lock would magically decide to yield. It did not.

He stepped back. There was only one solution. It was time for the tried and tested method of entry employed by the British redcoats. He lifted his leg, aiming the heel of his boot at the space just above the lock, then took a deep breath and slammed his foot against the wood.

The door crashed back on its hinges. Jack was in the room before it had stopped moving. He saw the scuffed and battered desk where Abdul's clerk worked for more than a dozen hours a day, but he had no interest in the neat, copperplate-filled ledgers littering the desk. He looked up and saw the door to Abdul's private room, and made straight for it.

It was time to retrieve what was his.

Chapter Seven

***

Abdul El-Amir woke with a start as the door to his clerk's office crashed open. He had been sleeping at his desk, the hookah he had been smoking lying still warm on the blotter next to his head.

He had run the Hotel Splendid for more than twenty years, fleecing his guests since the day he opened, overcharging for everything he could think of. Every type of crook and beggar was at his disposal and he was not above having his guests robbed, swindled or even, on one or two memorable occasions, murdered. In all that time, no one had ever dared to try to rob *him*.

He heard the loud footsteps in the outer office, the heavy tread making directly for his own private room. He reached for his desk drawer, his thin fingers fumbling with the lock before his shaking hands opened it to reveal the stash of weapons he kept inside.

He eyed the door before making his selection. As he lifted his weapon of choice from the drawer, he felt calm descend on him. He sat back in his chair and lifted the hookah to his mouth, sucking hard to breathe life back into its smouldering heart. He was no longer frightened. He lifted a hand and settled his red fez so that it sat neatly on top of his bald head. He was intrigued to know who had dared smash their way into the heart of his establishment. He would discover who it was, and then he would kill them.

The door to Abdul's private office was closed. This time Jack did not hesitate. He kicked hard, driving his heel into the heavy wood over the lock and sending the door flying back to smash into the wall behind it. He charged into the room, very aware that the noise he was making would bring servants scurrying towards their master's room. He would not have long.

He stopped in his tracks. He was staring into the barrel of a revolver.

'Ah, Lieutenant Fenris!'

Jack looked at the calm, smiling face of Abdul El-Amir. The revolver was aimed straight at his heart. It was a Dean and Adams five-shot, a twin to the one he usually carried himself. He knew how dreadfully effective the weapon could be. At such close range it would kill him.

The owner of the Hotel Splendid smiled wider as he saw the look of shock on Jack's face, and his finger curled around the trigger, the smooth action pulling it back the instant pressure was applied. In the cramped confines of the office, the explosion as the revolver fired was shocking. The gun kicked in Abdul's hand, the recoil throwing his arm backwards.

He was on his feet in a heartbeat, knocking his chair to the floor in his eagerness to check the body. He raced around his desk, keen to see how sharp his aim had been. To discover if his latest purchase had been worth the expense.

Jack lay on the ground, curled into a ball, his legs tucked to his chest. His ears rang from the blast of the revolver but he did his best to still his racing heart. He opened his eyes a fraction and saw the white robe rush round the desk. He could just make out the red velvet slippers underneath its heavy hem, and he watched for them to come to a halt as the man who had just tried to kill him stood over what should have been a bloody, tattered corpse.

He had felt a wave of terror rush through his veins as he saw the implacable face behind the weapon. He had believed he was entering an empty office. Instead he had found a room where death waited patiently for him to arrive. In desperation he had thrown himself to the ground just before Abdul pulled the trigger, gambling that the hotel owner would not be able to follow his movement in the excitement of opening fire. His breath had been driven from his body by the hard landing on the scuffed tiled floor, the hilt of his sword driven painfully into his ribs. But he had screwed his eyes tight against the pain, holding back the rage that followed the first icy rush of fear. His fingers closed over the weapon he had bought that afternoon in the bazaar, and he pulled it free, readying it for use.

Now he roared as he launched himself to his feet. The cudgel cut through the air and slammed into Abdul's belly. There was just enough time to see the horror and surprise on the man's thin features before the force of the blow bent him double, his fez tumbling to the ground and rolling to bump against the wall under the room's only window.

Jack chopped the cudgel downwards, bludgeoning the hotel owner to the floor. He was on him in a heartbeat, twisting the frail body around, his fingers digging into the sparse flesh without mercy as he forced the battered hotel owner on to his back.

'Hello, Abdul.' Jack leered down into the face of the man who had cheated him. 'That wasn't a very friendly way to greet your business partner, now was it?'

Abdul El-Amir's eyes were glazed. He opened his mouth but

nothing came out save a thin trickle of blood from where his lips had been crushed against his teeth by the hard landing on the floor.

Jack had no time for pity. He slapped the man once across the face, bringing him to his senses.

'Where's my bloody ruby?'

Abdul lifted his hands as if trying to shoo his attacker away, only for Jack to knock them to one side. The tall British officer straddled the hotel owner's thin body, his weight pressing down and threatening to suffocate Abdul where he lay. He would not move until he had what he had come for.

'I don't know—'

Jack slapped Abdul's face for a second time, cutting off the words in mid flow. 'Enough. Don't go kicking up a fucking shine. Where is it?'

Abdul closed his eyes in an attempt to escape his ruthless attacker, but Jack was in too much of a hurry to be merciful. He shook the man by the shoulders, careless of banging the back of his head hard against the floor.

He heard footsteps outside, and looked up in time to see the horrified face of a young boy of no more than ten years old peering into his master's office. The youngster shrieked in astonishment at what he saw before taking to his heels, screaming for all he was worth.

There was no time left.

Jack hauled Abdul to his feet. The man weighed nothing and Jack slammed him against the wall. He reached down and plucked the forgotten revolver from the floor before pressing it against the base of the shaking hotel owner's neck.

'You cheated me,' he snarled as he ground the barrel of the weapon into the man's flesh. 'You took what was mine and then you sent those dogs to kill me.' He heard a squeal of protest but he ignored it. 'I bet you got a nasty bloody surprise when you found the bodies. That wasn't part of your plan, now was it?'

He heard more shouts and screams echoing around the hotel. He knew he only had moments before some of the hotel's guards arrived to save their master.

'So now I am going to kill you. You understand?' He pushed his face forward so he could growl the words directly into Abdul's ear. 'I'm going to blow your fucking brains out.' Spittle was flung from his lips to land on the terrified man's face. 'And I hope it fucking hurts.'

He pulled back, stretching his arm taut as he prepared to fire the revolver. As he did so, he heard the sound of running water. Abdul El-Amir, proud owner of the Hotel Splendid, had pissed himself.

'This is your last fucking chance, you shit-eating toad. Where's my ruby?'

Jack's eyes kept flicking to the open door. At any second he expected to see a rush of people come running to their master's rescue. He was prepared to change his aim, ready to send a flurry of shots into the first men he saw.

Abdul was waving his arm, pointing to the wall furthest from the door.

'Where?' Jack screamed the word. He took up the tension on the trigger, making the gun's chamber revolve so that a fresh cartridge was beneath the hammer.

'Under the floor.' The words were barely intelligible. Jack risked a glance over his shoulder. He saw the rug on the floor against the wall. It was an odd place for a fine Persian rug, and at once he understood the hotel owner's terrified gestures.

'If you move one fucking muscle, you're dead.' He was already backing away as he made the threat. He kicked the red and gold rug to one side and saw the small ring handle buried in the floor. Keeping the revolver aimed at the hotel's owner, he squatted and tugged at the handle. The hidden cache opened easily, the mechanism well oiled and silent. The hiding place held a single wooden casket secured by a padlock. It was small, no bigger than an army shako, but it was heavy. He lifted it out and tucked it under his arm, then quickly scanned the room for a way out.

There were loud shouts coming from beyond the outer office and shadows flickering across the far wall. Jack raised his arm, aiming at the open doorway. As soon as the first figure appeared, he fired. The recoil snapped his arm back, but he was ready for it, and he readjusted his aim and followed the first shot with a second, and then a third.

The crash of gunfire was horribly loud. The smell of the powder smoke caught at Jack's throat and he coughed once before he was moving again. He dashed across the room and tore the grass tattie screen from the window, throwing it to the floor. The sudden gunfire had dampened the rescuers' ardour, and he heard nothing as he paused at the now open window.

He saw Abdul turn his face, risking a glance at the man who had threatened to kill him. Jack stared back into eyes that were white with fear. Carefully, he bent low and scooped up the fallen fez. He smiled at its owner as he placed it on his own bare head.

'Goodbye, Abdul.'

He turned and leapt through the window.

Jack's breath rasped in lungs that felt as if they were on fire. He had run without thought to direction, galloping through the maze of alleys that led away from the Hotel Splendid, thinking of nothing but escape.

Despite the pain in his lungs, he felt a sense of elation. The casket he had stolen was heavy. He did not care whether it contained his ruby, so long as it held enough money to get him out of Bombay. It was time to find a new identity; his time as Arthur Fenris was coming to an end.

He slowed his pace as he came to the wide thoroughfare that led from the Ghats on the northern edge of Bombay to the Fort at its heart. It was late at night, but there were enough carriages still making their way through the better parts of town to give him some security. He needed no more than an hour or two to gather his belongings, then he could begin his journey.

For the first time in as long as he could remember, Jack felt a sudden longing for London. He had been in India for too long. He needed a change. He needed to return to the security of the familiar. He smiled as he pictured his mother's expression when she saw her son return in the finery of a British officer.

If Abdul's casket contained enough money, Jack would try to find a way to book a passage on a steamer back to England.

He would go home.

The carriage pulled up sharply in a loud jangle of bits and traces. It was a stylish britzka rather than the more common lumbering shigram. The door was devoid of all decoration and Jack took a wary step backwards as it opened towards him. The inside of the carriage was dark, and for a heartbeat he was convinced that somehow Abdul had arrived to fight for his money.

Instead of naked steel or a raised gun, he saw an elegant gloved hand beckoning in his direction.

'Get in, Arthur.'

Sarah Draper, wife to the commander of the 64th Regiment of Foot, looked down and smiled. Her blue eyes sparkled with life, her mouth turned up in an impish smile, like a naughty schoolgirl about to break the headmistress's rules for the first time.

Jack didn't hesitate. He threw his stolen fez into the gutter and climbed into the carriage, all thoughts of his mother and home disappearing in a waft of French perfume.

Chapter Eight

———◆———

*J*ack lay on his back and stared at the ceiling. His body ached and the pit of his spine was on fire. But the bed was comfortable, the rumpled sheets cool and the pillow soft, so it was not too much of an effort to let out a deep sigh of contentment and enjoy the rare sensation of being at peace.

He felt the gossamer-light touch of hair on his cheek. He turned his eyes and stared into the pale face of Sarah Draper.

'Have I worn you out?' The question was asked with a teasing smile as she took hold of a single lock of her own hair and used it to trace a pattern across his face. She grimaced as it snagged on his thin beard. 'You should shave more often. You look like a navvy.'

Jack closed his eyes, savouring the sensation of the hair flitting across his skin. 'I hate shaving.'

Sarah laughed softly. 'So I can see. But I'm glad you don't have a beard. James is always leaving scraps of food in his. I can smell it when he kisses me.'

Jack felt a pang of guilt as his new bedmate mentioned her husband. To be a cuckold was a sorry affair. To be the one doing the cuckolding left him nursing a sense of shame, however much he had desired it. Draper's wife clearly thought nothing of it, and he wondered how many other young officers had been enslaved in her bed.

'Perhaps I'll ask him to shave it off.' Sarah laughed at the notion.

'I would advise against it.' Jack nestled his head into the thick pillow as he offered the advice. 'In my experience men are fiercely protective of their facial hair. You can offend their wife, mock their children and ridicule their ability to drink. But never, ever remark on their choice of moustache.'

Sarah leant forward, pressing the firm mound of her breast into his side. 'I expect you are correct. You are clearly a man of much experience, after all.'

He opened his eyes. Her face was only an inch from his. She arched her back like a cat, pressing the full length of her body into his.

'I wonder if your experience has taught you this.'

He felt her fingers wander across his chest before heading lower. He sighed. He would not be left to rest.

'Like this?'

'No. You're holding it wrong. Extend your arm.'

'It's heavy.'

'It's meant to kill people.'

Sarah Draper thrust her arm forward, lunging with Jack's talwar. She fought her imaginary adversary with a series of quick thrusts, her hair bouncing as she darted across the floor of the large bedroom. Jack watched in fascination. She was naked, and he could not tear his eyes from her. She showed no sign of minding his careful scrutiny.

'Was that better?'

'I have never seen anything more perfect.'

'Stop staring at my tits and teach me. I want to learn to fight.'

Jack curled his arms behind his head. He was sitting up in the messy bed, the tousled covers pulled to his waist. Sarah could practise all day as far as he was concerned. 'Why would you want to do that?'

'So I can protect myself.'

'You have me now. I'll protect you.'

Sarah snorted in a very unladylike manner. 'So will you now always be at my side? How very tiresome.' She turned as she reached the far end of the room, sweeping Jack's blade through the air and nearly knocking a fine porcelain vase from its stand in the process.

'Am I not to be your protector, then?' Jack tried to make light of the comment. He did not know what he wanted from her, but it still hurt to hear her dismiss him so casually. He shook his head at his own fecklessness. Taking the wife of a colonel to bed was a foolish and dangerous decision. His lust and desire might have overwhelmed his good sense, but that did not mean he could go on with it. As much as he still desired her, he had to quit Bombay and get far away from Ballard.

'Good God, no. I cannot imagine how I would explain that to James. Besides, do you not have to return to your regiment soon?'

'Not necessarily.'

Sarah seemed not to hear him. She lifted the sword close to her face, a faint sheen of sweat across her brow. Her fingers gently traced the swirling script etched into the blade. 'You are a strange fellow, Arthur. You intrigue me.'

Jack ignored the comment and ran his hand across his face. He noticed the thick growth of beard. Sarah had been correct. He did need a shave.

'Where did you get it?' Sarah asked as she continued to inspect the blade.

'Where did I get what?'

'Don't be obtuse. Your sabre.'

'It's a talwar, not a sabre.'

Sarah pouted. 'Don't be pedantic. Where did you get it? You don't appear to have a penny to your name, yet you carry a talwar that is clearly worth a small fortune.'

'How do you know I don't have a penny?' Jack was keen to change the topic of conversation. He did not want to dwell on his past. The talwar had been earned. Unlike nearly everything else he possessed, it had been neither bought nor stolen. It was his and his alone and it had been at his side ever since the Maharajah of Sawadh had presented it to him as a reward for his bravery.

'I had you investigated. I don't just leap into bed with anyone, you know. You are living on Lieutenant Knightly's charity. Why stoop to that when you have a sword . . . sorry, a talwar' – she pouted as she corrected herself; clearly she was a woman who did not like to be wrong – 'that you could sell?'

'It's not for sale.'

Sarah looked up sharply as she heard the warning tone in his voice. She smiled. 'How very intriguing. You don't want to talk about it, do you?'

Jack said nothing.

'Fascinating.' She dropped the blade and crawled on to the bed, sliding along Jack's body. She saw his obvious reaction to her approach and smiled. 'Completely fascinating.'

Jack forced the buttons of his scarlet tunic into their holes, lifting his chin high as he closed the high collar of his uniform coatee. It was close to mid morning. With her husband spending a few days with his regiment before he took up his staff appointment in Bombay, Sarah was at leisure, and she seemed fully intent on enjoying herself. She had been on her way back from a party when she had spotted Jack roaming the streets. He was grateful that she had whisked him away, but now it was time to make good on his decision to get out of the city before Ballard – or anyone else for that matter – could poke his nose into his affairs.

'Aren't you a little old to still be a lieutenant?' Sarah asked the pointed question from the bed, where she lay on her side watching her new lover dress as he prepared to leave.

'Rank isn't everything, my dear.' Jack quickly picked up the casket that he had hidden on a side table.

'Yes it is.' Sarah propped her head on one hand. Her hair fell on to her face and she used her free hand to push it behind her ear. 'A man should have ambition.'

Jack offered a wry smile at the comment. 'Oh, I have ambition. More than you could ever know.'

'Truly?' Sarah did not sound convinced. 'I will admit that you are not like the other junior officers I have met. Most of them can talk of little else other than their position in the battalion. Who is above whom, and who is buying out so-and-so. You don't seem to care.'

'I don't. You have to make you own fortune in this life.'

Sarah's eyes narrowed at the odd remark. 'Now you are doing your best to sound enigmatic. I wish there were more like you. Everyone else is just so damn dull.'

Jack was feeling awkward. He had dressed at her command; she had ordered him to be away before she left to attend on another wife whose husband served with her own. Now that he was ready, she didn't seem to want him to go.

'When you leave, please don't stamp around like an elephant.' Sarah smirked as she spoke, as if the comment were amusing. 'I don't want you to disturb my escort.'

'Escort? Why do you need an escort? I thought you were going to protect yourself. Are you going somewhere dangerous?'

'Perhaps. Who knows where I shall go?'

Jack smiled at her coquettish behaviour. 'Will you not accompany your husband, then?'

Sarah frowned at the notion. 'I have other plans. I have my own path to follow.'

'Such as?'

'I'm writing a book.'

'A book!' Jack could not help the exclamation. Sarah Draper had not appeared to be the bookish type.

She frowned. 'Yes. It should not astonish you that a lady is capable of writing a book.' Her cheeks flushed crimson; it was clear that she took his reaction to be mockery of her literary ambition.

Jack shook his head in denial. 'Don't be daft, it's not that. You took me by surprise, that's all.' He retreated as quickly as a broken skirmish line. 'I am not a book person.' He smiled and tried to appear interested. 'So what is your book about?'

'I plan to write a travel journal, so that I can record the details of the lands I visit before we improve them and destroy their cultures.'

'A worthy aim.'

'You sound sarcastic.' Her eyes challenged him.

'Not at all. It's a laudable ambition.'

'For a woman.'

Jack frowned. 'I didn't say that.'

'You didn't have to. Do you read, Arthur?'

'A little. The paper, that sort of thing.' Jack fought the blush he could feel on his neck. He could read, but not well. He was slowly improving, but it was still a struggle.

'For the first time, you disappoint me.' Sarah misinterpreted his reply. 'A gentleman should read.'

Jack smiled, ignoring the barb. He placed the casket under

his arm and bowed at the waist. 'Well then, it's a bloody good job I'm not a gentleman.'

He turned and walked from the room. He did not think he would see Sarah Draper again. He was not certain if he regretted it or not.

'I say, you there! Wait a moment.'

Jack was halfway down the stairs that led to the street when he was stopped in his tracks by a loud, hectoring voice. He turned and saw a young man moving across the upper landing to look down at him. He frowned at the rude command and started down the stairs again. He was not in the mood to chit-chat with a fool.

'Stay there, damn you.' The man chased after Jack, bounding down the upper staircase with a sudden burst of energy. He could not have been much above twenty years of age, but he had all the arrogance of a much older man. His blond hair was slicked back and he was clean-shaven apart from a fine pair of sideburns. He was dressed in a fine coatee of dark blue with a golden waistcoat and cream breeches. At his side hung a slender rapier, the kind of blade favoured by the young dandies who fancied themselves as swordsmen.

Jack turned and started quickly back up the stairs. The young man saw him turn and hurriedly came to a halt. Yet there was no fear on his face as his quarry marched towards him.

'Can I assist you in some way?' Jack's words were little more than a snarl. He kept walking up the stairs, his feet thumping heavily on to the polished wood.

'I would have a word with you before you leave.' The blond man stood his ground, facing Jack calmly, only the whites of his knuckles on the hand that gripped the banister betraying any tension.

Jack was not in the mood to be conciliatory. He knew he had wasted the day. He should have been on his way out of Bombay and far from the grasp of Major Ballard. Instead he had passed the time dallying in a woman's bed. He could not wholly regret the episode, but he was aware that he had behaved badly by taking another man's wife. He had set out to make good his ambition to be an officer and to prove that he could achieve so much more than society allowed. He was discovering that the longer he spent in his assumed station, the more he was becoming like the callow officers he so despised. The notion shamed him.

He stopped in his tracks. 'Well, out with it.' His hand slipped to the handle of his talwar, his fingers running over the coarse sharkskin that bound the hilt. The feel of it beneath his fingertips brought to mind an image of Sarah Draper cavorting naked with the weapon, and it took an effort of will to focus instead on the sneering face looking down at him.

The blond man shot his cuffs before speaking. 'I am aware you spent the night with my sister.'

Jack's face twisted in a wry smile. It was odd that Sarah had not mentioned the fact that her protector was also her brother, but at least it explained the younger man's acerbic reaction to Jack's presence.

'If you were here, then I'm sure you heard exactly how I passed my time with your sister.'

The other man grimaced at the vulgar comment. 'I would advise you to maintain your discretion in the matter. My sister is foolish. I am not. I will not allow her to become the subject of some braggart's tale-telling.'

'Are you warning me?' Jack felt the first stirrings of anger.

'Yes, I am.' The young man looked down his nose as he offered the pompous reply, preening like a morning cockerel proclaiming its prowess to the world. 'I am here to protect my sister and I shall not fail in that sacred duty.'

Jack snorted. 'And that includes warning off the men she takes to bed?'

'My sister's affairs are her own matter.' The man's expression betrayed his thoughts on the subject. 'But I will not allow her name to be dragged into the gutter. I suggest you remember that when you return to wherever it is you come from.'

Jack stepped forward, his anger threatening to boil over. 'Do not presume to tell me how to behave—' He stopped himself, taking a deep breath as he forced the rage back down. He could not draw his talwar and cut down every man who annoyed him. With his emotions barely contained, and without another word, he turned and went quickly down the stairs, suddenly keen for fresh air.

His last sight of Sarah's brother revealed a look of smug satisfaction on the young man's features. Jack savoured the notion of slamming his fist into the very centre of the arrogant turd's face. It was not as rewarding as carrying out the act itself, but it was as good as he was going to get.

Chapter Nine

Jack had to blink hard as he strode along the broad pavement in front of the mansion where the Drapers had rented a suite of rooms, the bright morning sunlight pricking at eyes that had become accustomed to the gloom indoors. The encounter with Sarah's brother had left him feeling drained, and as he headed back towards Knightly's lodging, he was looking forward to a few hours' rest to rebuild his strength before he left Bombay once and for all.

He had gone no more than a dozen paces when he felt the unyielding metal of a gun barrel being pressed between his shoulder blades.

'What the devil?' His hand instinctively made for his sword handle, his first thought to draw his weapon and fight the person foolish enough to risk trying to rob an armed British officer in broad daylight.

'Don't go raising up a shine, chum.' A calm voice came from behind him. The barrel of the gun was pushed forward, jabbing sharply into his flesh. 'And leave the poker where it is.'

'What the hell is going on?' Jack demanded. He could feel the barrel of the handgun pressing into his spine so he let his hand fall away from his sword. He felt the first fluttering of fear. This was no common footpad. The voice had a London accent, one from Jack's end of the city.

'My master wants a word.' The man who was holding the gun against Jack's back whistled once. Within moments, a black carriage had pulled up at the kerb.

Jack looked up as the door was thrown open. He understood at once, and cursed himself for being foolish enough to waste time. He should have been on his way the moment he left the Byculla Club. Now he would pay the price for allowing his prick to make his decisions for him.

'In you get, and don't try any funny business. I would hate to spoil that fine uniform of yours.' Without ceremony, the gun was pushed hard into Jack's back, forcing him to step towards the open door. For the second time in twenty-four hours he climbed up the steps into a waiting carriage not knowing what the future had in store. This time he had a notion that he would not be so pleased with the outcome.

'Good afternoon, Lieutenant Fenris, I am delighted you could join me.'

There was little warmth in the welcome as Jack entered the gloomy interior of the carriage with as much dignity as he could muster. Dark curtains covered the windows, and the inside was stuffy enough for him to draw a sharp breath as he tried to chew on the thick air. The man with the gun followed him inside, the barrel of his weapon never more than a few inches from Jack's side.

'I wish I could say I was pleased to be here.' Jack sat down heavily as the carriage lurched into motion.

Major Ballard smiled. 'I am not surprised. I expect you were looking forward to some rest after your day's exertions.'

Jack bit his tongue. He had known who had arranged for him to be lifted from the street as soon as he had felt the gun at his back. Major Ballard had clearly seen through his charade. Jack's future was suddenly bleak.

Ballard got straight down to business. 'Have you heard of a Reverend Youngsummers?' He asked the question mildly, as if he was merely enquiring after the weather.

Jack did his best to control the shudder that ran through him. He knew the man well. His denunciation had started.

'I don't recall the name,' he answered as calmly as his racing heart would allow. 'Should I?'

Ballard smirked. 'You are a fine actor, but then that comes as no surprise, given your choice of employment. It really should be the basic requisite for an impostor.' He stared at Jack, clearly at ease despite the situation. 'I believe you may know our friend the Reverend,' he continued as evenly as before. 'He was stationed at Bhundapur. With you.'

'I have never been there, sir.' Jack offered the lie knowing it would have little effect. He was certain Ballard knew who he was. All he could do was play the game and face his fate with dignity.

'The Reverend Youngsummers is a prolific writer.' Ballard leant to one side and peeked around the nearest curtain as if the topic was of little concern to him. 'He has written to the *London Gazette* at great length about his time at Bhundapur. It makes for turgid reading, but the story it contains is fantastical to say the least.'

'I shall make sure I look it out.' Jack risked a glance at the man who had forced him into the carriage. The gun-wielding enforcer was dressed in a thick tweed suit wholly unsuited to the Bombay climate. On his head was a dark green deerstalker pulled low over his face. He looked more suited to a day spent hunting in the wilds of Scotland rather than for life in the more extreme and vibrant temperature of Bombay. Jack looked down and caught sight of the Colt revolver pushed hard into his ribs. His abductor might have adopted a strange choice of attire, but Jack got the feeling that he would not hesitate to pull the trigger the moment Ballard commanded him to do so.

'I can lend you a copy if you like.' Ballard appeared to be enjoying himself, his tone convivial and almost jovial. 'At its heart is an account of the battle that was recently fought at Bhundapur between our forces and those of the Maharajah of Sawadh.' He smoothed a finger across his thin moustache. To Jack he looked like a cat cleaning its whiskers. 'It lacks detail and does little to add much to Captain Kingsley's report, but then I doubt the Reverend was involved in much of the fighting. What is more interesting comes after the description of the battle. Youngsummers goes to great lengths to chastise the cantonment's political officer for his handling of a most curious affair regarding the abduction of his daughter and her time spent as a prisoner in the court of the Maharajah of Sawadh.'

'This sounds fascinating, sir, but I really am rather busy. Could we not discuss this at a later time?'

'Indulge me for a moment, if you would.' Ballard smiled at Jack's bold reply, clearly unconcerned by the continued denial. 'Youngsummers offers us but one side of the story. Unfortunately the political officer attracting such criticism, a Major Proudfoot, died during the battle, so we do not have his account of the day.'

Jack kept his face neutral. He knew how Proudfoot had met his end.

'But if one adds the Reverend's account to that of Captain Kingsley, one does build up a most curious picture of events. I confess I find it all rather intriguing.'

Jack was spared from responding as the carriage bustled to a noisy halt. Ballard once again peeked past the curtain before turning back to face him. 'We have arrived. I suggest you behave yourself, otherwise my colleague here will be called into action. I can promise you he is a most excellent shot. He will not miss.'

The carriage door was thrown open and the steps were quickly and efficiently pulled down by a black-coated servant, who then stepped back and looked down at the floor, averting his gaze.

Jack felt the barrel of the revolver press hard against his ribs. He looked into the pugnacious face of Ballard's enforcer. The man had a broad nose that had clearly been broken a number of times. The rest of the face was fleshy and covered with fine pockmarks. The man's eyes were hard and they looked at Jack with the calm detachment of a butcher about to joint a fresh carcass. Jack did not think he would survive if he attempted to escape.

He let himself be led out of the carriage and through a doorway a few paces from the steps. It was clearly the back door to a fine building, but he had no notion of where he was being taken. He had a fleeting premonition that he would never leave the forbidding place that loomed up around him, but with the barrel of the gun at his back, there was little he could do to resist.

'Now then, to business.' Ballard pulled himself closer to the desk. It was devoid of any sign of recent work, the ink blotter unstained.

Jack sat opposite the major like an errant schoolboy summoned to the headmaster's study. Not that he imagined there were many headmasters who were guarded by armed men. He looked over his shoulder and saw the enforcer standing impassively by the room's only door with the Colt revolver in his hand. Escape was out of the question.

It had not taken long to reach the sparsely furnished room.

Jack had been stopped long enough to have his sword and his cudgel removed and the rest of his person searched by the unapologetic bodyguard in case he had any other weapons hidden on him. The heavy casket from Abdul's office was taken away, a single raised eyebrow the only indication of any interest in the odd object. He had then been led at gunpoint to the nearly empty office and left to wait until Ballard had returned.

Now the major reached into a drawer and pulled out a thick sheaf of paper, which he set in front of him. He flicked through the stack quickly, as if checking everything was in order, before shuffling the pages together and fixing Jack with his piercing gaze.

'Your name is Jack Lark. Is that correct?'

Jack felt his heart thump hard in his chest. 'No, sir. My name is Arthur Fenris and—'

Ballard lifted a hand to stop him. 'Do not take me as a fool. Lieutenant Arthur Fenris died at the battle at Bhundapur. Or at least he is presumed dead, as no one ever found his body. I rather fancy that you may be the only person who knows what happened to that unfortunate young officer.'

Jack said nothing, keeping his face neutral as his long masquerade surged to a conclusion around him.

'Kingsley and Youngsummers both speak of an impostor. A man called Jack Lark. This villainous cove stands accused of having stolen the identity of one . . .' Ballard paused as he scanned one of the pieces of paper in front of him, 'Captain Danbury. Now, as I am sure you are aware, the punishment for impersonating an officer is hanging, yet despite the risk, Lark attempted to pass himself off as Danbury, who we know died in the Crimea. Clearly the authorities in Bhundapur saw through this sham, but not before the impostor managed to escape and inveigle himself into the court of the Maharajah, taking the unfortunate Miss Youngsummers with him. They only reappeared in the hours before the Maharajah launched his attack. After the battle, Lark somehow managed to vanish again. Now here you are, masquerading as Lieutenant Fenris, a man we must presume died at Bhundapur.'

Ballard stared at Jack as he finished speaking. The two men sat in silence, neither seemingly willing to speak.

Finally Ballard returned his gaze to the stack of papers in front of him. 'There is a third account of the events at Bhundapur.'

He looked up to check for any sign of reaction. Jack did his best to look composed, but he was rattled. Ballard knew everything.

'This account also talks of the battle.' Ballard broke the spell only after a long study of Jack's face. 'It bears little resemblance to Kingsley's own report of the fighting. Indeed, it claims that Captain Kingsley had scarcely anything to do with achieving the victory that he so righteously claims. Does that surprise you, Jack?'

Ballard's thin eyebrows arched as he posed the question. Jack was becoming confused. He had expected to face an angry denunciation. Yet there was little censure in Ballard's manner. Indeed, the intelligence officer seemed genuinely intrigued by the matter that had captured his attention.

'This third account also goes to great lengths to talk of the miscreant impostor Lark,' Ballard continued, his eyes once again locked on Jack's. 'However, now we are told that the man is a damn hero. The account reads like a Greek fable, and our friend Lark is made out to be some kind of Hercules who takes control when Captain Kingsley is incapacitated, which I suspect is a rather polite way of saying that he shirked the fight. It is only down to the heroic actions of this mysterious impostor that the cantonment is not overrun. If this third account is to be believed, Jack Lark is the one who saved us from the embarrassment of a heavy defeat. If that is true, the British government owes him a great deal indeed.'

Jack met Ballard's scrutiny as calmly as he could. He had guessed who had written the account.

'Isabel Youngsummers is a determined young woman, is she not, Jack?'

Jack tried to hide his reaction, but he could not help but think of Reverend Youngsummers' daughter and smile. He owed the spirited girl a great deal. She had rescued him once already. It now appeared she was doing so for a second time.

'It is time to put my cards on the table.' Ballard broke the stare and shuffled his papers before opening the drawer and shoving them back into it. There was a finality to the action that caught Jack's attention.

'I don't give a damn who you may or may not be.' Ballard steepled his fingers and peered at Jack from behind them. 'My job here is not to police the country looking for common criminals. I am no more concerned with your identity than I am with the casket of valuables you appear to have in your possession.'

Jack maintained his mask of indifference, yet his heart was pounding away like a battery of artillery being charged by a Russian column.

'I am tasked with two things, Jack,' Ballard continued, 'both of equal importance. The first is to gather intelligence. To do that I maintain a network of informers, spies if you will, who pass me any information that they deem out of the ordinary, or that they think will be of interest to me. Should we go to war, this would of course mean that it would be my remit to gather intelligence about the enemy.' The major placed his hands on the now empty desktop and fixed Jack with a keen stare. 'However, I have a secondary role, one that vexes me a great deal and which to my mind is just as important as the first.'

Ballard paused and looked across to his formidable body-guard, who had stood silently throughout the questioning. The major gave the briefest of nods and the armed man turned and left the room. Jack and Ballard were quite alone.

Jack watched the armed man leave. It surprised him that Ballard would choose to dismiss his bodyguard. For the first time he gave serious consideration to the idea of trying to escape. It would be a simple affair to leap on the major and batter him into submission, but from there he had no idea what he would face or where he would go. The thought of another arduous and violent escape was an unappealing prospect, so he resolved to stay where he was and hear Ballard out. Besides, he was intrigued. He had the feeling something important was about to happen.

'My second role calls for absolute discretion at all times,' Ballard continued, his eyes boring into Jack's skull. 'It is a sensitive task and one that only suits a few, very rare individuals. Individuals with a set of skills that one simply does not find very often. Men like you, Jack. You don't mind if I call you Jack, do you?'

'You can call me what you like.' Jack had to fight the urge to lean forward as Ballard paused.

'Ha!' Ballard barked sharply at the reply. 'Well said, that man. As it happens, I quite agree with you. It does not matter what a man is called. I believe people round here refer to me as the Devil. I have no idea why, but I have never sought to correct them. I do not care what I am called so long as people do what I tell them.'

It was not hard for Jack to see how the rest of the staff had conjured the nickname. It suited Ballard. He had an unearthly calm, a quality of disinterest, as if he were watching events from afar.

'I have need of a man with certain unique talents.' Ballard

read Jack's expression and smiled at his obvious desire to hear more. 'The work of my department is not what you would call ordinary soldiering. It is a little more . . .' he paused, contemplating the next word, 'circumspect. You appear to have many of the talents that I require.' He paused once again before continuing. 'I would like to offer you employment, Jack. I want you to work for me.'

Chapter Ten

*B*allard rummaged in the drawers of the desk. The pause gave Jack a moment to collect the thoughts that had scattered as quickly as a routed column. He had believed he faced denunciation and ruin, with a trip to a lonely scaffold looming over his future. The offer of employment had taken him by surprise. Yet it was more than just a job. Ballard was offering him a way to live. A path away from the listless wandering that was all he had done since he had left Sawadh so many months before. He was delivering Jack the one thing he craved more than anything else: a new future.

'Have you heard of Herat, Jack?' Ballard finished his search and placed a thin leather folder on his desk.

'I have not,' Jack answered honestly. The conversation had changed direction. He felt his unease settle deep in his gut. Not yet gone, but at least contained.

'I am not surprised. Let me divert you with a little story. Herat is an independent city just the other side of the North-West Frontier. It is not a fine place; indeed, from what I hear, it has very little to recommend it. But it assumes an importance quite beyond its design. You see, it sits slap bang on top of the best route through the Hindu Kush, the only path a well-equipped army could hope to use to get through the mountain ranges. I do not need to tell you quite how much the bloody Russians would like to take it into their sphere of influence. As I am sure you can imagine, we simply cannot allow a foreign power to exert control over such a strategically vital city. That would effectively give them a direct route into India, and I am damn sure that if they succeed in their nefarious aim, then it won't take long for the Tsar to cast his beady little eye over the whole of the North-West Frontier. That thought gives the Governor, and most likely the Prime Minister, sleepless nights.'

Ballard paused and fixed his gaze on Jack, reassuring himself that his unwilling student was paying attention. 'Now, until very recently, all has been well. Herat was ruled by a fellow called Sa'id Mahommed. He did not like us very much and he was most certainly firmly in the pocket of the Shah of Persia, but we were quite content with the situation so long as the Shah lived up to the terms of an agreement we got him to sign back in '37 that forbade him from interfering in the city's affairs.'

'You said Herat *was* ruled by him. What has happened?' Jack was pleased that he had spotted the way Ballard had phrased his description of the ruler of Herat.

'So you are paying attention. That is something to your credit, at least.' Ballard did not seem in the least bit impressed. 'Well, unfortunately for poor Sa'id, one of the local princes, Mahommed Yusef Sadozai, did not take kindly to him being on the throne and bumped him off. Now our friend the Shah was not best pleased by this. He is no fool. He fully understands the importance of Herat. Indeed, he has long laid claim to the city, maintaining that it should fall under the power of his domain. He last made overtures to take it back in '52, but we managed to persuade him that his best interests lay elsewhere and we succeeded in maintaining its independence. You see, we have long cultivated our relationship with the Persians. For years we made ourselves friends of the Shah: we used to supply his army and we even sent in our officers to train his men. But over the last thirty years the ungrateful wretch has turned to the Russians for support. We know that they are forever whispering in his ear, and it seems he can no longer resist their call for him to take the city by force, especially as he has been led to understand that our commitments in the Crimea have somehow led us to take our eye off our affairs here in India.'

Jack had heard nothing of all this, but then he had been concerned with little other than keeping Knightly out of trouble for the past few weeks, so it was not altogether surprising. 'What has he done?'

'The Shah has used this revolt as an excuse to send a force to take the city.' Ballard's face was grave. 'According to our latest reports, he has the place besieged, but I shouldn't wonder if he has managed to take it by now. He claims he is merely acting to restore order. Of course, what he means to do is to take the city for himself and annex it. We simply cannot allow that to happen. In a matter of days, we will declare war on the Persians. We have no chance of being able to reach Herat itself – it is too far inland – but we can mount a punitive attack that will make the Shah sit up and realise that if he dares to flout our will, there will be a high price to pay. We already have plans to put together a force to launch an attack. We face two choices of route. One by land, the other by sea. I have argued long and hard against going by land. That would mean taking a direct route through the North-West Frontier, and, as I am sure you are aware, the last time we tried that, we were given a bloody nose for our pains. Therefore, as I see it, the preferable option is to strike at the Shah from the sea. The Indian navy is already planning an amphibious operation. We shall hit hard and quickly and force the Shah to seek terms. That should put an end to his nonsense and give those damn Russians a thing or two to think about. I am to join the campaign and be attached to General Stalker's command, where I shall run the intelligence department.' Ballard sat back in his chair, as if tired of the long lecture. He smiled at Jack. 'I want you to come with me.'

'I'm to be your bodyguard?' Jack was oddly disappointed.

Ballard shook his head, showing the first sign of animation since he had lifted Jack from the street. 'No. I have Palmer for that.'

'I presume he is the pleasant, chatty fellow I met?'

'Indeed. Although he also carries out other, more sensitive tasks as required.'

'Like abduction.'

Ballard grinned. 'Yes, like abduction. Murder too, if I order it.' The smile was gone.

Jack was beginning to understand the lie of the land. 'So what am I to do if it is not to murder innocent officers on furlough?'

'You are hardly the innocent, Jack. You have committed enough crimes to be hanged half a dozen times over.'

'Perhaps. If I really am Jack Lark, of course.'

'I think we both know that is the case. As I said before, I have no desire to hold you to account for any previous misdemeanours. I will provide you with a new identity, one that will actually stand up to more than a passing scrutiny this time.'

Jack felt the barbed comment keenly. Lieutenant Fenris was the third identity he had taken. Ballard knew something of the second. Jack felt an odd satisfaction that he knew nothing of the first. He would be the first to admit that his current guise was far from perfect, yet to hear his exploits casually demeaned offended him.

'I will also provide you with a new uniform,' Ballard continued, his voice betraying no emotion as he played his final ace. 'It can replace the blue lancer's coatee you appear to have in your possession.'

Jack felt Ballard's grip tighten around his future. The blue cavalryman's uniform belonged to the commander of the Maharajah of Sawadh's lancers, a rank and position that Jack had once held. Ballard's enforcer was clearly able to add burglary to his list of talents. They must have taken his knapsack from Knightly's rooms before they lifted him from the street. Ballard knew everything.

'How do I know I can trust you?' Jack asked the question despite being pretty certain that he already knew the answer.

Ballard snorted. 'Of course you cannot trust me. I have no idea why you would think you can.'

'Then why should I agree?'

'Because otherwise I don't think you have long left in the role of Lieutenant Fenris.' Ballard placed the threat on the table without a visible qualm.

'So, do as I am told or die?' Jack sat back in his chair.

'I'm glad you see the picture, Jack. It shows I am quite correct in choosing you for this role.'

'So then . . .' Jack plucked an imaginary piece of fluff from the cuff of his jacket. 'Now that that is out of the way, let's return to my earlier question. What am I to do for you?'

Ballard nodded slowly as he understood that he had secured Jack's agreement. 'I hate spies. I have my own, of course. I guard them closer than I would my children. But I simply cannot stand the thought of the enemy infiltrating men into our camp. A well-placed spy can endanger the success of an entire campaign, and I simply will not allow that to happen. I need an officer I can rely on to protect us from that threat. That will be your role, Jack. I want you to be my spy hunter.'

Jack felt the stirring of anticipation deep in his belly. 'And what do I do if I find any?'

'Why, you kill them. You will be my assassin.'

Jack stood in front of the mirror in the suite of rooms he had been assigned. He turned to one side, inspecting the new uniform that had just been delivered by Ballard's own tailor. It fitted him well, just as an officer's uniform should. On his collar he wore the crown and star of a captain; Ballard had been as good as his word and had provided him with a new rank to go with the new uniform. He had even returned the casket Jack had stolen from the Hotel Splendid. Jack's haul was a profitable one, and he had been able to lodge a good sum of money with one of the many agents who catered to the financial needs of the British officers arriving in Bombay. Quite whether he would live long enough to collect on his deposit was something he preferred not to dwell on.

As he looked in the mirror, he saw an officer wearing the uniform of the 15th Hussars smiling back at him. The 15th possessed one of the longest regimental names in the entire army. The 15th (The King's) Regiment of Light Dragoons (Hussars) was an awkward title, the legacy of their conversion from light dragoons to hussars some fifty years before. As hussars, they had won renown in the wars against Napoleon, before earning a different kind of notoriety for their role in the events in Manchester that the newspapers had cruelly dubbed 'Peterloo', a day in the regiment's history that it would rather forget.

The 15th were Major Ballard's own unit. He had told Jack that he had remained behind when the regiment had quit India three years previously, leaving the Madras Presidency for a more sedate life in Manchester. Like many officers, Ballard had chosen to forgo a regimental posting in the dull safety of the

English countryside, preferring to try his hand on the staff, where the prospects of advancement were much better. The army encouraged such postings, especially for officers like Ballard who had served long enough in their regiments to need to broaden their horizons as well as improve their prospects. It provided a corps of senior officers to fill the myriad roles required to administer the army's forces. Ballard now served with the Bombay Presidency, and his appointment as head of the intelligence department showed that he had chosen well. He was clearly going places, his current post merely a milestone on his route to the higher ranks.

A hussar captain was a suitable identity for Jack to adopt, and with no other officers from the regiment left in the country, it was unlikely that anyone would be able to denounce him as an impostor. With Ballard to vouch for him, Jack could feel safe, for the time being at least. What would happen when he no longer featured in the major's plans was anyone's guess, but he had learnt to avoid looking too far into the future. It had a habit of changing.

He wondered what Sarah Draper would make of his new appearance. As much as tried to forget her, he found himself thinking of her often. She had shocked him, and in some ways her wanton behaviour had offended him. But no matter his somewhat prudish values, he knew he would not hesitate to leap back into her bed if that was what she desired. He could no more shake off his infatuation than he could discard his talwar.

His fabulous sword hung at his side, attached to the black patent leather sword belt that he wore underneath his jacket. It was not the dragoon sabre that regulations demanded, but he refused to be parted from it. The dolman jacket fitted like a glove, the dark navy cloth cut to hug Jack's figure so tightly that it constricted his breathing. It would take time to come to terms with the snug fit, as it would to become used to the lines of heavy gold chain lace that decorated the front of the uniform coat and the fancy pouch belt that ran over his left shoulder and underneath his right armpit. Jack had never been a British cavalry officer before. He would have to adjust to his new gaudy uniform just as he would have to shelve his deep-seated infantryman's distrust of the cavalry.

The rest of the uniform was almost as tight as the dolman. The dark blue trousers, with the wide gold stripe running down the seam, clung to his legs, and he cautiously turned and looked at their fit over his backside. He was not pleased with what he saw, and not for the first time he cursed his weeks of inactivity.

However, he could not be wholly dissatisfied with his new uniform, and he began to understand why the cavalry officers took such pride in their appearance. He lifted his chin and turned his face from side to side. Perhaps he would grow a pair of the mutton-chop whiskers that were all the rage among the debonair young men who served in the cavalry. It would at least give him something to do.

The last weeks had passed with painful slowness. He had spent the days doing little. Ballard had handed over thick wads of documents detailing the current situation between the British and the Persians, and Jack had done his best to plough through the turgid texts, the dusty, dry language of officialdom testing his imperfect reading skill to its limits. What he discovered came as no surprise. Once upon a time he had supposed that highly able and competent fellows conducted the affairs of state, just as he had assumed that effective generals led the army. His opinion of the army's senior ranks had been shattered by his experience in the Crimea. Everything he read of the political affairs of the British government in India confirmed that it was no more fortunate in its own senior staff. As he read the long-winded reports, he was left wondering quite how his country had ever managed to carve out an empire, let alone hang on to it for so long.

Much of what he had read concerned the Honourable Mr James Murray, the British ambassador to Persia, and his ill-conceived affair with the wife of the Persian First Secretary. To put an end to the damaging scandal, the Shah had imprisoned the unfortunate lady concerned before demanding an apology from Queen Victoria herself for the actions of her representative. The affair spoke volumes for the strained relations between the two countries, a tension that had culminated in the British government declaring war a matter of days after the Shah had ordered the independent city of Herat to be placed under siege.

For all its tiresome and tedious nature, Jack relished his new role. To have been given a purpose filled him with a feeling of anticipation. He had drifted for too long, and it felt good to once again be part of the army, if only in the guise of a counterfeit captain. When the time came for the campaign to start in earnest, he was determined to seize the opportunity he had been given. He had become the Devil's assassin, and he could not have been happier.

Chapter Eleven

Hallila Bay, 7 December 1856

The sun was high in the sky, but the water was cold. It lapped up to Jack's shoulders, soaking the gold braid on the front of his hussar's dolman so that he was dragged forward. Had it been any deeper, it would likely have pulled him under.

'Don't let that get wet, Mr Fenris.'

Jack forced his arms straight, holding the heavy portmanteau as high above his head as his aching arms would allow. Palmer laboured along behind him, grunting with the effort of carrying a pair of small leather trunks, one balanced on each of his broad shoulders. A heavy splash further back told Jack that his new commanding officer had followed his small staff into the surf.

The landings had been going on for several hours before the three men of the army's intelligence department had been called forward to clamber down the thick rope net and into the small pinnace that would ferry them closer to the shore. They would be leaving the comforts of the steam frigate *Feroze* behind,

swapping their comfortable berths for the wild open countryside of Persia. At least that was how Ballard had described it
to Jack the previous evening as they contemplated their
departure. Jack had done his best not to snort in derision. They
would be serving on the staff. The only hardships they were
likely to endure were the heat and the insects. They would not
be expected to fight, nor would they be forced to sleep on the
ground without the protection of a tent. Staff officers lived
cheek by jowl with the men who would do the fighting, but
their conditions were a thousand leagues above the hardship
they expected the common redcoats to tolerate without murmur.

The British troops were coming ashore at Hallila Bay,
around twelve miles south of the town of Bushire, one of the
early objectives of the campaign. One full division had been
dispatched with the task of enforcing Great Britain's will.
Command of the expeditionary force had fallen to Major
General Foster Stalker, an officer who had enjoyed a satisfactory,
if not spectacular, career in the East India Company's army,
most recently commanding the 2nd Bombay European
Regiment. At his disposal he had five battalions of infantry,
two squadrons of cavalry, two batteries of field artillery, one of
horse artillery and two companies of the Bombay Sappers and
Miners. Drawn from the troops around Bombay, the small
army was already a close-knit group, with many of the officers
well known to one another.

Their orders were simple: teach the Shah that to flout British
influence was to court disaster.

Jack lifted his head and looked ashore. The air above the
beach seemed to shimmer, the haze created by the heat blurring
his view. The promise of the warmth to come sustained him as
he struggled towards the sand, his breath coming in ragged
gasps as he lumbered through the cold water. Despite the haze,
he could see enough to understand that the division was

disembarking in a calm and ordered fashion, with none of the chaos he had expected. The British landings in the Crimea had been a near disaster, the army thrown into the campaign in a display of utter mismanagement. It was clear that the Indian navy would not tolerate such standards on their watch.

As he stumbled through the surf, Jack could see the ranks of red-coated soldiers marching away from the landing area, heading towards their assigned bivouacs inland. Gunboats hovered in the bay, prowling backwards and forwards as they protected the exposed troops. The sailors had already been called into action. Some three to four hundred enemy troops had been waiting to contest the British landing, formed up in a grove of date trees around two hundred yards to the left of the beach. From their position they would have been able to pour a withering fire down on the heads of the first men coming ashore. Such resistance would have made the landings a bloody affair. The soldiers would have had to wade in from the small boats that brought them from the transports, enduring the enemy fire without being able to fight back until they were fully ashore. The casualties would have been horrendous.

Fortunately, the keen eyes of the young officers on the gunboats had spotted the Persian force. It had not taken long for them to engage the enemy, and their bombardment had scattered the waiting troops, killing dozens in the process. Jack had watched the attack from the comfort of the *Feroze*. At the time, he had applauded the calm demonstration of skill by the naval officers, a welcome spectacle for the soldiers waiting to go ashore. Now he was no more than one hundred yards from the target of the barrage, and he felt the shame of having joined in the celebratory cheers as other men had been dying and suffering on the receiving end of the cannon fire.

He staggered out of the last of the surf and trudged through the soft sand, grateful to feel the power of the sun after the chill of the water. He saw the scorch marks where the navy shells had landed. The date grove had been destroyed by the well-directed fire, the trees shredded. The ground was littered with bodies and abandoned equipment and the smell of smoke and spilt blood caught at the back of his throat. It had been months since he had last fought, and it churned his stomach to once again witness the destructive power of battle. Some of the corpses had been literally torn apart, whilst others lay in the grotesque and twisted positions of death. He forced his eyes away from the macabre sight and stepped around a puddle of vomit. Clearly he had not been the only one affected by what he saw.

'Good man, Jack, let's choose a place to set up, shall we?' Major Ballard marched past, the water cascading from his soaked uniform. If the commander of the intelligence department was concerned at seeing the first enemy casualties of the campaign, he gave no sign of it.

Jack traipsed after the major, using both hands to haul the portmanteau up the beach. Like the rest of the officers and men, the staff of the intelligence department carried the very minimum they needed. It would be some days before any of the heavier baggage could come ashore, so the troops marched without tents and with just three days' rations in their haversacks. Jack and Palmer had been forced to carry the other items that Major Ballard deemed essential; judging by the weight of the bag Jack had lugged ashore, they consisted mainly of bulging ledgers and thick sheaves of papers. Quite why he required the contents of a small library in the earliest days of the campaign was beyond Jack's comprehension, but he had long ago learned not to fight the whims of a senior officer.

The stove spluttered as it lit. The fowl stew had been a gift from a lieutenant in the 2nd Bombay Light Infantry who had come ashore in the first wave and who had sensibly carried a fowling rifle with him. It spoke of Ballard's standing that he had been given a share of the precious pot, and Jack was beginning to sense that he was fortunate to be connected with the cadaverous major.

'It's a marvellous thing, is it not?' Ballard poked the contents of the pan with the end of his pocket knife.

'I am looking forward to tasting it.' Jack's stomach growled as the aroma of the stew wafted his way. 'Should we save some for Palmer?' He had barely spoken to Ballard's burly bodyguard, yet it would not do to forget the man. Jack was keen to get the other half of Ballard's staff on side, but the major had dispatched his enforcer on an errand. He had not thought fit to tell Jack where or why.

'I am not talking about the stew, Jack, I doubt that will taste of anything much at all.' Ballard sniffed as he contemplated the bubbling mixture. It was becoming clear that the major had little time for food. He rarely ate, preferring to spend time reading the dozens of reports that came across his desk. It explained his sparse frame. 'In answer to your question, yes, I think we should save some for Palmer; the man eats like a veritable horse and we cannot possibly consume all this by ourselves. But I was referring to the stove, not to this concoction.'

Jack wondered at the mind of a man who could ignore a hot meal when faced with a night without shelter from the elements. 'It is a fine thing.'

'Fine indeed!' Ballard clearly did not share Jack's opinion. 'It is not *fine*, it is a marvel of modern engineering. It is a wonder that a Frenchman could have designed such a device. It takes but a morsel of combustible material, yet it produces the very maximum amount of output. Monsieur Soyer is a genius, and he is quite correct to name this a "Magic Stove".'

Jack was learning a great deal about Ballard's character. He was not interested in food, yet the machine that could cook it fascinated him. 'I wish we'd had these in the Crimea.' He shivered as he remembered the misery of the first nights of the campaign that had led to the terrific bloodletting at the Alma river.

Ballard looked up sharply. 'You fought in the Crimea? Where? At the siege?'

Jack scowled at his thoughtless remark. 'No, I was lucky. I missed that.'

The major would not let him off the hook so easily. 'So before that, then? At the Alma?'

'Yes.'

'Did you fight?'

'Yes.'

'It was a bloody affair, I hear.' Ballard was watching Jack closely. He frowned. 'You could not have been Arthur Fenris in the Crimea. He would have been with the 24th at that time.' His frown deepened as he realised he did not know all of Jack's story. 'You must have been someone else.'

Jack decided it would be best to steer the conversation away from his past. 'That looks done, sir.'

Ballard poked the thickened stew with his knife. 'You might well be right.' He leant forward and twisted the control knob on the stove, shutting off the heat that was condensed from the enclosed burner and channelled into the stove itself. 'Please help yourself.'

Jack did not need to be asked twice. He reached for the pan and started to eat. He was well into his third mouthful when he noticed Ballard staring at him.

'Will you tell me your story?' The major sat cross-legged on the ground, still watching Jack intently. 'The rest of it.'

'You know most of it already.'

'But clearly not all.' Ballard leant forward and swirled his knife around the stew. He extracted a thick nugget of flesh that he inspected carefully before gingerly nibbling at one edge.

'No. Not all of it.' Jack gave the admission grudgingly.

'Does anyone? Does anyone know the full story of Jack Lark, the infamous charlatan?'

'No. Only me.'

'That must be a burden,' Ballard said softly. He paused, looking at Jack closely before he spoke again. 'You scream in your sleep. I heard you on the ship.'

Jack said nothing. He had shared a cabin with his commander on the *Feroze*, but he had not gained the first indication that he had disturbed the major's rest. He felt his cheeks flush, the intimacy of Ballard's words disconcerting. 'You're lucky; *you* sleep like a bloody baby.'

Ballard looked straight into Jack's eyes, as if searching them for knowledge. 'That is the benefit of a clear conscience. Perhaps that is something you lack.'

Jack saved himself from replying by filling his mouth, something he immediately regretted as the hot mixture scalded his tongue. He was surprised at Ballard's insight, but he had learnt never to share his memories, no matter how tempting. He would keep his past to himself.

'So what next? What would you have me do?' Jack asked the question gruffly when his mouth was emptied, breaking the closeness that had been building between them.

Ballard snorted, but did not press further. 'It will take us one day to prepare to march, I imagine. Stalker landed this afternoon. He is an eager man and will be keen to get on before the powers-that-be decide this affair needs the services of a more senior officer with greater experience. He will want to garner some laurels before that happens. He is that kind of man.' The major made the observation seem like a criticism.

'I've never met him.'

'You will. Tomorrow. He has summoned me to his head-quarters. He will want to learn what manner of enemy we face. You can accompany me.'

'Do you *know* what we face?' Jack had no idea what Ballard knew.

'Of course!' He frowned at the question. 'I shall deliver the information tomorrow. I have everything I need.'

'Can you not tell me now? It would be good to know.'

Ballard snorted. 'You would not share your story with me. I think I shall now withhold my own.' He grinned with childish glee.

Jack smiled at the unexpected expression. Against all his better judgement, he was starting to like his new commanding officer. 'As you will, sir. What should I do now that we are here?'

'You must start sniffing around. You are clearly adept at fitting in no matter what your surroundings. Make yourself known to people. Ferret around a bit. I will tell you when I have suspicions for you to act upon.'

Jack contemplated the instructions. His new role was clearly not going to be the simple soldering he was used to. He had no responsibilities beyond Ballard's cryptic orders. He commanded no men and he would not be expected to lead anyone into battle Yet his instincts told him that his life was in danger. He just did not know from where.

Chapter Twelve

'**B**allard! You scrawny rogue, welcome.'

'Good morning, sir, I'm pleased to be here.'

'Then you are a damn fool. No one wants to be in a shithole like this. It is a festering cesspit. A godforsaken turd of a place that the bloody Persians are welcome to keep.'

'If you say so, sir.' Ballard did his best to smile at the ribald remarks.

Major General Foster Stalker twitched the thick moustache that dominated his face, clearly displeased with the mild response. The garrulous officer sat behind a folding field desk in a large bell tent, one of no more than a dozen that had been brought ashore. His temporary headquarters was a hive of activity. Staff officers bustled in and out, brandishing reports and scraps of paper as if they held the key to the entire campaign in their hands. Most were being filtered through an officer wearing the star and crown of a captain on his collar who sat at a separate desk near the tent's entrance.

'Hunter!' Stalker bellowed across the tent to get his aide-de-camp's attention. 'Come over here, you damn scoundrel, and listen to what the Devil here has to say.'

'Yes, sir.' Captain Hunter got to his feet. It was clear he was used to his general's domineering manner. He smiled pleasantly as he came across to join the pair of intelligence officers.

Jack had watched Ballard closely as Stalker delivered his forthright opinion on the local area. A casual observer would have noticed nothing on the major's face that betrayed his reaction, but Jack saw the slightest narrowing of the eyes as Ballard winced at Stalker's coarse tongue. He was becoming accustomed to the major's ways, and he knew Ballard would not enjoy such a vulgar display, even from his own commanding officer.

'Gentlemen, may I introduce Captain Fenris. He will be working for me.' Ballard hid his distaste well and introduced Jack to the pair of officers with urbane charm. They had discussed at great length what name he should take, and had decided to stick with Fenris rather than assume yet another false identity. It was unlikely that anyone else would make the connection between a hussar captain and a young lieutenant who had died in an unknown battle in the far north-east of the country. Moreover, Jack had already been introduced to some of the officers in Stalker's division as Fenris, and it would be harder to explain a change of name than a change of uniform.

Lieutenant Knightly was serving with the 64th, which now formed a part of Stalker's division. Jack had a mind to look him out as soon as possible, as much to check that the young officer was surviving the rigours of his job as to reveal his own new rank and position.

'What's he here for?' Stalker barked the question, already turning his attention to a piece of paper lying on his desk.

'He will assist me in my duties, sir, with a particular remit to ensure the security of our intelligence.' Ballard was careful in his reply.

'Sounds bloody dull.' Stalker scrunched up the paper and threw it to the floor. He fixed Jack with an uncompromising stare. 'If you want to do some real damn soldiering, let Hunter know.'

'I am sure Captain Fenris will be actively employed in the intelligence department, sir.' Ballard answered the general quickly, giving Jack no time to reply.

'I don't see how.' Stalker's bushy eyebrows knitted together. 'You already have that brute of a man with you. What's his name?'

'Palmer, sir.'

'And now you need someone else! God alone knows what you all bloody do all day.' Stalker shook his head. 'So, what do I face?'

'I have a full report for you, sir,' Ballard replied. He was clearly trying hard to avoid becoming nettled by his general, keeping his replies brisk and businesslike.

'I am sure you have. Hunter can read that later. I want a summary and I want it now.'

The slightest flush of crimson decorated Ballard's prominent cheekbones at the rebuke. To his credit, he rallied quickly. 'Very well, sir. We now know that the Shah's forces took Herat on the twenty-fifth of October. He has added the city to the twelve other foreign provinces under Persian imperial control. The closest enemy forces are still at the fort at Reshire, sir, as in my last report. Current estimate has them numbering around two thousand infantry. The Shah also maintains a strong garrison at the port of Bushire, twelve miles from here, but the bulk of his army is still inland. He will know of our arrival and initial reports claim that he is beginning to assemble his strength around the town of Borãzjoon, forty-six miles from here. It is this force that we will have to face in battle, and I would say that we should expect them to be ready to dispute our presence here shortly.'

'So you say there are two thousand in this fart of a fort.' Stalker sat back in his chair as he considered Ballard's assessment. 'Well, we have no choice in the matter. My orders are to strike inland and bring the Persians to battle. I am to destroy their forces and take and hold as much territory as I can until that dolt of a Shah sees sense and asks for terms. Before I can think of moving inland, I need to secure a strong base of operations, and that includes seizing the port at Bushire. Before I can launch an attack there, I need a secure foothold here so that I may assemble the division, and that means I have to take this bloody turd of a fort. Things are never simple.'

'That is why we need generals of your quality, sir,' Ballard replied smoothly. 'If it were easy, then anyone could do it.'

Jack tried not to smile at his commander's false charm. It was clearly wasted on Stalker, who nodded as if Ballard had offered him wise advice, but Jack noticed Captain Hunter's mouth twitch. Clearly the general's aide-de-camp was not cut from the same cloth as his master.

'That is the first sensible bloody thing you have said.' Stalker puffed out his cheeks as he accepted the praise. 'Now then, any changes in their defences?' He fired the question back. For the first time, Ballard had his fullest attention.

'Nothing new, sir. The remains of the old Dutch fort continue to be strengthened, but we have not seen any new trenches since our last inspection.'

'Ha!' Stalker laughed in a single syllable. He fixed Jack with a glare. 'Did the Devil here tell you about that?'

Jack shook his head before speaking for the first time. 'No, sir.'

'It still astonishes me. Ballard here visited Reshire a few weeks ago at the behest of the quartermaster general. He was supposed to stay aboard the damn frigate and inspect the defences from there, but for some bloody reason he came ashore and started surveying them. With a compass and measuring chains, can you believe? He only left when the bloody Persians told him to bugger off!'

Jack laughed along with Stalker. He'd had no idea that Ballard could be so brazen, or so brave.

'It seemed a good idea, sir. We weren't actually at war at that stage.' Ballard spoke as if he could not understand that there was anything remarkable in his exploits. 'It seemed expedient.'

'You're bloody priceless, Ballard. Expedient indeed. I only wish a few more of my officers were like you. We'd have the damn Shah on his knees and begging for mercy within the week. Oh, for Christ's sake, what now?'

Jack started at the admonishment before he realised it was directed towards a pair of naval officers who had entered the tent.

'Thank my lucky stars. The bloody webfoots have arrived.' Stalker turned to his aide. 'Hunter, it appears I shall have to delay my Persian lesson. Tell the damned teacher to wait around and to not bloody disappear like he did last time.'

The general looked hard at Ballard, who seemed amused to hear that the division's commander was taking the trouble to learn the local language. 'Don't look like you are trying to hide a fart at a wedding, Ballard. It was Commodore Fetherstone's idea, not mine. And we cannot have the bloody navy pretending they know better than we do, so I agreed to share their munshi, as did Hunter.'

'I think it is a capital notion, sir.' Ballard did his best to smile. 'I only wish I had the time to follow your example.'

Stalker snorted. 'You pompous ass. Off you go, Hunter. Tell the man to wait.'

'Very good, sir. Gentlemen, please excuse me.' Captain

Hunter took the opportunity to slip away. 'Good luck with it all, Fenris. Please do come and find me if I can be of any further assistance.' He gave Jack a genial smile as he escaped. Already a small group of staff officers were hovering at his desk, anxiously waiting for his attention.

Stalker thrust his chair backwards and lumbered to his feet to greet the approach of the two naval officers. 'What now, gentlemen?' he barked when the new arrivals were still several paces away. 'Can the navy not manage without my damn guidance for more than a few hours?'

'Good afternoon, Stalker.' The shorter of the two officers greeted the major general with a warm smile, despite the less than friendly greeting. 'We came ashore with a few of our guests and I thought I should do you the courtesy of paying you a visit.'

'A few guests! What does the navy think this is? A damn holiday?' Stalker slumped back into his chair, his face creased into a scowl. He waved a hand in Ballard's direction. 'You know Ballard?'

'Indeed, sir.' The two naval officers nodded in greeting.

'This is one of his men . . .' Stalker frowned for a moment. 'I have forgotten your name, Captain.' There was no hint of apology in the bland statement.

'Fenris, sir.' Jack reached forward and shook the hands offered in his direction. It was hard not to be overawed. He had been on campaign before, yet he had barely seen the senior officers at whose command hundreds, if not thousands, of men would march to their deaths. It was their decisions that would secure victory or else see the army shattered and broken, the troops fleeing for their lives. Generals on campaign were as close to being God as a mortal man could ever hope to be.

'May I introduce Rear Admiral Sir Henry Leeke, commander of our naval forces, and Commodore Fetherstone of naval intelligence.' Ballard made the introductions smoothly. Jack thought he detected a warning tone in his voice, but Stalker gave him no chance to dwell on the thought.

'Enough of this piss and wind.' The general was in the process of dispatching another dozen sheets of paper to their grave on the floor behind his chair. 'I have enough to bloody do without listening to you lot carrying on like we are at some damn garden party.'

The four officers shared a smile.

'We will leave you, sir.' Ballard seized the opportunity to depart. 'I will give my report to Captain Hunter.'

Stalker fluttered his fingers in the briefest acknowledgement. Jack followed Ballard out of the tent, happy to escape.

'Ballard, a moment of your time.' The voice called them to a halt before they had gone more than a dozen paces from Stalker's tent. They turned to see Commodore Fetherstone hurrying after them.

'Sir?' Ballard enquired politely.

The naval officer puffed his cheeks as he came to a halt. He was much older than Ballard, his thick mutton chops and thin crop of hair completely grey. His face was lined and weathered by a lifetime spent at sea, but his blue eyes were keen.

'I wonder if you could send me a copy of your report on the defences at Reshire. I would like to see how well it tallies with my own.' Fetherstone made the request seem trivial, but Jack saw Ballard's eyes narrow at the suggestion.

'Of course, sir. I would be delighted.' There was little hint of pleasure in Ballard's icy reply.

'Obliged to you. I will of course extend the same courtesy and send you the navy's own intelligence.' Fetherstone's small head bobbed forward as he replied. He looked like an undernourished starling pecking at a crumb.

'It is very kind of you to offer, sir, but there really is no need. I doubt we missed anything.' Ballard's opinion of the navy's intelligence-gathering skills was evident in his less than enthusiastic reply.

Jack realised that Fetherstone's role was similar to Ballard's. It was also clear that there was little love lost between the two rival intelligence officers.

'Our gunboats have drawn an accurate account of the enemy's position, with an estimate of their numbers,' Fetherstone continued, despite Ballard's belligerence. 'I appreciate it may not be quite as good as a survey on foot, but I warrant you could use the information, if only as a counterbalance to your own. We cannot risk any oversight.'

'Of course,' Ballard replied through gritted teeth.

Fetherstone turned his attention to Jack. 'Captain Fenris, I am surprised we have not met before. You must be a recent attachment to Major Ballard's department.'

Jack saw the keenness in the older officer's stare. Fetherstone missed nothing. 'That's correct, sir. My transfer came through shortly before embarkation.' He was smooth in his reply.

'How interesting. Where were you stationed before? The rest of the 15th are back in merry old England. I had no idea we had another of their officers still with us.'

Ballard took a step forward and spoke before Jack could respond. 'You must excuse us, sir. I am sure you have as much to do as we do. Perhaps we can continue this fascinating conversation when we don't have an enemy to fight.'

Fetherstone smiled at Ballard's sarcasm. 'Oh, we all have plenty to do. You would be amazed what we get up to in naval intelligence.' He said nothing more, and retreated to Stalker's tent with only a fleeting nod of farewell.

'Odd fellow,' Jack remarked. Something in the commodore's manner had struck him as strange. 'You clearly don't like him.'

'He's a webfoot. We really shouldn't expect too much.' Ballard was scathing. 'It's bloody typical of him to pry, the nosy old beggar. You would've thought he would have learnt some manners at his age.'

'At least he is trying to teach Stalker some new tricks, although I was surprised that he has agreed to learn Persian. He doesn't seem the type.' Jack was intrigued by the idea. He had spent a long time living amidst people without sharing their language, though he had picked up a little along the way.

'Don't let that act of Stalker's distract you. The man knows what he is about. The bluster is just a facade.'

'Well he does a bloody good job of playing the buffoon.'

Ballard shook his head. 'Do not judge so quickly. There is more to many men than one would first assume.'

Jack contemplated the advice. Coming from Ballard, it meant something. The Devil had a composure about him that Jack envied. Nothing appeared to surprise or shock him. The notion led him to think of Stalker's story. 'Did you really go ashore and measure the Persian defences?' He asked the question with genuine interest. He had done a few rash things in his time. It was nice to hear of another's madcap exploits.

Ballard looked at Jack as if he sensed mockery. 'I did. I cannot bear to get things wrong. It seemed the only way to be accurate.'

Jack shook his head. 'It is a good job you found me. I'll put a stop to that sort of bloody nonsense before you get yourself killed.'

Ballard gave his short bark of a laugh. 'Then I shall count myself doubly fortunate for having unravelled the mystery of your identity.' He leant forward and clapped Jack on the shoulder before leading him away.

They had gone no more than a few paces when a party of a dozen heavily laden sailors blocked their path. The matelots were weighed down with luggage, a bewildering assortment of portmanteaus, cases, hatboxes and canvas-wrapped parcels that looked more suited to a stay at a fine Bombay hotel than a dusty campaign field.

'I thought orders forbade any baggage.' Jack watched the procession with envy.

'They did. But I doubt they apply to her.'

Jack looked across to the rear of the party of sailors. A pair of civilians were strolling along behind the sweating men tasked with carrying their heavy luggage. They walked with calm detachment, as if on a pleasant excursion rather than in the midst of an army preparing for war.

Jack's breath stuck in his throat as he recognised the woman whose figure being admired by every red-coated and red-blooded man in the vicinity. He caught her eye and felt a tingle of lust shimmer down his spine as she met his stare, her own shock evident in the widening of her eyes.

Jack's lover had come to join the campaign. And from the look on her face, he was the last person on earth she had expected to find.

Chapter Thirteen

———— ❖ ————

'Arthur!' Sarah Draper raised her glove to her mouth in a delightfully demure gesture of surprise. 'I thought you were returning to your regiment?'

Jack felt the devilment stir within him. He was very aware how embarrassing his presence must be. He was meant to be safely on his way up country, far from Bombay and thus far from Sarah Draper's bed. 'I found new employment, ma'am. You know Major Ballard?'

'Mrs Draper.' Ballard took a step forward. 'How lovely to see you. I had heard a rumour that you were with the army, but I confess I am a little astonished to discover that it is true. I would have thought you would have preferred to remain in Bombay . . .' He paused. 'With your husband.'

Ballard was smooth, but Jack heard the bite in his words.

'James insisted that I come.' Sarah Draper smiled tartly back at the major. Clearly the two were well known to each other, and Jack got the sense that there was little love lost between them. He watched Sarah closely, spotting the flash of anger in her eyes as she fixed them on Ballard's face.

'I cannot write an account of the campaign from Bombay.'

She continued speaking with icy charm as she rose to Ballard's challenge. 'General Stalker was generous enough to listen to my plea and allow me to accompany the expeditionary force.'

Jack did his best not to laugh aloud as she dropped the general's name into the conversation. He didn't doubt that Stalker had readily agreed. Beautiful women tended to get what they desired. Even crusty old generals could not deny them. Not that he could blame Stalker. He was very aware of his own infatuation with Sarah. If she made demands, then Jack knew he would oblige, and be delighted to do so.

Ballard stiffened his back so that he stood ramrod straight as he responded to Sarah's tone. 'I would be delighted to offer my assistance should you require it. I would hate to see you inconvenienced in any way. An army on campaign is by its very a nature a rough and ready sort of affair. It may not be quite to your taste.'

'Why, thank you, Major, but I rather think I shall manage quite well. And if I find myself in any difficulties, well, I am not here alone.' She turned and beckoned her escort into the conversation. 'I should introduce my brother. Simon, you know Major Ballard, but I don't think you know his colleague.'

'No. He does. We met.' Jack spoke first, fixing his eyes on the young man who had accosted him on the stairs shortly before Ballard had abducted him. It appeared that although Colonel Draper had allowed his wife to join the campaign, he was not foolish enough to do so without making sure she was accompanied by a suitable chaperone. And who better than a brother to safeguard a lady's virtue? He let his hand fall to the handle of his sword, a gesture noticed by all. 'However,' he continued, 'I'm afraid he did not have the manners to introduce himself.'

The young man scowled. 'My name is Simon Montfort.

I suggest you remember it well.' He said nothing further, but came to stand protectively at Sarah's side.

'I am pleased to see you again, Simon.' Ballard was watching Jack closely. The tension between the two younger men was evident as they regarded each other like bull mastiffs, their hackles raised. 'This is Captain Fenris.' It was obvious that the major was doing his best to ignore the atmosphere.

'I shall not forget *your* name.' Montfort's tone was icy. He turned to Sarah. 'We must be getting on, sister dear. We have much to do. As I'm sure do these gentlemen.'

'Nothing that cannot wait.' Jack matched the other man's tone. He turned his body, subtly isolating Montfort on the periphery of the conversation. He had seen enough of polite society to know how to cut someone dead. He focused his attention on Sarah. 'Perhaps we can meet later on, at a more . . .' he paused, as if testing the next word, 'suitable hour.'

He was delighted at the reaction. Sarah's face flushed scarlet, a shade that sat well on her pale English complexion. Montfort looked as if he was being force-fed a turd. The lack of subtlety in the remark was not lost on Ballard, who raised an eyebrow.

'I am sure we will all have too much to do.' Montfort took a firm hold on his sister's arm and made to push past the two officers.

'Yes, of course.' Ballard took a step backwards.

Jack made no effort to move. As he expected, Montfort tried to barge his way past. Instead of forcing a passage, he bounced off Jack's shoulder, his hissed oath betraying the pain of the impact.

'Out of my way, dammit.'

Jack stared hard into the young man's eyes. It was only the second time they had met, and yet on both occasions it had seemed almost inevitable that they would come to blows. 'You should learn to curb your tongue.' He spoke in the calm tone of an adult dealing with an unruly child. 'Otherwise you could find yourself in a whole boatload of trouble.'

'Captain Fenris.' Ballard might not understand the source of the tension between the two men, but his anger was clear. 'You appear to be in the way.'

Jack continued to stare into Montfort's eyes. He could sense the evil in the man. Montfort met his gaze evenly. A look of mocking satisfaction appeared on his face.

'Do as you are told, old man. Stand aside.'

Jack held his position for a moment longer before taking a large step to one side and sweeping his arm in a theatrical gesture to show the path was clear. The two civilians hurried after their rapidly departing porters.

'What on earth was all that about?' Ballard asked under his breath as Sarah Draper and her brother moved out of earshot. 'You looked like you wanted to call the man out.'

'Just letting the little turd know where he stands.' Jack smiled at the look on Ballard's face. 'It had to be done.'

'No it did not.' Ballard scowled. 'Do not forget who you are or why you are here. You ogled that poor woman like a dog on heat and then you tried to force her brother into a fight. It really is too much, Jack, too much indeed. Your new duties require you not to draw attention to yourself and I expect you to remember that. I do not want to have to bring the matter to your attention again.'

Jack bowed his head as he weathered the lecture, but only to hide his delight. As she had passed, Sarah had flashed him a devilish smile that had sent a shiver of desire surging through his soul. It was all the invitation he needed.

Sarah lay on her back, her face sheeted with perspiration. It was stuffy and close inside her tent, the air thick with the smell of sun-ripened canvas laced with French perfume.

Jack nestled his head into the pillow. He was comfortable and contented despite the heavy air. He had arrived at Sarah's tent in the dead of night. She had been awake, sitting at her writing desk working on the first chapters of her account. He had been welcomed in silence, her kisses the delightful acknowledgement that he had done the right thing in sneaking to her bed.

'I don't know how you work for that man. You know they call him the Devil?' Sarah pushed herself up on to one elbow and looked at Jack, her fingers reaching forward to brush against his cheek.

'He is not so bad. Besides, I don't have much of a choice in the matter.'

'You could ask for a transfer.'

Jack smiled at the notion. He would have enjoyed the privilege of such liberty, something he had never had. As a redcoat he had gone wherever his regiment had been sent, no matter how dangerous or unpleasant. His attempts to become an officer had hardly improved his lot. 'It doesn't quite work like that.'

'Yes it does. Or you could sell out. Go back to England. Or purchase a commission in the Company.'

Jack scowled. 'Why? Are you so keen to be rid of me?'

Sarah's face did not change. 'I am merely thinking of how unpleasant it must be to work with that damn man. You should think of your future.'

'Now why would I do that?' Jack chuckled. He reached across and pulled Sarah to him. She came willingly, nestling against his side. The warmth of her body pressed into his flesh. He did not want to dwell on the future. He had to enjoy the here and now.

'Will you be involved in the assault on the fort?' Her lips

brushed against the skin of his upper arm as she asked the question. Jack shivered.

'No. The intelligence department does not fight.'

Sarah's head lifted and she returned to her position on her side so that she could look at his face. 'It sounds like you regret that.'

'What?' Jack closed his eyes and feigned indifference. 'No one wants to fight. Especially in an assault.'

'Why? You are soldiers. I thought you always wanted to fight.'

Jack found he could not answer. There was nothing in battle that was to be sought out. Yet he was drawn to it nonetheless, his skill in the brutal cauldron of the fight the one thing he was certain of. It was not something he could explain, not even to the woman who had taken him into her bed.

'I'm sorry.' Sarah broke the silence that had fallen over them. She had been studying his face, as if trying to read his thoughts. 'I think you know very well what battle is like. I do not, and it was thoughtless of me to make light of it. I know what it is to suffer, to have memories that you lock away.'

Jack looked at her. He thought he caught a glimpse of something more in her gaze, but it retreated quickly, pushed away by the sparkle of light that so captivated him.

'Will you tell me?' He asked the question honestly.

Sarah stared back at him. For a moment the faraway look returned, but then she smiled before moving close to him once more. 'So tell me what is to happen next. I need to understand, otherwise my account will make no sense.'

Jack thought of pressing her, but he knew what it was to have demons, to have a past that had to be shackled away lest it rule a man's soul. Sarah's body was against his skin, and he did his best to savour the feeling and to forget the look of pain in her eyes.

'Well, it will be a hard fight. The enemy are well dug in and they will know we have landed. They know we must attack them and from which direction. The only thing they *don't* know is when the attack is coming.'

'Surely it will take days for the army to be ready.' Sarah was fiddling with her hair, twisting her fringe into a short plait before letting it unravel. 'Stalker has only just landed. He cannot be prepared to launch an attack so soon.'

'We march tomorrow. These boys certainly know what they are about.' Jack could not hide how impressed he was. In the Crimea, it had taken days to sort out the chaos of the landings. The disembarkation on to Persian soil had only taken place the previous day, yet already the army was ready to march. The sailors of the Indian navy had worked tirelessly to bring the thousands of soldiers ashore, along with the equipment, provisions, guns and stores they would need to start the campaign in earnest.

'He does not need the whole army, surely?'

'He will use at least four battalions, maybe all five.' Jack was enjoying lying on Sarah's charpoy. It beat the sandy ground on which he had tried to sleep the previous night. The travelling bed had only been built for one, but he did not mind being pressed close to such a charming bedfellow.

'The whole division. Why so many?'

'The assault is making Stalker nervous, and he's right to worry.' Jack knew from bitter experience just how hard it was to remove an enemy from a fixed defensive position. 'He cannot risk failure. He knows that the longer the campaign goes on, the more likely it is that he'll be replaced by someone more senior. His only hope of remaining in command is to give his masters a swift victory. So he cannot afford to delay.' Jack enjoyed being able to recount the general's plans. It made him feel part of the campaign's inner circle. He only knew what was planned because Ballard had told him over dinner, but it did not matter. He wanted to impress the woman who had taken him to her bed, and prove that he was so much more than a typical junior officer.

'So the men will have to fight simply to keep Stalker in his job.'

'Isn't that always the reason?'

'Ah!' She purred in approval. 'You're a cynic.'

'No, I'm a soldier. We're all cynics when it comes to laying down our lives.'

Sarah looked at Jack out of the corner of her eye. 'You're no ordinary soldier, Arthur. You're quite different to all the rest.' She gave up her temporary hairdressing and lifted herself up one elbow so she could look at him properly. She reached forward to trace the thick scar on his left side, the legacy of a bullet that had been meant to kill him. Her fingers walked soft patterns over his skin as she stroked each scar and blemish, the tantalising, gossamer-light touch setting him on fire. She leant forward and kissed the thick raised line on his left arm, the legacy of a wound that had cut his flesh to the bone.

'Why don't you like my brother?' She whispered the question, her lips busy on his body.

'Who said I don't like him?'

Sarah lifted her head and pouted. 'I think you have made it rather clear, or do you normally barge into people you like?'

'He walked into me.' Jack frowned at her tone. He wanted her teasing his flesh, not picking at his mind.

'Don't be childish.' The rebuke was waspish. She pulled away, the memory of her touch leaving his skin tingling.

Jack sighed. He could not explain why he had taken such a dislike to Sarah's brother. It was based on nothing more than instinct, but he had long ago learnt to trust his judgement. 'He's not my type.'

'That's not an answer.'

'It's all I have.'

Sarah's eyes narrowed. 'So will you at least tell me how you come to be here?' She rolled on to her side to face him, once again reaching forward to stroke his flesh. 'One minute you're a lieutenant in an ordinary regiment of the line. The next you're a dashing cavalry officer and a captain.'

'I don't recall spending all that much time in conversation when last we met.'

Sarah pouted and her fingers stilled their delicate touch. 'The 15th are not with the division, so why are you here?'

Jack sensed the change in the tone of her voice. 'I'm on special duties.' It was hard to keep the pride from his reply. He was an urchin from the foulest rookeries of east London, but now he was serving on the staff of a general, wrapped in all the finery of a hussar captain. It was hard not to be proud.

The answer seemed to appease her. 'Special duties; that sounds intriguing.'

'So far it's been as boring as hell.' Jack thought of the hundreds of dull reports he had read. His life in Ballard's department was far from glamorous.

'I'm pleased you're here.' Sarah used her nails to trace the outline of the scar on his arm, sending shivers running through his body. 'I would've hated being alone.'

Jack closed his eyes to maintain control over his body. He had a feeling Sarah Draper was never alone for long. 'Why are *you* here?'

'For my book.' Sarah was earnest as she explained the reason for her presence. 'I plan to write a journal about the campaign. If that fat old sow Fanny Duberly can do it, then so can I. She was only the wife of a damn quartermaster and never got within a mile of the fighting, yet she is being treated like some Amazonian warrior.'

Jack grimaced at Sarah's turn of phrase. He was not accustomed to hearing a lady curse. He had heard a little about Fanny Duberly. She had successfully managed to avoid the authorities and stay close to her husband during the campaign in the Crimea. She had published her journal of the campaign the previous year and had become the talk of London. 'I'm sure it will be fascinating.'

Sarah jabbed a sharp nail into the soft flesh above his hip. 'Don't patronise me, Arthur.'

Jack opened his eyes to see Sarah staring at him coldly. 'I was not patronising. I think your book will be very good indeed. I don't think you would have it any other way.'

His words made her smile. 'It seems you're getting to know me, Arthur.' She leant forward, her fingernails tiptoeing down the side of his body. 'I always get what I want.' Jack gasped as she traced her nails lower, and Sarah smiled wider. 'You would do well to learn that.'

Jack let his eyes close, enjoying the sensation. He did not fully understand what he felt towards Sarah, but she enthralled him. He would happily submit to her will.

The hiss of a gas lamp woke him, and he blinked away sleep as he struggled to adjust to the light in the tent. He propped himself on his elbows and looked across to see Sarah bent low over a small table.

'What are you doing?' His voice was croaky and he cleared his throat as he came fully awake. He had been dreaming of the Crimea and he could feel the sheen of sweat cold on his flesh. He shivered as he forced the nightmare away.

'Writing.' Sarah didn't deign to turn round, but kept her nose pressed close to the page.

'At this time?'

'One must write when one has the muse,' she answered,

but it was clear she was concentrating on her work.

Jack rose from the charpoy and walked over to the table, where he stood in silence and watched as she wrote, listening to the scratching of her steel nib across the paper. Every few moments her free hand rose to push her hair back over her ear, where it remained in place for only a short while before it fell back, forcing her to repeat the gesture. Jack thought it was one of the most endearing things he had ever seen.

'You should go back to sleep.' Sarah lifted her head and turned to face him, speaking softly as she became aware of his continued scrutiny.

'I should be saying the same to you.'

'I'm a big girl, Arthur.'

'I can see that.' She was dressed in only a thin silk gown. With the gas lamp behind her, Jack could see every curve of her silhouette through the shimmering fabric.

His comment was not well received. 'Don't be tiresome, Arthur.'

She sounded weary, and Jack was made to feel boorish. He walked back to the bed and retreated under the covers, letting his head fall on to the pillow, doing as he was told. He was learning that it was the best tactic when faced with a resilient enemy. As he lay and listened to her pen working quickly and without pause, he wondered whether he would feature in her account.

He drifted off to sleep, the rare comfort of the charpoy lulling him to his rest.

Chapter Fourteen

◆—◆—◆

Jack panned his field glasses along the line of enemy defences. The ancient Dutch fort at Reshire shimmered in the heat haze, then came sharply into focus. The power of its defences made the breath catch in his throat. Stalker's division was lining up, readying for the assault. Jack and Ballard had found a vantage point on a small rise well out of the line of march. It gave them a fine view of both the fort and the army, allowing them to study the two forces as they prepared for the fight that both sides knew had been coming.

The Persian commander had had two days since the British division landed at Hallila Bay. Two days that he had used to gather his men and make sure the defences were as strong as he could make them.

They started with a network of trenches facing the direction the British army had to take if it were to storm the fort. They had been dug deep, the tops reinforced with sandbags, their path twisting and turning across the end of the peninsula. The long, wearing campaign in the Crimea had taught the world the most modern techniques of siege warfare. The Persian defenders had clearly employed the lessons the allied army had learnt, and now the redcoats would have to attack a series of well-constructed and scientifically designed trench systems packed with enemy soldiers. Hundreds of muskets were now aimed at the British troops who had formed up in front of them with ponderous precision. The power of their massed volleys would be brutal, the redcoats forced to advance into a storm of musket fire that would gut their ordered ranks.

Behind the trenches the ruins of old houses formed the next obstacle the attackers would face if they succeeded in breaching the first. The Persian soldiers had worked tirelessly to clear their fields of fire, and the redcoats would have to brave a storm of shot in the more open ground. There they would be forced to assault ruined wall after ruined wall, each one certain to be defended to the death by the fierce warriors who held them.

The Dutch fort formed the furthest part of the defences. It stood at the end of a rocky peninsula that jutted far out into the sea. The forbidding grey waters crashed around the heavy band of rocks at its base, the sound of the impact echoing across the peninsula like distant thunder. The old fort had been repaired and strengthened by the Persian defenders, who had seized upon its ancient defences to form the bedrock of their position. Broad ramparts lined the thick mud walls buttressed by bastions dotted at regular distances along their length. The whole was surrounded by a deep dry moat, a killing ground where any attackers would be exposed to constant fire from the defenders safe behind the ramparts.

Close to two thousand Persian soldiers were crammed into the network of defences. They came from the Dashti and Tungestoon tribes, the hardest of the irregular infantry in the Persian army. They were sarbaz infantry, the troops that made up the bulk of the Shah's armed forces, and they were deter-mined to stand firm and repel the invading red horde that had dared to venture into their homeland.

The Persian battalions were dressed for battle. Each fuadji wore a different-coloured cloth jacket, which created a gaudy kaleidoscope across the wide defensive line. The bright jackets were tucked into wide white pantaloons that were fastened above ankle-high boots with long stockings. On their heads they wore tall cone-shaped ram's-fleece hats called popakhs, which made them look distinctly foreign to the watching British soldiers. The rest of their uniforms were similar to those worn by the marching redcoats, the thick white cross belt worn over the chest a legacy of the decades now long past when British officers schooled the Persian troops in the art of war.

The sarbaz infantrymen were armed with long smooth-bore muskets. They were outdated when compared to the modern Enfield rifles carried by the British redcoats, but were still reliable and brutally effective. The Persian weapons used English-supplied flintlocks, another legacy of the British association with their army. The redcoats would come under fire from weapons sparked by the product of English manufacturing.

The enemy infantry waited for an assault they knew was inevitable. They trusted to their guns and their defences, confident that the red-coated army they faced would break itself on their walls and trenches. They would defeat the invaders and send them scurrying back to the boats that hovered on the horizon. Confident of victory, the sarbaz waited for the assault without fear.

But they hadn't reckoned on the Indian navy.

The gunboats, sloops and steam frigates had manoeuvred into position around one thousand seven hundred yards away from the fort, and now they opened the bombardment that signalled the start of the assault. Heavy artillery shells ripped through the air, their passage marked by a dreadful keening. They smashed into the network of trenches, great gouts of earth thrown high into the sky as explosions rippled across the defenders' line.

'Bang on time.' Ballard snapped shut his pocket watch and returned it to his pocket. 'Do pardon the pun. You have to hand it to our jolly Jack Tars. They certainly know how to shoot.'

Jack winced as a second salvo of shells roared out from the ships anchored close to the shore. He knew what it was to be on the receiving end of well-directed artillery fire. The terror of marching into a bombardment from a battery of heavy cannon still haunted his dreams, and he felt a pang of sympathy for the Persian soldiers. The second round of shells ripped into the trenches. Many exploded too early, the flash of the explosions bright even in the early-morning sunshine. But the navy gunners knew their trade, and a great number exploded the moment they entered the trenches. Even from a distance Jack could hear the screams as the shells tore men apart, their dreadful effect magnified in the closed confines of the trenches. The slaughter would have been terrible to behold.

A third, then a fourth salvo crashed out. Jack could picture the sweat on the smoke-streaked faces of the ships' gunners as they readied their enormous weapons. They would be going through the well-rehearsed drills without thought, the commands of the gun captains redundant after countless hours of repetition. The sailors were fortunate. They were far enough away to see their target as an abstract thing, not a living mass of humanity. They were spared bearing witness to the dreadful destruction they were bringing down on the Persian soldiers closest to the British assault troops.

Jack turned and looked at the long line of redcoats assembled to attack the fort. Major General Stalker had ordered his five battalions to form the assault in two lines of attack. The one regular British army regiment, the 64th Foot, were in the front rank, alongside the 2nd Bombay Light Infantry, a regiment of the East India Company's forces recruited from European rather than native soldiers. Two native regiments, also from the Company's army, the 20th Bombay Native Infantry and the 2nd Belooch Battalion, formed the second line, with a third native regiment, the 4th Bombay Rifles, positioned out on the left flank. Three thousand men, ordered to attack whatever remained of the Persian defences after the initial bombardment had finished.

As Jack watched, the army's own gunners opened fire. Two batteries of field artillery and one of horse artillery added their firepower to the barrage fired from the ships crowded close to the shore.

The trenches had now nearly disappeared under a thick cloud of smoke from the countless explosions. Yet it was not hard to imagine the destruction. All along the line, huge explosions threw enormous fountains of soil high into the air, as if some angry god was tearing holes out of the very earth itself. The ground shook with the power of the salvos, the watching redcoats shaken by the force of the barrage that never let up, shell after shell pounding into the enemy's defences in a remorseless demonstration of the brutal effectiveness of well-directed artillery fire.

'There they go!' Ballard squinted hard as he peered into the smoke. Shadowy figures were emerging from the battered trenches, moving quickly as the Persians ran to escape the ferocious barrage that was flaying their ranks and destroying their carefully constructed defences.

Still the artillery bombardment continued, tearing though the fleeing troops. It was hard to believe that each wraith-like figure was a living being. It was more like watching a shadow puppet show at the local fair, the spectacle seeming somehow unreal. Dozens of the dark shapes were thrown to the ground, the unceasing explosions gouging huge holes in the smoke, the navy pitiless in the execution of its orders.

The Persians were in full flight now. The battered battalions stationed in the trenches were unable to endure the dreadful storm of shot and shell that had torn their ranks apart. All notions of order and defiant defence were forgotten, the shattered bodies of their comrades abandoned without thought as they fled.

'Now's the time.' Ballard muttered the comment under his breath.

Jack could see the flush on the major's cheeks. He suspected this was Ballard's first taste of battle. Where the sight of the destruction turned Jack's stomach, Ballard had not yet seen enough to know the same revulsion. Instead, the smell of powder smoke excited him, like a schoolboy before his first rugger match.

'Advance!'

The brigade major bellowed the command. It was picked up quickly, the battalion officers repeating the order and stirring the five battalions into life.

Ballard turned to Jack as the long red line lurched into motion. 'Remember your orders, Jack. You are not going to fight, is that clear? Stay out of the way and search for any information that will be of use. You will most likely find it in the fort, so bide your time. When the enemy have been cleared out, go in and look for documents and so on that will tell us something of their plans. And don't give them time to destroy anything.'

Jack nodded. His throat had gone dry. The pungent powder smoke from the barrage was drifting over the British lines, its acrid tang sour in his mouth. Drums rattled and bugles blared amidst the red-coated ranks as they began the long advance, the bellows and shouts of sergeants and corporals loud

even over the cacophony of the bombardment that continued
unabated.

It was just as Jack remembered. The noise of the cannonade
was the same, assaulting the eardrums and reverberating
through the very fibre of his being. The fear returned. The icy
rush followed by the churn in the guts and the tremor deep in
the bowels. The terror of battle wormed its way in, twisting in
his belly as he faced the prospect of death. Yet there was also
the excitement, the fierce desire to enter the dreadful cauldron
of battle and once again prove his worth.

For Jack, battle was a place he both feared and desired.
He was no fool. He knew the reality of war. He had fought
enough to understand the sheer horror of the battlefield. He
was drawn to it nonetheless, the bitter talent he possessed
revealed in the sordid squalor of the fight. Only in battle could
he show his true self. Amidst the bloodshed and the death, the
shackles would fall away to reveal the steel hidden beneath. In
battle, Jack could show he was the leader of men that he knew
he could be.

'Good luck, Jack.' Ballard tapped him on the shoulder and
offered his hand. Jack could see a mix of conflicting emotions
on the major's face. Disappointment at not being involved in
the assault combined with relief at not having to face the
danger. He shook the hand, feeling the clammy sheen of sweat
on Ballard's fingers.

'I shan't need luck. I won't be fighting, remember.' Jack
forced a grin as he replied. Ballard had ordered him to stay out
of the assault, but he knew that anything was possible once a
battle had begun. He had loaded his revolver and paid a visit to
the 3rd Bombay Light Cavalry to have an edge put on his
talwar. He had learnt never to go near a fight without being
fully prepared, and he had an inkling that somehow he would
need his weapons before the day was done.

He stood and waited until the first ranks of redcoats had cleared his position before forcing his body into a trot, heading for the colour party of the 64th. The twin colours were huge, the gaudy, vibrant silk drawing him closer. One was the 64th's own regimental colour, a huge square of black silk surmounted with the red cross of St George. The other was the battalion's Queen's colour, a bright Union Jack with a laurel wreath in the centre, the regiment's number picked out in golden Roman numerals. Two young ensigns had been given the honour of carrying the colours into action, and they now unfurled their burdens, stirring the thick ash shafts so the silk caught the breeze.

There was grandeur in the spectacle. The two long lines moved forward, the men silent, their faces betraying none of the emotion that stirred inside every one of them. This was how the British army went to war. There was little fanfare, no martial tones used to inspire the troops other than the brazen call of the bugle and the hypnotic rhythm of the drums. The men advanced with calm precision, their eyes focused on their targets, their faces impassive as the assault of Reshire began.

Chapter Fifteen

———————◆———————

'Forward the 64th!'

Jack was close enough to hear the commander of the 64th urge his men on. The man was mounted on a light bay horse that pranced and skittered as it caught the infectious excitement that gripped the battalion. Jack supposed this was Major Sterling, the officer who had replaced Colonel Draper and who would now lead the men into battle.

The young ensigns carrying the flags marched forward with purpose, their arms straining to control the enormous squares of silk as they caught the wind to billow and flutter around their heads. They were guarded by the battalion's colour sergeants, each armed with a fearsome halberd, a relic of times long gone. The veteran sergeants were charged with the safety of the two flags, for to lose the colours was unthinkable and they would die to protect their battalion's pride.

Jack scanned the ranks for Knightly and caught a glimpse of the lieutenant marching in his station as the junior subaltern behind his company. He had not had a chance to find his friend in the hiatus of the landings or the swift departure that had followed. It was something he now regretted and he felt a sudden fear for Knightly, as if his inaction had somehow endangered the young officer.

The bombardment stopped.

The silence wrapped around the marching battalions. It was an unearthly quiet, and the faces of the redcoats turned pale as they imagined what was to come. The nine hundred redcoats of the 64th advanced two ranks deep, with a single company thrown out in front in a skirmish line. Behind the line, the sergeants prowled, their harsh voices snapping out to dress the ranks, keeping the advance steady, presenting an unbroken front towards the enemy.

The sandy ground passed swiftly under the heavy tread of the redcoats' boots. No enemy fire contested their advance. The trenches were ahead, a thick band of powder smoke enveloping them like a London particular. Had they still been manned, the redcoats would now be advancing into a maelstrom of fire. But the navy and the artillery had done their work, and instead the British marched into an eerie silence.

The skirmishers reached the trenches first. Jack saw the light company from the 64th scramble down, disappearing from sight for no more than a heartbeat before they reappeared on the far side, the dispersed ranks flowing across the obstacle with barely a pause. He could hear the officers' whistles as they led their companies on, the men moving with urgency now that the enemy fortifications had been reached.

The first shots rang out. Jack forced his pace, trotting forward so that he no longer wandered between the two lines of advancing redcoats. Ballard's orders to keep out of the fight were fresh in his mind, but he had felt exposed advancing alone. He wanted the company of the redcoats, and the steady ranks of the 64th drew him in like a moth to a candle. He did not want to die alone.

The 64th's skirmishers were taking cover as they left the

network of trenches behind. Working in pairs, they opened fire on the enemy sheltering behind the ruined walls of the village that had once clutched to the skirts of the Dutch fort. The Persian ranks were beginning to re-form, the remnants of the men in the trenches regrouping behind the men stationed in the second defensive position, the wild terror of their flight eased now that they had escaped the horrific bombardment. The officers started to reassert their authority, bringing order out of the confusion and rebuilding the shattered ranks so that their men would once again be able to join the fight.

Fresh Persian fuadji crowded behind the broken houses and piles of rubble, hundreds of muskets now aimed at the thin line of skirmishers. The leading redcoats were horribly outnumbered, but the 64th's light troops were not there to fight toe to toe with the packed defences. The skirmishers were trained to use cover and to fight independently. Their job was to pick at the defences, aiming their shots at the officers and sergeants who controlled the enemy soldiers, eroding the control and morale of the enemy before the thick ranks of the battalion arrived to deliver the shattering power of their massed volleys.

The Persian defenders opened fire, delivering a single huge volley as they sought to scour away the thin line of skirmishers. But the light troops knew their business. Their ranks were scattered, the extended formation leaving wide gaps between the pairs of redcoats, who ducked and twisted as they fought, using every bit of available cover to shelter from the enemy fire. Hundreds of musket balls flayed the air in a violent storm, but few skirmishers were hit, and they fought on, ramming and loading as they poured on their own fire, snatching men from all along the Persian line and exacting a dreadful toll on the enemy's leaders.

Jack saw the Persians' second defensive position disappear in the powder smoke of their opening volley before he came to the remains of the first trench. The parapet had been shattered, the sandbags used to line the top blasted apart by a well-aimed shell. The sand inside them had been scattered, dusting the ground, the soft yellow bright against the churned mud. He vaulted into the trench, knees bent to absorb the shock of the impact. As he thumped down on to the earthen floor, he reached for a handhold on the rear wall, his thoughts on nothing except the need to catch up with the fast-moving redcoats.

His foot slipped and he muttered a curse as he fell heavily against the side of the trench. He looked down in annoyance to see what had caused his boot to slide. The sight that greeted his eyes made him gag, and bile surged into his mouth, its acidic bite burning the back of his throat. A Persian soldier lay under his foot. The man had been hit by the naval bombardment. The same shell that had shattered the trench had eviscerated the unfortunate soul's stomach, and his entrails lay blue and pulsating on the ground, swamped in a sea of blackened blood. Jack's boot had landed on the gruesome mess, his heavy tread crushing the twisted guts into the mud.

'Dress the ranks!' The 64th's regimental sergeant major's voice thundered out from the far side of the trench, bringing the redcoats to a halt.

Jack tore his eyes away from the ruined body and forced himself up the side of the trench, emerging to see the British line halted whilst the officers and sergeants realigned the formation after the disruption of crossing the trenches. It was an understandable thing to do, yet it delayed the assault and gifted the battered Persian soldiers time to regroup after their retreat from the punishing artillery bombardment.

'Major Sterling!' Jack scrambled through the second trench before breaking free to run along the stalled line, calling for the attention of the 64th's commander. He saw the major turn as he heard his name, his face creased in concern as he saw a captain of hussars running towards him.

'What the devil . . . ? Who the hell are you?'

Jack slowed as he realised he had the major's attention. He could see the anxiety etched on the officer's face. It was no small thing commanding a battalion in battle, and Jack had sympathy for the man. But to halt the attack was folly, and he would be damned if he would sit on the sidelines and watch idly as the success of the assault was threatened by excess caution.

'Fenris. Stalker's staff.' He gave the lie easily. His lungs ached from the exertion of running and he was shocked at how out of condition he was.

'Quick, man, what is it?' Sterling leaned closer. He was young for his rank, his thick beard and moustache devoid of any trace of grey.

'You are to attack without delay.' Jack straightened up and looked Sterling in the eye. 'Don't waste time.'

'Damnation!' Sterling cursed, and a fleeting look of anger flashed across his face, but to his credit he controlled it quickly. 'You come from Stalker?' He snapped the question, waspish in the face of his commander's criticism.

'Yes!' Jack felt his own anger rise. 'Get a bloody move on!' This was not the time to dally. Decisions had to be made quickly now that the battle had started. Delay meant endangering the lives of the men. To Jack, that was inexcusable.

'Damn it all to hell!' Sterling snarled the words before turning away. 'Bugler, sound the advance! Come on, boys! Let's get at them!'

The rising call rang out and was quickly repeated by the company buglers. The sergeants and officers raced back to their places as the line jolted into movement.

Jack forced his temper down and trotted after the colour

party. He felt nothing at having assumed a rank far above his own. In battle, there was no place for niceties, or polite suggestion.

It was time to fight.

The second enemy volley crashed out. The air was suddenly alive with the whip-crack of passing bullets, a storm of musket balls slashing through the advancing redcoats. Jack flinched as a missile whispered past his ear, his body reacting to the fear that surged through him. Along the length of the advancing line redcoats were hit, their bodies thrown to the ground by the force of the impact, the whole battalion shuddering as it absorbed the enemy fire.

'Close the ranks!' The sergeants and corporals started the litany of battle. The line marched on, deaf to the screams of the men hit by the enemy fire. The pace of advance was relentless, the men callous now that the assault had begun.

'Forward the 64th!' Major Sterling exhorted his men onwards. A bullet had knocked his shako from his head and his dark hair stirred in the stiff breeze that billowed across the battlefield.

The 64th marched on. The Persians fired again, and more redcoats fell, their blood staining the foreign soil. This time the men seemed to surge forward after the fire swept along the line, their mood changing now they were close to the enemy. They tensed like a hound straining at its leash, ready for the order they expected at any moment.

'Now, my boys! Charge!' Sterling bellowed the command, waving his sword high above his head as he released his men.

The redcoats cheered as they stormed forward. The assault snarled into life, the tight line breaking up, and the wall of bayonets thundered towards the Persian line. The faces of the redcoats were twisted into dreadful grimaces as they were sent to do what they had been trained for: to close and kill the enemy.

The Persians saw the men charging towards them. Their frantic efforts to reload were forgotten as they watched the hundreds of bayonets coming for them. The redcoats were a dreadful sight. The terrified defenders had witnessed a dreadful bombardment, watching as hundreds of their comrades were slain by the remorseless barrage. Many of their officers and sergeants lay dead and bleeding, the work of the 64th's skirmishers taking away the voices that would have kept the defenders at their posts. Without firm leadership, their will to stand and fight evaporated in a heartbeat.

The Persian sarbaz ran. Many threw away their weapons in their haste, the urge to escape overwhelming. As they turned and fled, abandoning the second line of defences to the onrushing redcoats, they careered into the re-formed ranks of men who had been stationed in the trenches. The chaos was infectious, and it was too much for the shattered remnants of those who had endured the British barrage. The survivors joined the rout, any thought of rejoining the fight forgotten in the melee.

'Charge!' Jack added his voice to those of the 64th's officers. This was the time for madness, for the wild assault to race onwards. He knew they could not delay and risk losing the initiative. The officers had to keep the men moving fast, fanning the flames of the attack and giving the retreating enemy no respite. The redcoats had their foot on the throat of the Persian defenders. It was up to the officers to make sure they stamped down, crushing the last resistance without thought of mercy.

The redcoats reached the first wall and threw themselves over the top. A few stopped to discharge their rifles at the backs of the fleeing enemy but the bellows of their officers stopped them, ordering them to keep moving. Urged on by the officers, the men pressed forward, the last cohesion of the line disappearing as they thought of nothing but reaching the enemy.

Jack scrambled over the wall, ignoring the stab of pain in the palm of his hand as the coarse surface cut his skin. As soon as he was over, he pushed through the slowest redcoats, using his elbows freely to force a passage to the front. All thoughts of Ballard's orders to stay away from the fighting were forgotten. He drew his sword, the blade rasping from the leather scabbard as he released it.

'Come on!' He roared his challenge aloud, tasting the madness of battle. It was just as he remembered, the soul-searing joy of the fight filling his very being. He did not stop to see if the redcoats followed his lead. He ran forward, his left hand deftly unbuckling the flap of his holster as he moved and taking out the revolver.

'Follow me, 64th! Follow me!'

He felt broken tiles and bits of masonry crunch under his feet. He ran hard, forcing his tired legs to carry him onwards. Ahead he saw the press of enemy soldiers milling around the next barricade, their fear driving them away from the attacking redcoats. A few brave souls stopped to fire at the onrushing British troops, and the air was alive once again with the snap of bullets. Such courage was rare, though, and most thought of nothing but escape, fighting their own fellows to get over the wall and away from the steel bayonets rushing towards them.

Jack reached the next wall. He heard the thump of boots and the jangle of equipment behind him as the 64th rushed after him. He heard the shouts of the other officers as they urged their commands to greater haste, the fire of battle well alight in their bellies. Clumsy now that both hands carried weapons, he bundled himself over the wall, landing on the balls of his feet just in time to see the rush of soldiers charging towards him.

The men wore red jackets. For a single heartbeat, Jack had a terrible doubt that somehow another British battalion was attacking from the wrong direction, the similarity of the uniform making him pause. It only took a quick glance at the odd headgear of the leading ranks to recognise the enemy's counterattack.

He raised his gun, taking aim at the first figure rushing towards him. The face that appeared over the revolver's simple sight was twisted with rage, the hatred of a man fighting an invader of his homeland. He could see that the enemy soldier had dyed his eyebrows and eyelashes with henna, the oddness of the fashion registering in his mind as he opened fire.

The revolver's heavy bullet took the man in the face, snapping his head backwards. Jack switched his point of aim, firing for a second and then a third time, knocking two more of the red-jacketed enemy to the ground.

'Get the bastards!'

Voices screamed as the men of the 64th rushed past, their bayonets reaching for the enemy soldiers' flesh. They blocked Jack's aim, so he joined the charge, buffeted by the impact as the fast-moving redcoats surged forward. The opposing groups came together in a rush, the men from the two armies throwing themselves at each other with wild abandon, the violence sudden, sharp and brutal. The first men died in a heartbeat, the bayonets of both sides used with vicious precision. The bodies of the dead and the dying fell beneath the boots of the living, their bloodied flesh ground into the sandy soil without mercy.

Jack thrust himself into a gap and lunged at his first target. His enemy's red jacket had the three thick yellow chevrons of a vekil on the sleeve, the same badge of rank worn by British sergeants. The man was no naïve conscript, and he beat Jack's rushed blow to one side before thrusting his bayonet hard at

Jack's guts, his lips bared as he tried to kill the hussar officer with a disciplined attack.

Jack let the blade come. He knew the man would stamp forward as he lunged, the drill no different from the one Jack himself had learnt as a redcoat. The bayonet came at him fast, but he twisted away from the sharpened steel, letting it slide past no more than a single inch from his body. He slashed once with his talwar, a short, controlled attack aimed at the junction of neck and shoulder. The enemy vekil had no chance to recover, and Jack's blade thumped into his flesh, cutting deep into the man's body, bludgeoning him to the ground. Jack felt nothing as his opponent fell away, already seeking his next victim and deaf to the shrill scream of agony as the man he had struck down writhed once on the ground before lying still.

The enemy swarmed around him. Jack beat aside a bayonet thrust at his ribs, flaying his talwar at his attacker's face, driving him backwards. He saw the flash of fear in the man's eyes before the redcoat at Jack's side drove his bayonet deep into the Persian's breast, an explosive grunt escaping from the soldier's lips as he twisted the thick steel, recovering his stroke just as he had been taught in countless drills.

More and more redcoats were piling into the Persian infantry, overwhelming the determined counterattack. Yet still the Persian soldiers fought on, refusing to be beaten.

Jack flicked his talwar forward, driving the sharpened tip at another Persian. The man saw the blow coming and ducked underneath the fast-moving blade. His bayonet reached for Jack the moment he straightened, a quick, sharp jab that Jack only just managed to batter away with a desperate parry. The man roared with frustrated anger and came at him again. Jack saw the fury in his wild attack and parried the blow before stepping forward and punching the hilt of his sword into the man's face.

The Persian reeled away, his face bloodied. Before Jack could launch another blow, a soldier from the 64th attacked from the side, cutting the man down with a short, efficient stroke, punching his bayonet into the man's chest.

'Come now, sir. No need to fucking dance with the bastard.' The redcoat cackled with delight before he pushed on.

Jack made to go after him, but there was no longer any enemy to fight. The 64th had plunged into the melee without pause and fought with brutal efficiency. In the space of no more than a dozen heartbeats they had bludgeoned the counterattack to a standstill, the Persian soldiers' courageous attempt to thrust the redcoats back over the wall bloodily repulsed by the merciless bayonets.

'Forward the 64th!'

A captain roared the order, his sword flung forward to emphasise the command. He turned to Jack, a smile stretched across his blood-splattered face. 'Nice of you to join us, old boy.' He reached forward and clapped Jack hard on the shoulder before following his men forward.

Jack glanced once at the bodies that carpeted the ground before trotting after the captain. Around him the intermingled companies of the British battalion were surging forward once again, the redcoats stepping over the bodies of the dead as the assault stumbled back into life.

He looked ahead and saw the mud walls of the Dutch fort. The navy had obliterated the trenches, and now the redcoats had cleared the ruined village. The enemy soldiers were retreating to the last of their defences, their final bastion. The redcoats had fought hard, but it would all be for naught if they could not force a way into the fort.

Chapter Sixteen

*J*ack jumped down into the moat that surrounded the ancient Dutch fort. He landed hard and would have lost his footing if he hadn't blundered into the back of a soldier from the 64th.

'Mind your fucking feet.' The man's voice rasped in anger as Jack thumped into him.

Jack ignored the curse and tried to make sense of the confusion. The redcoats had followed their officers into the deep ditch, but once down, there was nowhere for them to go. They were pressed together in the confined space, and for the first time a ripple of uncertainty ran through the ranks. Ahead, a steep sand and shale embankment led up to the wall of the fort, which was lined with enemy soldiers firing down into the compact mass of troops in the ditch. Each shot found a target, and the battered Persian soldiers poured on the fire, knocking redcoat after redcoat from their feet. The assault stalled, the heavy fire and the ancient defences forcing the attackers to seek shelter.

Jack pushed his way forward, then pressed himself into the backs of the men lining the far side of the moat, where they were screened from the enemy fire. The redcoats had done well, covering the first hard yards quickly and clearing the first two lines of defence. Yet the final position was strong and they had baulked at the last hurdle, the impetus of the assault lost.

'This is no damn good.' Jack looked up at the enemy, searching for a gap in the defences. He saw none. He felt a body bump hard against his side and looked round to see the captain from the 64th who had passed him in the rush to the moat.

'We have to get them moving!' Jack bellowed to be heard over the cacophony of fire. He glanced at his fellow officer, noting the white wings on his uniform that told him the captain commanded the 64th's grenadier company. It was one of the two elite companies in the battalion, and Jack was pleased to have found the man in the midst of the melee.

'You have that right, old man.' The captain fixed Jack with a wild grin. His face was blackened from powder smoke and there was blood streaked on the sabre that he held. 'John Wood, grenadier company.'

'Fenris, intelligence department.'

Captain Wood whooped with delight. 'I was wondering what a dandy from the hussars was doing down here in the mire. I had rather supposed you had got lost.'

'I didn't want to miss all the fun.'

Both officers ducked as a Persian volley cracked out.

'Where are the 2nd?' Jack pressed his mouth close to Wood's ear, bellowing the question. He had no sense of the rest of the assault. The 2nd Bombay Light Infantry had been on the 64th's right flank. He had not seen them since the attack started and he had no idea if they had advanced or been beaten back.

'They're still with us.' Wood shouted the reply. 'But they are in the same bloody mess as we are. We have to get up that slope and drive the buggers back.'

Jack knew he was right. If the assault were not to fail, the officers would have to get the men to leave their shelter and throw themselves up the slope. The redcoats would have to summon the courage to charge directly into the face of the heavy enemy fire.

This was the responsibility that Jack had half forgotten: making the decision that would see men die at his command. Yet it had to be done. If they stayed where they were, the men would be cut down where they stood, the relentless enemy fire still finding targets no matter how hard the men pressed themselves into the dirt of the moat's wall. If they fell back, the blood the red-coated battalions had already shed would be wasted.

'Let's get this done!' Jack had to shout the words as the Persians' rate of fire increased. The enemy had sensed that the fight was balanced on a knife edge and had doubled their efforts to turn back the British assault.

'Bloody hell!' Wood flinched as a bullet punched past no more than an inch above his head. He took a step backwards, showing himself to the men huddling in fear against the wall of the moat. 'Advance, 64th! 64th will advance!'

Jack's heart thumped in his chest as he searched for the courage he would need. He looked back and saw the strain on Captain Wood's face. He risked a glance upwards and saw the Persians leaning forward trying to shoot directly at the redcoats who were partially hidden from view. There was little shelter in the moat. If they stayed where they were, they would die.

'Fucking hell.' He swore once under his breath and then pushed himself forward. This was the other responsibility of an officer in battle. The one Jack feared more than any other. Officers could shout and scream and give as many orders as they liked, but there were times when there was nothing for it but to show the men what was expected of them.

'Piss off!' The redcoat to his front cursed Jack as he elbowed his way into the press of bodies. Behind him he could hear Wood bellowing at his company to go forward. The redcoats were stubbornly clinging to the side of the moat, not one man willing to brave the dreadful barrage of musket fire.

'Shut your mouth.' Jack slammed his elbow forward, forcing his way through, ignoring the bellows of protest. He reached the wall of the moat. The side was not sheer, but it sloped up steeply away from him. Above it was a wide ledge that wrapped around the base of the fort's wall. If Jack managed to clamber up, he would be forced to stand in the exposed space where every Persian infantryman could see him.

He thrust his revolver back into his holster and pulled himself up as far as his arms could reach, the action made clumsy by the talwar he kept gripped tight in his right hand. His boots slipped on the sandy slope and he was forced to use his one free hand to pull himself forward, his progress reduced to little more than an undignified crawl. He screwed his courage tight and scrabbled his way up the side of the slope, then kicked hard and clambered on to the ledge. He flinched as bullets scorched past, but forced himself to his feet before turning to face the men of the 64th. He could see the fear in the whites of their eyes, the strain of enduring the enemy fire clear on every smoke-streaked face.

'64th!' His voice was huge. He saw men who had buried their heads in the sand lift their faces as he demanded their attention. 'You will advance!'

He recoiled as a musket ball smacked into the sand next to his feet, kicking up a puff of dust that splattered against his shaking legs. The terror was dreadful, but he fought against its embrace and stalked along the narrow ledge, showing himself to the frightened redcoats, demonstrating what it was he asked of them, flaunting the very courage they would have to find.

'64th! Follow me!'

It felt as if every Persian soldier was aiming at him personally. The sand around him was punched repeatedly, shot after shot coming perilously close to tearing his flesh. Somehow he survived and roared his orders, setting the example that the redcoats so badly needed.

'Follow that officer!' Wood screamed at his men, battering them with his fists, exhorting them to match the insane bravery of the hussar officer who had arrived in their midst. 'Move, move!'

Jack could not believe what he was doing. He had no place being in the fight, yet once he had seen what had to be done, he felt he had no choice. He was an officer. He was there to lead.

A dreadful roar erupted from the packed crowd of redcoats. It was a feral sound, a release of pent-up terror as they finally pushed aside their fears. As one they stormed forward, swarming up the treacherous slope and into the face of the enemy fire.

The Persian barrage faltered as the red-coated horde emerged from the cramped confines of the moat like a monster released from the depths of hell.

A ragged volley rang out. At such close range the Persian soldiers could not miss, and each bullet knocked a redcoat from his feet, the men falling like skittles at the fair.

The redcoats roared in defiance, hurling themselves out of the moat, the bodies of the fallen tumbling back to lie ignored and forgotten in the bottom of the ditch.

The Persian defenders wavered. Some turned and ran, abandoning their fellows to face the redcoats alone. Others looked down in horror at the horde that swarmed around the base of the wall, their muskets forgotten as terror took hold. A brave few cursed and reloaded, skinning their knuckles on their bayonets as they raced to be ready to fire again.

Jack reached forward and took a firm handhold on the wall in front of him. Decades of wear had left wide gaps and channels in its muddy facade. With his talwar still held in his right hand, he heaved himself up and started to scale the wall, terrified that he would drop his sword and reach the top without a weapon to fight with.

All around him the redcoats followed his example. They worked together, some bending double so they could be used as steps, others taking a firm hold of their fellows' cross belts before thrusting them up the wall to grasp the parapet. Jack could hear the bellows of a sergeant as he called men out of the assault, organising a firing party to scour the wall ahead of the climbing attackers. He flinched as their first volley cracked past him, driving the Persian defenders away from the edge of the rampart and clearing a space for the fastest redcoats to clamber up on to the top of the wall.

His lungs rasped with the strain of climbing. He glanced up and saw a Persian soldier lean over the wall and point a musket straight at him. He caught a glimpse of the clean-shaven face underneath the tall cone-shaped hat, and watched transfixed as the man aimed down the barrel of the musket, one eye screwed shut as he drew a bead on the officer who had inspired the attack. Jack braced himself, frozen in horror, his body tensing for the inevitable agony.

The musket coughed as it fired and Jack nearly let go of the wall in his terror. He felt the bullet snap past his body and screamed as he waited for the pain to come. To his shock, he felt nothing. He looked up. The man who had seemed certain to kill him had gone.

'Come on, old man.' Captain Wood flew past him, the commander of the grenadier company scaling the wall with the agility of a mountain goat. 'Forward the 64th!'

Jack hauled himself upwards, racing the 64th's captain up the wall, determined not to be second. Despite his best efforts, Wood reached the top first and Jack had to pause to avoid being caught by the scrabble of boots as his rival vaulted over and on to the parapet.

The explosion of a close-range volley assaulted Jack's eardrums, cutting through the air above his head, but there could be no turning back. With a final effort, he flung himself over the wall, a dreadful war cry blurting from his lips as he prepared to fight whatever waited for him on the other side of the parapet.

He stumbled forward, tripping over the corpse of the man who had aimed the musket at him just a few moments before. The man had taken a rifle bullet directly between the eyes, and Jack knew he owed his life to the quick-thinking sergeant who had dragged enough men from the assault to cover those climbing the wall.

There was no time to dwell on his deliverance. A blue-coated Persian soldier thrust a bayonet at his ribs, trying to strike him down while he was still recovering from his wild scramble on to the wall's summit. Jack could do nothing but watch in horror as the blade slid across his chest. He felt the edge score his flesh, but the inexperienced Persian soldier had thrust too soon and the bayonet went wide. Jack screamed in relief and with savage joy hacked his talwar forward, smashing the blade into the Persian's face. The man fell, his scream ringing out as Jack stamped forward, already searching for his next target.

He felt the madness of battle and let it take him, throwing himself at the press of Persian soldiers that milled in terrified uncertainty as the redcoats swarmed over the parapet. He slashed at the nearest enemy, the sharpened edge of his talwar tearing across his victim's cheek. He roared as he fought, snarling his hatred into the faces of the men who sought to block his passage.

He moved forward into the gap he had created, forced to step over the torn body of Captain Wood as he went. The man he had raced to the top of the wall had paid a dreadful price for having arrived first. The Persian volley had cut him down, but although his body was riddled with enemy bullets, somehow he had managed to fight on. A Persian infantryman lay across his legs, the officer's thin sabre buried deep in the man's stomach.

'Forward the 64th!'

Wood still lived. He shouted at his men to close with the enemy even as he lay in a pool of his own blood, fanning their desire for revenge.

A Persian sarbaz wearing the twin stripes of a dakhbash lunged at Jack. There was little conviction in the attack, and Jack laughed aloud as he simply twisted past the blade before hammering the guard of his talwar into the man's face. The Persian slumped to the ground and Jack stepped past, daring the other enemy soldiers to fight him.

Not one stepped forward to meet his challenge. The ferocity of his attack had forced the Persians back, creating more space for the redcoats who were spilling over the wall all round him. Already they had claimed the bulk of the parapet and now they looked to attack the last enemy soldiers, their bloodlust reaching fever pitch after enduring for so long under the Persians' relentless fire.

The respite gave Jack a moment's freedom, and he snatched his revolver from his holster. He still had two bullets left in its chambers and he emptied the weapon into the press of enemy bodies . The closest soldier crumpled as the bullets tore into his flesh, his body falling to lie at the feet of his fellows. More bullets followed as the men from the 64th finally had a target for their Enfields. At such close range, the effect of the modern British rifles was terrible. The ragged volley gouged through the Persian soldiers, tearing their bodies apart, each bullet passing through more than one man in a dreadful demonstration of the weapons' brutal power.

The sarbaz could take no more, and they broke. Still the redcoats fired, mercilessly flensing the retreating infantry, dropping more bodies to the ground.

'After them!' Jack's voice cracked as he roared at the redcoats. He led them forward, bounding down the ramp that led from the ramparts, his heavy boots thumping callously into ruined flesh as he ran across the bloody piles of torn bodies that smothered his path.

The redcoats went forward with a will. The companies were hopelessly intermingled, the chaos of the assault breaking their formation. They charged after the unknown hussar officer who had appeared to lead them, their voices screaming their challenge at the gods, their wild faces terrifying any of the Persian sarbaz foolish enough to try to stand against them.

The ground levelled under Jack's boots and he slipped and slid to a halt on the courtyard at the centre of the fort. The redcoats surged past him like a mob, chasing after the fleeing Persian soldiers who had tried so hard to keep the invaders at bay. The fight was over. Now all that was left was revenge.

'Arthur! What the devil!'

Jack turned and saw a face he recognised in the tightly pressed ranks of the redcoats racing past.

'Knightly!' He bellowed the greeting as the young lieutenant elbowed his way out of the crush and stumbled towards him.

Knightly's face broke into a wide smile as he saw his former guardian. 'What on earth are you doing here?' He followed the comment with a peal of laughter.

Jack laughed with him, releasing the joy he felt at having survived.

Knightly reached forward and clapped Jack hard around the shoulder. 'I thought you were off to re-join the 24th in the Punjab! Now here you are, larger than life and dressed in a bloody hussar captain's rig. How the devil do you explain that?'

'There's time enough for that later. Come and give me a hand.' The rush of victory surged through Jack. He knew that he had led the 64th to take the fort, certain that it had been his action that had forced the redcoats to continue the assault when they might have wavered and broken.

He laughed at his own arrogance, ignoring the bemused look on Knightly's face. He did not care what anyone thought. He had shown that no matter who he might pretend to be, he still had the ability to fight.

Now it was time to remember the orders he had forgotten in the wild melee of the attack. It was time to do the Devil's bidding.

Chapter Seventeen

———◆———

'Come on. This way.' Jack called over his shoulder to Knightly as he made his way towards one of the few doorways that led off the fort's central courtyard. He had no idea where he was going, but he could see a few windows above the doorway and it seemed the most likely direction.

Behind them, the redcoats were still piling over the ramparts. The 2nd Bombay Light Infantry had followed the 64th into the chaos of the assault, and now both battalions scoured the fort for any remaining enemy soldiers. Those they found they killed, their bayonets ending the last resistance without mercy.

In desperation, a handful of the beaten defenders took to the cliffs behind the fort, many plunging to their deaths as they tried to flee the victorious redcoats. The only alternative escape route was a network of steep ravines away to the west. As the redcoats piled into the fort, these gullies and slopes were filled with those sarbaz lucky enough to survive the assault. Yet even here there was to be no sanctuary.

As the enemy fled, Stalker released his cavalry, ordering them forward to harry the fugitives. The ground was poor and it would deny the cavalrymen the opportunity to massacre the fleeing infantry, yet they went forward willingly, the raucous call of their buglers urging them onward. Even from within the courtyard, Jack could hear the whoops and yells as they rode down any of the Persian infantrymen they could find, pursuing the remnants of the enemy force, their bloody sabres inflicting still more casualties on the broken ranks.

Jack pushed open the heavy wooden door with his boot, his muscles tensing as he half expected an enemy soldier to attack him the moment his hiding place was revealed. To his relief, the darkened interior was empty. He took a tentative step forward and peered inside. The small anteroom behind the door contained a number of ammunition crates, the wax paper that had protected the cartridges now scattered around the room. A single wooden staircase led upwards, and Jack felt a prick of fear as he realised he would have to scale it if he were to obey Ballard's orders and seek out any important documents before the Persians had time to destroy them.

He turned and saw that Knightly had followed him inside. The lieutenant's face was pale as he walked into the ammunition store, his Adam's apple bobbing up and down as he too looked at the dark stairway. For the first time, Jack noticed that Knightly's drawn sabre was still clean, the steel unblemished by blood.

'Are we going up?' The lieutenant's knuckles showed white as he gripped the handle of his sabre. He sounded like a small boy asking for permission to be taken to bed.

'I'll go first. Stay back in case I have to fight.' Jack gave the instructions in the clipped tones of an officer. There was no doubt who was in charge. 'Have you fired your revolver?'

Knightly shook his head and unbuttoned the flap of his holster before holding the weapon by the barrel and offering it to Jack. 'I never had the occasion to use it.'

Jack holstered his own empty gun before taking Knightly's. 'Is it loaded?'

'Of course.' Knightly spoke softly. He looked crestfallen, as if Jack had somehow questioned his bravery.

'Stay close,' Jack flashed Knightly a rakish smile, 'and follow me.'

The stairs turned to the right. The central wooden column blocked Jack's sword arm. If he were forced to fight, any defender would have the advantage of both height and the un-restricted movement of his own sword. It was just as the architect of the fort had planned. It was a design mirrored throughout the globe, from the dusty, damp stone fortresses of England to the splendid maharajah citadels of Hindustan.

Jack crept up the stairs, Knightly's revolver held steady in his left hand, the barrel pointing upwards. He would not hesitate to fire if necessary. In such an enclosed space the revolver would be deadly. He smiled as he tiptoed up the creaking stairs; the stopping power of the modern handgun had made a mockery of the antique defences.

He attempted to hide the soft scuffle of his heavy boots in the din of battle that still echoed through the fort. Yet no matter how hard he tried, every step seemed to thump against the ancient wood, so that it sounded as if an elephant was marching up the stairs. He paused and sucked in a deep breath, listening carefully, his ears straining to hear if anyone waited around the next turn of the staircase. He heard nothing. He closed his eyes and screwed his courage tight. He had endured enough pussyfooting around.

'Fucking hell!' He roared at the heavens as he threw himself forward, bounding up the staircase, taking the steps two at a time as he gave up the slow, nerve-stretching pace and gambled everything on violence and surprise. His boots thumped hard into the wood. He felt the effort pull at his thigh muscles and his breath rasped in his lungs in the moments before he burst round the last turn and into the simple room that mirrored the ammunition store below.

The scream took him by surprise. It was the piercing wail of terror released. He stumbled into the room, his eyes roaming the gloom for the source of the terrible sound. He heard Knightly crashing up the stairs behind him, yet there was no time to wonder if the lieutenant was close enough to help.

A flicker of motion caught Jack's eye and he twisted on the spot, his left hand swinging the revolver round in one smooth motion. He saw the flash of a weapon and pulled the trigger. The cough of the revolver was deafening, the sound echoing off the walls. He fired for a second time as he saw the rough outline of a figure stagger towards him. There was no time for thought, and he pulled the trigger once more, sending a third bullet into his assailant.

He stood still, his right hand tensed as he prepared to bring up his talwar, ready for the attack his instincts told him was coming. Yet none appeared. The silence stretched out, the quiet after the gunfire shrouding him. He ran his eyes around the room, searching for danger. He saw none; saw no one other than Knightly, who stepped belatedly into the room, his face ashen with fear.

Jack looked down at the figure that had leapt out at him. He supposed that the body now lying stretched out on the floor had been the source of the dreadful shriek of terror that had so set his nerves on edge. He saw the rusty sword that had caught his eye, the blunted edge and chipped tip that he had perceived as a threat. The robes the figure wore had once been white, but the simple cloth was now stained with so much blood that it had turned almost completely red. Jack's aim had been true, each of the three bullets tearing a huge hole in the slight body that had sought to ambush him. The corpse belonged to a young boy, no more than fourteen or fifteen years old. A childish dream of being a warrior now drowned in blood.

Jack sighed and turned away from the pathetic sight, forcing away the bitterness that threatened to crush him. Refusing to acknowledge the emotion that surged through him.

Knightly walked cautiously towards the corpse, as if uncertain whether the boy was alive or dead. He looked down in silence as he contemplated the victim of his friend's deadly skill.

'You killed him.' The lieutenant struggled to speak. He gagged as he broke the silence, as if the words physically sickened him.

Jack said nothing. He stalked across the floor towards a simple kitchen table positioned opposite the room's single window. Its top was smothered with stacks of paper. More was dumped carelessly on a battered dresser rammed hard into the corner behind the table. Jack had discovered what he had been sent to find.

'He was just a boy.' Knightly still stood over the body of the child. His sabre was held low in his hand, as if it was suddenly too heavy for the young officer to carry. 'He wasn't much older than me, yet you blew him apart.'

Jack laid the smoking revolver on a pile of paper and began to sift through the documents.

'You killed him, damn you!' Knightly raised his voice as he repeated the accusation.

The boy had fallen so that he lay on his back. Jack's bullets had hit him in the body, leaving his face untouched. His young features were twisted into a dreadful teeth-bared grin of terror. His upper lip was flecked with fine hairs that he had not yet been old enough to shave away. Dark ringlets curled down from his temples to whisper across his face, some errant strands catching and sticking in his staring eyes.

'He tried to kill me.' Jack's veneer of composure snapped. 'Now get a fucking grip and help me.'

Knightly shook his head, trying to dispel the nightmare, but he did as he was told, obediently sheathing his sword before coming to join Jack at the table.

'Is it always like this?' He picked up a single sheet of paper before tossing it away without so much as glancing at the text.

'No.' Jack swallowed the bitterness. 'It's usually much worse.' He was locking the memory away, securing it in the darkest recesses of his mind, where he hid all the horror that haunted him.

'He was just a boy,' Knightly said again.

'Then he shouldn't have been here. He was old enough to lift a sword.'

'He couldn't have hurt you.'

'Couldn't he?' Jack fixed the lieutenant with a cold, soul-searching stare. 'What would you have done had he attacked you? Spanked him and told him to go home? Or would you have hacked and flayed at the poor little bastard until he was dead.'

Knightly dropped his eyes. 'You're cruel.'

'War is cruel.' Jack's voice was harsh. 'You chose this as your career, so you'd better get used to it. Those bastards won't hesitate to kill you if you're foolish enough to give them the chance. So don't give them one. Fight as hard as you can and kill them before they kill you. It's the only way.'

He turned away, his bitterness choking off his speech. He prided himself on being a redcoat, on being able to thrive in the brutal bloodletting of battle. He glanced across at the pathetic corpse of the boy he had killed. The joy of the victory was gone. His fine words stuck in his craw. He felt nothing but shame.

Chapter Eighteen

———————————◆———————————

Major Ballard looked unimpressed as Jack deposited a small heap of paper on top of his travelling writing case. 'Is that all?'

'Yes. That's it.' Jack cared little for what he had found, his exhaustion after the fight finally getting the better of him.

He dumped his weapons and collapsed on to the charpoy pressed against the wall of the tent. As officers on the staff, he and Ballard had been able to lay claim to one of the first tents coming ashore. The navy was working tirelessly to supply the expeditionary force, despite a shortage of the native boats that they had hoped to find to assist with the effort. The small tent, which would ordinarily have housed a single officer, had become the less than salubrious headquarters for Ballard's intelligence department.

Jack lay back, not caring that he was filthy dirty. He heard Ballard sniff in disapproval but he left Jack alone and started work on the proceeds of his subordinate's morning's work.

The silence stretched out, but Jack was in no mood to talk. He wanted nothing more than to close his eyes and find rest. But the battle was too recent, the memories too fresh. It would take time for him to push them into the corners of his mind where he knew not to go. So he lay back and stared at the ceiling, trying to force the images from his mind and the shame from his heart.

At last Ballard spoke. 'Stalker is pleased.'

'We won. That's what he wanted. I should bloody hope he is pleased.' Jack's reply was flecked with belligerence. He felt his anger building. His commander had greeted him coldly and the reception had got under his skin. He was covered in the grime of the battlefield, his hands caked with the blood of the men he had killed. Ballard was immaculate, his uniform as clean as his soul, and Jack hated him for it.

'Of course we won.' Ballard snapped his reply, insensitive to Jack's mood. 'They had barely two thousand against a full division and half the bloody fleet. We should've been able to walk in there and wipe our boots on their doormat without losing so many damn men.'

Jack remembered the terror of leaping into the enemy trenches, the unbridled fear as the air hummed with bullets, the memory of standing alone to lead the 64th out of the shelter of the moat. 'It was a hard fight. Our men did well.' He bit his tongue, trying to hold back his fraying temper.

'The men did damn well.' Ballard shot Jack a frosty glare. 'Do not think that I denigrate the fine effort of our soldiers. They gave us the victory. Not General Stalker, and most certainly not us on the staff.'

Jack grunted in reply. In his experience, generals laid claim to victories no matter what the circumstances.

'And do not think I have overlooked your efforts.' Ballard continued his tirade. 'I have heard all about your damn exploits. You should not even have been in the fighting.'

'Where else should I have been?' Jack snapped the question.

'Out of the damn way and obeying the orders I gave you.'

'They needed my help.'

'What utter claptrap.' Ballard's face flushed as his own temper rose. 'It was not your job. Your orders were to stay out of the way and go in after the assault. If I had known you would want to play the hero, I would have let you rot in a cell in Bombay. I have no need of a soldier. Men who can wield a sword are ten-a-penny round here. Men who can do what you do are not. I suggest you remember that and next time do as you are bloody well told.'

Jack glared back, fighting against the urge to lash out. The image of the boy he had killed flashed into his mind. It shamed him. He had nothing to be proud of. He sighed and did his best to speak in an even tone, his words cutting through the atmosphere that had been building between them. 'I did what I thought I had to do. It might not be what you ordered, but I could not stand back and watch those men die.'

Ballard fixed him with a keen stare. For the first time, Jack saw a grudging respect. 'Very well. You are a brave man, Jack, if perhaps not a wise one. I would ask you to give my orders more consideration in the future.'

Jack nodded. 'I'll try.'

Ballard shook his head slowly. 'You will do more than try. Obey my orders or face the consequences. There is no middle ground. Is that clear?'

'Yes, sir.' Jack tried to sound chastised. He was too tired to fight any longer.

'Good.' Ballard sat back and breathed out as if releasing a hidden tension. 'So, it appears we have a problem.' His voice cracked as he revealed what had him so rattled. 'We have failed.'

'Stop being so damn melodramatic.' Jack's patience was wearing thin. 'How have we bloody failed?' He did not understand. Ballard had given the general a full account of the defences. They had been just as he had described.

Ballard paused. He stared at the paper in his hand for a long time before looking back at Jack, his eyes betraying the pain of what he had discovered.

'The enemy knew we were coming.'

'Of course they knew we were coming.' Jack felt his exhaustion slipping away as his anger rose. 'We were camped on their bloody doorstep. Their general would have to be bottle-head stupid not to know we were going to launch an attack.'

Ballard scowled. 'They knew more than that.' He brandished the paper. 'Our numbers, which battalions would lead the attack, even what Stalker had for bloody breakfast. They knew everything.'

Jack still did not understand. 'So they knew we would attack. None of that changes anything.'

'Perhaps it would not have affected the course of the battle, but it still means there is a spy in our camp.' Ballard threw the paper on to his desk in disgust. 'At the very heart of our operations.'

'How can there be a Persian spy in our camp?' Jack was tired and he answered more scathingly than he meant to. 'I rather think we would spot them.'

'They will not be parading around in their damn uniform.' Ballard's reply was biting. 'They will have a little intelligence.' He clearly doubted this was a trait shared by his subordinate.

'So what are we looking for?' Jack was finding organising his thoughts like wading through a swamp.

'If I knew that, Jack . . .' Ballard let the thought go unfinished. 'What I fear is that the enemy have already succeeded in placing a network of spies around us.'

'What the hell do you mean by that?'

'I am thinking of a number of spies, all working for a single spymaster. That is what I would do if I were them. Position a web of agents around our operation, all controlled by a single source.'

'Do you think the Persians are that clever?'

'Of course they are. Do not forget they have the Russians working with them. I shouldn't be at all surprised if the damned Russians control the spies. It would be quite up their street. They know the rules of this particular game better than anyone.'

'Better than you?'

Ballard scowled. 'No. I will find them.'

'Well you haven't found them yet.' Jack was quick to snipe.

'Thank you, Jack. I am fully aware that it is my job to prevent the enemy infiltrating our establishment. So that makes this my failure.' For the first time, Ballard's emotions were revealed. Despite his carefully constructed facade, there was a hint of shame in his voice.

Jack finally understood. Ballard blamed himself for the hard fight. Jack had been unfair. The major might not have smelt the smoke of the battlefield or slashed his sword at the enemy, but he still had blood on his hands.

'You were not to know.' Jack grimaced even as he spoke. He had never been good at delivering the polite blandishments that were expected of him.

Ballard fixed him with a withering stare. 'It's my job, Jack. I am supposed to bloody know. Fetherstone will be sure to make the most of it. As soon as he hears of this, that goddam man will demand my head.'

'It's easy to say what should have happened. It isn't the same as doing it yourself.' Jack's voice was full of scorn . He was beginning to understand Ballard's dislike of the commodore.

'Fetherstone always has an opinion.' Ballard was bitter. 'He pokes his finger into every damn pie yet never damn well bakes one himself.'

Ballard went quiet. He stared at the paper on his desk, as if rereading it would somehow change things. Then he stood up abruptly and stalked across the tent to take a bottle of vodka from his knapsack. He lifted the bottle to his lips and took a huge draught before offering it to Jack.

Jack accepted the bottle and took a more circumspect sip. He had never favoured raw spirits: a childhood spent dishing out the vile gin his mother supplied had turned him away from the taste of anything other than wine or beer. Yet the harsh liquor felt good as it burned down his throat.

'So at least we now have proof that there is a spy at the heart of this operation.' Ballard sat back down and picked up the sheet of paper he had been reading.

'How can you be so sure?' Jack's voice rasped with the after-effect of the fiery liquid.

'You found the evidence yourself.' Ballard passed the single sheet of wafer-thin paper to Jack. A fine copperplate script flowed across the page, the tightly spaced lines written in tiny letters.

Jack read the letter slowly. It told of the British army's preparations, listing the battalions with their current strengths, the number of cannon, the ready supply of ammunition, the details of the support ships and all manner of other details about the expeditionary force. Worst of all, it told of Stalker's intention to attack at Reshire; the expected dates, timings, forces, everything. The enemy had known every detail of the assault.

'Who wrote this?'

'That, Jack, is the question. You might want to read the last paragraph on the second side.' Ballard sat back in his chair before dropping his head into his hands.

Jack did as he was told and flipped the page. It took him a moment to find the passage Ballard had mentioned. When he did, he felt an icy hand place a grip around the back of his neck. The paragraph spoke of a formerly unknown captain of hussars who had appeared on the staff of the intelligence department. It was a brief reference, nothing more than two short sentences, yet it still made for hard reading. The author of the revelatory letter had damned Jack with a succinct turn of phrase, referring to him as a loutish rogue who was probably no more than a hired thug.

Ballard winced as he saw Jack's face. 'Do you still doubt we have a problem?'

'No.' Jack wanted to scrunch the paper into a ball, but he contented himself with tossing it back on to Ballard's blotter. 'So who the hell is it?'

'I would give a great deal to know that.' Ballard took the sheet of paper and lifted it close to his nose, as if he could discern the writer's identity from a closer inspection of the ink. 'But it is our job to find out and we had better do it damn fast.'

'And how do we do that?'

'You are full of questions.' Ballard closed his eyes as he thought. 'I have a few spies of my own and—'

'You do?' Jack interrupted.

'Really, Jack. Do you think I am a fool? I got to the bottom of your sorry little tale without too much difficulty, so it shouldn't surprise you that I know what I am about.' Ballard was condescending. 'I know my job, do not ever doubt that.'

Jack bowed his head. Ballard was right to remind him of his place.

'They have yet to provide anything useful.' Ballard snorted as he acknowledged his lack of success. 'Palmer has been in touch with a few of them. I have good reports on the enemy forces. I have nothing on any spy network.'

Jack had wondered where Ballard's shadow had been. He had barely seen the bodyguard since they had arrived. It was a sharp reminder that he did not know all of Ballard's affairs, something he would do well to remember.

'With Palmer engaged, it will fall to you to assist me here.'

Jack nodded. He did not know how he could help, but Ballard's scorn had shamed him. He was determined to prove himself useful, to demonstrate that he possessed the wit, and the ability, to be more than just a killer.

Ballard was watching him closely. 'You will have to be circumspect. I cannot have you blundering around like a bull in a china shop, and there had better be no more of your damn belligerence.'

'I understand.' Jack was thinking of Sarah. She was well connected. Perhaps he could use her to help him.

'You had better. Do not make me regret giving you this chance.'

'I won't.'

'We shall see.' Ballard's gaze rested on him. 'We shall see. So I expect you heard that the fleet bombarded the town of Bushire and forced them to surrender?'

'I did.'

'That gives us a secure foothold here. The navy will keep us supplied and Stalker will use the next week or two to build up the army's strength and prepare for a longer attack into the interior. That's if he is not replaced.'

'Is that likely?'

Ballard puffed out his cheeks and sat back in his chair, placing his hands behind his head. 'I would say it is now inevitable. He won his victory but the cost was too high. Colonel Malet of the 3rd Bengal Light Cavalry died in the assault, and we lost two other officers from the 20th. Worse, Brigadier Stopford from Stalker's own staff was killed. You simply cannot lose a Companion of the Bath and still consider yourself to have fought a small skirmish. I'm of the opinion that the government will now regard this as a more serious venture than they first thought. They will either need to hold us here indefinitely or reinforce us. If they choose the latter, Stalker is not senior enough to command more than a single division, so they must send a new commander-in-chief.'

'Poor Stalker.'

'He will not take it well.' Ballard did not sound overly concerned at the notion. 'He is doing his best to ensure he stays in command. He has written his dispatch praising every damn person he can think of. He is even recommending an officer from the 64th for one of the new Victoria Cross medals for bravery. A Captain Wood.'

Jack smiled as he remembered the officer who had beaten him to the top of the wall. 'Wood fought well. He deserves to be recognised.'

'Stalker also mentions another officer who led the assault and who many are saying inspired the victory. He has asked me if I know who it might be, so that he can be recommended for the same medal.'

Jack looked at Ballard keenly. 'What did you tell him?'

'What do you think I told him?' For the first time since Jack had returned, Ballard smiled. 'I said I had no idea who it might be. I had no one involved in the assault so this mysterious figure could not possibly have come from my department.'

Jack smiled despite the disappointment. 'You bastard.'

Ballard laughed off the insult. 'You don't exist, Jack. I can hardly have you listed in the damn dispatches. But you did well. All things considered. Well done.'

Jack threw back his head and laughed. If he had been a real officer, he would now be basking in the glory of receiving the newly conceived medal that was the highest accolade for bravery. But such a fate was denied him. He was no more than a charlatan masquerading as an officer. His only thanks would be a sarcastic nod from the man who had ordered him to stay out of the battle.

'So what now?' he asked, reaching to take back the bottle of vodka.

'Now?' Ballard smiled wolfishly. 'Now we find the enemy spies. I don't care if there are one or a hundred. We will find them all.'

'And then?'

'Then you can kill them. Slowly.'

Jack nodded in agreement. He was never going to receive a medal. He would have to find satisfaction in other, more visceral ways. He would hunt down those who had given the enemy the information that had certainly led to the deaths of many redcoats.

Then he would do the job he had been brought all this way to do.

Chapter Nineteen

———◆———

Jack walked towards the town of Bushire with pride. Sarah Draper had slipped her arm through his as they left the British encampment. It was an innocent enough gesture, yet he savoured the feeling of walking with such a beautiful woman. It had earned him many jealous glares from the other officers who were diverting themselves by visiting the recently captured town. He had heard little to recommend the place, but when Sarah had suggested paying a visit, he had been unable to deny her. Now that they had left the encampment behind, he had begun to enjoy the temporary reprieve from Ballard and his quest to find the spy.

The assault on Reshire and the subsequent capture of the nearest large town had given the army some respite from the rigours of the campaign. Yet despite their efforts, the men would not have an opportunity to enjoy their hard-earned rest. Stalker had issued orders for a wide defensive trench to be dug across the narrow neck of land that separated the swampy peninsula on which Bushire sat from the mainland. It was to be three feet deep and six feet wide, and the earth was to be thrown up to form a sturdy parapet. The redcoats might curse as they blistered their hands digging at the soft, friable soil, but the defensive position was necessary to protect the stationary army from landward attack.

In order to give them warning of any such Persian incursion, cavalry pickets had been established a few miles inland. The expeditionary force could only boast two regiments of cavalry, the 3rd Bombay Light Cavalry and the Poona Horse. Both had been worked hard. Thus far there had been little sign of the enemy, and it appeared that, for the moment at least, the British army would be allowed some time to recover from the exertions of their initial invasion.

The navy had used the lull in operations to bring the army up to strength, even though the largest ships in the fleet were obliged to lie three miles offshore, the presence of sandbanks close to the harbour at Bushire forcing them to ferry everything ashore on smaller craft. No matter what the difficulties, the navy had worked hard to build up the army's supplies. Thanks to their efforts, the tired redcoats now spent their nights under canvas, the long-awaited tents having finally arrived with the equipment and rations the army would need to strike inland.

With their men fully engaged digging the defences, the British officers had been granted permission to spend their time at leisure. Yet the Bushire peninsula failed to impress. Any hopes of the town itself being a pleasing diversion soon faded. The first few officers curious enough to explore its labyrinthine network of streets and alleys found little there to interest them. It was deemed a miserable place, full of mean peasant hovels, with the British residency the only substantial building of any quality. The town was surrounded by wide swathes of marshland and swamp, the only good land already occupied by the ever-growing British encampment. Heading further inland was out of the question, so the bored officers were limited to bathing in the sea and hunting the local birds and waterfowl.

The encampment echoed to the sound of gunfire as the over-zealous hunters amongst the officers slaughtered anything with wings. It might not have been good for the local wildlife, but at least the daily haul could be used to supplement the dreary rations provided by the ships.

Yet it appeared that change was in the air. The army was still reacting to the news that Major General Stalker had not long left in command. The government had decided to up the ante, and already a second division was on its way from Bombay to reinforce the troops that had carried out the invasion. With the second division would come the recently gazetted Lieutenant General Sir James Outram, an experienced officer who had made his name in the First Afghan War when, as a junior officer, he had captured an enemy colour at the Battle of Ghazni. Since then his career had flourished, and his defence of Hyderabad against eight thousand Baluchis during the Sind uprising had made him one of the most famous of all Queen Victoria's generals.

Outram and the second division would land in the coming days with express orders to take the fight to the Persians. The objectives of the campaign had not changed. With two divisions at his disposal, Outram could maintain a more aggressive operation, and the larger force would help convince the Shah that the British would not back down until he had agreed to terms that would force him to relinquish his hold on Herat.

The arrival of their new commander would surely put an end to the expeditionary force's temporary respite. Already orders had arrived for the battalions to begin a series of daily route marches once the defensive preparations were complete; Outram seemed determined to prevent the redcoats and the native infantry from going soft.

'Captain Fenris!'

'Excuse me a moment.' Jack made his apology to Sarah and turned to face the hectoring voice that had interrupted their stroll. To his disappointment, she let go of his arm as he did so.

'Captain Fenris, it is good to see you again.'

Jack felt his back stiffen as he recognised the naval officer walking towards him.

'Good afternoon, Commodore.' He saw the pointed look Sarah shot his way as she heard the ice in his tone. He was in no mood to be conciliatory. He had spent the last few days in pointless inactivity, searching the documents he had rescued from the fort at Reshire for any further clue as to the identity of the spy in the British camp. He had found nothing, and the task had him chafing at the bit to do something, anything, other than sit and read more of the same.

'Mrs Draper, how lovely to see you again.' Fetherstone bowed at the waist and fixed Sarah with a warm smile that, much to Jack's annoyance, she returned in equal measure. If Fetherstone spotted anything awry in finding a lady he knew to be married in the company of an officer who had only just joined his rival's department, he hid it well. Indeed, he seemed pleased to have bumped into the oddly matched couple.

The naval officer was close to a foot shorter than Jack, who stood straighter to emphasise the difference. Fetherstone seemed not to mind being forced to stare upwards as he tore his eyes from Sarah and focused them on her companion.

He was older than Jack remembered, his grey hair and whiskers thinning and his face weathered. Yet his eyes twinkled as he saw Jack's obvious belligerence, the spark of life still very much alive in the clear blue eyes.

'I hear Ballard has been working you hard. It cannot be easy for a man of action to be forced to spend his days behind a desk.' Fetherstone half smiled as he passed comment, clearly hoping to rub Jack up the wrong way.

'It's part of my job, sir.' Jack snapped at the lure. 'I do not mind it.'

Fetherstone guffawed at the stiff reply that was just what he had hoped for. 'I can see he has got you well trained, at least. Did he give you a royal rollicking for joining the attack?'

Jack scowled at the criticism of his commander. 'I did not take part in the assault.'

'Come, come, Captain. Please credit naval intelligence with knowing a few things. Your bravery has not gone wholly unnoticed. I hear your actions quite saved the day. I cannot think why Ballard would not let you garner the credit you so clearly deserve, unless he means to punish you, of course. That, at least would make sense, however churlish it may be.'

Jack caught a glimpse of Sarah looking closely at him as the naval officer alluded to his part in the assault on Reshire. He hoped the revelation would impress her. Despite his instinct warning him to be careful, he felt a spark of pride at the recognition that Fetherstone was giving him. Yet it was still a dangerous topic, and he knew he needed to steer the inquisitive intelligence officer away to safer ground.

'Major Ballard ordered me to remain out of the fighting, sir. You must have me mistaken for another man.'

'I rather fancy you are the one who is mistaken if you think I am going to believe that. I am no man's fool, believe me.'

'I'm sure you are no fool, sir.'

'I am glad to hear it. So, have you found the spy?'

This time Jack struggled to hide his surprise. 'I don't know what you mean, sir.'

Fetherstone's snort revealed his opinion of Jack's denial. 'You would do well to leave the politicking to Ballard, Captain Fenris. You are not cut out for dissembling. You should not be astonished that I know of the presence of a spy. It comes as no great surprise that the Persians have men in our camp.

We all know that the Russians are supporting the Shah. They will have taught him all he needs to know about handling such things. Indeed, I would be more surprised if there were no attempts to garner information. What concerns me is that the enemy appears to have access to the very heart of our enterprise here. That is a danger to the success of the campaign, and it is my duty . . .' he smiled thinly at Jack before continuing, 'our duty to discover their identity and root them out before any more harm is done.'

'Then may I ask what the navy is doing about it?' Jack lifted his chin as he asked the pointed question.

Fetherstone was not at all put out. 'Why, the same as you, I imagine. Judging from your reaction, we are both having the same amount of success.'

'Perhaps.' Jack tried to remain non-committal. The commodore was right. He was out of his depth. 'So you think there is just the one spy?'

Fetherstone scowled. 'I think it unlikely that even the army is foolish enough to allow more than one. Does Ballard think there are more?'

'Major Ballard keeps his own counsel.'

'I am sure he does.' Fetherstone seemed to give the matter some thought. 'No. It does not make sense, to me at least. One well-placed spy could do much more damage than a dozen poor sources. Why would the enemy risk placing more than one agent? We are looking for one man, I am sure of it.'

Jack made a note of Fetherstone's certainty.

'It really is a shame Ballard is so secretive.' Fetherstone shook his head at Jack's reluctance to be drawn. 'It would be better for everyone if our two departments could find a way to work together.'

'I'm sure Major Ballard has his reasons, sir.'

For the first time, Fetherstone scowled. 'The man is clearly paranoid, or deluded; perhaps both. I would like to ensure you are not prejudiced against us. My door is always open to you. If you feel you have information that would be best shared, you must not hesitate to come to me.'

Jack said nothing.

Fetherstone smiled at the reaction. 'You are a loyal soul, Captain. It does you great credit. But sometimes you must think of a higher purpose. You must do what you know to be right, no matter what the cost. Isn't that so, Sarah?'

Sarah's brow furrowed. 'I would like to believe I would do what is right.' Jack heard an unfamiliar trace of timidity in her voice.

Fetherstone looked at her sharply before continuing, leaving no time for Jack to dwell on her reply. 'Anyway, I would not wish to delay you. I can see you are out to enjoy a pleasant afternoon's excursion, although I must warn you that you may not find Bushire to your taste. It is a mean place. There is little to recommend it.'

Jack nodded politely. Fetherstone reminded him of a hungry sparrow pecking at the ground in the hope of finding a delicious morsel. No matter how many times he was disappointed, he could not resist pecking some more.

The commodore turned back to Sarah. 'Mrs Draper, I was wondering if you and your brother would do me the honour of dining aboard tonight. The place hasn't been the same since you left us.'

Sarah bobbed her head in acknowledgement of the gracious comment. 'We would be delighted.'

'Wonderful.' Fetherstone clapped his hands. 'Until tonight, then.' He bowed at the waist and left Jack and Sarah alone.

'Do you really like him?' Jack asked when he judged Fetherstone to be out of earshot.

Sarah slipped her arm back through his as they turned to

resume their walk towards Bushire. 'He is good company. He looked after me when we were on board his ship. It would've been rude to refuse him. Do you mind?'

'Of course not.' Jack was surprised she asked the question.

'I shall not stay late.' She nestled her head against his arm, like a cat brushing against its master. 'We shall have the night together, I promise.'

The idea made Jack smile, and he pushed the meeting with Fetherstone from his mind. 'Perhaps when you are there you could do something for me.' He asked the question softly. He was thinking of Ballard's instruction to help him discover more about the spy plaguing the army. It was clear from their conversation that Fetherstone was working on the same thing. Sarah was certainly clever enough to be able to help him, and if she was going to spend the evening with the leader of the naval intelligence department, perhaps he could ask her to garner some useful intelligence for him.

'I rather think I am doing enough things to you,' Sarah teased, lifting her face. 'I am shocked you would consider asking for more.'

'Not *to* me. *For* me.' Jack shook his head at her coquettish behaviour. He did not fully understand her wanton streak. He was no shy virgin, but he sometimes found her behaviour somewhat unbecoming. He sensed that she had a deep need for his company, something more than just a desire for the nocturnal activities they shared. Yet she guarded her emotions well, almost as well as he did his. He had yet to penetrate her protective shell, the hard carapace behind which she hid her true feelings. He hoped that with time she would let him.

'When you dine with Fetherstone, it would be helpful if you could find out what he knows of any enemy spies.' Jack made sure he looked at her as he asked the question, trying to read her reaction to his words.

Sarah pouted, his request clearly not to her liking. 'What is all this fuss about spies? James told me they are almost inevitable in a campaign on enemy soil. I am sure half the local people are reporting back. Surely it makes little difference. It is no great secret that we are here to attack.'

'No. It is more than that.' Jack wondered how much to reveal. 'The enemy is somehow getting more than just general observations. It is becoming serious.'

'How delicious,' Sarah purred as she began to understand the intrigue. 'What about Captain Hunter? You know his father was forced to sell his commission?'

Jack was interested. 'I had no idea.'

'It was over some affair with his regiment's accounts. The poor fellow never got over the shame and killed himself when Hunter was a child. They say his ghost haunts their family home, his tortured soul unable to find rest.'

'That sounds like bollocks to me.' Jack had no time for such gossip. 'Hunter seems a decent fellow.'

'So that precludes him from being a spy?'

Jack shook his head. 'I think for now we should concentrate our attention on finding out just what Fetherstone knows rather than throwing slurs on every officer on Stalker's staff. This is not a game. If the Persians do have a well-placed spy, men will die because of his information.' He paused, letting the seriousness of his words sink in.

Sarah was silent. It was some moments before she spoke. 'Cannot Ballard not simply ask Fetherstone what he knows?'

'No. They don't trust each other.'

'So it is up to us?' Sarah was quiet a moment longer before she rallied and squeezed his arm tighter. 'How very exciting. It will add some wonderful spice to my account.'

'You mustn't write about it!' Jack was appalled. Ballard would have his balls if he found out he had asked Sarah for help. 'At least not yet. Not until this is all over.'

'I shall be the soul of discretion.' Sarah was clearly delighted at being involved in Jack's scheme. 'There really is more to you than meets the eye. I think I may have underestimated you.'

Jack smiled at the notion. He was pleased to have Sarah on his side. He had a feeling she would be a powerful ally.

They walked in silence as they entered Bushire, content in each other's company. The street was narrow, with windowless buildings pressed hard on either flank. It was a dank, foreboding place and the muddy ground underfoot was liberally scattered with filth.

'Fetherstone was right.' Jack acknowledged the commodore's warning about Bushire. 'This place has little to recommend it.'

'Fetherstone is often right. You would do well to remember that. You can trust him. You cannot place all your faith in Major Ballard.'

'Why do you say that?' Jack stopped in the middle of the road. There was no one else around. Many of the town's inhabitants had taken to staying in their houses now that the invading army had made its camp on their doorstep.

'He has a reputation as a ruthless man who will stoop to any depths to achieve his aims. He will not serve you well.'

Jack said nothing. He could understand why Ballard was thought of in that way, yet during his time with the major he had come to like the man. There was something refreshing in his forthright manner, especially when compared to so many of the callow buffoons Jack had encountered in the British army.

'You must be careful not to be used,' Sarah continued, 'for he will discard you without a qualm when he has finished with you.'

Jack kept his face neutral. He could have levelled the same accusation at Sarah herself. He knew where he stood. He was aware that the time would come when he would be cast out.

By both of them. He had been alone too long for that thought to worry him.

'You do not agree?' Sarah's mouth twisted in vexation as she noticed that Jack was ignoring her advice. Jack saw the flash of temper in her pale blue eyes.

'I do not.'

'You think you know it all, don't you, Arthur? You know about Ballard, about Fetherstone, even about my brother. Is there anyone that surprises you?'

'No.' He spoke with blunt honesty.

'How very sad.'

Jack turned and began the long walk back to the British encampment. He had gone no more than a dozen paces when he heard footsteps as Sarah trotted after him. She slipped her arm through his, but said nothing.

He thought about what she had said. He did not know if he could trust Ballard, but he was certain he could not trust Fetherstone. He sighed and placed his hand over Sarah's, feeling the warmth of her skin underneath his fingers. Fetherstone had been quite correct: he was not cut out for politicking. He could do nothing but trust his own judgement and place his faith, and indeed his life, where he thought it best.

Chapter Twenty

---◆---

The 78th Highlanders arrived with glorious fanfare. To the skirl of their bagpipes they led the new division into the encampment outside Bushire, the locals looking on in astonishment as the kilted warriors marched in. The Highlanders were impressive. Their usual feather bonnets and hackles had been left behind at their barracks at Poona, but even in just their hummel bonnets they still looked imposing. The people of Bushire had never seen anything like the fabulous MacKenzie of Seaforth tartan that the Scottish soldiers wore, the dark green standing in vivid contrast to their red jackets with their bright buff facings.

The rest of the second division were less spectacular. The red-coated battalions of the 23rd and 26th Bombay Native Light Infantry marched to their allotted areas with calm order. With them came more artillery and more cavalry, the arrival of a second full division filling the encampment to capacity. For the weary redcoats of the first division, the new troops created a welcome spectacle, although few had any strength left to greet them. That day, the division had endured a twelve-mile route march to the town of Charkota, so that it was a drained and weary audience that watched the reinforcements arrive.

With the second division came the new commander-in-chief, Sir James Outram. Outram had been on convalescent leave in England, but his new appointment had led to a remarkable recovery, and he had arrived in time to sail from Bombay with the reinforcements. Major General Stalker, his ego sorely battered, remained to command the first division, with the sixty-two-year-old Major General Sir Henry Havelock arriving to take charge of the second. The new command structure took its place swiftly and with little fuss.

The encampment filled with rumour as quickly as it filled with fresh troops. The newly arrived redcoats told of a plan to advance almost immediately, Outram's desire to get on with the campaign certain to force a rapid pace. For the men who had spent the last week digging and marching, it was exactly what they wanted to hear. Within hours of his arrival, Outram had dispatched a party of officers to reconnoitre the nearby town of Mohammerah, and the army saw this as confirmation of their new commander's desire to get on with the second stage of the campaign.

Not all the rumours brought by the second division were so positive. Others predicted nothing but a bloody disaster for the expeditionary force. These stories told of an immense enemy horde – thousands upon thousands of infantrymen supported by countless regiments of cavalry and hundreds of pieces of artillery – waiting just inland and preparing to counter the invaders the moment they stepped away from the apron strings of their navy. The numbers grew with each retelling, until defeat seemed inevitable, followed by a harrowing evacuation if the British were to escape annihilation.

Yet one thing was clear, no matter which rumour held sway. The arrival of the fresh division meant that the period of inactivity was over. The next stage of the campaign was about to begin.

Jack lingered outside Sarah's tent. He could see her shadowy form moving around inside and he took a moment to savour the image. He had anticipated the moment through the long, dull afternoon, thinking of little else but seeing her again. They had agreed he should come to her tent around midnight, and he had made sure to be there on time.

He heard a scuffle of boots on the ground and turned to see Simon Montfort staggering back from the bivouac's designated latrines. The young man had clearly enjoyed the navy's entertainment, and his footing was unsteady, as if he believed he was still on board ship rather than on the solidity of dry land. He looked up and spied Jack loitering outside his sister's tent.

'You!'

'Good evening, Mr Montfort.' Jack kept his voice even. He was not there to fight.

Montfort looked round, as if checking that he had not been followed. When he faced Jack again, he was vibrating with barely controlled anger.

'I suggest you leave.'

Jack scowled at the suggestion. 'That's not very friendly.'

'You are not welcome here.' Montfort's words were slurred by drink, but he stood steadier as he faced Jack.

'I think your sister would disagree.'

'She has foolish ideas. That is why I look after her. And I know that a damn pleb like you has no place here.'

'I rather believe she knows her own mind.' Jack tried to control his temper. Sarah had accused him of believing he understood everyone. It was time to see if he was wrong about her brother.

'What the fuck would you know? Just because she chooses to rut with you . . .'

Jack felt his anger begin to simmer. 'Mind your mouth, boy.'

'Why? Are you going to shut it for me?' Montfort's hand fell to the rapier at his side.

'If need be.'

Montfort laughed. 'You really are nothing but a thug, but then my sister has a taste for a bit of rough. You are just her type.'

The talwar whispered from its scabbard. Jack had not fully formed the decision to draw his weapon before it appeared in his hand. The beautiful blade glimmered in the light of the campfires scattered through the bivouac. The fiery reflection seemed to glide up and down its length, making the steel shimmer, the tight script engraved on the blade coming alive.

He stepped forward, holding the sword out so that the point was aimed directly at Montfort's throat.

'You are quite right, Mr Montfort. I am a coarse bastard. I may not know how to behave in polite company, but I do know how to use this sword. I know how to batter any bugger to death with it.'

He stepped forward again, rotating his wrist so the talwar turned in the firelight. Montfort took a hesitant step backwards, and then another, his eyes focusing on the glimmering blade, his bravery silenced by the sight of the naked steel.

Montfort was forced to a halt by a stack of ammunition crates, and Jack stopped and straightened his arm so that the point of his sword was no more than a single inch from the young man's throat.

'I have killed so many men, Mr Montfort, that I have quite lost count.' He snarled as he spoke, his mouth twisted as he talked of death. 'I could kill you now and I would barely remember your name.'

An involuntary shudder ran down Jack's spine. The face of the boy he had killed in the fort at Reshire sprang unbidden into his mind. The image haunted him.

Montfort saw the tremor on Jack's face and it gave him courage. 'You wouldn't do it. It would be murder. You'd hang.'

The words brought Jack back to the present. He looked at Montfort's face. He saw the fear in the boy's pallid complexion, and he felt the bloodlust wash out of him. He could not kill another boy.

'Arthur, is that you?' Sarah Draper's voice called out from behind them.

Jack turned and saw Sarah peering out from behind the entrance flap of her tent. She had already undressed, and was wearing nothing more than a simple cotton shift that clung to her body. With the light inside the tent behind her, he could make out every curve, and the sight made his breath catch in his throat.

'What on earth do you think you are doing? Simon, what is going on?' Sarah's voice rose as she saw the drawn sword.

Montfort found the courage to knock the talwar away with the palm of his hand before pushing his way past Jack. He said nothing as he stalked past his sister and into the night.

'Arthur, tell me what is going on this instant,' Sarah demanded.

Jack sheathed his sword and walked towards her. 'It was nothing.'

'It didn't look like bloody nothing.'

'I was just giving your brother a piece of friendly advice.'

'It looked to me like you were scaring the poor boy witless.'

'It's not your concern.'

'Of course it's my concern.'

'It's nothing.' Jack growled the denial. He was not used to being with a woman. He had forgotten the nagging. He walked forward and took Sarah around the waist, pulling her to him, crushing her body against his. The confrontation with Montfort had made him angry, and he leant forward and pressed his lips against hers, not caring if he was rough.

Sarah pushed him away, her neck and throat flushed scarlet with anger. She opened her mouth to speak again, but before she could utter a sound, Jack kissed her again, this time with nothing but passion. He swept her into his arms and carried her into the tent.

'How was your evening with Fetherstone?' Jack asked as he pulled his boots on. The snug-fitting cavalry breeches were cutting into his thighs as he perched uncomfortably on the edge of a wooden travel chest, and he drew in a sharp breath as the action of tugging on the boots caused the fabric to tighten around his balls. 'Did you manage to find anything out?'

Sarah sat on her travel cot and smiled at the sight. 'I think I prefer you as a hussar. The uniform is much more becoming.'

Jack grimaced as he saw the target of her gaze. In his current position, the tight breeches revealed everything. 'I asked you a question.'

Sarah threw her head back and laughed aloud. She was still naked, and Jack stopped what he was doing so he could take a last lingering look.

'It was dull, if you must know.' She pushed her hair back behind her ears as she studied Jack intently. 'Fetherstone was rather boring.'

Jack had to force himself to stop staring at her nakedness. 'Did you manage to steer the conversation around to the matter of the spy?'

'I tried, but he was having none of it. I told you he was

clever. You said I should be circumspect, so I did not press the issue.' Sarah lolled on her back and stretched. 'He may have said something of interest, but it was just a passing remark, nothing substantial.'

Jack tugged on his second boot and came to stand over her, his heart beating a little faster. 'You heard everything. You always do.'

Sarah looked at his serious expression and laughed. 'Look at you. Why, you appear quite cross.'

Jack snapped his arm forward and gripped her tight around the wrist. 'Tell me what he said.'

'You're hurting me.'

'I'm sorry.' Jack apologised but did not let her go.

'There is a teacher with the army.' She tried to pull her arm free, but Jack held it fast. 'A munshi. He is teaching some of the officers Persian.'

Jack let go at last and perched on the corner of the cot. 'I've heard of him. Go on.'

Sarah drew away from him, nursing her wrist where he had grasped it. 'He is passing messages to the Persians. He teaches a number of officers, including General Stalker. Fetherstone supposes he uses it as an opportunity to find out about their plans.'

'Who else knows?'

'No one. Fetherstone said he had only just discovered the information. The final link in the chain, he called it, or something like that. I didn't hear it clearly.'

Jack recognised the importance of the news. He looked at Sarah. 'Thank you.'

He saw her eyes flash with temper. 'You hurt me.'

'I'm sorry. It was important. I didn't want to play games.'

Sarah's eyes narrowed. 'You used me. That hurts more than any damn bruise.'

'I didn't use you.' Jack scoffed at the idea. 'You helped me. You have my gratitude.'

'Your gratitude.' It was Sarah's turn to scoff. 'So I am well rewarded, then.'

Jack scowled. 'I would have hoped you would help me willingly.'

'Then why grab my arm?'

'I . . .' Jack searched for the reason. In truth, he was not sure he trusted her, though he did not know why.

'I understand.' Her voice changed. 'I don't trust easily either.'

Jack looked at her sharply. 'Who says I don't trust you?'

'Come on, Arthur. I am not a naïve little girl. You never speak of your past or your future. You make no reference to family or friends, nor do you seem to care that you have no one in your life save Ballard and that thug of a bodyguard. I see how alone you are. I saw it the first moment I clapped eyes on you.' She stood and came closer to him, her fingers reaching out to run through his hair. 'You are not alone any more.'

Jack said nothing. He could not form the words. His loneliness was ever-present. It had been that way since he had first taken an officer's uniform from its peg and placed it on his shoulders. He refused to ever think of it, for if he did, he knew it would crush him.

'I know what it is to be alone.' Sarah spoke softly. She bent forward, laying her cheek against the top of his head. 'My life before I met James was . . .' She paused, and Jack felt her body tremble. He slid his hands up, placing them around her waist and holding her tight. 'My life was different before.' Sarah took a breath, holding it for several long seconds before she continued. 'I do not like to think on it.'

She said nothing more. They stayed close together, each taking much from the contact.

'Now you should go.' Sarah pulled away, her hands clasped together in front of her waist.

Jack stood up. He looked at the woman in front of him. He had seen her vulnerability. It drew him to her. He felt more than lust, and the strength of the emotion shocked him.

'Sarah . . .'

'Hush.' She stopped him by placing a finger on his lips. 'We have said enough for one night. Take the information to Ballard. Do your duty. I am not going anywhere. I will be here.'

Jack knew that she was right. He had to deliver the information she had gleaned from Fetherstone. For he now had what he needed. He had found the spy.

Chapter Twenty-one

———◆———

'W ake up! Wake up, man, for God's sake.' Jack shook Ballard, manhandling his officer without care.

'What the devil!' Ballard came awake roaring with anger.

'Get dressed, quick.' Jack rushed across the tent and pulled at his knapsack, digging for his revolver's ammunition, careless of spilling his spare clothes on to the ground.

'What is going on? Are we under attack?' Ballard staggered to his feet. To his credit, he rallied well and immediately reached for his breeches.

'I've found the spy. I know who it is.' Jack grunted in satisfaction as he tore open a packet of fresh ammunition. His hands started to load his revolver with practised ease, the movements instinctive. He took a deep breath to calm himself. Loading a revolver was not a thing to be done with passion. He carefully poured powder into each chamber of the revolver before following with a ball that he forced home with the loading lever held beneath the barrel. He worked as quickly as he dared, doing his best to make sure each bullet was tight in the chamber. It was a delicate task and Jack knew he had to take care if he was to avoid a misfire. The weapon had saved his life on more occasions than he could recall. Yet it had also let him down. He had learnt to treat it with care.

'Well, who the devil is it?' Ballard snapped the question as he forced his legs into his tight boots. There was little light in the tent but Jack could see the eager anticipation in the major's eyes.

'Stalker's teacher.' Jack returned his attention to his revolver, working quickly as he sealed each of the five chambers with a dab of wax to prevent the risk of a flash fire, before pushing the firing caps into place.

'What! What manner of teacher?'

'That Persian. The damn munshi.' Jack snapped the revolver shut before thrusting it into its holster, leaving the flap unbuttoned. 'That bugger who has been teaching the officers on Stalker's staff the language. It all makes sense.'

Ballard stopped midway through buttoning his breeches, his arm outstretched as he reached for his dolman. 'How do you know?'

'Sarah told me.'

'Sarah? You mean Mrs Draper?' Ballard's face creased into a frown as he understood Jack's explanation. 'If you have been letting your prick do your thinking, then I shall have it removed.'

'It's not like that. She dined with Fetherstone and he let it slip.'

'Fetherstone revealed it.' Now Ballard was interested. 'It does not make sense. Just one spy?'

'It does make sense.' Jack was buoyed up by his success. 'Stop seeing grand schemes and spy networks, or whatever it is you call them. This man has had direct access to Stalker and God alone knows which other senior officers. He listens carefully and keeps his eyes peeled. Whatever he discovers he passes on.

Come on, you see how it fits? You saw Stalker's tent. The place is bedlam. The man could have seen and heard everything.'

Ballard was nodding, his fingers clasped over his chin as he contemplated Jack's information. 'You say Mrs Draper got this from Fetherstone?'

'Yes. He referred to it at dinner and she happened to mention it to me.' Jack delivered the lie smoothly. He had no intention of letting Ballard know that he had asked for Sarah's help.

Ballard sat back down on his charpoy and began to remove his breeches.

'What the devil are you doing?' Jack could not believe what he was seeing. 'I have found the spy. Surely to goodness we need to get our hands on him before he can do any more damage.'

Ballard smiled at Jack's eagerness. 'My dear Jack, you really are a simple fellow.' He tossed his breeches on to his knapsack and tugged the blankets over his knees. 'Go to bed.' He turned his back on Jack, settling himself to his rest. 'I thank you for your information.'

'You are not going to act on it?' Jack was stunned.

'I will consider it.' Ballard did not bother to turn to face Jack. 'Perhaps I will find some other uses for this spy of yours. It would be a waste to take him straight away without giving it some more thought.'

Jack stared at his officer's back. 'This man is dangerous. He is passing secrets to the enemy, yet you are going to leave him to it?'

Ballard ignored him.

Jack turned on his heel and strode out of the tent. Ballard was making a dreadful mistake. For all they knew, the spy was passing the army's secrets to the enemy at that very moment. Jack would not let it happen. He would not endanger the lives of any more redcoats. He remembered Ballard's instruction to him after the battle for Reshire. He had been brought out on campaign to do one job and one job only. When the spy was found, it was Jack's duty to deal with him.

He marched into the night, his mind set. He would do as he had been ordered. He would kill the enemy spy.

'Captain Hunter, I need your help.'

Jack had been kicking his heels in the operations tent for several long minutes waiting for Stalker's aide-de-camp. The captain had finally appeared, and Jack elbowed past the young ensign who had also been waiting patiently for the officer's attention. Despite the ungodly hour, the tent was still busy, the general's staff working through the night to issue the orders that would be needed if the army were ever to strike inland.

'Captain Fenris! What's going on?'

'I need to find the munshi.' Jack strode to Hunter's desk. 'Where is he?'

'Who?' Hunter rose to his feet. His face showed the strain of the campaign. Puffy dark pouches circled bloodshot eyes, and his pallor was the dull grey of a winter's morning.

'The damn teacher. The one teaching Stalker Persian.'

'It's not the time of day to be trying to book a lesson, old man.' Hunter offered a thin-lipped smile as he teased Jack.

'This is not a bloody game, Hunter. Where will I find him?'

Hunter scowled at Jack's tone. 'How the devil should I know?'

'You run this damn place, you should bloody know.'

'He shares a tent with some of the servants, I think, but I do not know which.' Hunter spoke in clipped, businesslike tones. He looked at the young ensign who had been listening to the conversation as he waited patiently for his turn. 'Fitzwilliam, do you know where that is?'

The young officer quailed as both captains turned to stare at him. He was little more than a boy, his attempt at growing a pair of mutton chops wispy and threadbare. He looked thoroughly petrified, his thin Adam's apple bobbing up and down at a great rate. 'Yes, sir.'

'Then let's go.' Jack clapped the youngster on the shoulder. The junior officer staggered with the force of the blow. He was as thin as a rake and looked like the first fresh breeze would blow him away. To his credit, he nodded firmly as he turned to lead Jack out into the darkness. The chase was on.

'It's over there.' Fitzwilliam pointed at a cluster of tents that had been given over to the servants employed to cater to the needs of the staff officers at divisional headquarters. With time, the locals had been all too willing to serve the foreign invader, and the three stone-coloured tents were now the temporary residence of more than a dozen men.

'Which one?' Jack started forward before stopping and turning to fire the question at the junior officer.

The ensign paled. 'I'm not sure, sir.'

'For God's sake. What does he look like?'

Fitzwilliam had been staring at the three tents as if he could summon divine intervention to tell him which one contained the man they were after.

'I beg your pardon, sir?'

'What does this bloody teacher look like?'

'Well, sir,' Fitzwilliam stammered. 'He's a tall fellow. Bearded, of course. Dusky skin and dark around the eyes, you know, with that henna muck they all seem to use.'

'You've just described every goddam servant in this entire fucking army.' Jack's patience was quickly becoming exhausted. He grabbed Fitzwilliam by the arm and frogmarched him to the first tent. 'See if he's in there.' He shoved the officer forward and stood back, hands on hips.

Ensign Fitzwilliam hesitated. He had been in India less than six months. His mother had insisted he go, the purchase of his commission arranged through an uncle he had never met but who had agreed to see the young man on his way. The same uncle was a friend of Stalker, and so Fitzwilliam had become attached to the major general's staff without ever having served in his battalion. He had never seen battle or done anything more serious than run errands for the officers on the staff. Now this tall captain, who looked ready to commit murder, had dragged him into the night and was glaring at him as if the whole sorry situation was somehow his fault.

He turned to face the entrance to the tent, pulling hard at his scarlet jacket as he tried to compose himself. He risked a final glance over his shoulder and saw the look of thunder on the captain's face. He did not need to be told to get on with it.

He lifted his hand and rapped on the tent pole. 'Excuse me. I wonder if I might come in?'

'Oh for fuck's sake.' Jack's temper was fraying. He strode forward and pushed the ensign to one side before snatching open the tent flap. 'Everybody out. Now!' His shout roused the startled occupants of the tent. 'Move!' He ducked inside and hauled the closest man to his feet. 'Out! Now!'

The frightened servants did not need to be told again. They staggered to their feet, elbowing each other in their haste to do as they were told. Jack was forced to step back as they came out of the tent in a rush before stumbling to a halt in front of the two officers.

'Well?' Jack twisted on the spot and fired the question at Ensign Fitzwilliam.

The young officer scanned the anxious faces that had immediately turned towards him. In the darkness it was hard to discern each man's features, but the light from the few campfires still burning made a hasty identification possible. Fitzwilliam shook his head as he failed to spot the man they sought.

Jack was already moving. He pushed through the crowd and tore open the flap to the second tent. The men he had forced from their rest milled around uncertainly, their voices rising in fear and anger, the quiet of the night disappearing in a hubbub as they all started speaking to one another at once.

'Everybody out! Now!' Jack roared again. This time most of the tent's occupants were already awake, the ruckus outside too loud to ignore. They rushed past Jack, their own bellowed queries adding to the chaos.

Jack turned and pulled Fitzwilliam closer, forcing him to stand at the entrance as the men piled out around him. The tent was close to empty when the young officer jerked in Jack's grip and uttered a squeal of recognition.

'That's him!'

Jack turned and spotted the dark-faced man Fitzwilliam had pointed out. There was enough time to see the flare of white in the man's eyes as he realised he was the target of the ensign's raised finger before the munshi turned and ran.

'Shit!' Jack pushed his way through the crowd of servants. He felt hands claw at his clothes, but he was in no mood to be gentle and he used his elbows freely as he forced a passage through the melee. As he broke free, he saw the shadowy form of the Persian teacher racing away.

He forced himself into a run, leaping over the treacherous guide ropes that would have sent him sprawling in an ignominious heap and sprinting after the fleeing man.

'Oi! You! Stop there!' A voice accosted Jack from out of the darkness. He recognised it in an instant but paid it no heed. He would not stop now, not for anyone.

A red-faced Palmer staggered to a halt as he saw his quarry race off into the darkness. Ballard's bodyguard was struggling to breathe and he bent double, his hands clasped to his knees as he sucked in huge lungfuls of air.

Ballard strode to his side. He had not taken kindly to being woken twice in the same night. Captain Hunter had sent a runner to inform him of his subordinate's odd behaviour. Ballard had understood Jack's intention instantly. He had summoned Palmer and they had come after Jack in an attempt to stay his hand. The intelligence officer was not best pleased to discover that they had arrived too late.

'Well get after him, man. Whatever you do, don't let him kill that bloody spy.' Ballard snapped the order, pointing after Jack to show Palmer the way.

Palmer heaved in a final lungful of air before lumbering off again. Ballard turned his attention to a white-faced Ensign Fitzwilliam, who was surrounded by a crowd of jabbering servants.

'You. Come with me.' Ballard summoned the young officer to his side before striding after his bodyguard.

Fitzwilliam did what he was told. He had no idea what role he would have to play in the drama unfolding around him. He wanted no part of it, but the look on the hussar major's face had left no doubt in his mind that he had to do as he was told. He did not understand what was happening but he could sense the violence in the air. He jogged to keep up with the major, his heart hammering in his chest. He had anticipated the first time he would see battle, his imagination conjuring a dozen scenes of brave redcoats routing a stubborn enemy. He had never supposed that his first fight would come in the very heart of the British encampment.

Chapter Twenty-two

Jack's lungs rasped as he struggled for breath. It had been a long night already, and he could hear his own tortured gasps echoing in his ears as he raced along.

The fleeting shape of the fleeing Persian teacher was still ahead. The detritus of the British camp flashed by as Jack's boots pounded into the hard-baked ground. He blundered through the areas between the tents, careless of knocking into stands of rifles, the clatter of the falling weaponry barely registering in his mind.

'What the fuck!'

He crashed past a redcoat staggering back from the latrines, the shouted oath left to linger in the quiet of the camp as he raced onwards, never once taking his eyes from the figure ahead. He could feel the muscles in his thighs beginning to burn. His breath scorched as he forced it into his straining lungs. He would have cursed against the pain, but it was all he could do to maintain his pace.

Then the Persian teacher turned.

Jack saw the flash of a knife, the blade reflecting the light of the nearest campfire. His boots scrabbled for purchase on the dusty soil and he slewed to a halt no more than half a dozen paces away from the man he had been chasing. They were close to the edge of the camp's lines, in an open area free of tents where the nearest battalion would form up when they stood to with the dawn. It gave the Persian room to manoeuvre. Space to fight.

'Put it down.' Jack's voice rasped in his throat. He would have dearly loved to bend double and suck in a revitalising lungful of air, relieving the pain in his abused body, but he could sense the sudden change in mood and his hand moved instinctively to hover over the hilt of his talwar.

The Persian said nothing. Jack saw the man's tongue flicker nervously over his lips, his eyes roving around, looking for a way to escape. He was in the midst of a British army encampment. There were sentries to all sides; Outram had issued orders that the camp should be well protected at all times, no matter that the enemy army was supposed to be some fifty miles distant. There was no escape for the munshi.

'There's nowhere to run to.' Jack spoke more clearly as his breathing started to return to a more normal level. 'Come with me. You won't be hurt.'

The Persian spat on the ground. He did not reply. He did not need to. His face revealed exactly what he thought of Jack's offer.

'Don't be a fool.' Jack felt the first prick of anger. 'Do as you are fucking told and drop the knife.' He had never been good at diplomacy.

The Persian looked around once more before dropping into a crouch, the knife held low in his right hand.

'You stupid bastard.' Jack's left hand slipped to his side. In one practised movement he pulled his revolver from its holster, bringing it up smoothly so that it pointed at the Persian's heart.

He saw the flicker of disappointment on the man's face. The

munshi straightened up and let the knife fall from his hand.

'Sensible fellow.' Jack felt the stirrings of anger sliding away. 'Step over here.'

The man didn't move. His eyes flickered nervously over Jack's shoulder.

'What is going on here?'

The voice had the clipped, urbane tones of an educated man. It was a voice Jack recognised.

'Stay away, Mr Montfort, if you please.' Jack kept his eyes on the man he had been sent to capture. Carefully he switched his revolver to his right hand and took up the tension on the trigger.

'I am not some bloody ranker, you cur. You cannot order me around.'

Jack heard the slur in the voice. Montfort was still drunk, the after effects of the navy's hospitality forcing him back to the latrines and into Jack's path for a second time that night.

'Stay out of it.' Jack snapped the words. He could not afford to take his eyes off the Persian teacher. Already the man had stopped moving forward, and Jack could see the calculation on his face. He was not alone in sensing the change in the situation.

'I will not.' The words were delivered with arrogance. 'And put the damn gun away. I can vouch for this man. He is teaching me Persian.'

'That's not all he's been up to.' Jack took a step forward, closing on the munshi. He wanted to subdue the man. He had a notion that the barrel of a five-shot revolver pressed into his spine would encourage obedience.

'Damn your eyes,' Montfort howled as Jack ignored him, like a child beginning a tiresome tantrum. 'Stop, I tell you.'

Jack sensed the approaching disaster. A hand clasped his shoulder, the fingers clawing into the flesh underneath the dolman, and he felt himself spun round on the spot. He caught a glimpse of the petulant face beneath the crop of wild blond hair, and as he raised his arm to knock the interfering young man away, his eyes momentarily left the Persian.

It was the opening the man needed. He snatched the knife from the sandy soil and threw himself forward, thrusting the blade at Jack, aiming to drive the long blade deep into his heart.

Jack saw the blow coming out of the corner of his eye. He twisted on the spot, slicing his right hand across his body in a desperate attempt to batter the knife away with his revolver. He caught the blade with the gun's barrel, deflecting the sharpened steel to one side. But the impact knocked the weapon from his hand and the revolver went flying.

The Persian was on him in a flash. The blade whispered through the air, slashing at his face. He tried to twist out of the way but the tip of the knife sliced across his cheek. He felt a searing flash of pain as the blade scored through the soft flesh under his eye, the blood hot on his skin. With a roar of agony, he threw himself backwards, careless of colliding with Montfort, thinking of nothing save getting out of the blade's path. He hit Montfort hard and the two men went down, their bodies slamming into the ground with a bone-jarring impact.

There was little time to recover. Jack punched down hard, slamming his fist into Montfort's face before crushing the young man's body underneath him as he levered himself back to his feet. He staggered to one side, twisting fast as the Persian lunged again. The blade cut through the air, missing him by a hair's breadth. He spun round as he found his footing and battered his fist forward, slamming it against the Persian's head. His knuckles screamed in pain at the impact but he ignored it and threw himself at the enemy spy, catching hold of the man's wrist and tugging with all his strength, pulling the blade round and bringing the Persian's face in front of his own.

He didn't hesitate. He smashed his forehead forward, slamming it into the centre of the Persian's face. He felt the crunch as the man's nose broke, the stickiness of blood splattering across his skin.

As his vision greyed, Jack felt the Persian's body slump. He pushed forward, keeping the man's right wrist in a tight grip. The munshi fell backwards and Jack went with him. The two men scrabbled on the ground, writhing and punching, both hurt but both still fighting. Jack's head rang as his foe caught him with a blow. It felt like it had been split in two and he could feel the blood running freely from the wound to his face, but he hammered it forward again regardless, into the ruin of the Persian's own bloodied face. He yelled as the impact drove red-hot needles of pain through his skull. Yet his hands were trapped and he had no other weapon, so he smashed it forward again, pulping the remains of the spy's nose.

He felt the body underneath him go limp. He tensed, waiting for the fight to continue. But his enemy's hands fell away and the Persian teacher slumped unconscious to the ground. Jack had beaten him into oblivion. He staggered to his feet, snatching away the blade that had come so close to killing him.

Blood smothered his face and he wiped it away with the sleeve of his hussar's dolman, turning the dark blue fabric black. He spat out a wad of phlegm and fixed Simon Montfort with an intense glare, feeling the weight of the knife in his right hand. Montfort still lay prostrate, blood trickling from one nostril, a legacy of the punch Jack had thrown as he leapt from the spy's blade. The red was bright against the pale flesh.

'You fucking idiot.' Jack spat the words out. His head throbbed, the pounding echoing round his skull. And it was all Montfort's fault.

'Fenris!'

Jack heard his name being called, but still he hefted the knife. He looked into Montfort's eyes and saw fear.

The sound of a revolver being cocked was very loud in the quiet after the fight. Jack turned and saw Palmer staggering towards him, the maw of a gun's barrel aimed directly at his head.

'Put the poker down, mate.' Palmer's voice rasped as he spoke, the strain of chasing Jack showing in his flushed and florid face. But the barrel of the gun was rock steady in the man's huge paw.

Jack looked into Palmer's eyes. He saw no sense of comradeship, no bond of shared experience. He saw only the flat stare of a man used to death. He spat once before he tossed the knife to one side.

'Good choice.' Palmer used his free hand to wipe the sweat from his eyes. 'You don't half move fast. You fair nearly killed me.'

Jack was in no mood to be chummy with a man aiming a gun at his head. He heard movement behind him and turned to see Montfort pushing himself to his feet. If he was relieved to have been saved, it did not show. He stared at Jack, the hatred naked on his face, then turned and scurried from the scene without a word, pushing his way through the crowd of onlookers and disappearing from sight. Jack stared at his back, aware that the business between them was unfinished. Then he heard the voice of his commanding officer, and sighed.

'You damned fool!' Ballard walked out of the darkness and stared at Jack, his eyes boring into his subordinate.

Jack was not easily cowed. He pointed to the body of the man he had beaten into submission. 'There's your spy.'

Ballard glowered at Jack before finally walking forward to inspect his victim. 'The poor bastard, did you have to do that to him?' He used the toe of his boot to poke the body lying spread-eagled on the ground. The slightest groan came from the slack mouth. 'At least you didn't kill him.'

Jack snorted and then cursed at the pain it caused in his head. He looked into the crowd and saw Ensign Fitzwilliam staring at him as if he were a monster from a child's nightmare. He smiled. He could feel the blood oozing from the thin knife wound on his cheek. 'We couldn't leave him, sir. He had to be stopped.'

'You did well, Captain Fenris.' Ballard spoke loudly, letting the onlookers hear the praise, then walked forward and clapped Jack hard on the shoulder, leaning forward so that he could speak directly into his ear. 'The next time you do not ask my permission before you act, I shall throttle you myself.'

Jack looked up sharply. But there was a hint of a smile on Ballard's face, an indication that he was not to take the threat too seriously. He lifted his right hand so that he could point at the body of the Persian teacher. 'I told you I would get him.'

Ballard looked at the blood-smeared hand and grimaced. 'You did. I suppose I should thank you.'

'Yes, you bloody should.'

'You are a man of action, Jack. I should have known what you would do. Palmer,' Ballard addressed himself to his winded bodyguard, 'when you have quite finished panting, be a good fellow and take that poor man into our custody. Guard him well.' Orders delivered, he clapped Jack on the shoulder once more. 'It might not have been my preferred method, but you have identified and captured the spy, and for that you should be thanked.'

'But why would you leave him?' Jack still did not understand Ballard's reluctance to root out the canker at the heart of the army's operation.

'I was going to use him, you dolt.' Ballard shook his head at his subordinate's lack of vision. 'Did you never stop and think how we could turn a spy like this to our advantage?'

'No,' Jack answered honestly. 'I saw him as a danger, so I wanted to remove him.'

'Well you certainly managed that. At least I can have Palmer ask him some questions now. He has proven to be rather persuasive in the past. If there is a network of spies then I should be able to discover more from that unfortunate fellow.'

'And if there isn't?'

'Then you have captured the one man causing all our problems and we will have to thank you.'

'So I will have done what I came here to do?'

'Yes.' Ballard offered his thin-lipped smile.

Jack felt relief wash over him. It numbed some of the pain. He hoped it had all been worth it, for he had paid a high price to reveal the identity of the enemy spy. He was convinced that Ballard was wrong about there being a network of agents. Fetherstone had believed that the munshi had been acting alone and Jack saw the sense in that opinion. Now the man had been stopped. Jack had done his job and saved many of his fellow redcoats from a needless death. He had finished what he had come all this way to do.

Chapter Twenty-three

'Gentlemen, I am grateful for your time. Now, what have you got for me?'

Lieutenant General Sir James Outram fixed the two officers with a piercing stare. Major Ballard had brought Jack with him when he had been summoned by the commander-in-chief to deliver his latest assessment on the build-up of enemy forces that had been the talk of the army ever since the second division's arrival the day before.

Ballard handed over a thick sheaf of paper, laying it almost reverentially on Outram's campaign table. 'Sir, this is my latest report.'

Jack stood as straight as he could as he felt Outram's gaze wash over him. His body still hurt from the fight and he did his best to hide the inevitable wince as he tightened his battered muscles.

'Thank you, gentlemen. I'd be grateful for a brief summary whilst you are here.' Outram sat back in his chair and lit a fresh cigar. The tent was fuggy, the air still ripe with the smell of the general's previous cigars, which he smoked at a prodigious rate.

'Certainly, sir.'

Jack could see Ballard savouring the request. The commander of the intelligence department loved an audience, and he preened before beginning his briefing.

'My sources indicate that the enemy is beginning to assemble at Borãzjoon, some forty-six miles from here. Thus far he has gathered around six to seven thousand men, including at least two thousand cavalry and around eighteen guns.'

Outram sighed. 'So they have two thousand sabres.' He pondered the news. 'That is many more than I have.' He nodded for Ballard to continue.

'The force is under the command of Shooja-ool-Moolk and includes at least two Karragoozloo regiments of guards, four regiments of Sabriz and one of Shiraz. More men are expected to arrive in the coming weeks, and already the enemy is building up the quantity of supplies they will need for a campaign against us. This amounts to at least forty to fifty thousand pounds of powder, small-arms ammunition, and what appears to be enough shot and shell to keep their guns supplied for a year of fighting. In short, sir, the enemy is massing his strength. When the whole is assembled, he will fall upon us with the intention of driving us into the sea.'

Outram said nothing as Ballard delivered the dour news. He sat back in his chair and puffed contentedly on his cigar.

'So the enemy is preparing to attack but he is not yet ready to do so.' He leant forward and propped his cigar on the already overflowing ashtray on his desk. 'That is good news indeed.' He fixed the two intelligence officers with a firm glare. 'It is necessary to understand the nature of the enemy and then overawe him with bold initiative and resolute action. I am of a mind to attack immediately.'

He picked up his cigar again. Holding it in his teeth, he flipped open the wooden case on his desk. 'Please help yourselves.'

'Thank you, sir.' Ballard bent forward and selected a fat

cigar, rubbing it under his nose to savour the scent.

'Captain?' Outram gestured towards the box, inviting Jack to take one.

'No thank you, sir. I do not smoke.'

Outram puffed out his cheeks, letting a cloud of blue-grey smoke escape in a rush. 'You are probably wise.'

Ballard smiled at Jack's temperance. 'It is the only vice he lacks, sir. We have to thank Captain Fenris for providing the intelligence that led to the discovery of the Persian spy.'

'The teacher?' Outram's eyes narrowed as he replied.

'Yes, sir.' Jack cleared his throat as his voice cracked. He could taste the cigar smoke and he had to try hard not to cough as it filled his mouth.

'That was good work.' Outram looked hard into Jack's face, which still showed the effects of the fight with the Persian spy. His forehead sported a fresh blue and yellow bruise right in its very centre, and the cut to his face had barely had time to scab over. The knife wound would likely scar, but Jack knew the rest of the wounds would heal quickly; at least he hoped they would. Ballard would likely have called it a small enough price to pay for ridding the army of an enemy spy but to Jack's mind he had done more than his fair share.

'So have you put an end to the problem of the enemy knowing our every move?' Outram puffed on his cigar as he asked the question, his face half hidden by the cloud of smoke that he exhaled at regular intervals.

'We believe so, sir.' Ballard glanced once at Jack before continuing. 'We are still investigating whether the man was working alone, but we are certain that he was working for the enemy. He relied on the local populace to take his messages to the enemy's camp. Unfortunately there is nothing I can do to stop such a thing happening; there are simply too many locals with us.'

Jack had seen the hint of discomfort in his commander's face. The Persian spy had revealed little of any use and Palmer had extracted nothing that added credence to Ballard's notion that there was a network of enemy spies in place. Everything pointed to the munshi acting alone, but still Ballard remained to be convinced.

'Very good.' The major had at least been able to reassure the army's commander that the problem was in hand. 'It seems you have the matter under control. I would ask you to keep me informed of any developments.' Outram nodded once before placing his cigar to one side. 'So we must take the initiative and strike before the enemy gathers his full strength. If he discovers that we are coming, he will either scurry away or meet us on ground of his choosing. You may have dealt with this one spy, but the country is still against us and there will be no shortage of people riding to warn the enemy the moment we march.'

Ballard nodded in agreement, listening intently to the general.

Jack cleared his throat. He was as nervous as he had been when he had been the first out of the moat at Reshire. 'Then don't let them know, sir.'

Outram looked at Jack sharply. 'I think it is rather hard to disguise the movement of a few thousand infantrymen, Captain. Not to mention the enormous baggage train that follows. Even a blind man would know we were marching.'

Jack shook his head in denial. He saw Ballard's face go pale as his charlatan subordinate chose to give advice to a general. Jack forced down the nerves. It was the same as digging deep for the courage to lead men into battle. It had to be done, no matter how much you feared the first step.

'Then don't march with a baggage train. The army has been conducting route marches for days now. General Stalker even had the whole division out last week. The locals must think we are either bonkers or too frightened to advance. It need not be any different when you march to attack.'

'What of supply?' Outram steepled his fingers.

'We leave it behind.' Jack was speaking with confidence now. He forgot Outram was a lieutenant general and he nothing more than a deserter and a fraud. 'The men march light, carrying just enough for a few days. The enemy are but fifty miles away. We can be there in two days. We strike hard and fast and catch them before they are ready.'

Ballard looked aghast, but the general seemed intrigued. He took up his cigar and drew on it, his eyes never once leaving Jack's face.

'How long have you been in the hussars, Captain Fenris?'

Jack's heart thumped in his chest. 'It's a recent transfer, sir. I was with the 24th.'

'So the 24th's loss is Ballard's gain?' Outram turned and looked at the intelligence officer. 'You are lucky to have Captain Fenris on your staff, Major.'

Ballard recovered well. 'I thank God for it daily, sir.'

Outram laughed. 'As well you should.' He looked back to Jack. 'What happened to the spy?'

Jack smiled, his fears receding. He liked Outram. 'I believe he is still with the surgeons, sir.'

Outram seemed delighted by the response. 'Major Ballard was correct. Smoking might be the sole vice you lack. Thank you for your briefing, gentlemen. It was very enlightening. You may go about your duties now.'

The two officers snapped to attention and saluted before beating a hasty retreat from the general's presence.

Outside the tent, they both took a deep lungful of clean air.

'Don't ever do that again, Jack.' Ballard exhaled deeply as he spoke. 'I think you forget who you really are.'

Jack laughed at the major's expression. 'I sup with the Devil.

Do not complain when his devilment rubs off on me.'

The use of his nickname made Ballard smile. They walked together in companionable silence through the encampment. As they approached their own tent, Palmer saw them coming and walked over to greet them.

'This just arrived for you.' He held out a letter addressed to Captain Fenris.

Jack nodded his thanks before noticing the tears at the envelope's top. 'You opened it?'

'Fucking boring it was.' Palmer laughed at Jack's expression. 'You really should get some more interesting friends.'

'And you should mind your fucking manners.' Jack's anger rose quickly. 'The next time I receive a letter I suggest you leave it alone.'

Palmer shrugged, clearly unconcerned by Jack's belligerence. 'Orders is orders, chum.'

Jack turned his anger on Ballard. 'So you told your ape here to open my letters?'

'I did.' Ballard raised a single eyebrow at his subordinate's display. 'Do not forget where I found you. I had to treat you with a certain degree of caution.'

'Well, you know me better now.'

Ballard cocked his head as he considered the notion. 'Yes. That is a fair comment.' He looked at Palmer. 'You can stop opening his mail.'

Palmer nodded, clearly not bothered either way.

Jack scowled, despite having won the argument. He would have liked to have opened the letter for himself. Unlike the rest of the officers, he never got mail. Those with families received post by the bundle, thick wraps of letters and hefty packages and parcels arriving every few days thanks to the efforts of the Indian navy. Jack received nothing, ever.

He reached into the envelope, a strange excitement building, and flipped the letter over, scanning the contents to see if he recognised the signature. He did. It was from Commodore Fetherstone.

He sat and read slowly, making sure he understood every word. It was a letter of congratulations. Fetherstone thanked him for finding the spy and for ending the problem that had dogged the army ever since it had arrived. The note was no more than a few scribbled lines, but Jack detected the sarcasm thinly veiled in the polite phrases. He had stolen Fetherstone's thunder. He had prevented the navy from gaining credit for capturing the enemy spy, something the commodore would surely have savoured.

He folded the letter tightly before returning it to the envelope. He would show it to Ballard that evening although Palmer was sure to have let the major know its contents already. It would do Ballard good to know they had put one over on the naval intelligence commander. Jack felt pride at all he had achieved. He had been brought here to do a job and now it was complete. He could sit back and watch the campaign unfurl knowing he had saved many of the men under Outram's command from enduring extra suffering. It was almost a pity that the Persian spy was no longer able to communicate with his masters. In the message Jack had found in the fort at Reshire he had been written off as little more than a hired thug. It would have been pleasing to know that the Persians would now know that the man they had written off so glibly was actually the one who had broken their power.

Chapter Twenty-four

———————◆———————

The army slipped away in the late afternoon. There was little grandeur to the departure, no martial spectacle to awe the inhabitants of Bushire.

The baggage and supply carts stayed behind. The encampment was trusted to the care of Lieutenant Colonel Shepheard, whose men were reinforced by a party of seamen from the ships moored in the harbour. Outram was gambling on a quick march to take the Persian general by surprise, but he was cautious enough to ensure that he had a secure base to fall back to.

The men marched with no more than two days' rations in their knapsacks, bread and beef for the redcoats, chapattis for the native infantry. Their pouches and cartouches were full of ammunition, their rifles and muskets cleaned and ready for battle. Once again they were left to find rest without their tents, the need for speed overriding any thought of comfort.

Close to four thousand men marched in two long lines of contiguous quarter columns. Most came from the force that had achieved victory at Reshire. The daily route marches had hardened them. The fight at the Dutch fort had proved that they could best the enemy. They advanced with confidence, eager to bring the enemy to battle, ready to prove that Great Britain's will could not be flouted.

The force would march through the night. It would be a treacherous process. The land they would cross started out as little more than a swamp. The damp air was full of deadly exhalations, the men certain that the foul smell was sure to carry disease. The choice of route left the redcoats wondering at the sanity of their masters for subjecting the army to such a deadly miasma. Yet it was the only way off the Bushire peninsula. Once they had marched around the head of the Bushire creek, they could strike inland, into the desert that separated the coastal lands from the dry, featureless interior.

They would have to cover the ground quickly and then summon the energy and willpower to fight. For the Persian army was gathering its strength. The Shah's orders were clear. His commander, Shooja-ool-Moolk, was to force the invaders back into the sea. The invasion must be stopped.

Jack enjoyed the feeling of being back in the saddle. He had borrowed a roan mare from Outram's stables and had joined the procession of staff officers surrounding the commander-in-chief. It felt strange not to be marching with a battalion, though. He missed it. There was a security in being in the midst of hundreds of redcoats. A knowledge that whatever you faced, you faced it together. This time he rode towards battle accountable for no one other than himself. He would not be expected to show the courage that defined a true leader. In all likelihood he would not even be called on to fight. Ballard had stressed the need to keep out of the battle, no matter what urge came upon him. He would not be allowed to transgress again.

The ground underneath his horse's hooves gave out an obscene squelch as the weight of horse and rider squashed the matted fibres of the earth together, forcing up small puddles of water that slowly disappeared back into the swampy soil. It would be hellish for the redcoats and the native infantry, who would be forced to march straight through the marshland. The sodden soil would all too soon turn into a quagmire, the rearmost battalions left to slog their way through a sea of mud.

But Outram's orders had been clear. The enemy awaited and so the army must march with haste, lest the chance to bring them to battle was lost.

The wind howled across the barren plain. Bushire was far behind them and the redcoats were battling their way inland. The marshland of the peninsula had given way to scrub, the featureless terrain affording the men nothing to look at other than the occasional scattering of date trees, or an ancient fortified tower standing guard over the precious wells that gave life to the desolate land. Not that they could see much in the impenetrable gloom of the night.

The wind-battered troops were covered in muck. The relentless wind kicked up huge clouds of dusty soil, which swirled and twisted across the arid plain. Still they trudged onwards, gritting their teeth against the tempest, forcing their legs to move, each heavy tread taking them one pace closer to their objective.

Jack was suffering. He had not been in the saddle for weeks, and it felt as if his backside had been rubbed raw by the constant contact. His tight-fitting hussar's uniform chafed, making every movement of the horse a misery. The wind drove the sandy soil into his face, the dusty, friable surface that had seemed such a boon after the morass of the swampland transformed into a virulent enemy by the gale that had assaulted them for hours.

When he could take no more, he left Ballard and the staff

behind and forced his tiring horse to catch up with the 64th, who marched at the front of one of the twin columns. He went to seek company, to find a friendly face to stave off the monotonous suffering of the advance.

Lieutenant Knightly was with his company. The men had long been allowed to march easy. Few had the energy to chatter with their mess mates, the long trudge wearing down their reserves of strength.

'I say, you lucky blighter.' Knightly spotted Jack's arrival and lifted his face to peer up at his friend, who enjoyed the fortune of being mounted. 'Have you come to gloat?'

Jack ignored the barbed comment and slid from the saddle, wincing as the movement burned his tortured flesh. It was a relief to be on the ground, but his legs thought differently and nearly gave out underneath him as they were forced to take his weight for the first time in hours.

'Steady there, sir.' A strong arm reached out and set him on his feet. The sergeant gave him a friendly smile, accepting his thanks with the briefest nod of his head. Like all officers, Knightly was covered by an NCO, an experienced sergeant whose job it was to make certain that their officer survived in battle, giving the battalion's leaders the freedom to do their job without having to concentrate solely on their own safety.

'It's a crappy night, Sergeant.' Jack stretched his spine, his hand kneading the small of his back that was cramped and aching from the hours in the saddle. 'How are the men?'

'Don't worry about us, sir.' The sergeant shot a gap-toothed grin back at Jack. 'A scrap of wind ain't going to bother the likes of us. You should save your worry for the cavalry. Your lot don't take kindly to this sort of thing.'

Jack smiled at the comment. He still thought of himself as an ordinary foot soldier, no matter what type of uniform he happened to be wearing.

'That's because the horses have more sense.'

The troops marching around them found the energy to laugh, or at least grin, at the exchange. Jack relished the contact. He had not appreciated how much he would miss being with the men who made up the rank and file of the army.

Jack reached into his saddlebag and fished out a bottle of brandy, which he handed to the sergeant. 'Share this around, Sergeant.'

The man looked at Jack and grinned in appreciation. 'That is rare kind of you, sir. Much obliged.' He took a huge draught before handing the bottle and its precious contents to the man at his side. Then he turned and, without missing a step, called to the redcoat marching behind him, 'Thatcher, take the gentleman's horse.'

Jack handed the reins of his borrowed mare to a boy who looked no more than sixteen years old. The youngster smiled nervously and took a firm hold on the greasy leather.

'Don't let her go, lad. You'd be paying her back for the rest of your service.'

The boy paled at the words. Jack laughed and clapped him on the back before turning and placing an arm on Knightly's shoulder and steering him a few paces away from the column.

'You're good with the men.' Knightly looked pale.

'They are good boys. You're lucky.'

'They terrify me.' Knightly was too tired to hide his anxiety. 'They only do what I say because Sergeant Rogerson tells them to.'

Jack smiled. He knew the feeling well. 'You'll get the hang of it. Show them that you are willing to share every hardship and danger they face. Make sure they know what you expect them to do and then show them how to do it. That's it. It's that simple.'

'You should write a book.'

Jack would have laughed, but a spasm of pain seared down his spine and for a heartbeat he thought his legs would give out. He kneaded the tense flesh in the pit of his back until the feeling passed, then stretched, arching his spine in a vague attempt to ease the discomfort. 'I doubt I have the right credentials to write a book aimed at young gentlemen.'

'What's it like?' Knightly asked the question quietly.

'What's what like?'

'Battle. Real battle, I mean.'

Jack heard the fear in the young officer's voice. He sounded like an earnest schoolboy asking a friend what it felt like to kiss a girl. The two of them walked on together in silence, both hunched forward as they battled through the sand that flayed into their faces.

'Nothing will prepare you for when you first go under fire,' Jack began hesitantly. He had never spoken so seriously of battle before. It was not the done thing, especially for an officer. All such talk was done in jest, the whole grisly affair discussed lightly, as if it was nothing more than a game.

He recognised Knightly's terror. There was little he could say that would assuage the young man's fear – Knightly would have to wrestle with that alone – but he wanted to help if he could, and so he forced open his soul, delving into the darkness that he usually kept locked away as he searched for the words to comfort his friend.

'At first, it is worse than you can ever imagine.' He looked up and saw Knightly staring at him intently. 'But then the fear goes.' There was doubt on the young man's face. 'Truly. It goes. You forget to be afraid and you do what you have to.'

'That's when you kill them.'

Jack heard the tremor in Knightly's voice. 'Yes. That's when you kill them.'

'I'm not sure I can do that.'

'You can and you will.' Jack tried not to sound harsh, but he heard the steel in his reply. 'Because if you don't, they will kill you.'

'I understand.'

'You had better. It's not as easy as you think.' Jack sighed. 'Men die hard. They go down kicking and screaming and they will still try to kill you even if you have your sword buried in their damn guts.' He looked across at Knightly and saw the younger man hanging on his every word. 'Don't hold anything back when you fight. Go at them with everything you have.' Jack grimaced as he remembered the harder fights he had lived through. 'And don't forget to turn your bloody wrist.'

'I won't forget.' Knightly looked appalled at the idea.

'You had better not. I've seen a dying man drive a bayonet straight back though the officer who had struck him, just because the stupid fool forgot to turn his wrist.' Jack glared at Knightly, reinforcing the message.

Knightly looked at him, his eyes betraying the terror in his soul. 'I don't want to die. When I think of not existing . . .' His voice tailed off.

'There is nothing you can do about that. Everybody dies.'

Knightly sniffed, barely in control of his emotions. 'It's easy for you. You've done it before.'

Jack laughed grimly. It was not a pleasant sound. 'Oh, it doesn't get easier. I sometimes feel I have a ration of courage. There are times when I think it's gone. Then, in battle, I feel this madness. Nothing matters then. I suppose I lose my mind. And that terrifies me even more the next time.'

Knightly watched Jack closely as he confessed his fear. He nodded slowly, as if coming to an understanding with his own emotions.

'I don't know how you can go back. To battle, I mean.'

Jack shivered, despite the warmth of the night. 'At first you think you are immune, that nothing can happen to you. It will always be some other fellow who will die. Then you see so many men get hit that you realise it could happen to you. So maybe the only way to survive is to be more careful. But then, when the lead is flying and the enemy come at you, you find that you fight just as hard anyway, no matter how much you have told yourself to take it easy and let someone else do the crazy stuff. That's when you realise that one day it is going to happen to you. No matter what you do. And that's when it gets tough, when you know it's just a matter of time.' He looked at Knightly, trying to see the effect of his words. 'Then you can either carry on or give up. And some of us don't have the option of giving up.'

Knightly didn't speak. He seemed lost in another world. It was several minutes before he looked at Jack and forced out a tired smile. 'What a life.'

Jack smiled in return. 'You chose to be an officer. The men have called you "sir" and done what you tell them. Now it's your turn to pay for that respect. You have to do your best because that's what they deserve. That, my friend, is the key. Your responsibility to the men comes first. Even before your own life.' He reached out and placed his hand on the younger man's shoulder. 'Don't worry. You'll be fine.'

They marched on in silence. Every step taking them closer to the place they both feared most of all.

Battle.

Chapter Twenty-five

The sand got everywhere. It chafed against the red-coats' skin, the seams of their trousers turned into abrasive weapons of torture that scoured the delicate flesh from their bodies and made every step an unrelenting agony. It filled their eyes, leaving them red raw and sore, the men blinking and squinting in the fierce early-morning light. The sand had become the enemy, its painful presence adding to the misery of the long advance.

The columns marched on, the officers relentless as they drove their commands forward, ignoring the complaints and the men who slid silently from the ranks, their bodies dragged out of the line of march lest they be crushed under the merciless boots of their comrades. These unfortunate souls were abandoned to the musicians from the battalions' bands, who had stowed their instruments so that they could take up their secondary role as stretcher-bearers. The fallen were taken to the surgeons and the pitifully small collection of bullock-pulled wagons, their passing unremarked amongst their fellows, who could do nothing but march onwards, forcing out step after step, the need to cover the distance overriding the need for compassion. The long columns had walked through the night, carrying on until the sun touched the horizon, the men waiting stoically for the order to halt. Still they marched on, advancing into the morning sunlight, forcing their aching bodies onwards, the miles crawling past.

It was nine o'clock before the command to halt was passed along the line. The exhausted men had no energy for the horseplay that would usually follow a march or the banter that would see them find something to laugh about no matter how dreary their temporary home. The exhausted redcoats slumped to the ground, even the rock-hard soil a welcome respite after the hours they had spent, heads down, grinding through the miles. They would spend the day where they were, the men left to pile their weapons and seek what respite they could whilst still remaining in the order of march. They had covered nearly twenty-six miles, but they were barely over halfway.

The men lay down and rested, baked by the sun, waiting for evening. Waiting for the command to march once more.

Late in the afternoon, the battalions formed up. The twin columns snaked back across the barren plain like two lines of red ants, the sense of the individual lost in the vastness of the whole.

The drummer boys picked up their sticks before rattling them against the taut skin of their instruments, beginning the mesmerising rhythm of the march that would continue until the men were finally allowed to march easy. The two columns lumbered into life. Like a pair of enormous beasts they lurched forward, the braying voices of the sergeants rippling along the ranks as they forced their men to order.

As if at a secret signal, the weather changed. What had been a clear blue sky darkened as the redcoats slipped into the rhythm of the march. Huge banks of dark grey-blue clouds rolled in from the horizon, smothering the last of the sun's rays and casting an ominous shadow over the advancing troops.

The men marched in silence. Heads down. Trudging through the miles.

In the gloom there was little to see, the few trees and olive groves soon lost in the darkness. The men could only make out their fellows, their world reduced to nothing more than the back of the man in front and the heavy sand beneath their feet. The only sound the thump of their boots hitting the hard-baked soil, the jangle of their equipment and the occasional rasp as men forced air into their tired, aching lungs.

The last of the light was soon gone and the redcoats advanced into the night. They marched on, each man surrounded by hundreds of fellow soldiers, yet still alone.

A single voice began to sing.

It came from the ranks of the 64th, the lead battalion in the left-hand column, and cut through the silence that had settled heavily over the redcoats, like a single ray of sunshine piercing a storm cloud.

'And to my heart in anguish pressed, the girl I left behind me.'

The men recognised the words. The voice sang them well, the purity of the sound only wavering as its owner drew breath. The notes of the familiar tune flowed over the marching troops, a balm that soothed away the misery of the relentless advance.

'I shared the glory of that fight, sweet girl I left behind me.'

A deeper voice picked up the melody. The two voices sang together, the words blending, the tones merging into one. More men joined in, the song spreading quickly through the tight-packed ranks. They sang softly, using the music to lift their flagging spirits.

'Dishonour's breath shall never stain, the name I leave behind me.'

Lieutenant Knightly closed his mouth and listened to what

he had started, the men picking up the tune and taking it for their own. The redcoats sang well. They kept their voices low, but the song settled over the noise of the march so that the tramp of heavy boots was lost in the beautiful lament.

When it ended, the men fell silent once more, sharing the moment, each thinking his own thoughts, savouring his own memories. The feeling of camaraderie was complete, and Knightly was not sure he had ever experienced an emotion as pure or as heartfelt.

Then a loud voice in the centre of the column lifted to bellow the first lines of 'Cheer Boys Cheer' and the spell was broken. The men hooted aloud before joining in with gusto, the deep, sombre melody replaced by the raucous joy of bellowing out the cheerful song.

Knightly smiled at his men's spirit. His redcoats could take anything. He knew that he would never fully understand their indomitable spirit. They came from the meanest of backgrounds – they were the dregs of society, the flotsam and jetsam, the scum from the jails and the boys from the workhouse – yet they were willing to fight and die for their country. As they cheered their own singing prowess, their faces betraying the simple delight of being with their mates, he remembered what Fenris had told him about the responsibility of leading the men, of putting them first, even over his own life. To fail them was becoming unthinkable, no matter what the cost.

It was long after night had fallen that the redcoats were ordered to halt. Once more they would seek their rest in the order of march, so that they were ready to advance with the first light of the new day.

They were not to be left to rest in peace.

Thunder rolled across the sky, the deep, resonating crashes echoing through the empty landscape, the ominous booms rousing even the most exhausted man from his rest. Lightning followed, slashing through the darkness, the brilliant flashes searing the sky into temporary daylight before plunging it back into an all-enveloping blackness. It was a display of raw power, the forces of nature providing a spectacle of natural violence.

Then came the rain.

It fell in solid sheets, a deluge that soaked the redcoats to the skin. Without shelter, the men could do nothing but endure the tempest as best they could, each man's misery self-contained, bodies wrapped in their greatcoats, faces hidden under their shakos. They sat in silent misery and waited for dawn, looking to the sky and wondering at the power of the gods. Asking themselves if the angry display was a prophecy; a dire warning of what was to come.

Chapter Twenty-six

T he sound of rifles firing awoke Jack with an uneasy start.

He scrabbled to his feet, his boots slipping on the damp earth so that his heels gouged thick crevices into the topsoil, a sudden nervous energy searing through his veins. He looked around, his eyes running over the rest of the staff officers, who had made their beds wherever they could, those still at rest looking like so many corpses, their bodies hidden away under their blankets.

He searched for the danger, for the enemy that had appeared to make the sentries open fire. He saw nothing but the miserable faces of exhausted and sodden redcoats. The grimaces and scowls as the bedraggled soldiers in the nearest battalion pulled themselves to their feet and began to prepare for the march. He suddenly understood the rifle fire and sat back heavily on the ground before running his hands over his face, rubbing vigorously in a vain attempt to bring himself to life. Within moments the bugles sounded reveille, the loud call echoing around the barren ground where the battalions had spent the night.

'What's that all about?' Ballard had not moved. He sat next to Jack, hunched deep into his greatcoat, a horse blanket draped over his shoulders. It was difficult to discern the man huddled underneath.

'The sentries are discharging their wet cartridges.' Jack sighed and forced his aching joints into action, this time taking more care as he began to move. His back ached, the base of his spine on fire as if red-hot pokers jabbed into the very fibre of his being.

Ballard grunted in reply.

'Come on.' Jack turned and offered his commander a hand. 'Time to get up.'

He hauled the major to his feet and the two officers stood in silence as they contemplated the dreary scene around them. The few hours' rest had done little to revitalise them, the long night hours spent enduring the misery of the thunderstorm that had raged without pause until shortly before dawn.

Jack busied himself doing his best to brush off the worst of the mucky crust that was caked on to the seat of his overalls. He knew the army faced another long march, the enemy still miles away inland. He remembered his enthusiasm when he had told Outram that the men could advance with ease. Back then, the fifty or so miles had seemed an easy obstacle to overcome. Now, with his body aching and his sodden uniform stuck to his skin, it was hard to see how they could make it to their destination intact, let alone fight a battle when they got there.

If Ballard's intelligence had been correct, the enemy was no more than eight miles distant. Outram had gambled everything on a quick dash across country. If the enemy had been forewarned, they would be ready for the British advance. The redcoats would either be forced to fight on ground of the Persian general's choosing or they would see nothing more than the rearguard of an enemy long gone in flight.

If the Persians chose to pick a fight, it would be a close-run affair. After the long march, the redcoats were in a poor condition. Tired, battered and outnumbered, they would be forced to assault prepared positions on terrain that would inevitably favour the defender. It would be a hard fight, with defeat as likely an outcome as victory.

But if the gamble had worked, the enemy army would be caught in disarray. The British expeditionary force would be able to sweep forward and force the Persians either to fight unprepared or to flee in chaos and disorder. If they could catch the enemy and bring him to battle quickly and without forewarning, victory was almost assured.

'There they go!' Ballard twisted in the saddle so he could watch the British cavalry rushing forward. The 3rd Bombay Light Cavalry passed to the left of the column, moving from their position covering the flanks to the front of the now stationary column.

The enemy had been sighted.

The men had marched with the sunrise. The anticipation of battle had quickened the pace, the troops eager to end the long, wearisome trudge across barren country. Rumours had spread swiftly. Every redcoat now knew that the Persian encampment was only a few miles ahead. Yet no one, not even the commander-in-chief, knew whether the enemy was waiting, ready for their arrival, or whether they had been thrown into chaos by the sudden appearance of the invading army.

Staff officers put their spurs to the sides of their horses, a sudden bustle replacing the calm of the morning march. Orders needed to be delivered to the brigade and battalion commanders to move the battalions out of the marching column and into the long lines in which they would engage the enemy. The junior officers whose role it was to deliver these messages burst away from the huddle of senior officers, each one puffed up with self-importance as they went on their vital errands.

'May I go with them?' Jack chafed at his impotence. He had fidgeted in the saddle as the blue-coated cavalry had ridden past, the sudden flurry of activity infectious.

'No you may not.' Ballard let out a disapproving humph at his subordinate's suggestion. 'Must I remind you of your proper station again?'

Jack sighed and settled into the saddle, letting his horse's reins go limp. 'No.'

'You sound like a petulant child.' Ballard smiled at Jack's pathetic expression. 'You will have soon have things to do. We will be called upon again.'

Jack sat straighter in the saddle as he peered ahead. He could not make out the enemy. All he could see was the cloud of dust kicked up by the fast-moving horses of the light cavalry rushing forward to drive off the enemy vedettes.

'This is a gloomy place for a battle.' Ballard chewed his lip and looked at the terrain to the sides of the column. The high hills were certainly forbidding. They had funnelled the advance, forcing the column to march directly for the enemy's encampment at Borãzjoon. There was no room for deft manoeuvre, for the subtlety of a flanking march. A handful of men could hold off an army in the hills, the narrow gullies and ravines a nightmare for an attacking force. Outram had had to order the advance on the flatter ground between the hills. It was his only choice, but it meant the army would have few options when they came across the enemy. If the Persians knew they were coming, the fight would be brutal in its simplicity.

'Maybe the enemy chose it that way.' Jack enjoyed the grim comment. It was his way of paying Ballard back for his refusal to let him join the cavalry.

'Perhaps.' Ballard lifted his hussar's busby with its glorious eight-inch scarlet osprey feather plume before settling it back in a more comfortable fashion on his head. 'Perhaps they are not ready for us.'

'They had better not be. Outram would have my guts for garters.'

'I think you take too much on yourself.' Ballard smiled, enjoying his own turn to send a barb towards his fellow intelligence officer. 'I rather fancy the general had his own ideas. I doubt you swayed his mind.'

Jack scowled. 'Perhaps.'

Ballard laughed and then fell silent, cocking an ear as he listened intently. The sound of rifle fire rippled down the column, echoing around the empty hillsides.

The huge voices of the regimental sergeant majors followed the gunfire, and the column shook itself into life. With all the precision and martial splendour of the parade ground, the battalions manoeuvred into line. The left-hand column would form the second rank, the right-hand column the first. With the drummers marking out the time, the hundreds of red-coated soldiers swung into the formation they would use to attack.

Each battalion formed into a line two men deep. With four battalions in the first line and three more in the second, the army snaked across the plain, the exposed flanks protected by the limited number of cavalry at Outram's disposal. The battalions' skirmishers broke from the formed ranks and took their place to the front of the tightly packed line, ready to screen it from any enemy skirmishers. The tactics Outram employed had changed little since the days of Wellington and the battles fought in Portugal, Spain and France. Manufacturing had improved the weaponry, the Enfield rifles carried by the regular British army regiments more powerful than any weapon previously brought to the field of battle. Yet their leaders clung to the anachronistic principles of a dead general and the battles he had fought over forty years earlier.

The British line bustled with purpose. This was what they had come all this way to do. The redcoats looked at one another as they heard the sounds of fighting ahead, the men of the light cavalry and the rifle battalion that formed the vanguard of the army already engaging the enemy's troops. Soldiers fiddled with their equipment, making sure everything was just so, their fears building as the order to advance rippled down the line.

Each man's belly squirmed with terror, the clammy hand of death suddenly present at every shoulder. Faces flushed with the exertion of the march paled as they contemplated what was to come, the thought that these might be their last minutes on earth sending icy flushes through their veins.

The battalion colours were unfurled. The gaudy silk caught the morning light, the bright reds, blues and golds adding grandeur to the display. To the beat of the drum the lines marched forward. The sight was like a grand painting, the long, steady rows of grim-faced soldiers marching into battle with stoic grace.

The rifle fire died out.

The men sucked in their breath and stiffened their sinews as they braced themselves for battle.

A flurry of staff officers galloped past the marching redcoats, the sudden activity sending a spurt of excitement flashing through the tight ranks. Sergeants and corporals bellowed at their charges as heads turned to watch the fast-moving gallopers. Yet the whispers flowing through the battalions were impossible to stop.

'What the devil is going on?' Ballard twisted and turned in the saddle as he tried to watch all of the sudden comings and goings around him.

A cornet from the 3rd Bombay Light Cavalry galloped into the gaggle of officers clustered around Outram. His light blue tunic was covered in a fine layer of dust and streaks of sweat had carved thin channels in the layer of grime coating his face. The young officer handed a scrap of paper to the general, his horse skittish as it was forced to an abrupt halt.

Jack leant forward in the saddle as he tried to listen to what was being said. He and Ballard sat close to Outram's staff, on the periphery of the officers charged with running the day's affair. Without any direct involvement, they had no more idea what was going on than the humblest redcoat marching in the centre of his battalion.

'I cannot hear.' Jack's face twisted in vexation.

The cornet was on the move once more. He had snatched an order from the hand of Captain Hunter before forcing his mount into a tight turn and beginning the long, fast ride back to the vanguard. Another half-dozen staff officers left in the moments that followed, each bearing a fresh message for the brigade commanders.

'Something's up.' Jack slapped his thigh in frustration.

'Your powers of deduction are a wonder, Jack.' Ballard scowled as his irritation threatened to boil over. He hated not knowing what was happening.

Jack had opened his mouth to reply when a new series of orders were bellowed out in the nearest battalion.

They were orders to halt.

The attack was being reined in. The redcoats' fears had been unfounded. There would be no fighting. No great battle to mark the start of the campaign.

The enemy had fled.

Chapter Twenty-seven

———◆———

The enemy encampment was enormous. It covered the ground outside the town of Borãzjoon, its half-dozen acres liberally smothered with abandoned supplies. The engineer officers who had travelled with the column made a quick tally and estimated there was nigh on forty thousand tons of black powder. There was food enough to feed a dozen armies the size of the expeditionary force, with sacks of flour, rice and grain stacked in vast heaps like some bizarre offerings to a pagan god.

'Damnation!' Ballard kicked an abandoned stand of muskets, stepping back quickly as they tumbled to the ground, the sudden clatter causing a dozen faces to turn in their direction.

Jack looked around at the encampment. The mud wall that surrounded it was not much more than two feet high. It was barely substantial enough to slow a man on foot, let alone deter a force of charging cavalry. It was a place of shoddy workmanship constructed with little thought and even less care. Now that it was abandoned, it looked pitiful.

'It makes no sense.' Jack glanced at his commander, his bewilderment clear. 'Why not use that damned town?'

He pointed towards Borãzjoon. With little or no effort it could have been turned into a stronghold for the Shah's army. Even the most basic preparations would have made it a horrendous place to attack. Regularly spaced tower bastions protected the high walls, with a wide ditch that was at least fifteen feet deep surrounding the whole village. Beyond this were wide fences made from thorns and cactus bushes, obstacles that would have slowed any attacker. The town could have been readily converted into a nearly impenetrable fortress, yet it had been ignored.

Ballard sighed. 'Perhaps they never expected us to attack them.'

'Then they are fools.' Jack scowled.

'Perhaps. But they knew we were coming. That means they are not totally without merit.' Ballard's voice was bitter.

'That's madness. No one knew we were coming. And they left all this shit.' Jack waved his arm to encompass the supplies scattered across the encampment. 'Why not take it with them if they were warned? They cannot have known.' He poured scorn on his commander's opinion. He did not want to think what it meant if the enemy had been warned. He had captured the spy himself and paid a bloody price for doing so. He did not want to believe that his efforts had been for naught.

'Of course they bloody knew.' Ballard was struggling to contain his anger. 'If we had caught them by surprise, they would still be here! They would have been forced to fight or else they would now be running like a bunch of frightened schoolchildren.'

'How can you be so sure that's not what happened? It certainly looks to me like they left in a damn hurry.'

'Because it's so bloody obvious a child could see it!'

'Perhaps you'd care to enlighten me, since I am too bottle-head stupid to see it for myself.'

Ballard placed his hand to his forehead. 'Where are their guns, Jack? Where is their bloody artillery?' He swept his hand around the encampment. At regular intervals along the low wall were prepared artillery positions. The Persians might not have chosen the wisest place for their camp, but they had taken the time to site their guns with care, building a number of protective enclosures for their precious cannon. It would have taken time and effort to extricate the heavy guns, something they could only have done if they had been given warning of the British approach.

'There is no way they could have dragged all the guns away in time.' Ballard looked distraught. 'It would have taken them hours. This,' he kicked at a sack of powder to emphasis his point, 'is almost worthless. They have food and powder to spare. They can rebuild another supply dump like this in a few days. They must have been warned.'

Jack finally understood. The British advance had been swift. Even a rider on a fast horse would have struggled to keep pace with the column, let alone beat it to the enemy camp. By rights they should have caught the Shah's army with its drawers around its ankles. Instead they had seen nothing but the enemy's rearguard. They had captured the camp, and with it supplies that the Shah's army would need to begin its campaign to drive the invaders back into the sea. But the enemy had been given enough warning to escape to the hills. Ballard was correct. Rice, grain and even powder could be replaced. Artillery could not.

Shooja-ool-Moolk had been given a vital warning. He had pulled his army back to the formidable heights, where it was impossible for the British force to attack him.

Jack had thought that the capture of the Persian munshi had ended that particular threat to the success of the campaign. He had been wrong, and now Ballard's suspicions were proved to be correct. The enemy had more than one spy at the heart of the British expeditionary force.

'This is an intolerable situation, gentlemen. Completely and utterly intolerable!' Major General Stalker delivered the damning indictment. He had summoned the two officers from the intelligence department to attend on him the moment his command tent had been erected and had launched straight into a tirade as soon as they had taken their seats.

'Sir. We are doing all we can.' Ballard scowled as he defended his department. 'We believed that by finding the spy we had put a dent in the enemy's supply of information, either ending it completely or at least damaging their efforts sufficiently to give us time to work on discovering the rest of the network.'

'Well, you clearly failed. That much is damn clear.'

Jack watched Stalker's face turn purple as he berated the two officers. He felt the shame of the failure keenly. He had been so proud of his efforts, happily accepting the plaudits for having denied the enemy their spy. To have been so mistaken hurt his pride. Enduring Stalker's invective was humiliating enough. Yet their disgrace was not to be delivered behind closed doors. The general had invited an audience.

'Fetherstone, you are uncommonly quiet.' Stalker turned his attention to the naval commodore. 'General Outram asked your department to join this campaign so that you can share what information you have at your disposal and assist with the analysis of the facts gathered by our patrols. Thus far you seem to have added precious little. May I enquire quite what you are doing to resolve our predicament?'

'We believed it to be an army matter, sir. Thus far I have left it in Major Ballard's most capable hands. He seemed quite content with the arrangement. Indeed, I would go so far as to say it was by his design. We offered to assist yet we were quite forcefully rebuffed.'

Ballard snorted in derision. 'I did not seek your assistance as you had nothing to offer. Every man jack in this damned army was brought here on your ships, yet you claim to have no damn idea who anyone is.'

'I fail to see how that has any bearing on the matter.' Fetherstone's reply was icy.

'There is no need for the navy to be here, sir.' Ballard turned away from the commodore and faced Stalker. 'They clearly have nothing of relevance to pass on.'

'The general has asked for their assistance.'

Ballard looked like he had been slapped in the face. 'I hardly think that is necessary, sir.'

'Well, the general does.' Stalker was curt. 'You are in no position to argue.'

'I believe it to be an eminently sensible course of action.' Fetherstone preened with self-importance. 'Thus far the army has failed. It is time to let the navy sort this mess out.'

'You would say that.' Ballard scowled.

Jack sat forward in his chair. He could not stay silent any longer. 'Did the navy not come to the same conclusion? That the information we discovered pointed to the man they themselves had identified?' He stared at Fetherstone sharply as he spoke. The commodore had been the source of Jack's intelligence, yet he was giving no sign of accepting an iota of responsibility.

Fetherstone simply smiled. 'I cannot think why you would say that. Would you care to explain?'

'You know damn well what I mean.' Jack felt the futility of the argument, but he could not let Ballard fight alone.

Stalker slammed his fist on to his makeshift desk. 'Enough of this damn bickering.'

'Sir,' Jack ignored the warning, 'I believe Commodore

Fetherstone knows exactly what I mean. His own intelligence pointed to the same suspect.'

Fetherstone remained calm. 'The plans that are being leaked pertain to the army and its operations. To date these have not been the direct concern of naval intelligence. Captain Fenris is merely trying to palm off some of the blame.'

'How very convenient,' Ballard sneered.

'I do not think you are in any position to be so damn high and mighty, Ballard,' Stalker intervened. 'Fetherstone is quite correct. It was an army matter. But I promise you this. That is not the case any longer.'

'What do you mean?' Ballard's face flushed as his own temper rose.

'What I mean, Major Ballard, is that I am handing the matter over to naval intelligence.'

'Sir!' Ballard rose to his feet. 'You cannot do that. It is not in their remit to—'

Stalker cut him off in mid sentence. 'I can do what I bloody want. You and your chum here fucked up. You told the general you had rid him of the enemy spies, and he believed you. We would never have embarked on this expedition if we had known the truth.'

Ballard slumped back into his chair. He had nothing more to say.

'I will require the army's files.' Fetherstone was not slow to twist the knife. 'All of them.'

Ballard could not bring himself to speak. He nodded, his mouth clenched tight shut.

'You had better get this sorted, Fetherstone.' Stalker had not completely forgotten which branch of the Queen's forces he belonged to. 'The navy must find this canker and rip it out.'

Fetherstone smiled. 'I think you can leave us to handle the

affair, sir. I trust you will order Major Ballard to offer me every assistance?'

'Of course.' Stalker's reply was clipped.

'Then I see no reason why we cannot resolve this deplorable situation.'

'You had better. This has been one colossal waste of time.' Stalker prowled around the operations tent, which had been emptied of his staff officers whilst he dealt with the thorny problem that Outram had thrust into his lap. 'We are going to march back to Bushire taking as much of this damn junk as we can. Then at least we can claim this bloody march as some sort of victory.'

'I am certain the army will find something satisfactory to write into the dispatches.' Fetherstone's sarcasm was biting. 'You usually do.' He stood up, signalling the end of the meeting, and nodded to Stalker before sweeping out of the tent. His own victory was complete.

Ballard made to rise to his feet too, but Stalker waved him back into his place. The three officers watched Fetherstone leave in silence. Only when he was gone did Stalker speak again.

'Well, gentlemen, I must offer you my sincerest bloody thanks. I assure you I like nothing better than letting that fucking webfoot think he has got one over on us.' The general's sarcasm was biting.

Ballard opened his mouth to protest, only to shut it again as Stalker fixed him with a thunderous stare.

'From now on, counterintelligence is the navy's business. You are not to be involved at all. Is that clear?'

Ballard looked like he was sucking on a lemon. 'Yes, sir.'

'Your role will be to analyse the incoming intelligence regarding the enemy's activities. Nothing more.'

'Sir.' Ballard simply nodded, barely able to speak.

Stalker turned his baleful glare upon Jack. 'Captain Fenris, do not think I overlook your role in all this. You are to report to Captain Hunter immediately.' He turned away before he had finished, as if speaking to Jack was distasteful. 'You are to be reassigned.'

Ballard was back on his feet in a heartbeat. 'Sir, Captain Fenris is on my staff. He should not be reassigned without my permission.'

'You lost that right when you fucked this up.' Stalker was cruel in his denial. 'Fenris will be posted to the 3rd Bombay Light Cavalry. Poor Malet was killed at Reshire. That leaves them short of senior officers and I am damned if I will allow a captain of hussars to sit around on his fucking arse when there is proper soldiering to be done.'

Ballard looked at Jack. There was nothing further to be said.

Chapter Twenty-eight

'Captain Fenris to see you, sir.' The young cornet announced the arrival of the regiment's newest officer with the calm assurance of a junior officer familiar with his superior.

'Thank you, Combe.' The razor-thin officer who had been seated behind a camp desk leapt to his feet. Both men wore the smart uniform of the 3rd Bombay Light Cavalry. Even after days on campaign, their light blue tunics were immaculate and the dark blue overalls with the thick yellow stripe down the seam looked freshly pressed. Jack took in the detail as he waited for his new commanding officer's own rapid scrutiny to be completed, pleased to see that his adopted regiment was maintaining its standards, even on campaign.

The cavalry commander smiled thinly at Jack. 'Welcome. I'm Forbes. I'm running the show here.'

Jack shook the hand offered towards him and felt the discomfort of joining a new body of men. The last time he had done so he had been revealed as a charlatan within days. He just hoped his assumed identity would last a little longer this time.

'I'm glad you could join us.' Forbes was trying to sound genial. 'After Colonel Malet fell, we have been a little short. We have all been stepping up but I must say I was glad when I heard you were coming our way. Perhaps our luck has changed.'

Jack did his best to hide his uneasiness. The commander of the Bombay Lights was being welcoming enough, but there was a terse tone underlying his greeting. Forbes would be unlikely to relish the arrival of a newcomer into his regiment, especially as he had only just taken command following the death of Lieutenant Colonel Malet during the attack on Reshire. New men were always an unknown quantity, and any threat to the stability of the regiment was to be avoided if at all possible.

'I am sorry not to have joined you at a better time.' Jack was uncomfortable. He had never served with light cavalry before. He had been taught how to ride by the son of a maharajah, and had even ostensibly commanded a regiment of lancers in the father's service. But that did not qualify him to lead British irregulars. He was out of his depth and he knew it.

'Now then, there is no sense in shilly-shallying.' Forbes did his best to force his face into some semblance of a smile. He cast a final, somewhat longing, glance at the pile of papers he had been working on before giving Jack his full attention. 'As you probably know, we have two squadrons, both made up of four troops. As of today, our strength is two hundred and forty-three sabres. We are down on numbers but on the whole we are in good shape. The men are in fine fettle and I am lucky that the officers know what they are about. We have been fortunate to avoid many changes in recent months, so we all know each other and rub along nicely.'

He gave Jack a pointed stare as he spoke. There was a warning veiled behind the cursory introduction. Jack would do well not to rock the boat.

'I think you would be best suited to staying with me as my second. The squadrons are all settled and the men acquitted themselves well in the affair at Reshire. Young Moore is doing a good job as adjutant and I am reluctant to change things around on the hoof, so to speak.' Forbes forced out a half-smile at his tired pun.

'Very well, sir.' Jack nodded his agreement. He saw no value in saying anything else. In his time he had been an ordinary redcoat, a fusilier, a lancer and a hussar. He would now join the irregular cavalry. Only time would tell if he would be any good at it.

The darkness wrapped its arms around the cavalry vedette, crushing them in its cloying embrace. Its ominous presence pressed against their senses. It was impossible to see more than a dozen yards. Shapes that in daylight would have meant nothing became fear-inducing shadows, every moving shape a potential enemy, every figment of an overactive imagination a threat to the slumbering army.

'Fancy a nip, sir?'

Jack tore his eyes from a patch of darkness that had seemed to be growing in size the longer he stared at it. The commander of the vedette, Lieutenant Ross Moore, was offering him a small silver hip flask.

'You may find the contents a little unsophisticated, but at the very least it staves off the chill.'

Jack accepted the flask and took a cautious sip of its contents. The lieutenant had been correct. The rough brandy caught at the back of his throat but he was grateful for the fire it ignited in his belly. The days might have been hot but the nights quickly got cold. It was not something he had really noticed when serving on the staff; the tent he had shared with Ballard had been warm and snug. Now he was back at the sharp end of the campaign, he would have to make the best of it, no matter what the conditions.

He nodded in appreciation of the friendly gesture. 'Thank you.'

'Think nothing of it, old man. It's my brother Arthur's anyway. He doesn't know I took it.'

'Your brother is here?'

Moore took a mouthful of the brandy, puffing his cheeks out as he sucked down the fiery liquid before replying. 'They call him the young Moore. He's our adjutant.'

'I had no idea I was joining a family firm.' Jack's discomfort had yet to release him. He was amongst strangers and it had put him on his guard. It also made him sound somewhat caustic, and he regretted the bile in his reply the moment he said it.

'Oh, I know we are not as grand a regiment as the 15th, but we are a tight bunch and we know what we are about.'

Jack saw the glimmer of annoyance in the way Moore narrowed his eyes as he spoke. He tried to lighten the mood. 'I meant no offence.'

'Of course not, old man, none taken. It must be hard being a fish out of water. I know how I would feel if I got dumped into the middle of a group of bally hussars.'

Jack nodded his head in acknowledgement of Moore's understanding. 'I am glad to be here. Truly. It's better than being on the damn staff.'

The lieutenant threw his head back and barked a short laugh at Jack's candour. He was a handsome young man and something of a Goliath; he must have stood at least six and a half feet tall, with a broad, muscular frame. He wore his beard full, but it was neatly trimmed and clearly tended with pride. The eyes above the thick bush of hair twinkled with a devilish spirit. 'Well said, that man.' He tucked the flask away in the inside pocket of his light-blue tunic.

The small patrol of cavalrymen was hidden in a fold in the ground a good quarter of a mile from the Persian encampment that had become the expeditionary force's temporary home. Captain Forbes had suggested that Jack join the men charged with warning of any enemy attack. Major Ballard had written at length to describe the Persians' favourite tactic of launching a night attack against an unsuspecting enemy. His stock might have fallen with the generals, but Outram had still heeded his warning and doubled the usual chain of picquets, pushing his cavalry vedettes far into the darkness of the surrounding plain.

Jack had been a bystander as Moore placed his chain of vedettes, each pair positioned close enough to one another so they could remain in sight, even in the gloom. Moore had kept half a dozen men back to form the patrol that would prowl along the line, checking that his men stayed alert and in place whilst keeping the Bombay Lights in contact with the other cavalry vedettes on their flanks. It was no easy feat in the darkness and it had been a relief when Moore had ordered a halt and let the small patrol take a breather from being in the saddle, although he was still cautious enough to leave two men on guard to watch the nearest pair of sentries.

It had already been a long, nerve-shredding night. Jack had peered into the darkness and seen all manner of danger, yet Moore had seemed totally at ease and Jack had done his best to match the junior officer's calm sangfroid. The men of the 3rd Bombay Light Cavalry were clearly used to their duties, going about their work with a quiet competence. They needed few orders and, from what Jack could see, the daffadar in charge had his troopers well in hand. There was little for the officers to do and Jack felt like a spare part simply brought along for the ride.

'Sahib!' The sudden call brought him sharply to his senses.

One of Moore's men was pointing into the darkness. Jack screwed up his eyes and did his best to find what it was that had startled the sentry into action. He could see nothing.

Lieutenant Moore jogged across to stand at the sentry's shoulder. He stood almost on eye level with the trooper even though the man was mounted and Moore was on foot. 'What do you see, Wazier Khan?'

The trooper swallowed hard as he felt his commander's presence at his shoulder. But he was a steady man, and when he spoke, his reply was clear and precise.

'There, sahib, number five vedette.'

Jack stared hard into the darkness. He followed the direction of the pointed arm and saw a pair of troopers walking their horses in a tight circle to the right. It was the signal that meant they had spotted the approach of cavalry. Had they been turning to the left, it would have meant they had spied infantry. If each man turned in a different direction, it meant that the widely spaced vedettes faced a mixed force.

Lieutenant Moore had recognised the signal in a heartbeat. He walked forward quickly before going down on his knees and pressing his ear to the ground. He listened intently before bounding to his feet with surprising grace for such a large man.

'Time to mount the boys.' The lieutenant jogged across to where he had hobbled his horse next to Jack's own. He flashed Jack a smile. 'Might be nothing, but we cannot be too careful. My brother would never let me forget it if I cocked up.'

Jack nodded in agreement and made to mount his own horse. He felt a flutter of fear deep in his belly. It was up to the 3rd Bombay Light Cavalry to discover what had disturbed the night.

The noise of moving horses echoed around them as the patrol mounted quickly and without fuss, the men pausing only to tighten their horses' girths, which they had loosened off when they had been allowed to rest. The jangle of tackle was loud and Jack could not help but think that the cavalrymen were doing a fine job of announcing themselves to any enemy that was daring to encroach on the slumbering British camp.

He turned and was about to say as much to Moore when he heard something else. He cocked his ear, straining his hearing as he tried to pick out a sound amidst the noise of the patrol.

There was no mistaking it. It was the noise of hooves drumming on the hard-baked sand of the plain. It was the sound of cavalrymen on the move.

Above them the clouds had begun to thin out, and for the first time, a small amount of starlight was filtering through the sky. It was still too dark to see clearly but there was no mistaking the shadowy forms that were silhouetted against the far horizon.

Lieutenant Moore rode close to Jack's shoulder. On horseback the man looked like a hero from an ancient fable. His horse was huge and the pair loomed over Jack so that he was forced to angle his head far back as he told his subordinate what he had seen.

'There's movement. Away to the west.'

Moore listened for a moment, then nodded his head in agreement. He turned and signalled to the daffadar. The patrol had formed into two lines behind the pair of officers and now they drew their swords. The rasp of the metal being withdrawn from their scabbards could have been heard for hundreds of yards, but there was no longer any value in remaining hidden. If the enemy was close, then the Bombay Lights wanted to be ready for a fight.

Jack drew his own sword. The blade felt snug in his hand, the familiar weight reassuring. He twisted in the saddle and looked at the line of men behind him. He saw the steadiness in the ranks, only the movement of the horses spoiling the stillness of the troop.

Moore raised his hand. Behind him the men tightened their grip on their reins, preparing to respond to the order he was about to give.

The young officer waited. The small gap in the cloud closed, plunging the men back into almost complete darkness. The shadowy figures disappeared, hidden by the gloom, yet the sound of their movement was still clear. There could be no doubt that another troop of cavalry was moving through the night.

Jack eased his horse forward, peering into the black.

'Can you see them?' Moore's voice was hoarse. 'I can't see a bloody thing.'

Jack said nothing but continued to walk his horse on. His mind remembered a battle on a faraway hillside. The redcoats had just captured the enemy's great redoubt when a column had advanced against them. In the confusion of battle it had been hard to identify the nationality of the soldiers, the smoke of the battlefield obscuring the detail of their uniform. When panicky shouts had announced the arrival of their French allies, no one had been certain enough to gainsay the command to hold fire. It had been a dreadful mistake. The column had been Russian and the redcoats had broken, abandoning what had been hard won without a fight. Jack was not about to let history repeat itself.

'Are they ours or theirs?' Moore hissed the question, his anxiety clear.

Jack turned in the saddle and fixed his gaze on the enormous lieutenant. 'Stay here.'

Without another word, he spurred into the darkness.

The ground flashed by underneath the hooves of his fast-moving horse. Jack could barely see anything, yet he urged his mount to pick up speed. He felt the fear build in his belly, squirming and twisting in his guts, but he forced it to be still, ignoring the icy flush that poured through every fibre of his being.

If the cavalry they had seen were indeed the enemy, Jack was likely to be riding to his death.

He pulled up hard, yanking on the reins to bring his horse to a halt. He saw the shapes of men close ahead. He knew they must also be able to see him. He was close enough to hear the noises of their horses. He gripped his sword, screwing his courage tight, steadying himself so he was ready to fight. He heard the murmur of a language he did not understand in the low tones of men trying to remain quiet.

He planned for the fight he thought was inevitable. He would throw himself forward, trusting to surprise to keep him safe, gambling on a desperate, lonely charge as his only hope of survival. It was worth the risk. He would not sit idly by and watch another disaster unfurl around him. The mysterious force simply had to be identified, and Jack had endured enough of sitting on the sidelines.

He bunched the reins into his left hand and sucked in a last mouthful of the sweet night air. He prepared himself to spur hard into his horse's flanks, his muscles tensing as he braced for the charge.

'Come forward and be identified.'

The clipped tones took him by surprise. He nearly gouged his spurs back regardless, so keyed up was he to fight. It took him a moment to force himself to breathe, to let the tension leave his body.

With a deep sigh, he thrust his sword back into its scabbard. 'Fenris. Bombay Lights.'

He saw the shadowy form of a rider emerge from the blackness, the white of his face bright in the flickering starlight.

'Now there's a spot of luck. We nearly shot you.'

The cavalry that had caused Jack so much trepidation emerged from the gloom. They wore long dark blue tunics with wide red sashes. Jack recognised the uniform of the Poona Horse, the other cavalry regiment at Outram's disposal.

He heard the jangle of horse tackle behind him as Moore's troopers advanced. Jack turned and waved to the lieutenant, summoning him forward. He sat deep in his saddle and breathed in a deep lungful of the cool night air, feeling the nerves flutter deep in his belly. It would take time to settle them down and still the tremor in his hands.

He thought of the risk he had taken and shivered, cursing at his own foolishness. He was acting like a griffin. He saw Moore's furrowed brow as he brought his patrol forward. There could be no doubt that the younger officer was not impressed. There was no place for heroics on the front line. Foolish actions cost lives. Jack knew he would have to do better if he was to make a new home for himself with the Bombay Lights.

Chapter Twenty-nine

'A door?'

'I'm not jesting, I swear.'

'Why would anyone think a door posed a threat?' Ballard steepled his fingers and contemplated the outrageous tale.

Jack had sought out his former commander and had discovered him in a corner of Stalker's operations tent, half hidden behind a stack of paperwork. He had greeted Ballard with the tale of a vedette from the Poona Horse that had nearly set the whole camp to alarm when one of their nervous troopers mistook a discarded door as an enemy about to attack. It made for a better tale than the one about a foolish cavalry officer who had come close to charging headlong into a vedette from his own side.

'It was pitch black.' He sighed as he was forced to explain the story, quite spoiling its effect. 'They couldn't see what it was. God, you do know how to suck the life out of a tale. It was meant to be amusing.'

'Still.' Ballard shook his head. He was obviously not convinced that Jack's story was true, and he clearly found nothing remotely humorous in a tale of such rank incompetence. 'Not even I would think of a door as a threat.'

Jack sighed at the major's ability to pick the bones out of everything he heard. He had hoped the light-hearted story would put a smile on Ballard's face, but he had been disappointed.

'I take it things haven't improved here, then?' He pulled over a camp chair and sat down heavily. 'Is it bad?'

'Bad?' Ballard tasted the bland word; it was sour. 'It's not bad. It's bloody awful. They don't even invite me in when Fetherstone arrives to deliver his reports. They've cut me dead.'

'But you are still called on to advise on the enemy's movements?'

'What enemy! The buggers appear to have disappeared. They are hiding up in the hills daring us to attack them.'

'Will we?' Jack was all ears. Now that he was back at the army's sharp end, he was keen to know if he faced a fight.

'No. That much I do know.' Ballard tossed his steel pen to one side and pushed his chair back. 'We are going back to Bushire. The orders are being drafted even as we speak. We will march tomorrow, taking what supplies we can. The rest will be blown to high heaven to deny it to the enemy.'

'So we scurry back to Bushire with our tails between our legs.'

'Nonsense!' Ballard stood up and grabbed his cap from the corner of his desk. In camp, the officers wore their undress uniform, which meant that the two officers could forgo the heavy busby that made the hussars so distinctive. The small light cap with its scarlet top was much more comfortable for daily wear. The busby would only be worn if they went back into action, something that seemed to have become a great deal less likely now that the Persian general had retreated into the hills.

'I've seen Outram's dispatch.' Ballard stood beside his desk, as if reluctant to leave the reports he had been working on. 'This has been a glorious expedition that has put a serious dent in our enemy's ambition to counter our presence here. It is a success, Jack. A resounding success.' He closed his eyes, as if in sudden pain. When he opened them again, he fixed Jack with a hard, flat stare. 'Come on. Let's go and find a drink. I need some fresh air.'

The two officers made their way out of the bell tent that was the centre of Stalker's divisional operations. Outside, the early-morning light was warming away the chill of the night and the army was waking to a day of hard toil as they prepared to march back to Bushire. If Ballard was indeed correct, the next few hours would be spent loading whatever provisions they could on to the collection of mismatched carts and wagons that was all the commissariat could find in the local villages. The infantry would be pressed into service as temporary porters, and for the first time Jack was glad that he now served in a cavalry regiment.

'You understand this spy business is not finished.' Ballard opened the conversation as they made their way from the bustling encampment and headed towards the major's private tent. 'I didn't want to talk of it back there. There are too many beady eyes and eager ears.'

'I thought it had all been passed to Fetherstone.' Jack was wary in the face of Ballard's statement. The commander of the intelligence department had a worrying intensity about him. Jack had been in the army long enough to know that was never a good sign in a senior officer.

'And what if it has?' Ballard was gruff as Jack was quick to remind him of the shame of their failure.

'Do you think it wise to become involved in something that no longer concerns you?' Jack asked the question pointedly.

He wanted no part in the scheme he sensed Ballard was dreaming up.

'Of course it still damn well concerns me.' Ballard shook his head as Jack questioned his reasoning. 'Just because Stalker stomps and shouts doesn't mean I have to let it all go.'

'I rather think he made his point of view clear.' Jack sensed danger. Ballard was clearly close to disobeying Stalker's orders. 'He has given the whole damn thing to Fetherstone. You are a fool if you intend to meddle.'

Ballard looked sharply at Jack. 'I am no fool. You would do well to remember that.'

Jack saw something of the man who had abducted him from the streets of Bombay. It was a reminder of how precarious his position was. It was easy to forget that he owed everything, including his continued survival, to the intelligence officer. 'I apologise. I am merely concerned for your career.'

Ballard waved the remark away, but Jack knew he had been warned.

'So what do we know?' Jack asked the question gingerly.

For the first time, Ballard smiled. 'I have discovered a little. I may be out of favour, but Captain Hunter is a good fellow and he tells me what he can.'

The mention of Stalker's aide made Jack think of Sarah's gossip. Hunter's family had been disgraced. Was that enough to make a man turn his coat and spy for the enemy? He shook his head to clear his mind of the notion. It was not the time for idle speculation. He tried to concentrate on Ballard's news.

'I have learnt that the enemy have a Russian officer in their ranks.' Ballard continued to share what he had discovered. 'We don't know his name, but we think he comes direct from the Tsar. We know very little about him, although rumour has it that he is a hard bastard who fought us in the Crimea. He makes no attempt to hide; he serves on the staff of the

Persian general, Shooja-ool-Moolk. We think he is the ring-leader. The spymaster, if you will. Whoever our spy is, he sends his reports direct to this man, who can then pass on whatever he pleases to the Persian command.' Ballard scowled as he summarised the situation for Jack's benefit. 'The presence of this Russian complicates matters. It means that not only do the Persians seem to know our every move but they get the information from the Russians, which can only further increase their damned influence here.'

'Perhaps we should pop over to the Persian camp and ask the bugger what he is playing at.' Jack chuckled at the idea, but the look on Ballard's face silenced him quickly. He would not put it past the intelligence officer to be contemplating exactly that.

'No, we cannot do that.' Ballard eventually conceded the idea. 'But we can finish the job we were given. This is my mess. I fully intend to be the one who sorts it out.'

They arrived outside Ballard's tent, where Palmer was seated on a stool, sharpening a knife. The bodyguard looked up as they approached, a wry smile on his face as he saw Jack.

'So, you're back.'

'He is not staying.' Ballard was quick to reply.

Palmer grunted. He clearly did not care one way or the other.

Ballard turned to face Jack. His face was serious. 'Just because you have buggered off to the Bombay Lights doesn't mean this isn't your fight too. Do not think I have forgotten your role in apprehending the spy. If you had not rushed in, perhaps we would have unravelled this whole sorry mess.'

'You do not know that. And the poor bastard revealed nothing when your man there got his hands on him.'

'Perhaps.' Ballard frowned. 'We shall never know. So, your orders—'

'I am not sure I can help,' Jack interrupted. He could sense where the conversation was headed. He may have been seconded to the light cavalry, but he had been wrong to think his tie to Ballard had been severed. Like it or not, the major still held the reins to his future.

'You cannot wash your hands of me that easily.' Ballard flashed his thin, wolfish excuse for a smile. 'Or have you forgotten who you really are?'

Jack grimaced as he felt his past tighten around him. 'I see.'

'I'm glad you do. Now, when we get our arses back to Bushire, I want you to talk to Sarah Draper or her brother. They seem to have Fetherstone's ear. See what they know.'

Jack smiled at the notion. He had missed Sarah more than he'd thought possible. His thoughts were no longer solely lustful. He had begun to sense that they shared more than just a physical connection. The idea of seeing her again, and asking her to help him once more, sat well in his mind. 'I'll try.'

'You had better do a damn sight more than that!' Ballard scowled at Jack's meek answer. 'I'll be damned if I leave that bloody webfoot to make a mess of this. You and I will discover the identity of these bloody spies and then you can do what I brought you here to do.' He fixed Jack with a determined stare. 'We will find out who is betraying us and you will kill them.'

The army marched that night. The screech of the ungreased axles on the simple peasant carts grated on the ears of the redcoats, the dreadful cacophony underscoring the sound of hundreds of men marching. Every type of conveyance had been pressed into service as the British attempted to take away as much of the vast amount of supplies as they possibly could. The carts and wagons slowed progress, the heavily laden transport dictating the pace so that the column was forced to halt repeatedly, the delays adding to the frustration of the men who had marched so far to fight only to be denied by the enemy's refusal to meet them in battle.

The long trudge back to the main force's base at Bushire began in silence, every man aware of the long, difficult route they must follow over the coming days and nights. Their officers had promised an easy pace, the need for speed long since gone, yet the redcoats were wise to the ways of their commanders and knew how quickly the situation could change.

They had spent the day piling up the supplies they could not carry into a single heap in the very middle of the enemy's meagre encampment. It was enormous, a man-made mountain. At its base were stacked the hundreds of barrels of black powder they could not hope to take back to Bushire. The whole lot was to be fired, Outram ordering its destruction to garner some credit from the wasted march.

The detonation was entrusted to two officers from the engineers, Lieutenant Gibbard and Lieutenant Hassard. They planned to use a pair of Jacob's shells, a new type of exploding ammunition, the brainchild of Major John Jacob. A copper percussion tube filled with fulminate of mercury was contained in the fore part of the bullet and would explode on impact, igniting the shell behind. The new ammunition promised much. If it worked, it would allow riflemen to annihilate any field battery of artillery from a distance, something that would revolutionise the battlefield. *If* it worked. The ammunition was still very much at an experimental stage, and this would be one of the first occasions it had been used in anger.

The British might be retreating, but they would at least depart with a bang.

The blast split the night asunder, the roar rolling over the marching redcoats in a dreadful explosion of violence. As one, the column halted, turning to stare at the spectacle.

A single column of flame leapt into the sky, like a fiery finger pointing in accusation at the gods who had denied the British the battle they had so desired. It seared through the darkness, banishing the night and lighting the sky so that the world was bathed in a warm orange glow. Cloud after cloud of bright silvery smoke billowed from the base of the flames, rolling out at a terrific rate so that it smothered the entire encampment, before rushing on to blanket the town of Borãzjoon. Explosions punctured the smoke cloud as the enemy's store of ammunition went up. Each burst like a sky rocket in a shower of sparks and flame, punching a hole in the heavy smoke for a single heartbeat before disappearing, only the flicker of falling shards a legacy of its brief but vibrant display.

The concussion of the massive explosion shook the ground. The soil under the redcoats' boots seemed to shimmer, the very fibre of the earth shaken by the power of the exploding black powder. The weary infantry looked at the fabulous scene created by their engineers and saw nothing but shame, their failure displayed to the world.

The order to resume the march echoed down the column. The redcoats ignored the fiery mountain and trudged on into the night, turning their backs on the legacy of their daring incursion into the enemy's heartland.

The Persian army watched the British depart. They had seen their supplies go up in flame, their encampment laid waste by the single massive explosion. They saw the men who had invaded their homeland marching away, the long column snaking for miles across the flat, barren landscape. They sensed fear in the retreat, the hated pale-faced foreigners and their native levies lacking the courage to face them in battle.

As the invaders' column made its way away from Borãzjoon, the Persian army appeared from the safety of the hills and set off after the enemy, huge blocks of infantry marching in close column whilst vast swarms of cavalry led them forward and pressed close to the rear of the retreating British.

The force the Shah had assembled was easily twice the size of the British column. Five thousand infantrymen of the Karragoozloo, Shiraz and Sabriz regiments, the best soldiers in the Persian army, marched with pride, their ranks dressed and ordered just as their British instructors had once taught them. Nigh on two thousand cavalrymen of the Sufenghees, the Shiraz Cavalry and the Eilkhanne Horse were ready to pounce on the enemy, the handful of cavalry at the foreign general's disposal a mere morsel that could be snapped up and devoured before the Persians took their sabres against the broken ranks of the red-coated infantry.

Shooja-ool-Moolk would not let the invaders skulk away unmolested. He had bided his time, waiting for the moment to strike. Now he watched the undefended column and the tiny rearguard that protected it. He saw the opportunity and he thought of the victory his master the Shah so desired.

The British army would not be left to retreat in peace. They would get the battle they had marched so far to find.

Chapter Thirty

The enemy came out of the blackness. Their screams echoed across the plain, drowning out the sound of their galloping horses. The cries swirled around the British rearguard so that it seemed as if they were being attacked from all sides. The suddenness of the attack shook the men of the 3rd Bombay Light Cavalry. They had expected a dull, routine march back to Bushire. They were roused from their lethargy by an eruption of violence, the vicious war cries of the Persian cavalry leaving no doubt that their complacency had been ill founded.

The column was under attack.

The first shots rang out. They snapped through the air, stinging past the ears of the light cavalry protecting the last of the marching infantry. The gunfire drove any indecision from the minds of the officers charged with the security of the column. It was time for action. The rearguard would be the first to fight, their job to protect the column long enough for the infantry to re-form and face the enemy threat.

'Fenris! With me.'

Jack heard Captain Forbes bellow his name. He turned his

horse round and spurred it hard, chasing after the commander of the Bombay Lights. He had been lost in his thoughts, imagining his reunion with Sarah Draper, even though it would likely mean another clash with her arrogant prig of a brother. He emerged from his reverie to the chaos of an ambush.

He saw fast-moving shapes in the darkness as the enemy swarmed around the rearguard. The Persians were screaming and yelling like fiends, the dreadful cries seeming somehow inhuman, as if the column was under attack from the denizens of another world. Their frantic trumpets blared out, the strange calls piercing his ears and scattering his thoughts as he tried to make sense of the confusion that had erupted from the dark.

He reined in hard next to Forbes. There was just enough moonlight to make out the light blue tunics of the troopers as they re-formed their ranks to face outwards into the night. He saw Moore, the adjutant, riding away from his commander, bearing away the first report of the contact to the senior officers who would need to know of the sudden threat to the marching column.

'Take number five and six troop; protect the left flank.' Forbes snapped the order at Jack. Another flurry of shots stung the air around them and both officers flinched, the sudden strain of being under fire written large on their faces. 'The Poona Horse have the right flank. I shall hold the rest of the regiment here to protect the rear. Is that all clear?'

'Sir.' Jack acknowledged the order. He was about to ram his spurs back when Forbes grabbed his shoulder.

'And for God's sake keep the enemy away from the column. Whatever it takes, we cannot let them past.'

Jack nodded and galloped towards the ranks of the Bombay Lights.

'Five and six troop with me.' He glanced along the length of the line and saw the older Moore acknowledge the order.

He looked for the officer in charge of the other troop he had been ordered to command. A thin-faced lieutenant raised his hand: John Malcolmson, an officer Jack barely knew. It was a pity their introduction to one another would come in such dangerous circumstances.

He brought his horse to a stand so he could watch his men as they responded to his orders. The animal pranced and skittered, sensing the building tension, and Jack had to work hard to keep it in hand. He forced the beast into a tight circle and observed the daffadars issuing the orders to their men as they prepared to take the two troops out of the formation. He looked for signs of panic or confusion but the men responded calmly, their stony faces betraying none of the excitement the sudden attack must surely have caused. He was impressed. He just hoped they were as calm in a fight.

'Follow me!' Jack waved his arm and signalled the two troops to move to the left flank. His horse tried to gallop away and he was forced to haul on the reins to keep it in hand. He heard the drumming of hooves behind him as the troops followed his command, and he hoped the darkness saved the men from seeing their commander wrestling to control his horse like a raw recruit fresh from the depot.

He led the men quickly towards the column's left flank, or at least where he believed the left flank to be. In the darkness it was nigh on impossible to know exactly where anyone was. He brought them into position, formed into a single line two men deep so that they could screen the tail of the column from attack. He could hear the first shouted orders as the infantry awoke to the sudden threat. They would need time to re-form. In the column of march, they would be unable to fight back and repel the sudden ambush. The formation was perfect for advancing across country, the men moving in one solid, compact oblong. But it was vulnerable to attack. They needed to reorganise themselves into a square, the one formation that would protect them from the ravages of enemy horsemen. With a wall of bayonets facing out on all four sides, the infantry would be secure, the ring of steel certain to force any attacking cavalry to veer away. It was a tactic that had worked for Wellington, and it would work for the British generals who had learnt from the old duke.

The light cavalry would have to buy the infantry the time they would need to complete the change in formation, no matter what it cost them. If they failed, the infantry would be easy targets for the hard-riding Persian cavalry. They would be butchered, the mournful retreat turned into a rout, the campaign coming to a bloody end with an ignominious defeat.

A bugle sounded from the darkness. Its rising call demanded attention, the signal to retire clear even over the dreadful cacophony of the enemy's screams and yells.

Jack looked in every direction, trying to find the source of the urgent call. He twisted in the saddle and saw his own trumpeters lifting their instruments to their mouths, their instincts telling them to echo the order.

'Hold fast!' he bellowed. The rising call came again, the notes sounding with absolute clarity. There was no mistaking the command.

'Should we retire?' Lieutenant Moore had raced forward so that he could call to Jack. His face was etched with tension.

'No. It's a trick!' Jack forced himself to smile. 'Hold the men here. Two lines, facing west. Quick, now. We are not going to stay here for long. We need to drive these bastards off.'

Moore looked at Jack, a moment of doubt showing in his expression, before he turned away and bellowed the orders to the two troops.

Jack could feel dozens of eyes boring into his back as he tried to discern the enemy in the darkness. He was sure he had made the correct decision. He had read enough reports of the Persian army to know that they had been trained for many years by British officers. It was natural to assume that the enemy trumpeters would know the British army's bugle calls, and he was certain that the command to retire had come from out of the darkness and not from the direction of the British column. He pushed the doubts away and summoned the courage to trust his instincts. He would not obey the orders of the enemy.

A volley of gunfire shattered the calm. The bullets whistled past him, the air suddenly alive with the storm of deadly missiles. A single trooper slumped from the saddle, his left arm shattered by a ball fired from an enemy carbine. The darkness was saving the men from taking more casualties. The enemy horsemen were armed with carbines, and were wasting their time delivering weak volleys of gunfire when they should have been pressing home their attack and relying on cold, hard steel. Jack intended to show them just how light cavalry should fight, a demonstration that he hoped would shatter the enemy's ranks and buy the British column some much-needed time.

'Draw sabres!' He faced his new command, parading his horse in front of the troopers, showing them that he was braving the danger. There was enough moonlight filtering through the thin clouds for them to see their new captain, to witness the example he was trying to set.

He felt his shoulder blades twitch as he turned his back on the enemy. A cold rush of fear surged down his spine before settling in the nagging pain in the small of his back. He forced it from his mind, concentrating on watching his men. He might have only just learnt the sequences of commands the British cavalry employed, but this was what he was used to. He knew how to fight.

The sabres flashed in the meagre light. The Bombay

Lights were issued with straight, heavy swords. They were brutal weapons, the steel capable of cutting through a man's flesh with ease. The troopers endured countless hours of training as they built up the strength they would need to be able to wield the swords effectively in combat. A skill Jack was about to put to the test.

He studied the ranks of faces staring towards him, his eyes roving across the men who had fallen under his command. He saw their determination, the grim set of their jaws as they braced themselves for what was about to come. Moore had ordered them into two lines, each two men deep. The second line had pushed to the rear, leaving a gap between it and the front rank. The men had re-formed quickly, without fuss. For the first time, Jack felt a spark of pride at leading them into battle.

He drew his own sword. The talwar rasped from the scabbard and he brandished it high in the air, letting every man see the fabulous weapon.

A young trooper rode forward, taking his place at Jack's side. His face was pale in the darkness, his eyes wide. He held a trumpet in his hand, and Jack could see the whites of the boy's knuckles as he held the instrument in a vice-like grip.

'Stay close, lad. Watch for my command.' Jack spoke softly so that only the young trumpeter could hear him. He looked into the boy's eyes and saw the fear bright inside them.

Slowly and deliberately he turned his horse on the spot so that he once again faced the darkness. He could see the shadowy forms of the enemy horsemen as they prowled around the rearguard. It told him all he needed to know.

He lowered his sword, pointing it forward.

'Bombay Lights!' His voice was huge, his hidden terror given voice. 'March!'

He tapped his heels into the flanks of his willing horse,

keeping the bit rammed hard into the animal's mouth, curbing its instincts to race away. The two lines of cavalry lurched into motion behind him, the men obeying his orders without hesitation.

'Trot!'

The rhythm of the hooves pounding into the sun-baked soil changed as the men hastened their speed. The line was moving rapidly now, pulling away from the rearguard, advancing into the dark.

'Gallop!'

Jack pushed his spurs backwards, urging his horse on yet still keeping the bit hard in its mouth, holding it back, keeping it in hand.

'Charge!'

He was supposed to give the final command when the enemy was no more than forty to fifty yards distant. In the darkness, it was impossible to tell, but he screamed the order anyway, the need to close with the enemy overriding the need for precision.

He racked his spurs back and finally let the bit fall loose, giving the horse its head. The valiant animal threw itself forward. The young trumpeter echoed the order, his instrument blaring the notes of the charge as he raced after his commander.

Jack galloped into the darkness. The movement was mesmerising, the motion of the horse's gait sending a rush of exhilaration flushing through his veins and banishing the last of his fear. He heard the sound of hundreds of hooves hitting the ground as the two troops followed his lead and felt a heady rush of excitement, the intoxication of the charge like nothing he had ever experienced.

He looked ahead and saw the shapes of the enemy horsemen scattering in every direction as the sudden charge took them by surprise. He sensed the panic engulfing the Persians, the reversal in fortune so quick that it snatched away their initiative in a heartbeat. He felt the flare of success. He was doing what he did best.

A shadowy shape flashed towards him. Without thought, he changed the angle of his horse's charge, his body reacting just as it had been trained to do so many months ago. He brought his talwar around, acting on instinct, slashing the blade forward, slicing it across the back of the body that had erupted from the darkness.

His arm jerked with the impact. He felt the blade slide through flesh before it bounced off bone. He caught the impression of an enemy rider being thrown from the saddle before he was past, the speed of his horse's gallop taking him away from the man he had slain.

He heard a visceral thump as his men hit the loose formation of the enemy. They swept on with barely a pause, scything the Persian riders from their saddles, their heavy swords battering the enemy into bloody ruin.

There was no time for anything more than the brutal collision. Jack knew he had to halt his men almost immediately. He could not afford for them to become scattered, their cohesion broken as they chased down the enemy horsemen.

'Walk!' He bellowed the command, immediately reining in hard, slowing the mad headlong rush. The two troops had covered the ground fast and already they were some distance from the column they were protecting. The young trumpeter drew up beside him, his instrument already pressed to his lips.

Jack lifted his arm high, signalling his command. 'Sound the halt!' He snapped off the order.

The two troops came to a breathless standstill as the bugle called for them to stop. Jack flashed a smile at his trumpeter. In the darkness, the boy's instrument was vital as the only practical way of issuing commands to his men, the youngster's skill the only thing between him and chaos.

Jack twisted in the saddle, taking one last look into the darkness. There was no sign of the enemy riders. He nodded at the trumpeter. 'Signal retire.'

It was time to rejoin the column. The Bombay Lights had scattered the enemy troops. They had bought their comrades some time to re-form. For the moment, that was all they could do.

Chapter Thirty-one

*J*ack led his two troops back towards the column.
He could sense the men's exhilaration at having
charged the enemy, and the horses tossed their heads
and snorted loudly as they joined in their masters' excitement.
He was proud of his new command and he relished being back
where he belonged.

At the rear of the column, the 4th Rifles had formed a thin
skirmish line facing out into the darkness. Their officers
prowled behind the line, steadying the troops, readying them
to fight. Ahead, Jack could hear the bugles and drums of the
main column. The cumbersome infantry battalions were still
re-forming, moving out of the column of march and into
the square that would protect them from an enemy attack. The
column was performing well under the stress of the night-time
ambush, but the change in formation was taking longer than
Jack could have imagined. They needed still more time.

'Well done, that man.'

Jack looked up and saw a mounted officer waving them in,
his enthusiastic greeting an unexpected boon.

'That's the way, boys. Show them some bloody steel.'

The officer was clearly delighted at their performance. He lifted his hand in greeting as he saw Jack. 'Captain, form your men up on the left, if you please.'

Jack recognised the voice. He rode forward as his men manoeuvred to obey the command, leaving them to the care of their officers.

'Good evening, sir.' He greeted the army's commander whilst he was still too far away to be properly identified in the dim light. He was pleased to see the general look round, squinting in an attempt to discern Jack's features as he approached.

'You!'

Jack smiled as he saw the flare of recognition in Outram's eyes. 'Yes, sir.'

'That was fine work, Fenris. Fine work indeed.' To Outram's credit, he rallied fast, even remembering Jack's name. He was clearly not going to let Jack's past failure stop him from giving praise where it was due.

'The men knew what they were about, sir. I just tagged along for the ride.'

Outram laughed at his modesty. 'You did well; it was just what was needed. I had a feeling you were wasted working with Ballard. You are a man of purpose, Captain Fenris. A man of action. I could see that the moment I clapped eyes on you.'

'Thank you, sir.' Jack tried not to look too pleased.

'Well, I am sure you will be given another chance to show what you are made of tonight. This is a nasty business. These buggers seem to know what they are doing.'

There was no time for Jack to reply. A staff officer rode up to the general, thrusting forward a scrap of paper the moment he came to a halt. Jack rode back to his new command. Outram was right. The enemy were still swarming around the rearguard, their yells and cries building in intensity once again as they re-formed. It was only just after midnight. It would be a long night.

'Re-form the ranks!' Jack gave the order to his trumpeter. The two troops had become more scattered on the third charge, the men's tiredness beginning to have an effect on their cohesion. He felt his own exhaustion pressing down, numbing his brain so that his thoughts became turgid and slow.

The call to re-form was ragged and uneven, and he flashed an angry glare at the young boy who had been at his side throughout the charges. It was enough of a warning for the youngster to find a reserve of energy, and the call steadied, the notes sounding clear once again.

For the third time, the two troops trotted back to their station on the left flank of the rearguard. For the last two hours they had ridden hard to drive away the enemy cavalry, keeping them at bay. Their frustration was building as quickly as their exhaustion. The enemy had learnt fast. They refused to stand and fight, preferring instead to melt into the darkness as soon as the Bombay Lights pressed close. Thus far Jack's men had only caught the Persians with their first attack, and they were tiring of the need to re-form when they had barely got going. Despite their frustration, Jack was determined to keep them on a tight leash. The British had pitifully few cavalry; they could ill afford to allow two troops to disappear on some fruitless chase into the night.

A deep boom resonated through the night sky. The enemy had brought up four guns and had begun shelling the halted column shortly after the Bombay Lights' first charge. It was an ill-directed fire, the shells exploding harmlessly away from the column. Yet the constant barrage was wearing away the men's nerves. It had to only be a matter of time before the Persian gunners got lucky and managed to land a shot on target.

The column had re-formed into an enormous single square, each of the four sides facing outwards so that no matter where the enemy attacked they would be greeted by the massed ranks of the British infantry. A single brigade formed each of the long flanks, with a demi-brigade making up the two shorter faces at the front and rear. The supply wagons were huddled together in the centre, sheltered from attack by the long walls of rifles and muskets that surrounded them. In this new tight formation, Outram's men could wait for dawn and for the daylight that would allow them to take the battle to the enemy.

'Here they come again, sir.' Lieutenant Moore called for Jack's attention.

Some of the cloud had been blown away so that more moonlight made its way on to the plain. There was enough to see the enemy cavalry pressing forward again. For the fourth time they approached the rearguard. The screams and yells that had typified the initial attacks were gone, the enemy calmer as the night wore on and the impetus of the early ambush faded. It was as if the Persians had accepted the standoff and now both sides were reduced to going through the motions as they waited for the dawn and the battle that seemed inevitable.

'Prepare the men. Dress the ranks.'

'Will we charge again, sir?' Moore asked the question cautiously, sounding his captain out.

Jack looked closely at the lieutenant. 'I see no other option.'

'The men are tired, sir. So are the horses. We aren't coming close to catching the buggers. Perhaps we can hold our position for the moment. Give everyone time to catch their breath.'

Jack sighed. He well understood the weariness. 'We cannot risk meeting the enemy from a halt if they do decide to charge us. We must have momentum. We have no choice. Prepare the men to charge again.' He gave the order confidently. He was in command.

'Yes, sir.' Moore accepted the argument.

'The men are doing well, Ross. You should let them know that.'

Moore smiled. 'They are good boys. You mustn't listen to all the nonsense about the Company's men being at odds with their officers. I would trust my boys with my very life.'

Jack heard both pride and complacency in Moore's reply. He had seen how the East India Company officered its native battalions. He had not been impressed. Bombay had resounded with dire tales of the lazy, indolent Company officers treating their men with appalling brutality. Talk of discontented jawans disobeying their officers was becoming commonplace, as was rumour of unrest. The native soldiers' list of complaints was long, from the threat of being forced to serve overseas to the attempts to convert them to Christianity. Jack had seen first hand how hard the native infantry fought. He had every respect for their ability as soldiers and he could only wonder at the senior Company officers who steadfastly refused to listen to their men's complaints.

This was no time for such a political discussion. Jack summoned the energy to sit straight as he gave his next orders. 'Form the men. Send me the trumpeter. We charge as before.'

Moore stiffened in the saddle as he acknowledged the command. 'Very good, sir.'

Jack's tired squadron would have to fight on.

'Charge!'

For the fourth time that night, Jack bellowed the command. The trumpeter picked up the order and blew the rising call beautifully. Despite his exhaustion, Jack felt his body respond to the warlike melody. He did not doubt that the notes would haunt him for ever; he could not imagine a time when they would not resonate deep in his soul.

His horse went forward willingly. He felt the change in gait as the restraining bit loosened to give the animal its head.

Just as before, the enemy turned and raced away. The light had improved as dawn crept ever closer, and Jack got a better look at the men who had plagued the rearguard for so many hours.

They were dressed in a similar fashion to their infantry: light blue tunics with red collars and cuffs, and the same white cross belts and popakh hats. They were armed with thin lances decorated with scarlet flags. From what little Jack had seen, they were not as well trained as the infantry, their scattered formation easily broken by the disciplined charges of the Bombay Lights.

'Walk!'

Jack shouted the order, the words grating in his throat. The Bombay Lights eased their horses into the slower pace, the repetition of the manoeuvre lessening the disappointment at being unable to bring the enemy to meet their sabres.

'Halt! Re-form the ranks.'

Jack felt the tiredness take hold. He watched his men as they re-formed. He could see their exhaustion, their tired mounts having to be worked hard as they were forced back into the ordered ranks. The charge had taken them close to half a mile away from the rest of the rearguard, and Jack wanted to get his small command back to the safety of the main position. But even once back with the other troops, there would be no opportunity for any kind of rest. There were simply too few cavalry with the expeditionary force. The Bombay Lights would have to stay in the saddle until daybreak, and God alone knew what they faced when the morning revealed the full extent of the enemy's preparations.

'Sir! Beware right!' Cornet Combe, stationed in serrefile rank behind six troop, called for his commander's attention, his adolescent voice squeaking as he did so.

Jack felt a flutter of fear. His squadron was exposed, its flanks unguarded and open. It was the necessary evil of scattering the enemy cavalry with a short, sharp charge. If a large body of enemy horsemen caught them now, they could be quickly cut off from the rest of the expeditionary force. He forced his horse to a trot. From his position at the centre of the two troops, he couldn't see the threat that placed his new command in danger.

'Sir!' Combe waved his arm frantically. 'Cavalry to the east.'

At last Jack spotted what had captured his subaltern's attention. A body of enemy horsemen was trying to slip around the flank of the squadron.

'Sound the retire!' He snapped the order at his trumpeter.

The boy's eyes widened with fear at the urgency in his officer's voice. He raised the trumpet and tried to sound the order, but his lips were dry and the notes stuttered and died.

'Spit, boy, spit!' Jack admonished, knowing full well that any delay placed his men and the rest of the rearguard in danger.

The boy did as he was told, his tongue flicking nervously over his lips. He replayed the command, and this time the notes sounded clear.

'Sir?' Lieutenant Malcolmson reined in at Jack's side. 'Orders?'

'We have to retire. Those bastards are trying to cut us off.' Jack snapped off the instruction.

'Very good.' Malcolmson understood instantly.

'We ride hard.' Jack reined his own horse round. 'If we are quick, we can hit them in the flank before they work out that we have seen what they are up to.'

Malcolmson said nothing, merely nodded quickly before heading back to his troop.

Jack's squadron had to move fast. The large body of Persian cavalry was attempting to sweep around and cut them off from the rest of the rearguard. The Bombay Lights would have to react quickly. It would be a race between the two groups of horsemen. If the Bombay Lights lost, they would be cut down and massacred. If they won, they could hit the enemy cavalry in the flank. But only if they were quick.

The ground flew past under the hooves of Jack's horse, every impact hitting the arid soil like a gunshot. Jack could feel the film of dust covering his face, stretching his skin taut and drying out his eyes and nose.

The front rank was close behind him, and they brought their sabres down to the engage position as they thundered towards the rearguard. Jack could see enough to spot the tremor in the enemy cavalry's ranks as they finally awoke to the sudden appearance of the squadron of charging horsemen they had been attempting to outflank. The confusion was immediate, the cohesion of their loose formation disappearing in a heartbeat as most of the terrified Persians immediately turned and raced away.

Yet there was not enough time for them all to escape the charging Bombay Lights. Jack would have bellowed in delight if he had had the breath. His men had reacted fast and had snatched the initiative from the enemy. They were no longer the quarry but the hunter. His head whipped back and forth as he tried to judge time and distance, then he raked back his spurs and led his men into the charge.

The Bombay Lights raced forward, letting their horses use their reserves of strength in a final, muscle-stretching burst of speed. They smashed into the Persian cavalry's ranks, their greater momentum driving them into the enemy horsemen with a sickening thump.

Jack was at the forefront of the melee. He slashed his talwar at a fast-moving figure to his left. The blade scythed through the air and he howled in disappointment, the speed of his horse taking him past the enemy before the blow could land. He wrenched at the reins, slowing his mount and searching out another target. A trooper from the Bombay Lights rushed past him, riding across his line. Jack could do nothing but watch in grim approval as the man spurred his horse hard, driving it at a Persian horseman slow to react to the counterattack. The trooper shouted once, a yell of frustration released, before he chopped his heavy sabre down on to the enemy's head, bludgeoning him to the ground with a single vicious blow.

Jack urged his horse on, looking for danger, though his desire to fight was overridden by the more urgent need to understand the chaotic melee. His men had broken the enemy ranks, the bulk of those left in the saddle in full flight to the rear. A dozen scraps were still going on, his troopers trading blows with the Persian riders who had been unable to escape the charge. It would soon be time to re-form, the wild dash to their rear having left the Bombay Lights' own ranks badly disordered. Jack opened his mouth, preparing to issue the orders that would bring those men not engaged with the enemy back under control.

The words died on his lips. Not all the enemy cavalry were in flight. The men on the flank furthest from the Bombay Lights' charge had ridden on, their officers driving them past the British cavalry and towards the rearguard.

Jack saw the danger. Any notion of success was lost. He twisted, desperately looking for his trumpeter, yet knowing it was already too late. There was no sign of the boy; the melee with the Persian cavalry had separated him from his commander. Jack cursed and forced his horse around, turning it to face the sudden threat to the British rear.

He was not alone in spotting the danger. A small group of British officers were spurring hard as they saw the Persian horsemen racing towards the 4th Rifles' undefended flank. They would be horribly outnumbered, but they rode at the attacking cavalry nonetheless, throwing themselves into their path in a courageous attempt to save the riflemen, who were still unaware of the danger, their thin defensive line dreadfully vulnerable to the marauding Persians.

Jack's heels worked vigorously to force his exhausted mount back into the gallop. He had no choice but to risk everything on a madcap dash back across the plain. If he was too late, the British officers would die and the Persian cavalry would have a clear path to the rearguard's undefended flank.

Chapter Thirty-two

There was no time for the niceties of regular orders.

Jack's men swirled around him, some still fighting the enemy horsemen, others looking for their mates and their officers, ready for the next set of instructions. Their ordered ranks were broken, the violent contact with the Persian cavalry shattering the neat lines in which they had charged.

'Follow me!'

Jack screamed the command. It was one more suited to the chaos of an infantry assault than to the ordered world of the cavalry, but he did not have time to gather an organised group. He did not wait to see if anyone understood. He simply rammed his spurs into his horse's flanks, cruel in his mastery, the need for speed doing away with any notion of gentility. The willing horse responded well, and Jack raced past his disordered troopers, catching fleeting glimpses of astonished faces as their new commander powered to the rear, exhorting his men to follow.

He could see at least two dozen enemy horsemen swarming around the handful of red-coated officers. Even from a distance he could make out the flash of a sabre as the heavily outnumbered officers fought desperately to stop the enemy attack. With such odds the result was a foregone conclusion. Even as Jack raced towards them, he saw one of the red-coated figures topple from the saddle. The man hit the ground hard, the impact jarring his sword from his grasp.

The fallen rider's horse twisted on the spot, its dark pelt matted with blood from a dozen wounds. It bravely lifted its head, trying to obey the training that was buried deep in its instincts, but the valiant animal was too badly wounded and its legs buckled beneath it. It screamed as it fell, an animal shriek of mortal agony, then toppled on to its master, crushing the man to the ground.

Jack watched in horror as the closest Persians slashed at the fallen rider, trying to finish him off, whilst their fellows traded blows with the other red-coated officers still in the saddle. Swords thrust downwards, but the body of the dying horse frustrated them, its flesh absorbing the vicious attacks meant for its master.

Jack screamed as his mount closed the last of the distance. He caught a glimpse of one of the Persian cavalrymen turning in surprise as he became aware of the lone rider charging towards them.

He slashed his sword from right to left, slicing the sharpened edge across the closest face. He felt the blade catch as it drove through flesh, the bright spray of blood telling him his aim had been true. He tugged on the reins, turning his horse's head round, avoiding the body that tumbled from the saddle, his first victim falling without a sound. He saw a second rider come into range and he drove his sword forward, thrusting the tip into the man's stomach. The blade slid into the Persian's guts and Jack twisted it, releasing the talwar from the inevitable suction, tugging it free as he rode past.

He thought of nothing as he fought. He saw not other men

but merely targets for his sword. The first attacks had slowed his horse, and now he spurred it on, making it lurch into motion once again. It bounded forward, pushing past enemy riders, its forelegs scrabbling as they fought for purchase on the friable ground. He felt a tug on his uniform and glanced down to see the tip of a lance score through the side of his jacket before it was ripped free by the sudden movement of his horse.

He felt the madness build. He let his horse run, rushing past the body of the fallen British officer, narrowly missing the hooves of the man's horse, which thrashed in pitiful agony as the animal writhed in its death throes.

He roared as he attacked a crowd of Persian cavalrymen surrounding one of the officers. He flashed past the mob, slashing his talwar into one man's side and only just missing a second as he backhanded the blade.

He turned fast, riding back at the enemy, the anger driving out the last of his control. He could hear his own war cry, but it sounded as if it came from far away. He crashed into the melee, his bloodied sword whispering through the air as he battered it at the closest enemy. His arm jarred as his target blocked the blow with a fast parry. He bludgeoned the sword forward again, hacking at the man who had defied him, avoiding the Persian's own desperate lunge before driving the blade into the man's breast. His opponent fell with a scream, his hands clawing at the steel, his face twisted into an awful grimace of horror as he realised his death was upon him.

The surviving Persian horsemen turned to escape. Jack's lone attack had been fast and brutally effective. Four of their number had been slain in minutes, and the rest had no stomach for the fight now that their easy victory had been snatched away by a single blue-coated hussar. They threw their mounts round, giving the animals their heads as they tried to flee.

The slowest to turn howled in frustration as his tired horse staggered, its balance thrown by the desperate manoeuvre. Jack was on him in a flash. It took barely a heartbeat for him to catch the Persian and bury his sword in his spine. The man reared in the saddle, his body arching against the sudden agony, his hand flapping at the talwar embedded in his back. Jack pulled the blade away and the man fell, his horse galloping free.

Jack let the broken enemy go. He felt the madness of the desperate melee begin to slip away, rational thought once again taking control of his mind. He rammed his bloody talwar back into its leather scabbard with a grimace, his right hand cramped and sore from having held the weapon so tightly as he fought. Only then did he turn and face the officers he had saved. He recognised one man at once and called across in greeting.

'Captain Hunter!'

Hunter looked at him without any sign of recognition. Jack's face was flecked with blood flung from his talwar. He looked like a grotesque spectre that had escaped from a charnel house.

'Fenris!' The name emerged from the shocked captain's mouth as he belatedly recognised the bloodied rider who had come to his aid. 'Help me. It's the general.' He immediately slipped from his saddle and raced to the fallen officer.

Jack heard the panic in the aide's voice. He jumped down and ran to help Hunter, who was doing his best to drag the general from underneath his fallen steed. Jack thrust his shoulder against the dead animal's flank, ignoring the slick sheen of blood that covered its hide. He shoved with all his strength and managed to create enough of a gap for Hunter to haul Outram free.

'Is he alive?' he asked as Hunter leant forward and laid his cheek against the general's nose.

Hunter nodded quickly before bending down and lifting Outram into a sitting position.

Jack squatted down. He looked into the general's eyes and saw them open.

'Sir. You are safe.' He spoke reassuringly.

Outram's eyes failed to focus. He had been knocked insensible by the fall. His head lolled forward and Hunter was forced to cradle him like a mother holding her newborn child for the first time.

'I'll get help.' Jack leapt to his feet and turned, looking for his horse. Like all well-trained cavalry mounts, it had stayed in place when he had left the saddle, and now he vaulted on to its back.

As he mounted, the first of his troopers arrived at the scene. He saw the look of approval on the dark faces as they rode around him, their horses picking carefully over the bloody remains of the men he had killed.

'Dekho, sahib.' The closest rider, a kot-daffadar, nodded with satisfaction at the slaughter he found scattered around his new officer. The man's drawn sabre was smeared with blood, his white uniform belts bespattered all over. 'You gave those bastards a jewab for killing Malet Sahib Bahadur, and no mistake.'

The other troopers roared their approval. They raised their bloodied sabres, brandishing them to the sky, and cheered their new commander, celebrating his exploits.

Jack felt his heart constrict as he listened to their loud approval. It meant more than any medal. It was a vibrant recognition of his ability to lead men in battle, and he had never known such pride.

He turned to the kot-daffadar and began issuing the orders that would bring the command to order, before sending Cornet Spens on his way to summon a litter for Outram.

Daylight was beginning to creep into the sky. The long night was coming to an end. The new day was just beginning.

Chapter Thirty-three

———————❖———————

The thin morning light crept across the British ranks. The redcoats looked at one another and shared grim, thin-lipped smiles at their deliverance. The night had passed with infinite cruelty, the men forced to stand staring out into the darkness for hours, waiting for a sudden attack or the dreadful explosion of a well-directed enemy roundshot. Their nerves had been stretched thin.

Thanks to the efforts of the rearguard, the enemy had been unable to reach the main ranks of the column whilst they were still dangerously exposed in a marching formation. The cavalry and the 4th Rifles had remained steady, no matter what the enemy threw at them, and they had bought enough time for the unwieldy battalions to form the defensive formation that had seen them safe through the night.

Thus far, they had been fortunate. The Persian gunners could have caused much destruction, the tightly packed formation the perfect target for artillery. The redcoats had been saved by the darkness, the black of night denying the enemy the chance to see what they were firing at. Barely a handful of rounds had hit the expeditionary force, but as the early-morning light pushed back the gloom, the four guns deployed against the British were finally able to see the huge target ahead of them.

Lieutenant Knightly stood in his allotted station behind the line of redcoats, doing his best to look calm and unconcerned now that his men could see his face once more. His captain was on the right flank of the company, with the senior lieutenant on the left, leaving Knightly alone with his covering sergeant to prowl behind the line. His main task was to keep the ranks tight, making sure that the files closed together if the company took casualties. The need to keep the line steady and unbroken was paramount.

He had drawn his sword when the men had been ordered to fix bayonets. It had been a long time ago and he now felt rather foolish walking around with the naked steel in his hand. He had yet to even catch a glimpse of the Persian attackers. Even as the sun crept reluctantly into the sky it was hard to see anything beyond the ranks of tall redcoats to his front. He was beginning to believe he would go through the whole battle without once casting his eyes over the enemy.

The Persian cannon fired again. Knightly looked up and saw the roundshot searing through the grey morning sky. He watched transfixed as they raced towards the British ranks, smashing into the ground to the side of the 64th with appalling violence, gouging thick crevices in the soil before bouncing back into the air and careering forward. He shivered as he realised the morning light would let the enemy gunners aim with greater precision.

He looked up and saw Lieutenant Greentree leave his allotted station on the left of the line. The senior lieutenant flashed Knightly a friendly smile as he made his way over to talk to Captain Mackler, the company commander. For a moment Knightly considered joining the two officers, but the long night had worn him out and he couldn't find the energy to move. Instead, he finally decided to sheathe his sword, hoping he wouldn't be bawled out for doing so before the battalion had been ordered to unfix their bayonets.

He barely registered the boom as the Persian guns fired again. His eyes felt as if they had been filled with grit, and now that he had both hands free, he balled them into fists and rubbed them, savouring the sensation of scrubbing them clear.

He opened his eyes just in time to see the roundshot as it hurtled down, moving at a terrific rate before smashing into the right-hand file of his stationary company. The red-hot shot ripped into the tight files, sending a grotesque shower of blood and bone into the air and knocking men down like skittles before it sped away, its dreadful momentum barely altered by the vicious contact.

Knightly felt the gorge rise in his throat as he saw the tumbled heap of men writhing on the ground. He ran forward, his body lurching into motion by itself, and reached the gory spectacle as the first victims were being dragged backwards, their shattered bodies belching so much blood that it had stained the pale sandy soil black.

Captain Mackler, Lieutenant Greentree and four other redcoats had been hit, the single roundshot working a dreadful destruction on the company. Six men snatched from the fight in no more than a single heartbeat.

Knightly shook his head to clear the gruesome sight from his eyes. He turned away from the horror and met the uncompromising stare of the company's colour sergeant, who had arrived to sort out the bloody mess.

'Mr Knightly. You're in charge now, sir.'

The words cut Knightly's soul like a knife. It had taken one roundshot to thrust him into command of a company of redcoats, just fewer than one hundred souls now his responsibility and his alone.

'Form line.'

The regimental sergeant major bellowed the order. Knightly forced away the tears that had sprung unbidden to his eyes. There was no time for self-pity. He stood back and watched as the battalion musicians came forward and removed the casualties from the line of march. All the victims of the enemy roundshot were alive, despite appalling wounds to their flesh. Greentree had lost a foot, and Knightly had to tear his eyes from the gory stump that pulsed blood with every beat of the lieutenant's heart.

'Come along now, sir.' The colour sergeant reached forward and placed a surprisingly gentle hand on Knightly's shoulder, steering him away from the carnage. Behind them the battalion drummers were already beating out the pace of the manoeuvre. The first light of day signalled an end to the long, nerve-shredding night. It was time to re-form, to bring the redcoats out of the defensive square and into an attacking formation so they could take the fight to the enemy.

Knightly trotted forward, obedient to his sergeant's instruction.

'On the right, if you please, sir.'

He blushed and altered his route. He had been heading to his regular station behind the line, but now that he was in charge, he would have to take Captain Mackler's place on the right. The position of command was now his.

'Form line!'

The redcoats responded to the order with a will. They shook away the effects of having been under fire for so long, their heads lifting now that they could finally see their surroundings. As they manoeuvred, the enemy artillery fire finally stopped. It was time for both sides to re-form, the two armies bracing themselves for the real battle that had yet to begin.

With staff officers racing around the manoeuvring troops, the redcoats and their native infantry formed into two long lines facing back the way they had come. In the front rank, the 4th Bombay Rifles took the left flank, with the 2nd European Light Infantry, the 26th Native Infantry and the 78th Highlanders stretching away to their right. Behind them, in the second line, the Belooch battalion marched on the left, with the 20th Native Infantry on their right and the 64th on the far flank.

The early-morning air resounded to the call of the bugles and the rhythm of the drum, as the British expeditionary force came to life. Officers galloped between the battalions, ferrying orders from the senior officers and collecting reports from the battalion commanders. The beautiful regimental colours were unfurled and the gaudy silk squares billowed in the stiff breeze that flowed across the plain.

'Battalion. Battalion, load!'

The huge voice of the 64th's regimental sergeant major bellowed out. To his command, the battalion began the process of loading their Enfield rifles. The weapons were new, the battalion only having been issued with them in the weeks before their hurried departure to join the campaign. The native infantry battalions were still armed with smoothbore percussion-capped muskets, weapons that were little changed since the days of Wellington and Waterloo.

There had been rumours circulating through the division that the native soldiers had concerns about accepting the new weapons. The Enfield rifles came with a cartridge that was greased to allow it to glide over the rifling in the gun's barrel, the twisted grooves that spun the bullet and made it so much more accurate than the outdated smoothbore muskets. It was said that the cartridges were waxed in pig fat, something that was totally abhorrent to both the high-caste Hindus and the Muslims who made up the bulk of the native infantry's ranks. Yet the concerns had been pushed to one side in the rush to embark on the campaign, and for now the native infantry would fight with their trusted, if less effective, muskets. The dispute over the cartridges would have to wait.

'Battalion, prepare to advance.'

The words dispelled any last doubts. It was the final command they would be given before the order to attack.

The battalion fell silent and the men stood with their weapons ready for the fight. It was the time to wrestle with the fear that was stirring in their guts, the presence of death haunting many. This was this moment for silent prayer, for the men to seek forgiveness or to beg for protection in the battle that was now inevitable.

All along the line the redcoats fidgeted with their equipment, going through the superstitious rituals that they believed would keep them safe in the fight. Each man was surrounded by thousands of fellow soldiers, yet each was alone.

The sudden strident call of the bugle cut through every man's thoughts. The drummer boys rattled their sticks against the taut skins of their instruments, summoning the men to action.

'Battalion, battalion will advance. Advance!'

As one, the long lines strode forward. The men forced away their fears. The brilliantly hued silks of the battalion colours stirred in the freshening breeze so that the huge squares spread to their fullest extent, the pride of the regiments on display. To the beat of the drums, the redcoats marched to take the fight to the enemy.

They advanced as only the British advanced, the ranks stoic and steady. There was no pomp, no cheers or wild yells.

The line walked forward in silence, the grave, stony faces of the redcoats betraying none of the emotion that seared through their veins. No matter how heavy the fire, no matter how many men were struck from the ranks, they would march on, ignoring their fallen comrades, the line moving forward with resolute purpose, unrelenting and unstoppable.

The enemy had belatedly chosen to give battle. The British redcoats would not shirk from the fight.

Chapter Thirty-four

With the drums and bugle calls muffled by a damp morning mist, the army marched back along the path it had taken the day before. The night attack had revealed the Persians' intention to fight, but if they expected to see a tired, half-beaten enemy, they were to be disappointed. The redcoats' advance was slow and steady, their boots thumping hard against the dusty ground as they retraced their steps. It would be a short march. The enemy's attack had stopped the British column before it had gone more than a few miles towards Bushire, and the red-coated army marched with purpose, the men looking ahead with anticipation, waiting for the enemy to be revealed. This time they advanced knowing they faced battle.

A sharp, cold wind blew over the redcoats as they advanced. It soon dispelled the morning mist, stirring the battalion colours and revealing the enemy army drawn up and ready for battle. Whilst the Persian cavalry had been harassing the British column, the bulk of their infantry had marched down from the safety of the high ground and taken up position between the column and the village of Khoosh-Ab. They formed one long continuous line, their left flank tethered on the walled village itself, their right secured by a thick grove of date trees.

There were two hillocks in the centre of the line, and the Persian commander had wisely chosen these as the best position to site his artillery. The raised ground gave them a clear line of sight towards the British force, which would be forced to advance across the open plain if they chose to assault the Persian line. The two hillocks would become the bastions of the enemy line, natural redoubts that would shore up the centre of the formation. With two strongpoints in the centre and both flanks secure, it was a powerful defensive position.

The redcoats looked ahead and wondered what it would be like to attack the Persians' position. Their fears built as they saw what they must endure, the British command certain to order an attack now that the enemy had finally obliged and offered them the battle they sought. The Persian general had chosen to fight. He had picked his ground and his army now waited to see if the British commanders would take the bait and attack.

With Outram still shaking off the effects of his fall, command of the army had reverted to General Stalker. He would not disappoint the enemy. The British infantry advanced and took up position opposite the Persian line. As they waited, the men sucked on their canteens of precious water while the rest of the British expeditionary force manoeuvred into position.

The light cavalry were sent to guard Stalker's right flank. He had far too few sabres to cover all his options, so he massed his cavalry opposite the bulk of the Persian general's horsemen. The two regiments were under strength and horribly outnumbered, but he could not risk letting the Persian general unleash his own troopers without opposition. The 3rd Bombay Lights and the men of the Poona Horse would have to protect the infantry's flank no matter what the cost. The success of any assault, indeed the success of the entire campaign, relied on their willingness to hold back the horde of enemy horsemen.

The infantry would not be left to advance alone. The expeditionary force had two batteries of foot artillery and one of horse, a total of eighteen guns. The three batteries had been sited along the length of the line. The gunners' job that day would be simple: they would fire as the infantry advanced, their roundshot and shell certain to work a dreadful destruction on the tightly packed ranks of the Persian defensive line. But to succeed, the artillery officers would have to be unerringly accurate and demonstrate the very highest level of skill, with not a single shot wasted. Stalker was relying on his artillery to batter the Persians into submission before the infantry arrived to launch their assault. If they failed and the enemy line was left intact, the Persian infantry would be able to deliver volleys of such power that the redcoats would be butchered no matter how courageously they advanced.

The plan was simple, but it relied on each of the three branches of the army working together. If one should fail, the whole expeditionary force would be hard pressed to avoid being destroyed. Stalker and his officers had done all they could; it was now down to the rank and file to achieve the victory they so desperately desired.

The enemy cannon opened fire.

Even from far out on the right flank, Jack could see the pencil-thin trace the roundshot left as they seared through the pale blue morning sky, racing towards the two red lines that advanced towards the Persian position. They smashed into the ground in front of the first rank before flying high into the air and over the heads of the rearmost. The redcoats marched on in silence, ignoring the temptation to jeer at the enemy's failure.

The British artillery replied. Their guns were of a smaller calibre than those of the Persian army, the roundshot they fired lighter and less powerful. The British gunners had waited to be called into action. They had sweated as they hauled their beloved cannon across country, their trial so much greater than that of the marching infantry. They had endured the same bitter night as the infantry, forced to suffer the enemy barrage without being able to reply. Finally they had been given the order they had waited so long for, and they served their weapons with a will as they opened fire on the strongly positioned Persian army.

The British gunners had not been given long to study the distances. They had been forced to rush the guns into the line as the expeditionary force moved on to the attack, the hasty advance denying them the opportunity to plot their barrage with their usual mathematical precision. Still their first volley smashed into the Persian ranks with dreadful effect, every roundshot working a terrible slaughter on the packed ranks of the enemy.

'Bloody good shooting, what?'

Jack turned and saw that Lieutenant Arthur Moore, the Bombay Lights' adjutant, had ridden across to join him. Jack had been given little chance to converse with any of his fellow officers. He had given Captain Forbes a terse summary of the night's activity when he had finally brought his squadron back to join the rest of the regiment. If his new commander approved of his efforts during the long, wearing night, he made no mention of it. He said little before leaving Jack in command of his squadron and riding to take his place at the head of the regiment as it formed on the right flank of the advancing infantrymen. Now the regiment's adjutant had found a moment to ride across and spend a moment with their new captain, and Jack was pleased to be able to share his thoughts with another officer.

'It's about time the damn gunners made themselves useful. It would have been a waste to have hauled their sorry backsides all this way for nothing.' Jack welcomed the adjutant with a wry observation.

Moore guffawed at the forthright sentiment. 'You have that right, old man. Still, let's hope they save some for us. We don't want the enemy skedaddling before we have the chance to be about them.'

Jack had to bite his tongue at the naïve words. 'Let's hope.' He tried to sound enthusiastic. He did not think he succeeded.

Moore nodded in approval anyway. He sat at Jack's side gnawing the ends of his moustache, and Jack saw the tension in the younger officer's body. Moore held the reins so hard that his hands quivered with the effort, and there was the faintest sheen of perspiration on his forehead.

The lieutenant might have been the product of a privileged upbringing, but that would not save him when the lead started to fly. Jack had known many such officers. Some were brave souls who readily shared their men's danger and demonstrated the true qualities of a leader. Others were callow fools who shirked the fight once the battle had started and deserved nothing more than scorn and derision. Jack had learnt not to make a judgement simply on the basis of a man's accent or manner. Battle would reveal his true character, and until then Jack did his best to keep an open mind.

'The men did well last night. You must be proud of them.' He offered the praise in an attempt to get the lieutenant talking. He could see the man's fear.

'They are good fellows,' Moore answered, but his mind was clearly elsewhere. The young officer shook himself before fixing Jack with a cheery grin that went nowhere close to his pale eyes. 'I think you did a pretty good job yourself. I heard Kotdaffadar Khan call you a devil. He said he had never seen a faster blade.'

Jack smiled tightly. He was not good at accepting praise. 'I did what had to be done. Nothing more.'

'If slaying half the bloody Persian army by yourself is doing what had to be done, then I am bloody glad you are on our side, old man.' Moore held his reins a little easier as he spoke. 'Here we go. I bet that's for us.'

Both officers had spied the fast-moving galloper riding up to Captain Forbes. The arrival of one of Stalker's staff meant that orders were being delivered.

'Let's see what his lordship has in store for us, shall we?' Moore invited Jack to join him as he rode forward towards the small gaggle of officers surrounding Captain Forbes, waiting to find out what Stalker was asking them to do.

The 3rd Bombay Light Cavalry advanced in a line, its two squadrons riding side by side. Jack led the second squadron, comprising number five and six troop. He rode in the centre of the formation, with Lieutenant Moore at the head of one troop and Lieutenant Malcolmson on his left at the head of the other. The two troops advanced behind their officers in a line two men deep. Both were under strength; together they numbered just over one hundred and twenty sabres. Behind the line of troopers the trumpeters and the two cornets rode with their covering non-commissioned officers in the serrefile rank, their eyes roving over the men, the daffadars pouncing on any whose horse was even a fraction out of its spacing.

'March!'

Forbes ordered the line forward, the command echoed by the troop leaders. The regiment eased forward, the horses moving gently, their slow, rolling gait needing to be controlled carefully as the roar of the cannons unsettled the mounts.

To the regiment's left, the lines of infantry advanced steadily, the redcoats covering the ground rapidly. The enemy cannon fired without pause, their roundshot roaring towards the twin lines like express trains thundering at full speed down the line. Each drove into the ground, digging wide channels in the soft surface before bouncing high in the air, careering onwards before striking the ground again and again, their impetus driving them on with an unstoppable fury.

So far the first line was untouched, the enemy shot wasting its power on the ground around them. The second line was not so fortunate. Roundshot aimed at their colleagues in the front line might have missed their target, but the heavy shot skipped back into the air, their trajectory lowered by the violent contact with the ground. They smashed into the second line, the force of the impact barely diminished, knocking men down so that the passage of the redcoats' advance was marked out with the crumpled bodies of the fallen.

Jack looked back over his shoulder, studying his own men. The lines were already ragged, the troopers' exhaustion after the long night in the saddle taking its toll on their discipline.

'Steady in the ranks.'

Jack was not the only one concerned about what he saw. Lieutenant Moore snapped a series of orders, his face a furious scowl, his displeasure at the disorder in the ranks obvious. The line steadied, the daffadars barking at any man who let his horse move out of the precise formation, the frontage once again as regular and ordered as it would have been on the parade ground. Jack caught Moore's eye and acknowledged his subordinate's action with a nod of approval.

'Trot!'

Forbes ordered the increase in pace. Once again the command was repeated by the troop commanders and echoed by the trumpeters. The horses picked up speed, the noise of their advance increasing. Tackle chimed and clinked as men and mounts went into the trot, the noise of the hooves drumming into the ground getting louder as the speed built.

Jack looked ahead. The Persian line was covered in a thin cloud of powder smoke, the dense ranks of the waiting infantry wafting in and out of view as the brisk breeze blew the rolling smoke along the enemy ranks. The British gunners kept up their rate of fire, their barrage puncturing the smoke cloud as roundshot after roundshot pounded into the Persian infantry. Even from a distance Jack could see the damage they were inflicting. All along the enemy line, dozens of men were being hauled backwards, their bodies left in bloody heaps behind their fellows. The British artillery was exacting a dreadful toll on the huge blocks of men waiting for the red-coated line to arrive.

Jack's horse threw its head, fighting the bit that he kept rammed hard in its mouth. The animal was caught in the passion of the advance. It could sense the tension in the air, its nostrils flaring as it caught the whiff of powder smoke being blown across the battlefield. It was as if the animal knew what lay ahead.

In front of the Bombay Lights, the enemy cavalry waited. They numbered in the thousands. Jack could see the pennants on their lances fluttering in the breeze, the dense ranks appearing to shimmer, the constant movement mesmerising to the eye. They stood watching the British cavalry advance, their ranks packed several men deep, their frontage much wider than that of the two squadrons of the Bombay Lights. If the enemy commander had known what he was about, his cavalry would already have been moving forward to counter the British advance. Meeting a cavalry charge from a stand was to invite disaster. But as yet the Persians gave no sign of moving.

Jack looked to the rear and saw the dark blue coats of the Poona Horse advancing behind his own regiment. They were a fine sight, the bright colour of their tightly woven pagdi adding a splash of gaudiness to the disciplined appearance of the ranks. The Poona Horse were the Bombay Lights' support, and they held their own advance back, keeping a gap of around four hundred yards between the two regiments. The spacing was vital. If the Poona Horse were too close behind, they ran the risk of being disordered by the shock of the Bombay Lights' charge. Too far behind and they would be unable to offer support if the enemy started to gain the upper hand. It took fine judgement to maintain the right gap, and Jack hoped the commander of the Poona Horse was up to the job.

The two British cavalry regiments might have been outnumbered, but they had no choice but to advance. Left unopposed, the enemy cavalry could sweep forward, forcing the advancing British infantry into a square. The Persian horsemen would be thwarted, unable to close on the foot soldiers, yet once in their defensive formation, the infantry's advance would be stopped. The square would also leave the redcoats exposed to a dreadful danger. It might have been the best defence against cavalry, but it left the packed ranks horribly vulnerable to artillery fire and the musket volleys of the Persian infantry. Any enemy fire would shred the dense formation, the tight files blown apart. The cavalry could then return and pour into the gaps, spreading a dreadful carnage amongst the remnants of the square.

If the British infantry were forced to form a square, the battle was lost.

The two British cavalry regiments had to advance and counter the superior numbers of enemy cavalry, or the whole attack was doomed to failure.

'Gallop!'

Jack heard the tremor in Forbes's voice as he bellowed the penultimate command in the series of orders that would bring the Bombay Lights into action. He could feel his horse quiver underneath him as it increased its speed, the beast shuddering with the sheer joy of being allowed to run.

'Charge!'

With fifty yards to go, Forbes screamed the last command. The trumpeters challenged the gods as they sounded the beautiful, haunting call. The troopers released their horses, giving them their heads, summoning the very last vestiges of speed. They hammered towards the stationary enemy cavalry, their sabres reaching forward, every man thrilling to the wild glory of the charge.

Jack was filled with the madness. He could feel it searing through his veins. It resonated deep in his soul, every fibre of his being tingling with the insanity of galloping against an enemy horde.

The regiment raced forward, their voices roaring out as the men unleashed the cheer saved for this moment. The last yards flashed past and the 3rd Bombay Light Cavalry charged into action.

Chapter Thirty-five

The Bombay Lights pummelled into the Persian cavalry. The sound of the impact was dreadful, the fast-moving horsemen smashing into their stationary enemy.

Some of the British riders were driven on to the lance points of the waiting enemy, the speed of the charge leaving them no time to swerve away from the razor-sharp weapons that waited for them. But once past the tips of the lances the British riders were safe, and those still seated crashed their mounts into the Persian formation, flailing their weapons at the now defenceless enemy horsemen.

The shock effect of the charge was brutal.

The British cavalry's speed drove them deep into the enemy's ranks. Without any momentum of their own, the Persian horsemen were easy targets for the British, who cut their swords left and right, slashing them at the enemy. Dozens of Persian horsemen were scythed from their saddles in the first moments of the fight.

Horses fled from the melee, their masters dying in the saddle, heads drooping on to their breasts, their bodies torn and bloody. Dying men and beasts fell to the ground, their final agonies ruthlessly crushed beneath the hooves of the horses left standing, their ruined flesh trodden into the dust.

Despite the carnage, the Bombay Lights continued to pound forward, driving the attack home.

Jack had rushed past the lance points in a blur of movement, the terror of the moment flaring bright, a single prick of icy fear stabbing deep in his guts, before he was safe. He hacked his sword at the first enemy, a wild swing driven by anger and the lust for battle. It cut through the air before slicing into his target's face, the sharpened steel meeting no resistance as it found its first victim.

The impetus of the charge drove him forward so that he never saw the man fall. He was past another enemy before he could recover his sword, his horse moving faster than he could react. He swung the blade back and forth, cutting at the figures that raced past, the enemy ranks splintering around him as he drove deep into their formation.

A riderless horse thumped into his flank, its eyes wide in terror, its flared nostrils caked in foam. It slowed his momentum and he reined his own horse hard round, spurring it into the enemy that surrounded him.

He yelled as he fought, the wild battle cry forced from his lips. A face turned towards him, the henna-edged eyes bright beneath the tall conical hat. The man's fear was obvious and his mouth opened to scream in terror as Jack rode straight for him.

The scream never came. Jack thrust his talwar forward, punching it into the man's throat, silencing the shriek of horror with a torrent of blood. He rode on, forcing his horse into the press of bodies. He aimed his sword at another Persian rider, but the man swerved his horse to one side and Jack's blade flashed past. He was given no chance for a second blow as the man gouged his spurs backwards, galloping his horse free of the melee and away from the vicious sabres that had slain so many of his comrades.

Not all the enemy were so quick to flee. A lance was thrust at Jack, its sharpened point scoring across the top of his thigh. There was no time to see who had attacked him, so he simply thrust his sword at the closest enemy. A fast-moving lance parried the blade and he bellowed in rage as he failed to land a telling blow.

A trooper from the Bombay Lights barged past, his face splattered with blood from a wound to his scalp. The man rose in his saddle, standing tall before thumping his sabre down on to a Persian's head, the sickening sound of bones crunching clearly audible over the roar of the fighting.

The trooper rode on and Jack spurred his horse, driving it into another group of Persian horsemen. They tried to turn from his path but they were slow and he was fast. His talwar snatched away the throat of the first, the spray of blood bright in the morning sunlight. He recovered the blade and cut it hard above his horse's ears, slicing it into another man's side, screaming an incoherent curse of anger and fear, fighting like a creature from a nightmare let loose on the battlefield.

His arm ached from the blows he had landed. His stomach churned with fear. His throat choked on the dreadful stench of battle, the air thick with the reek of blood and opened bowels. But still he hacked at the enemy, slashing and cutting with his talwar, fighting any who did not run.

The press of bodies around him eased and he twisted in the saddle, seeking more victims for his blade. But the last of the enemy were backing away, forcing their trembling horses from the horror of the British charge.

The Persians broke, throwing away their lances in their haste to escape. The Bombay Lights slashed at the enemy, mercilessly cutting men down even as they tried to flee. The carnage turned the retreat into a rout and the Persian horsemen streamed away in a wild mob, their ranks shattered by the dreadful power of the controlled charge.

'Walk!'

Jack heard Forbes but could not see him. A dazed Persian horseman staggered past on foot, his sabre hanging uselessly from its strap around his wrist. The man's face was a mask of blood and Jack let him go, the mad lust of the charge slipping away as quickly as the Persian cavalry had retreated.

'Halt!'

Jack looked round the disordered ranks of the Bombay Lights. He could see the delight on the troopers' faces. They raised their bloodied sabres, shouting to the heavens as their victory sank in, whooping and cackling in delight, the spectre of death that had ridden with the regiment retreating as they realised that they had come through their first fight unscathed.

're-form the ranks. Officers to me.'

Forbes rode past. His stern face betrayed no joy at his men's celebration. He repeated the instruction as he continued on through his command, demanding order. The Bombay Lights might have broken the enemy's cavalry, but the battle was far from over.

'Captain Fenris!' Forbes had to bellow to be heard. The gunners from both sides were engaged in a deadly duel, neither side slackening the pace of their cannonade. The British infantry marched into the fire, their bloodied ranks advancing no matter how many were gouged from the lines.

'Sir!' Jack rode forward.

Forbes fixed him with an eager stare. The captain's face was slick with sweat, and Jack saw the bloodstained sabre held at his side. The commander of the Bombay Lights was clearly leading his men from the front.

'I am sending one squadron after the enemy to ensure they do not rally. I want you to take your squadron and bring them behind the enemy's flank. Try to get behind their gunners on that closest hillock.'

Jack saw immediately what Forbes intended. With the cavalry streaming away, the Persian flank was dangerously exposed. The 3rd Bombay Light Cavalry was perfectly positioned to exploit the advantage.

'Sir!'

He turned his horse and rode back to his command, which was quickly and efficiently re-forming after the chaos of the charge. Both of his lieutenants were there, their swords bloody testament to their having joined in the fight. Half a dozen men were missing, their bodies strewn across the ground where the squadron had fought the enemy cavalry. There was no time to wonder who had fallen and who had survived. If the Bombay Lights were to make good on what they had won, they had to move and move swiftly.

Knightly felt his hands shaking. He could see his sword quivering and he tried to force his muscles to stay still. He couldn't do it. Another volley of artillery slashed across the sky. He could see the trace of the roundshot. They arced high into the clear morning air before racing downwards and rushing towards the twin red lines that marched across the sandy plain.

He had never known a fear like it. He wanted to turn, to run to the rear. Yet he was firmly tethered by the responsibility of his command. No matter how much the fear built, he could do nothing but march onwards, like some new-fangled automaton, step after step, striding towards the oblivion of his death.

His terror bubbled up. He felt it swallow his soul in its remorseless black grip. He wanted to cry, to release the emotion, but he could do nothing but walk forward, the pace of the advance relentless. More roundshot smashed down behind the foremost line. The ground erupted in an enormous fountain of broken earth and shattered rock before the shot leapt back into the sky, screaming onward, its force barely altered by the violent contact.

Knightly watched it ricochet high over his company before it crashed uselessly into the ground behind them. He forced his body to move, focusing his mind on placing his feet down on the sandy soil, each step an effort of will.

The Persian artillery roared again, flinging more roundshot at the long red lines that refused to turn. Knightly stayed in his place and walked forward into the enemy's fire.

'Gallop!'

Jack bellowed the command. He had led his men forward, sweeping them behind the Persian ranks towards the enemy's artillery. The sudden appearance of the British cavalry had an immediate effect on the Persian infantry. Under a dreadful barrage of artillery fire, and with their rear threatened by rampaging horsemen, the closest of them took the only option open to them.

They ran.

It was like watching a dam break. Jack was forced to speed up his squadron's pace lest they get caught up in the fleeing troops. It was tempting to turn his men and drive them at the broken infantry, who would have been easy targets for the hard-riding horsemen, but it was not what he had been ordered to do. Forbes had seen the opportunity, and so Jack moved his two troops in a wide arc, ready to bear down on the rear of the Persian artillery, which was still exacting a dreadful toll on the advancing British infantry.

The troopers upped the pace of the advance, responding to their commander's lead. The rattle of equipment and the clink of the metal scabbards increased as the horses pounded onwards, the men lowering their sabres to the engage as Jack led them towards the enemy guns.

The Persian artillerymen never saw them coming. They were serving their weapons with intensity, thinking of nothing but loading their pieces as fast as they could, preparing the heavy guns to send yet another volley searing across the plain and into the red tide that flowed so steadily towards them. The thick cloud of powder smoke that billowed around the cannon hid the arrival of the Bombay Lights until the last moment.

The British horsemen erupted from the smoke like creatures emerging from the depths of hell. Their horses were covered in gore, with still more splattered across their light blue uniforms, and their sabres were bloodied to the hilt. They charged towards the enemy gunners, who could do nothing but stare in horror as their worst nightmare unfolded around them.

Jack led his men from the front, his teeth clenched as he rode hard to the slaughter. There was none of the wild joy of the first charge. The enemy was defenceless and the Bombay Lights were merciless as they charged for the second time that day.

Their precious guns forgotten, the Persian gunners broke and ran for their lives. Yet there was nowhere for them to run to, the barren hilltop that had seemed such an advantage when they had sited their guns now turned into a killing ground. The gunners twisted and turned, trying to dodge the British horsemen. But for every rider avoided there was another sabre attacking, the cavalrymen going about their bloody task with ruthless efficiency.

A man tried to run past Jack's saddle. It took him no more than a heartbeat to slash his bloody talwar downwards, bludgeoning the unfortunate Persian to the ground with a single blow to the head. Another man dashed past on the other side, and Jack lashed out with his foot, kicking the man hard so that he stumbled into the path of a trooper's sabre.

Jack held fast, leaving the rest of the butchery to his men. The task sickened him. The Persian gunners stood no chance. He watched a man with the stripes of a vekil on his sleeve kneel beside his beloved cannon, weeping with the shame of the defeat. A trooper rode past and severed his head from his neck. Another gunner lay on the ground, his hands clutched to the ruin of his face, his feet thrashing the ground with the dreadful agony. A British horseman rode past with a stolen Persian lance balanced in his hand. With a whoop of delight he thrust it downwards, driving it into the wounded gunner's chest, the shaft left pointing upwards like a gruesome standard.

A cluster of gunners huddled together back-to-back, their rammers and handspikes held out like spears in an attempt to keep the marauding cavalry at bay. As Jack watched, one of his troopers rode hard at the group, his sabre held at the full stretch of his arm and pointing towards the closest gunner. At the last moment his horse twisted away, unable to charge the vicious weapons that faced it. With a scream of victory the gunner stepped forward and rammed a spike into the rider's side, striking him from the saddle.

The action condemned the brave artillerymen. The gunner's attack left an opening in the pitiful huddle, and a group of Jack's troopers tore into them in a heartbeat. Sabres flashed and the gunners were cut to the ground, their resistance finished in a brief flurry of sword strokes.

The fight was over. The gunners had been massacred, their cannon silenced. Jack peered through the smoke and saw the Poona Horse charging at the next hilltop, the second battery of Persian artillery about to be taken out of the fight.

Far out on the plain, the British line still advanced, the pace faster now that the enemy barrage had been stopped. The redcoats no longer marched to fight. They had been denied the opportunity by the valour of the cavalry and the ruthless precision of their own artillery. The Persian army was broken, the huge blocks of infantry running for their lives. Only the right flank of the enemy horde remained at least partially intact. Three battalions had escaped the British barrage, and now they were trying to withdraw in good order whilst the rest of their army ran in a mob, all cohesion gone, their ranks shattered, their morale ripped to shreds. Three battalions, all that remained of an army. A few hundred left out of thousands.

Chapter Thirty-six

Captain Forbes galloped on to the hillock where the Persian gunners had been butchered. He fixed his attention on Jack and rode straight for him.

'Fenris! Re-form your squadron. Quickly, now.' He snapped the order before turning and riding away.

Jack had no breath left to reply. His throat was parched and his body felt like it had been battered from head to toe. A thin line of blood traced across his thigh from where the Persian lance had scored into his flesh, and now the wound was starting to hurt in earnest. He closed his eyes, forcing away the tiredness and the pain. The time for rest would come later.

'Re-form the ranks.' He bellowed the command, forcing his spine straight. The small of his back flared in agony, so he sheathed his bloody sword and pressed his fingers into the knotted muscles, trying to relieve some of the ache.

He turned and saw the two Moore brothers shaking hands. The adjutant had ridden in with the regiment's commander and had seized the opportunity to share a moment's contact with his older brother. To Jack's surprise, he felt a spark of jealousy as he saw the bond between the two men. He had been alone for so long that he could scarcely understand what it would be like to share such an intimate connection. For him, relationships were fleeting, as substantial as a silk veil. They hid the loneliness for a while, nothing more. The thought of his loneliness made him think of Sarah. Although she was married, he sensed that she too was alone. They had clung to each other, aware of each other's need. He summoned the picture of her face. He smiled as he conjured the spark of life in her eyes that so captivated him. He wanted nothing more than to see her again, to be with her once more. The image faded, the noise of the battle interrupting his thoughts.

He opened his mouth to order his troop commander to his place, but shut it before the words could be formed. He would let the two brothers enjoy each other's company for a moment longer.

Captain Forbes reined in beside him. Jack looked across and saw the strain on the young commander's face.

'The regiment is doing well, sir.' He offered the encouragement, watching Forbes carefully.

'Thus far, perhaps.' Forbes kept up his facade. 'The day is not yet done.'

'True.' Jack wanted to somehow reassure the captain that he was leading his regiment on a day that would live long in its annals. But he did not know the man well enough and he could not find the words that would break down the barrier of unfamiliarity.

The squadron was re-forming. It was slow, the men's tiredness obvious, their lathered horses close to exhaustion. Yet Forbes was correct. The day was not yet over. The left and centre of the Persian line might have been in full retreat, but its largely untouched right flank was still formed and ready to fight.

Forbes looked Jack hard in the eyes. 'We have more work to

do, Captain Fenris. The Poona Horse are to pursue the enemy infantry. I want us to harry their right flank.'

Jack said nothing. He turned and looked back at his squadron, the ranks now standing silent and ready for orders. They had fought all night and had charged twice that day, but they would not be allowed to rest.

He faced Forbes. 'We're ready, sir.'

'Good.' The commander of the 3rd Bombay Light Cavalry offered a tight-lipped smile. 'We are going to attack over there.'

He turned and pointed to the massed ranks of infantry battalions on the enemy's flank. The Bombay Lights had fought cavalry and artillery. Now they would face a horseman's worse fear. They would charge the bayonets of the Persian infantry.

The squadron moved quickly and with purpose. They trotted down the hillock and turned to face the enemy's flank. The two lines of red-coated infantry were close now. Yet they were still too far away to join the fight, the distance too great even for the power of the 64th's Enfield rifles.

'Trot!'

The cavalry wheeled to the left as Forbes led them towards the Persians' surviving flank. Their line was ragged and the files were forced to work hard to maintain their spacings as they realigned the ranks so that they could sweep on to the Persian infantry. The formation lacked the regimental precision with which it had started the day, the effects of the two vicious engagements showing in the bloodstained uniforms that had been slashed and battered by the enemy. Yet they still displayed a purpose that was chilling.

The Persian infantry saw them coming. With the rest of their army in disarray and the steady lines of British infantry moving ever closer, the enemy foot soldiers had been forced to begin a long and lonely retreat. Unlike their comrades, the three Sabriz battalions moved in good order, marching in tight columns. They had witnessed the destruction of their artillery and seen their cavalry driven from the field. Yet they were determined to fight on, to show that not all of the Persian force was so easily defeated.

As the British cavalry trotted towards them, the Persian infantry saw only one course of action. The closest battalion, the 1st Khusgai Regiment of Fars, stopped and immediately began to re-form, leaving the rest of their comrades to carry on the retreat. To the hoarse screams of their vekils, the side of the battalion closest to the British cavalry turned to face outwards, the men shuffling into three deep ranks. Around them, the rest of the troops marched to form the other three sides of the square. Calmly and without fuss, the battalion moved into the defensive formation that would keep it safe from the advancing British cavalry.

Jack watched the manoeuvre as the Bombay Lights headed straight for the enemy infantry. He was impressed by the steadiness in the Persian ranks. The infantry battalion had seen its comrades routed, yet still it stood its ground, determined to see off the small band of cavalry that had already caused so much destruction that day.

It was an easy decision for the Persian commander to make. The single squadron of horsemen numbered just over one hundred riders. The square was made up of more than five hundred infantrymen each armed with a musket and a bayonet. The odds were so heavily in the Persians' favour that not even the sight of so many of their fellows retreating had deterred him from halting and preparing to fight off the remains of the British cavalry.

At any moment Jack expected Forbes to sound the halt, to bring the squadron to an impotent stop, far out of the range of the enemy's muskets. Yet for a reason Jack could not fathom, the commander of the 3rd Bombay Light Cavalry showed no sign of even pausing. The younger Moore rode at his shoulder, the adjutant belatedly drawing a sabre unblemished with blood. The two officers advanced a little way in front of the squadron, their attention focused on the force of Persian infantry that stood resolutely in their path.

The Bombay Lights were at least five hundred yards away when the front rank of infantry squatted to the ground, the butts of their muskets rammed hard into the soft, sandy soil, the bayonets held ready to rip out the guts of any horse foolish enough to venture close. Behind them, the two standing ranks presented their muskets, the tips of the bayonets reaching past the heads of the front rank. Still the Bombay Lights rode on. If Forbes ordered the charge, they faced a long gallop right into a volley from the Persians' muskets. When the horses swerved away from the wall of bayonets, as they surely must, they would be forced to ride past the other sides of the square, giving the rest of the Persian infantrymen the chance to open fire. It would be a massacre. If Forbes ordered the charge, he was committing one hundred men and their horses to certain death.

Still they pressed on. The line flowed swiftly across the plain, the steady trot closing the distance with surprising speed. Forbes stayed silent, never once looking away from the square. He sat his horse easily, his sabre held almost casually in his right hand, as if on an afternoon's hunt rather than heading directly into a Persian volley.

Jack felt the fear churn in his stomach. He had once taken his place in a square, standing shaking as a force of enemy cavalry rushed towards his company. It was a memory that still haunted his dreams. His men had stood firm, defiant in the face of the enemy horsemen. The square had not broken and they had blasted the cavalry from their saddles as they swirled around them, the horses unable to close on the wall of bayonets.

Now he was riding towards a similar formation. He knew what would happen, yet he was powerless to stop it.

He saw Forbes lift his sabre and point it at the sky, preparing to give the command to begin the gallop that would soon give way to the madness of the charge.

Jack fought off the fear. He went to draw his talwar, but the blood on the blade had congealed in his scabbard and it would not come free. He tugged harder, breaking it loose before he raised it high, mirroring his commander's gesture.

'Bombay Lights!' Forbes's voice cracked as he shouted for attention. 'Bombay Lights!' The voice hardened, the words coming clear above the noise of the moving horsemen.

Jack's exhaustion slipped away as he prepared for the final charge. He had come so far. He had stolen a place in society far above his own and proved that an unwanted child from the foulest rookeries of London could achieve so much more than his station in life allowed. Now he would likely die on a foreign field in the service of his Queen. He glanced round quickly. He saw the look of stony determination on the face of Lieutenant Moore, and the grim expressions of the troopers, who were following their officers into almost certain oblivion.

He turned to face the front, focusing his attention on the tightly packed ranks of Sabriz infantry, who watched in astonishment as the fragile line of blue-coated cavalry advanced to attack.

Forbes slashed his sword forward, pointing it at the square.

Jack repeated the gesture, opening his mouth to echo the order that was about to follow.

He was leading his men into battle. There was nowhere else on earth he would rather be.

Chapter Thirty-seven

'**G**allop!'

Forbes bellowed the command. The squadron picked up speed. The horses moved willingly, carrying their masters to the slaughter without hesitation.

Jack never once took his eyes off the Persian square. Even as his horse powered forward, he watched the barrels of the muskets that pointed towards him. He was pulling away from his men, his charger faster than the mounts issued to his troopers, but he did not care. Nothing mattered save the need to reach the enemy and try to force a way into the wall of bayonets.

The distance closed with terrifying speed.

He could see the muskets wavering as the infantrymen struggled to hold them still, the heavy bayonets at the tip making the weapons unwieldy. A Persian officer stood with the second rank. Jack watched the fear etched on the man's face as he stared aghast at the racing cavalry. He saw too the determination as the enemy officer waited for the British horsemen to come into range.

The Persian officer opened his mouth. Jack was close enough

to see the muskets steady, the infantry stiffening their muscles as they braced for the brutal kick that would follow a heartbeat after they pulled their triggers.

Forbes turned and glanced at his command. He caught Jack's eye. Jack tried to read the emotion in the man's gaze, but the stare was too intense. Forbes was still looking at him when the Persians fired.

The storm of musket balls tore through the air. Jack flinched uncontrollably, his body reacting to the sound of the missiles scorching past.

The volley smashed into the line of galloping troopers.

Men were snatched from the saddle as the musket balls tore into their flesh. Horses were struck down, their bodies crashing to the ground, their riders thrown to the dusty soil. The sound of the dozen or more impacts was dreadful, like the meaty slap of a butcher slamming a fresh carcass on to the chopping block.

The screaming began.

Horses shrieked, their bellows of agony tearing at the hearts of the troopers who rode past the carnage unscathed. Men screamed, their bodies shattered by enemy bullets or by a violent connection with the ground.

The Bombay Lights did not falter.

Even as they galloped forward, they closed the ranks, callously ignoring the fallen, thinking of nothing but reaching the enemy. They raced on, their bloodied sabres held ready for the Persians who stood in their path.

Forbes still led them. His breeches ran with red from a bullet wound to his leg, but he charged onwards nonetheless, throwing his head back as he bellowed the final order that would send his precious regiment against the enemy that had killed so many of the men under his command.

'Charge!'

The men responded. They roared as they went, their terror released, and the regiment surged forward.

Jack let the madness take him. He screamed as he raced forward, the certainty of his imminent death releasing a soul-searing shriek that came from the very core of his being.

The Persian soldiers held their ground. The smoke of their volley billowed around them. The closest flank of the square stood firm, the vicious weapons bristling outwards, creating an obstacle that no horse could penetrate.

Adjutant Moore was in the van. Forbes fell behind, his tiring horse slowing his progress. The younger of the two brothers would have seen the wall of bayonets ahead of him, the hundreds of faces standing behind the seventeen inches of steel bayonet.

He did not turn away. He held his line, spurring his horse hard. The willing animal tore towards the wall as if it were nothing more than a hedgerow on a day's hunt.

Moore set his horse at the square. He released his sabre, letting it fall, trusting to the thick cord around his wrist to keep it at his side, both hands needed to control his mount. With a final desperate yell, he urged the animal to jump.

It soared up, its hooves scrabbling at the air as it tried to vault the wall of bayonets. They came for it the moment it left the ground. Dozens of sharpened steel blades tore at its flesh, the vicious points ripping through its soft underbelly. The Persian officer who had controlled the volley lifted his pistol and fired at the madman who had tried to break the square. The bullet took the animal in the side of the head, smashing through skull and brain, killing it in an instant.

The stricken beast crashed into the Persian soldiers, crushing the nearest men, whole files smashed by the impact. It kicked out as it died, knocking more men to the ground, its iron-shod hooves breaking bones as they lashed out. Moore was thrown, his final roar of anger turned into a scream of terror as he went down with his horse.

Captain Forbes watched in horror, yet still he did not pause. He shortened his reins, bunching them tightly into his left hand before spurring his own horse forward and leaping at the square, following Moore's line so that he jumped over the chaos the adjutant's dying horse had created.

He was lucky. With so many Persians struck down by the falling horse, there were few bayonets left in position. He surged over the wall, landing on the far side without coming to harm.

He turned hard, slashing his sabre at the rear rank. He fought in silence, jaw clenched, teeth bared, attacking the files that had been crushed by Moore's wild charge, thrusting his horse at the last men left standing. His sword took a man in the face, and a visceral roar escaped his gritted teeth before he struck another Persian infantryman to the ground. He urged his horse forward, riding it over the bodies of the men he had killed, forcing an opening in what remained of the square's flank. His bloodied sabre hacked at a musket, battering it to one side before he thrust the point into the man's neck.

He turned, his war cry faltering as he found no one left close enough to fight.

There was a gap in the square.

Jack had seen the two officers jump the wall of bayonets. He had watched in mounting horror as Moore fell. The sight sickened him and he cursed the fool's courage that had driven the young officer to the hopeless act. Then he saw Forbes land unharmed. He pulled at his own reins, realigning his horse so that he was heading for the place where the two officers had leapt, a sudden rush of hope surging through him.

The wall ahead was blocked, the rear ranks still standing,

their bayonets holding the line. Then Forbes struck. More men fell, and Jack saw the opening.

He raced for the gap. He saw the look of terror on the Persian soldiers' faces as they realised what had happened. A thin-faced officer stepped forward, blocking the hole in the ranks, trying to seal it off alone.

Jack roared in anger. He spurred his horse hard, urging it to find a final surge of speed. More Persian infantrymen were rushing to close the gap, their muskets raised, bayonets pushing forward.

With a valiant effort, his horse responded. Jack felt its body tense beneath him as it strained with the last of its strength. The final yards rushed past, then Jack was slashing his talwar downwards, beating away the bayonets that reached for him as he raced through the opening. He felt a blade slice through his left calf, the blinding flash of pain the last thing he noticed before he was through and into the centre of the square.

He had been prepared to die, certain that the decision to charge the square would send the squadron to its doom. The sudden release and the hope of life surged through him, mixing with the horror and the fear to fuel the intoxicating madness of battle.

He cut down the nearest man, his blade ripping away the Persian's throat. He felt nothing as the man fell, his only thought to find more of the enemy to kill. The thin-faced officer who had tried to seal the gap came at him. His curved sabre slashed forward but Jack blocked the blade, knocking it to one side, then kicked out, driving the point of his boot into the officer's face. The man reeled backwards and Jack spurred forward, standing tall in his stirrups before smashing his sword down on to the man's skull, killing him with the single blow.

He reined his mount away, turning it back into the gap that had been created. There were bodies everywhere. Some lay still, their bloody flesh a testament to the skill of the two British officers who had made it into the square. Others were staggering to their feet, rushing to recover after having been knocked to the ground by Moore's falling horse.

The gap was closing. Men from the opposite face were rushing forward, led by an experienced vekil who had grabbed a section from the third rank without waiting for orders, knowing that his battalion faced destruction if they let the British cavalry into the square.

Forbes had been surrounded and forced into a desperate defence against half a dozen bayonets. More men were being summoned to the unequal fight, the Persian officers trying to end the resistance of the British cavalrymen who had found a way into the square.

Adjutant Moore was pinned under his fallen horse. He fought on, slashing his broken sword against any who came close, his body twisting and writhing as he tried to keep open the channel he had created.

Jack saw the fresh rush of infantrymen coming and drove his horse at them. He slashed his sabre hard, cutting at the leader of the group, but the man was ready for him and blocked the blow with his musket, then grabbed at Jack's leg, trying to throw him from the saddle. Jack felt the man's fingers digging into the flesh of his thigh like claws, and he roared in building frustration as he brought his talwar down, chopping the hilt on to the top of the man's head. The vekil fell away and Jack threw his horse round, thinking to rush back in a final attempt to keep the opening free and give his troopers a way into the square.

He was too late. The rest of the vekil's squad had rushed past as their leader wrestled with the foreign horseman. Already they were reaching the opening. The gap was being sealed off. The British officers would soon be trapped. Cut off and alone, they would not stand a chance.

Chapter Thirty-eight

Lieutenant Moore hit the square like a knight of old. The huge officer was mounted on the biggest charger in the battalion and he thundered into the Persian infantry's re-forming ranks, using his horse as a living battering ram to force an opening. Men were knocked flying as the huge animal smashed through their files, their bodies broken by the force of the impact. Moore slashed at those left standing, cutting a bloody swathe through the Persian flank.

As soon as he had broken through the shattered ranks, he reined his horse round hard, turning into the wall of bayonets that stood on his flank. He battered his sword down as he turned, the heavy blade a vicious weapon in the hands of such a powerful man.

Jack rode into the melee. He cut down a man from behind, mercilessly slashing his talwar against the back of the man's undefended head. He pushed his horse into the gap, cutting at another Persian infantryman, who stood in mute horror as he saw his comrades dying at the hands of the British officers. He caught the man in the neck, slicing his blade deep into the man's flesh, killing him before he could fight back.

Moore fought like a man possessed, his blade never still as he thrust at the men around him. With dreadful skill he hammered his way through the Persian ranks, walking his horse over the bodies of the men he had killed, pressing forward, clearing a path that he lined with bloodied corpses.

Jack realised what his lieutenant was trying to do, and he forced his own horse to follow, battering away the bayonets that reached up to stab at him. His horse staggered as it stepped on a corpse but rallied quickly, steadying its footing just in time to allow Jack to thrust the point of his talwar into a man's face moments before the Persian had been about to drive a bayonet into the animal's breast.

He urged his mount on, joining Moore in his attempt to reach his fallen brother. Together they forced a path through the files, kicking out or thrashing their sabres at anyone who tried to block their path. The Persian infantrymen began to step back, terrified of the two bloody warriors who fought with such intensity.

They reached the younger Moore's fallen horse and Jack rode past the trapped officer, forcing the closest enemy soldiers away. One man risked an attack, coming at him from his left-hand side. Jack saw the blade and slashed his sabre round, but he was tiring, his reactions dulled by the constant struggle to stay alive, and the bayonet slipped past his parry and drove deep into his horse's chest. The animal staggered and the Persian soldier shrieked in triumph, but it was a short-lived moment of joy.

Jack kicked his feet free of the stirrups the moment he felt his horse stagger and vaulted clear, landing on the balls of his feet as his mount toppled to one side. He hammered the hilt of his sword forward, smashing it into the enemy soldier's face and bludgeoning him to the ground. He felt the rage course through him and punched the sword down, driving the tip deep into the fallen man's heart.

The solidity of the ground beneath his feet came as a relief. This was this type of fighting he knew best, and he threw himself at the closest enemy. The bayonet-tipped muskets lunged forward, but he had seen it all before and it was easy to let them come, swaying out of their way before counterattacking, slashing his own blade forward and cutting down the men who were trying to kill him.

The closest men backed away and Jack snatched his revolver out of its holster. In one practised move he swung it up and aimed at the press of bodies to his front. There was just time to register the horror on the dark faces before he opened fire. At such short range, the revolver was brutally effective, and each shot knocked a man to the ground.

The rest of the Bombay Lights hit the square. Their officers had rushed ahead, using the speed of their superior horses to take the fight to the Persians. Now the troopers poured through the square's broken face, riding over the bodies of the dead and the dying. A handful of Persians still stood in the shredded ranks, and they fought hard, striking men from the saddle or stabbing at the horses that raced past them. But there were too many gaps and the line collapsed as the Bombay Lights cut their way in.

The rest of the square did not stand a chance. The British cavalry attacked without pause, the pace of the charge barely checked by the men they rode down. They smashed into the backs of the other flanks, cutting down the men in swathes, their bloody sabres working furiously. Without pause they rode back and forth, striking man after man from their feet. The centre of the square became a charnel house, the ground churned into a bloody quagmire.

With his revolver empty, Jack turned and ran to the side of the younger Moore, who still lay trapped under his fallen horse. The Persian troops were trying to run, but the British horsemen

were everywhere, spurring mercilessly over any man who tried
to flee, their faces twisted into dreadful masks of hate as they
went about the bloody task with brutal efficiency.

Moore slashed his broken sabre upwards as he sensed Jack
approaching. 'For fuck's sake, it's Fenris,' Jack bellowed as he
was forced to dodge back sharply. The adjutant's weapon had
snapped midway up the blade, but the blood that was smeared
on what remained showed that he had still used the weapon
to effect.

Jack saw the flare of recognition on Moore's face, and he
bent forward and heaved at the body of the dead horse that
had the younger officer trapped. The animal was smothered in
blood and his hands slipped as they tried to get a grip on the
slick, matted coat. He lowered his shoulder and pressed it hard
against the animal's flank. He grunted with the effort but
managed to move the beast a fraction. It was enough for Moore
to scramble free. The lower half of his uniform was sodden
with blood, but he appeared to be largely intact.

His brother left the slaughter and came towards them, his
huge horse lathered in sweat.

'You're a damn fool!' The older Moore's face was twisted
with anger, and for a moment Jack thought he would strike his
brother down.

The younger sibling threw his head back and bellowed with
the sheer joy of being alive, then stepped forward and slapped his
brother hard on the thigh. 'You always were a soulless bastard.'

Jack turned away. He walked across to the body of his dead
horse, feeling the remorse of having led the brave beast to its
death.

'Are you coming?'

Jack turned to face the two brothers. The adjutant had
slipped a foot into his brother's stirrup and taken a firm hold
on the back of the saddle.

Jack shook his head.

'Thanks for your help, old man.'

Jack waved the brothers away. His attention was focused on two figures who were trying to flee unnoticed amidst the rout of the Persian army's centre. The men wore a strange uniform, one wholly different from that sported by the rest of the Persian army. A uniform that had no right to be there.

Jack had recognised it at once. He had fought against men with similar dark blue coats and spiked helmets. Then he had been a red-coated officer, leading his troops against the enemy's prepared position on the far bank of the Alma river. Now he saw two men wearing the same uniform and he broke into a run, forcing his tired body to move, chasing after the officers dressed in the uniform of the Russian Empire.

He forgot the broken square and the staggering victory the Bombay Lights had earned. Ballard had taught him well, and Jack knew that the men trying to escape the blood and carnage of the battlefield held the answer to the riddle of the Persian spy.

Chapter Thirty-nine

———◆———

Outram stood close to the British artillery as they limbered up their guns now that the fight was done. He surveyed the field of battle, his glasses panning slowly from side to side as he tried to understand the fight that he had missed. He had only returned to command the army once the attack was well under way, the injury he had suffered the previous night keeping him from the field until the day was nearly done.

His men had won him a spectacular victory, the efforts of the artillery and the heroism of the cavalry ending the Persian resistance before the bulk of his army could even be brought into play. Outram had achieved the first aim of his campaign. The Persian army would never again be able to face the British expeditionary force without remembering the fight at the village of Khoosh-Ab. He might not have been able to inflict a complete defeat and utterly destroy the Persian field army, but he had secured the foothold he needed so that he could launch the second phase of his campaign, which would see his force strike further inland. He would keep fighting until the Shah accepted defeat and sued for terms. The British public would be pleased and his masters at Horseguards would nod in approval. He might have hoped for more, but for now his men had done enough.

Outram lit a cigar and watched as the British infantry marched towards the remains of the position that the Persian army had occupied. The enemy battalions had fled, leaving behind their dead and wounded. The British had been allowed to complete their advance in peace, the horror of the enemy bombardment fading as they pressed forward, the beat of the drums the only sound marking their passage.

The redcoats were marching into a butcher's yard.

The British artillery barrage had been dreadfully effective. Corpses lay in heaps, the mangled bodies a testament to the skill of the gunners. The ground was soaked in blood. Shattered limbs and ragged flesh smothered the sandy soil. The bowels of hell were revealed for all to see.

The first British line marched on, driving after the remnants of the Persian infantry, which streamed away on to the plain behind where they had made their failed stand. The redcoats would not go far, for the enemy was retreating too fast, the Persian soldiers running from the victors in disarray, discarding their weapons as they fled for their lives.

The British cavalry rode after the broken ranks, doing their best to harry the retreat and add fresh impetus to the rout. Yet they had fought hard that day and their horses were blown, the riders exhausted. Without fresh cavalry coming after them, much of the enemy infantry would be able to make good their escape, the shattered ranks heading back to the haven of the high ground and the places where they would be able to re-form. The British army's shortage of cavalry was hampering the pursuit, denying Outram the ability to turn the Persian retreat into a catastrophic defeat.

The general began to issue his orders. The young officers on his staff were sent galloping across the plain as they carried his instructions to the battalion commanders. The second line of British infantry was to halt as soon as it reached the ground where the Persian army had made its fateful stand. The three battalions in the rearmost line of the assault had taken the majority of the day's casualties and Outram wanted to give them time to regroup and tend to their wounded. The men in the first line would be recalled to spend the rest of the day and the night that would follow on the field of battle. Outram had his victory and now, finally, his men could rest.

Lieutenant Knightly tried very hard not to be sick in front of his men. He walked amongst the bodies of enemy soldiers who had been living just a few hours before. He wondered how they had felt as the British barrage crashed into their ranks. Had they believed they would be the fortunate ones; that they could not be amongst the fallen? Or had they sensed death coming for them, somehow foreseeing what was going to befall them?

He shivered as he remembered the long advance. The sight of the broken bodies made a mockery of his pathetic hopes that he would not die; that it would always be someone else whose body was broken, whose blood would flow to run into the dusty soil. He saw death in all its grotesque butchery and knew then that it was only a matter of chance whether he lived or whether his own flesh was to be tattered and torn, his corpse left to lie forgotten on some foreign field.

'Sir?'

Knightly looked up into the calm face of his covering sergeant. He saw the pity in the man's eyes and it shamed him. He forced himself to stand straighter and fight away the horror.

'Yes, Sergeant?'

'Isn't that your chum over there?'

Knightly looked in the direction of the sergeant's pointing

arm. He was not surprised to see a hussar officer who had no business being in the field of battle. He shook off the dread that had crushed his spirits since the first cannon had opened fire. The battle was over and he had survived. It was time to move on.

He ordered his sergeant to fall the company out and to wait for orders. With his duty completed, he forced his fears away and trotted over to see just what his friend was up to.

'Arthur! What the devil is going on!'

Knightly puffed out his cheeks. The run had left him out of breath and the hurried question had him gasping for air. He had arrived to see his friend holding two officers prisoner at gunpoint. Both were dressed in a uniform he did not recognise, but he was sure that neither would pose much of a threat. To see a raised weapon seemed rather melodramatic now that the battle was done.

'Arthur, if these men have surrendered, you should put your gun down.'

He watched his friend's face closely. He saw the grime that covered his face, the flecks of blood that had been splattered across his cheeks. His uniform was filthy and there was a thin crust of blood across one thigh. Knightly looked into his bloodshot eyes and saw the anger burning deep within.

The taller of the two prisoners spread his arms, showing the British officers that he was unarmed. His face twitched, a spasm of what might have been fear twisting his mouth. Knightly had seen enough.

'Arthur. Put the gun down.' He spoke slowly, as if to a difficult child. He was ignored. 'Arthur!'

The prisoner looked at Knightly, his eyes beseeching the red-coated officer to come to his aid. He opened his mouth, releasing a torrent of words. It was a language Knightly did not understand, but the meaning was clear. His fellow officer was tormenting the two men. Now that the battle was over, it was a gratuitous display, and Knightly knew he would have to bring it to an end.

He thought about calling for his men to come to his aid. Jack and his two prisoners were partially hidden by a fold in the terrain that kept them out of sight of the redcoats, most of whom had already sunk to the ground, finding the few clear spaces not littered with bodies. Knightly did not have the heart to march over and force them back to their feet, so he sucked up his courage and tried to intercede once again.

'Arthur. You are scaring the poor fellows witless. It's over now. The battle is finished. Let me take them back to battalion. You look done in.' He tried to sound light-hearted, and even offered a short laugh as he attempted to shake off the tension in the air. He took a step forward as if he were going to push the gun aside.

'Stay where you are.'

The command was snapped and angry. It stopped Knightly in his tracks. The young lieutenant felt the first flutter of fear deep in his belly. The battle was over, but he sensed the presence of death.

Jack did his best to keep his gun steady. The exhaustion threatened to overwhelm him, and his arm was aching from shoulder to wrist from having fought for so long. He had heard Knightly arrive but he did his best to pay the junior officer no heed. He kept his eyes fixed on the taller of the two Russians, who stared back without fear. It was only when the British lieutenant started to intervene that Jack was forced to act.

'Stay where you are.' His voice rasped as he gave the order. He looked into the Russian's eyes as he spoke to Knightly, sensing that the man understood his words. 'I'm going to shoot

these bastards if they don't tell me what I want to know.'
He saw the flicker of understanding, the slightest narrowing
of the eyes as the Russian officer planned his next move. He
knew he could not afford to drop his guard, not even for a
single heartbeat.

The Russian had a hard face. His left cheek bore a single
thin scar that linked the corner of his mouth to his ear. His
black hair was flecked with grey, his thin moustache showing
the first signs of losing its colour. He looked more like a
veteran soldier than a diplomatic observer. He stared at Jack
for a long time. Jack met the scrutiny calmly, revealing
nothing. The second officer, who was much younger, took a
tiny half-step backwards, as if trying to edge away from the
wild-eyed British officer of hussars who threatened murder on
a battlefield.

'I surrender.' The older officer spoke in English for the first
time. He spat to one side, as if the language had left a sour taste
in his mouth. 'Now put the gun down, Captain, and I will offer
you my parole.'

Jack smiled, the dirt that crusted his face pulling at his skin.
'So you do speak English. But then of course you would. You
wouldn't be here otherwise.'

'So let us go.' The Russian sneered, defiant even with a
revolver aimed at him. 'We are not here to fight. My country is
not at war with yours. We are here as peaceful observers,
nothing more.' He scowled as he offered the response. It was
clear that surrendering was not an easy thing for him to do.

He turned his gaze back on Knightly. His eyes were like
steel. There was no trace of fear. Just a quiet, simmering anger.
'Tell your friend he is to let me come with you. Tell him to let
us go.'

'Arthur.' Knightly used his friend's name gently. It was clear
that both men terrified him. He looked like a small boy

summoned to bear witness to his first bare-knuckle fight. 'I'll take them back to our lines.'

'You will do no such thing.' Jack lifted the barrel of his gun an inch, aiming it directly at the Russian officer's forehead.

The Russian turned away from the fresh-faced young officer who was being so roundly ignored and focused his attention on the lean face of the man with the gun. 'What do you want, Englishman?'

'Tell me why you are here.'

The Russian smiled. It did not come close to reaching his eyes. 'I am an observer.'

'Bollocks.' Jack raised his voice for the first time. 'You're a fucking spy.'

'And you are a madman.' The Russian turned his pale eyes on Knightly again. 'Get this man away from me.'

'Shut your fucking muzzle,' Jack snarled. 'I know who you are and why you are here. I want to know the identity of the spy in the British camp. The spy who reports to you. You will tell me or I will kill you.'

'Arthur!' Knightly had gone pale.

'Be quiet!' Jack turned his head to glare at Knightly for the first time.

It gave the Russian the opening he had waited for so patiently. He stepped forward and punched Jack hard, the blow rising fast and connecting squarely with the side of his head. Jack staggered away from the impact, his ear ringing and his vision clouding. The Russian closed on him quickly, fists hammering away at his body. Jack tried to twist away from the blows, but the Russian was relentless. Another punch smashed into his stomach, followed by a further one that knocked the revolver from his hand, sending it spinning away. He lifted his arms and tried to fight back, but he felt the strength leaving his body as the Russian pummelled at him without pause. A fist connected with his jaw and he fell.

He hit the ground hard. He tried to get back to his feet, but the Russian gave no quarter, kicking out with his heavy boots as Jack scrabbled in the dirt in a futile attempt to escape.

A kick caught him in the pit of his gut, driving the air from his lungs. The pain flared bright and he couldn't breathe. He opened his mouth, but the dust choked him. He writhed on to his side, desperate to get some air into his lungs, but the Russian flopped on top of him, straddling his battered body. He tried to push him away, but the other man laughed and batted his flailing fists aside before reaching forward to take his throat in a vice-like grip.

Jack was choking, his neck crushed under the Russian's thick fingers. His lungs screamed, the last of his breath roaring in his ears. In desperation he tried to hammer his head forward, seeking to batter his way free. The Russian saw the attempt and forced Jack's head backwards, grinding it into the dust.

Jack's vision faded. His lungs screamed out in agony, the need to breathe torturing him. He let his body go limp, his mind still trying to find a way out even as the Russian throttled him. He had one last chance, a final, desperate gamble. A glimmer of hope as the darkness rushed forward to claim him.

The younger Russian had leapt at Knightly in the moments after Jack had fallen. Knightly had not moved, unable to do anything but stare in horror at the sudden eruption of violence in front of him. The Russian officer was as fast as a viper and he had his sword held at Knightly's throat before the British lieutenant could even think of drawing his own. He tried to step away, but the Russian pushed the blade forward, scoring it into the soft flesh at the base of Knightly's neck. The sharpened steel drew blood and Knightly went completely still, held fast by the threat of death.

He felt his body begin to shake. He watched the Russian batter Jack into bloody submission, powerless to intervene. He felt frozen, his whole being mesmerised by the vicious blade that hovered under his chin. He could smell the sheen of oil on the polished steel, the metallic tang catching in the back of his throat. With the point cutting into his flesh, he could do nothing but watch events in stupefied terror.

The hard-eyed Russian officer stepped away from Jack's body. Knightly felt his throat close in horror as he saw the limp figure on the ground. His friend was dying no more than half a dozen paces away and he could do nothing to save him.

The Russian officer glanced once at Knightly before bending to snatch the fallen revolver from the ground. With practised ease he brought the gun around, aiming it at the body of the hussar officer who had tried to capture him.

'No!' Knightly screamed, the dreadful sound exploding from his lips.

He saw a thin smile appear on the Russian's scarred face as he cocked the weapon. He lifted the revolver a fraction of an inch and then turned to look at Knightly. His eyes bored into the young officer, daring him to move. The revolver remained pointing at Jack's skull. At such close range the Russian couldn't miss. He smirked at Knightly, relishing his distress.

With a final twist of his lips, the Russian pulled the trigger.

Chapter Forty

The trigger clicked on to an empty chamber. Jack had used all his rounds in the final fight with the Persian infantry and had not had the opportunity to reload. The weapon was useless. He had been bluffing when he had threatened his two prisoners.

The Russian's face betrayed his shock. He pulled the trigger again and again before throwing the gun to one side, his hands reaching for the sabre at his side.

Jack rose from the ground, roaring like a madman. He threw himself at the Russian, punching his right fist into the foreign officer's throat. It was a brutal blow and the Russian staggered backwards, his hands clutching his crushed windpipe. Jack went after him without a moment's pause, his fists flashing at the man who had tried to kill him, smashing blow after blow into the Russian, who crumpled under the onslaught, his legs giving way beneath him. Jack lashed out as he fell, kicking the tip of his boot viciously into the man's throat, driving the clasping hands into the abused flesh, choking off the last of his breath.

Knightly saw the fear flash in the younger Russian's face as he watched the man he had thought beaten rise from the ground and batter his fellow officer insensible. The tip of his sword wavered and Knightly reacted without thought, slashing his arm upwards, knocking the blade to one side. The Russian fell backwards, giving Knightly the freedom to finally draw his own sabre. It rasped from the metal scabbard and he slashed it forward, forcing the Russian to jump away.

As he cut at the Russian, a yelp of childish glee burst from his lips. He was fighting for the first time and he felt invincible. He stamped forward, hammering his sword at his enemy, forgetting his fear. The Russian parried the blows but the effort caused him to stagger, and Knightly thrust the point of the sword forward, sliding the sharp steel into the man's flesh. He could barely believe how easy it was. He pushed his weight behind the blade, driving it deep into the Russian's chest. When he looked up, he saw the agony reflected in his foe's eyes, his bitter surprise revealed in a look of abject horror.

Knightly let go of the blade. It was stuck fast in the Russian's flesh and he could not find the strength to wrench it free. He stared at the man's hand as it flapped at the blade, the fleshy tips of his fingers torn as they clasped the sharpened edge. The joy of killing faded and the heat of victory was replaced with coldness, the shock of having killed a man freezing his soul.

The Russian staggered forward. He yelled as he lurched into motion, a spew of foreign words rushing from his mouth before they were cut off in a torrent of blood.

Knightly screamed, shrieking like a child confronting a monster from a nightmare. He was still screaming when the Russian rammed his own sword forward. It was thrust with the last of his strength and it cut deep into Knightly's body. The Russian fell, his hand falling away from the blade he had buried in the British lieutenant's flesh.

Knightly's fingers scrabbled at the Russian's sword. A wave

of panic engulfed him and he fell silent, unable to comprehend what had happened. He felt his strength ebb and he fell to his knees. He tried to pull the blade from his own body but it was stuck fast. Blood spilled down the length of the steel, smothering Knightly's clutching fingers. He screamed again and then again, releasing the horror that surged through him.

Jack had turned as soon as he heard the sounds of the fight. He watched as Knightly fought, recognising the rage that took hold of the young officer. The struggle was short, the two men trading barely half a dozen blows before Knightly struck the Russian down. It was only when the lieutenant let go of his sabre that Jack lurched into motion. He knew what was about to happen and he rushed forward, his cry of warning stuck in his tortured throat.

He could do nothing as the Russian made his final thrust. He saw the sword pierce Knightly's flesh and he moved quickly, reaching his friend's side just as he fell to his knees. Knightly's hands pawed at the blade in his flesh but Jack knocked them to one side and eased him to the ground, setting him down in the dust as gently as he could.

He didn't need to look at the thin sabre buried in Knightly's chest to know what was going to happen. He drew the young's man head into his lap, cradling him in his arms, the bitter futility of what had happened sending a surge of anger coursing through him. As he held Knightly close, he looked down at the ashen face of a boy about to die.

'I'm sorry.' Knightly choked as he spoke, the breath refusing to come.

'You're going to be all right.' Jack ran his fingers through the young officer's hair and hugged his head to him as if he could stop what was to come.

Knightly could not speak. A tremor ran through him, his

body convulsing with fear. He was sobbing now, an incoherent stream of terror, as he realised he was about to die. Jack could do nothing but hold him tight, fighting against the darkness that threatened to lay claim to his very being.

The young man's body went still. Jack looked down and fixed his eyes on the face that stared up at him. He was still watching as the final spark of light fled, to be replaced by glazed nothingness.

Knightly was dead.

'I told you to twist your bloody wrist.' Jack felt a blackness engulf his soul. He placed Knightly's head gently on the ground and closed his eyes, trying to hold fast against the wave of bitter grief.

The feeling passed. He opened his eyes once again and felt nothing.

He slipped his hand forward and unbuckled the flap of Knightly's holster, pulling free the revolver that he knew had not been used that day. Then he got carefully to his feet and walked towards the first Russian officer. The man lay on the ground, gasping for breath, his hands twisted around his broken throat. Jack straddled his chest, crushing the man's tortured lungs, then threw the Russian's arms backwards and pinned them under his knees, leaving the man completely at his mercy.

He looked down at the beaten officer. The man's eyes were glazed, so Jack slapped him hard around the cheeks, hitting him again and again until his vision focused.

'So, where were we?' He spat a wad of bloody phlegm on to the Russian's chest. His own throat burned and he could feel the place on his neck where the other man's fingers had dug into the soft flesh. He felt no compassion, no mercy. 'Who is the fucking spy?'

The Russian said nothing. He simply stared at Jack, the air

rasping in his gullet as he tried to breathe through the ruin of his throat.

Jack felt the solid shape of Knightly's revolver in his hand. The weight was reassuring and he brought it around, placing it with care so that the barrel rested against the Russian's temple.

'Tell me who the damn spy is or I'll blow you to kingdom come.' He pressed the barrel into the soft flesh just under the Russian's hairline. He felt empty, his soul drained of all emotion. 'Tell me, you by-blow of a whore, or I'll fucking kill you.'

The Russian spat. The thick globule landed on Jack's chest and stuck there, hanging from the gore-splattered dolman before slowly falling away and landing on his bloodstained thigh.

Jack leant forward. 'Then go to hell.' As he whispered the words, he saw the flare of fear deep in the man's eyes. He pulled the trigger.

The crash of the gun going off was loud. The retort echoed around them, the sudden noise somehow out of place even on what had been a field of battle.

The Russian jerked in terror and Jack nearly lost his balance. He had turned his wrist as he pulled the trigger. The bullet had scorched through the Russian's hair, missing his scalp by no more than half an inch.

The other man went still. Jack stared down into his eyes, betraying no emotion. Slowly, carefully, he cocked the revolver for a second time, bringing another chamber under the hammer.

'Tell me who the spy is.'

The Russian began to shake. Jack could feel the tremors running through the man's body, yet he felt no remorse. He steadied his wrist and pulled the trigger for a second time.

Again the sound of the gun firing exploded around them.

This time Jack's aim had not been as careful, and the bullet caught the Russian's scalp, tearing a path through the man's hair, parting the delicate flesh on the very top of his head.

The Russian screamed, and jerked like a landed fish, but Jack did not move. He waited until his captive went still before he leant forward and spoke softly.

'There are three bullets left. One of them will kill you. Tell me who the spy is.'

The Russian closed his eyes. The blood from the wound to his scalp ran freely down his face, streaming in thick rivulets down his cheeks so that it looked like he was crying tears of blood.

Jack waited. He counted to ten and then slowly prepared the revolver to fire again. The click of the rotating chamber was loud in the silence. The Russian's eyes snapped open, blinking away the thick covering of blood.

'In my pocket.' The words were slurred, fear thickening the man's accent, his crushed throat barely letting him speak.

Jack didn't move. He simply stared down at the Russian, as if unmoved by the words he had waited so long to hear. Then, with a sudden flurry of movement, he cracked the revolver hard against the man's skull. The sound of the vicious impact was sickening.

Jack leapt to his feet, immediately covering the Russian officer with the still loaded revolver. But the brutal blow had bludgeoned the man insensible. A thick stream of blood ran from his temple, and his head sagged to one side, all signs of consciousness gone.

Jack tossed the revolver to the ground, then bent forward and started to rummage through the Russian officer's uniform, grunting in satisfaction as he tugged a thick sheaf of papers from the man's pocket. He stood back and flicked through them, his eyes scanning the neat copperplate script, the elegant sloping letters revealing to him what he had come so far to find. He had discovered the identity of the spy in the British camp.

He looked down at the body of the man he had beaten senseless. He contemplated picking up the revolver and blowing the Russian to kingdom come. He turned his head and saw Knightly's staring blue eyes. The sight sickened him. He turned his back on the scene of so much blood and so much horror and walked away.

He went to do murder.

Chapter Forty-one

———◆———

$\mathcal{J}$ack rode at Ballard's side on a horse borrowed from Outram's stable. It had not taken long to reveal all that he had discovered. If Ballard had been shocked by the revelation, he had not shown it. It had taken barely thirty minutes to secure Outram's permission for the two intelligence officers to leave the army and race back to Bushire to apprehend the enemy spy. They had left Palmer behind, the bodyguard ordered to guard their possessions and Ballard's papers. The two men would deal with the spy themselves.

It was still not past midday but already the redcoats were going about the gruesome task of sorting the dead from the still living. The battlefield was theirs, the victory complete. Jack and Ballard left the British army as victors of the field and went to finish the job they had started but which had been left unfinished for too long.

The heavens opened. The afternoon sun was hidden behind a bank of thick, rolling clouds that had rushed across the sky to smother the brightness and shroud the land in a dark cloak. The two officers rode on regardless, paying the deluge no heed. They faced a long journey. They would ride on into the night, pushing their horses hard as they sought to cover the miles back to Bushire as quickly as they could.

The crash of thunder and the crack of lightning split the sky. It was as if the gods had been angered by the slaughter and now raged in the heavens, their displeasure manifest in the violent storm. The road the two officers followed became little more than muddy slurry and sand, the slop splattering the horses and riders with a thin covering of foul-smelling muck. The rain fell constantly, driven almost horizontal by the biting northerly wind. The officers could do nothing but endure the tempest and ride onwards, their mission too vital to be turned aside by even the foulest conditions.

Jack could not ever remember being so weary. His sword arm felt like lead, the muscles deadened by a night and day of fighting. His leg throbbed from the lance wound that was still untended, his throat burnt from the throttling the Russian officer had administered, and his spine felt as if it had been severed, such was the pain in the small of his back. He ignored it all, driven on by the need for revenge on the person he blamed for so much of the suffering, the power of betrayal fuelling his body past the point of exhaustion.

The storm raged around him. Every minute was a torment, a torture that would never cease. He endured, staying in the saddle and forcing his horse forward, each step taking him closer to the confrontation he sought.

He thought of nothing. He refused to dwell on the bitter battle or on the fight that had led to Knightly's death. He felt nothing. No anger. No grief. No remorse.

He rode through the tempest, his soul empty. He rode to exact revenge. He would find the British spy whose identity the Russian papers had revealed. And he was ready to kill.

They arrived in the dead hours before dawn. It was the time

when the camp was at its quietest, the men left behind slumbering through the last of the night. No one remarked on their progress, the two weather-beaten officers left to pick their way through the empty spaces. With so many men with the main column, the camp felt eerily still, the tents silent, only shadows moving through the darkness.

Ballard looked across at Jack. They had not spoken for hours, the only exchanges coming when they passed through the network of vedettes and picquets that ringed the British base, keeping it safe from marauding enemy cavalry.

'Let's get this done.'

Jack nodded. His did his best to force away the exhaustion. He had one last duty to perform. Then he could rest.

They rode into the staff headquarters. Lieutenant Colonel Shepheard had been left in command of a combined army and naval detachment to safeguard the encampment whilst the column made its lightning attack on the Persians. In the small hours, the headquarters was quiet, only a handful of men left to work through the night.

It did not take long for Ballard to rouse the duty officer, a Captain Campbell, who bustled out of the tent, his surprise at the summons clear. He took one look at the two officers' bedraggled attire and shouted for an orderly to bring coffee.

'Do you want a detachment?' Campbell was brisk and to the point. Ballard had explained to him that they were going to arrest the spy who had dogged the campaign since the beginning.

'No.' Jack spoke for the first time. His voice was brittle.

'As you wish.' Campbell yawned, smothering his mouth with a meaty paw. 'The first dispatch from the battle only arrived about an hour ago. You must have ridden hard.'

Jack said nothing. He reached for Knightly's revolver and set about reloading it. His exhaustion was like a lead bar pressing down on his soul. It took an effort to open the pouch on his belt that contained the ammunition, his hands fumbling with the clasp. The cartridges were dry under his fingertips, kept safe against the deluge.

Campbell nodded at Jack's reaction. He had been in the Crimea and he knew what it felt like after a hard-fought battle. He turned to face Ballard. 'Do you want anything further from me?'

Ballard was looking at Jack, his face creased with concern. He was gambling his career on the events of the next hour. His only weapon was a battered and bloodied charlatan. For the first time, he had doubts.

'No.' Ballard spoke with finality. He turned and fixed Campbell with a grim smile. 'We will deal with this ourselves.'

Sarah Draper sat at her writing table. She had risen early, long before dawn, unable to sleep any longer. She barely slept at all these days. Her nights were long, the charpoy she tried to rest in becoming a bed of thorns when she did lie down. So she wrote, passing the hours of darkness with only the hiss of a gas lamp for company, her paper and ink a solace against the loneliness that swamped her.

The words she wrote comforted her. They had become her release, her salvation. There was a joy in creating images with nothing more than words, the dry, scribbled lines taking on another life as she recorded her thoughts and feelings. When she wrote, she could forget her life, passing into another place, where the choices she had made meant nothing. There was just her and the words she chose. Nothing more.

She heard footsteps outside her tent. The heavy tread of army boots, scuffing the wooden boards she had arranged outside the tent's flaps so that she would be spared from muck being traipsed into her abode. She heard the footsteps stop, the boots stomping loudly on the boards.

She felt a frisson of fear. She expected no one. She spent the nights alone now, no longer seeking to force away her loneliness by taking a lover to her bed. She shook off the feeling of dread, forcing the anxiety from her thoughts. She was in the heart of the British camp. She was safe.

The tent flap was thrown open. The rush of air was cold on her skin. She had time to stand and wrap her linen robe tight around her body before the intruder strode into the tent.

'Hello, Sarah.'

Jack took a step forward, moving out of the shadows and into the meagre light cast by the solitary lamp. He heard her gasp of shock as she saw who had come to disturb her rest.

He took another step, and then another. He knew how he looked. How he smelt. He was dressed in the horror of the battlefield, the grime and the blood a visceral reminder of the violence of the fight. He had not taken the time to clean himself, wanting to confront Sarah with the stain of other men's lives on his clothes; their blood on his hands. He wanted to shock her. To scare her. To somehow communicate just what she had done when she had intervened in the affairs of soldiers.

For Sarah Draper was the spy that Jack had come all this way to kill.

'Why do it?'

Jack blurted out the question. He had spent hours thinking of what he would say when he confronted her. The long, miserable hours of the ride had given him plenty of time to imagine this moment, to taste what it would be like to denounce the woman whose bed he had shared. He had considered every emotion, but as she rose to face him, he felt nothing but the bitterness of betrayal.

The question hung in the air. Sarah turned her back on him and carefully placed the steel pen she still carried on top of the paper she had been working on. She leant forward and straightened the papers, leaving them in a neat stack with the pen positioned carefully as a paperweight to stop them being disturbed in the storm she knew was coming.

Her hands fell away from her robe and it opened round her, so that when she turned back to face Jack he would see the outline of the body that had once been the source of such pleasure. She looked into his eyes, searching for an escape.

Jack said nothing. He raised Knightly's revolver. The weapon was covered with dirt, the heavy handle still stained with the blood of the Russian officer. He saw Sarah's face appear over the tip of the barrel, her eyes filling the sight. Her hair was scraped back, tied behind her head so that he could see the whole of her face. She took his breath away, the simple symmetry of her features making her one of the most startlingly beautiful women he had ever seen.

He stared into her eyes, just as he had done so many times before. He saw the vitality, the spark of life they contained, the force that still captivated his soul. His finger curled around the trigger, taking up the slack. A single ounce of pressure and the gun would fire. Then the beautiful eyes would glaze over, the life force fading to nothingness before it was replaced by the blank, lifeless stare of death. He had seen it before. He had watched the flicker of life leave Knightly's eyes, and now he would be the one who would end the same spark in Sarah's.

He never saw her hand slip behind her back. He was lost in his thoughts, his mind in such turmoil that he didn't notice her slim fingers slide into the drawer of her writing desk.

'I'm sorry, Arthur.' Sarah spoke for the first time.

The words meant nothing.

Jack could not know that she was apologising not for what

she had done, but for what she was about to do.

The slim pistol only fired a single bullet. It was small, tiny enough to fit into a man's pocket or a woman's purse. It was an expensive object, crafted by the best gunsmith as a lady's weapon of last defence.

Sarah Draper did not hesitate. She did not bother lifting the weapon, but instead fired it from her hip.

The bullet hit Jack before he was fully aware of what was happening. It spun him round, the force of the impact knocking him backwards. His own gun roared, his finger tightening on instinct. But he was already falling backwards, and the bullet went wild, blasting through the tent's canvas roof.

The agony seared through him. He felt the rush of blood pouring from the wound. The bullet had taken him high on his right arm, searing through his flesh, filling his world with pain. He went down, his bloodied body hitting the floor with all the grace of a falling brick.

Sarah moved fast. She stepped past Jack, barely glancing at the man she had struck down, and threw back the tent flap thinking of nothing but escape.

A strong hand reached from out of the darkness and grabbed her arm, the fingers clawing into her flesh, stopping her headlong flight with a vice-like grip.

'Going somewhere?' Ballard pulled hard, dragging her back into the tent.

Sarah screamed. She shrieked a single word in the darkness, her anguish complete.

Ballard was in no mood to be gentle. He smothered her mouth with his free hand. Without mercy he twisted her arm behind her back and thrust her ahead of him into the tent. She struggled under his grip, trying to free herself, but Ballard was too strong. He pushed her backwards, sending her sprawling on to the charpoy.

She leapt to her feet, her hands twisted like claws, and went for Ballard's face, her screech of rage like that of a wounded animal. She came at him fast, but he slapped her cheek, battering her back on to the camp bed.

'Stay there!' He growled the words. His hand stung from the blow he had given her, but he would not hesitate to repeat it if she tried to escape.

Sarah lay sprawled on the charpoy. Her cheek was scarlet, the imprint of his hand clearly visible on her pale skin. Her robe was open, and Ballard saw the lithe body beneath.

He turned away, refusing to be drawn by the sight. He saw Jack trying to get to his feet, blood oozing from the wound just below his shoulder. His face was pale, drained by the agony of the bullet.

Ballard heard footsteps. He had time to turn to face the tent's entrance just as it was thrown open and a man burst in. He carried a naked blade, the bared steel glinting in the light of the gas lamp.

Sarah had not screamed in terror. She had called for help.

Chapter Forty-two

Simon Montfort rushed into the tent, his weapon drawn. He had been summoned by Sarah's dreadful scream and he came in fighting.

Ballard was no warrior. His hands fumbled clumsily for the sabre at his waist. He had never once drawn the weapon in anger, and now that danger loomed in front of him, he was terribly slow.

Montfort bellowed as he struck, giving Ballard no chance to defend himself. The blow speared through the major's sparse flesh, the blade grating on the edge of a rib. Montfort recovered the sword immediately, his face contorted with the rage of battle as he prepared the next strike.

The commander of intelligence staggered to one side, his sabre undrawn, his hands clasping at the bloody tear in his side. The rapier came for him again as he stumbled away, but he was moving too fast and the sharpened steel only managed to gouge a deep crevice in the flesh of his upper arm. His balance failed him and he fell, sliding into the slick of blood already spilt across the tent's floor.

Montfort was after him in a flash. Yet he held back the

killing blow, giving his victim enough time to twist on the floor so that he lay on his back, his face lifting towards the man about to kill him.

Ballard looked up and saw Montfort looming over him. The younger man's mouth twisted in a dreadful grimace as he prepared to thrust his sword into his opponent's heart.

Montfort aimed the blow. His arm tensed and drew back as he gathered his strength for the killing strike. Ballard lifted his own arms, a final act of defiance as he saw his death reflected in the eyes of the man summoned to protect the spy. He watched the rapier coming for him, the tip aimed squarely at his heart, and he braced himself for the blow even as his mind recoiled from the thought that he was about to die.

But he had forgotten the charlatan.

Jack had dragged himself to his feet. The pain in his arm seared through his veins but he refused to stay down. He saw Montfort looming over Ballard in the moment before he attacked hard and fast. He hammered his talwar at Montfort's rapier, driving the blade wide even as it reached for Ballard's flesh.

'Come on!' Jack fanned the flames of his anger. He recovered his sword and attacked again. The blow missed but it drove Montfort backwards and Jack stepped into the space, putting himself between his foe and his fallen commander.

He cut his sword through the stale air, forcing the younger man into a desperate defence. He shouted again, his pain and anger released into one dreadful banshee wail as he flailed his sword at his latest enemy.

Sarah screamed as he went past her. He looked like a creature from a nightmare. Blood dripped from the wound to his arm, and he was coated in the grime and filth of the battlefield, the stains of combat covering his uniform. Yet worse was the look on his face. It was the look of a killer. The face of a man who had witnessed so much death that he lived in a world of ghosts and shadows. The man she had taken to her bed had returned, and he terrified her.

Montfort moved backwards. There was little room for manoeuvre and he could not retreat for long. Jack hammered blows forward, flowing through the impacts. He had killed so many men. Their faces flashed in his mind. He relived the moments when he had struck them down, when they realised they were about to die. He screamed as he fought, haunted by the memories, driven half mad by the legacy of the deaths he had caused.

He parried a half-hearted counter, twisting his wrist so that he deflected the rapier to one side. It gave him the opening he needed and he thrust his talwar forward, going for the killing stroke just as he had done so many times before.

But Montfort was young and fast, and Jack was hurting and slow. Montfort threw himself to one side, a final, despairing ploy to avoid the blade that reached for his flesh. Jack missed, his talwar hitting nothing but air. Montfort saw the opening and punched his sword's guard into the wound to Jack's arm.

The force of the merciless blow knocked Jack to the floor. His talwar fell from his hand, his arm losing all sensation, agony flaring across his vision. He cried out, the explosion of sound torn from his lips. He saw Montfort's boots step forward, knowing the killing strike would follow.

'No!'

Jack heard the cry but he did not know what it meant. He forced himself to move, levering himself to his feet, hearing his own sobs as the pain seared through him. His right arm was useless, so he snatched his talwar from the ground with his left hand, lifting it up in a pathetic attempt to be ready to fight.

But it was over.

Ballard had come to his aid. He had plunged his sabre deep

into Montfort's body, driving the steel in hard. Montfort's mouth opened to scream, but no sound came out. He staggered, staying on his feet even with Ballard's blade buried in his flesh. Still he tried to fight, bringing his rapier round, his eyes flaring wide as he thrust it forward one last time.

Jack saw the blow coming. Ballard's sabre was stuck fast, the naïve mistake trapping the blade, leaving him defenceless. Jack would not watch another man die from the same feckless error. He lashed out, flailing his talwar in a clumsy parry. The blow was awkward, but it swatted aside Montfort's rapier, blocking the thrust that would have struck Ballard's heart.

Jack staggered, the impact jarring his battered body. But he had done enough. He forced himself to stand straight so that he was face-to-face with Montfort. The younger man's features were screwed tight against the agony. For a moment he stared into Jack's eyes, his hatred naked and exposed. Jack met the stare, not flinching from the younger man's gaze until it glazed over, death arriving fast to steal another life away.

Montfort fell silently. As his body slipped to the floor, Jack saw Ballard's grim, bloodied face. It wore a look of horror, the closeness of death and the enormity of having killed a man for the first time only now registering in the man's mind.

But Jack knew the fight was not yet over.

He turned, ignoring the pain in his arm. He dropped his talwar as he spied the fallen revolver. He bent to snatch it from the floor, cursing as the motion set off fresh waves of agony. But the familiarity of the weapon tethered him to who he was and why he was there.

He stood straight. His right arm hung useless from his side, the searing, torture of his wound denying him its use. So he held the revolver in his left hand, just as he did in battle.

He walked forward, stepping carefully towards the cause of so much pain. He remembered the sight of the shattered bodies on the battlefield. The pathetic, twisted remains of men who had died at the hands of the enemy; an enemy who had been forewarned of the army's movements. He saw again the bloodied face of Knightly as he died, the dreadful terror in the boy's eyes as he rushed towards the nothingness of oblivion.

He took another step, and then another. He tried to calculate how many deaths could be laid at the door of the woman who now cowered away from him. He was close to her. He could see her sobs of terror. He could smell her fear. She raised her hands, trying to ward him away, but he would not be denied.

He lifted the revolver. He felt nothing, his emotions scoured away from his soul. He had killed so many times before. One more death would barely be a blot on his mind, one more stain amidst a thousand.

He aimed the gun, filling the simple sight with the face of a woman he had once kissed and caressed with lust and desire. The gun's movement was still smooth and the chamber moved with greased precision to bring a fresh cartridge under the hammer. He felt the trigger beneath his forefinger, the metal cool against the heat of his flesh.

'Stop!'

The order cut through the silence.

'Do not shoot.' The voice of authority wavered slightly as Ballard found the strength to get to his feet. 'Jack Lark, I order you to hold your fire.'

It was the use of his own name that brought Jack up short. It resonated through his being, a tie to a past he barely remembered. The image of a young girl flashed into his mind. She was beautiful. A complex network of pins just about held her unruly curls in place. A few had escaped to whisper across her face. He savoured the image, his memory replaying her smile as she saw him watching her, her lips pursing as she blew the errant hairs away from her face. Yet the girl was dead, the

vital spark of her life stolen away. Her eyes stared at him devoid
of all life; the blank, sightless stare of death. The girl Jack had
loved was dead and the memory of the grief surged through
him.

The image fled and he looked at Sarah Draper. He pictured
her face stricken with the same waxy pallor, the same lifeless
eyes that would bore into his soul. He shuddered, the nightmare
so real that he gasped. He lowered his weapon and closed his
eyes against the vision, trying to blot the images from his mind.

Ballard stepped past him. He clasped his left hand against
the sword cut to his side, the blood oozing past his fingers. Yet
he gave no impression of caring about his wounds. He slipped
on to the edge of the charpoy, sitting carefully, close to the
woman he had come so far to denounce.

Chapter Forty-three

'Why?' Ballard asked the question simply, searching for an answer. 'Why do all this?'

Sarah Draper curled her legs up to her chest, wrapping her arms around them, and stared into the distance, as if seeing nothing.

'Because I was bored.' She spoke suddenly, her words cutting though the silence. She fixed Ballard with an intense stare. 'You have no idea what life is like for someone like me. I can do nothing. I'm paraded around the place like some damn trinket, an accessory, like the bloody swords you are all so proud of.'

Ballard eased himself forward. 'You don't become a spy because you are bored.' He spoke gently, but he refused to be thwarted by her attempt to keep up the pretence of being a lady.

'No.' She hung her head. 'You do that for money.'

'That is all?' Ballard seemed genuinely shocked.

'Ha!' Sarah was cruel. 'You are a man, how could you understand?'

'But what of James?'

Sarah's mouth puckered in distaste. 'What of him?'

'Was life with him so very bad?'

'You have no idea.' Sarah laughed. It was a bitter, cold sound. 'He married me because I was pretty. Because he wanted the adornment. I was born poor and I would have died poor if I had said no.'

Jack stood in silence. Sarah's words had struck him with more force than her bullet. She was echoing what he had once said of his own life. He had embarked on his long charade to make something of himself, to achieve more than he was allowed. Sarah Draper was claiming to have done the same.

She cackled unpleasantly. 'You look so shocked.' She crooked a finger in Ballard's direction.

Ballard shook his head, his hard eyes never leaving hers. 'You married a man for money. No, that does not shock me. It is your betrayal, of him, and of your country, that disgusts me.'

Sarah's eyes blazed in genuine anger as she heard the repulsion in Ballard's voice. 'What would you know?' She displayed her scorn openly. 'I had nothing. If I had not married him, I would have gone back to the life I had lived before he came along.' For a moment there was a trace of pain in her eyes. 'I would not return there.'

Jack struggled with Sarah's confession. Was she any different from him? What would he have done had he not been able to start on his long charade?

'So you married an officer for money and for station. But that was not enough for you. So you became a spy. You betrayed the country of your birth for money.' Ballard was bitter. He could not imagine the circumstances that would drive anyone, least of all a woman, to sell their soul for so base an ambition.

But Jack could. He lived in the shadows, where nothing was certain. He knew desperation. Yet he had never turned his back on the country of his birth. No matter what temptation he had faced, he had stayed true to that at least. It was one of the few certainties in his life.

Sarah stared into space, lost in the past. It was only when she turned her gaze on Jack that she seemed to come back to herself.

'You were a whore.' Jack spoke evenly. He came from her world, and he knew.

Sarah bit her lip. Her eyes were pitiful.

Jack stared at her. He was starting to understand. Ballard was truly the Devil, but he did not know everything.

Sarah met his gaze. She searched his eyes, her suffering revealed yet still half hidden behind a mixture of anger and shame. Finally she nodded.

Ballard snorted, but Jack held up his hand, silencing his commander with the gesture. 'Where?'

'On my back.' Her scorn was biting.

'London?'

'Does it matter?'

Jack sighed. The woman in front of him bore little relation to the fascinating creature who had taken him into her carriage and into her bed. She had infatuated him, tormenting and tantalising his every thought. Now the veneer of beauty was gone. The ugliness of her life was revealed. Yet it did not repulse him as he sensed it did Ballard. For he understood it.

'How old were you? When they forced you.'

'Old enough.'

Jack felt his exhaustion pressing down on him. He wanted to lie down but he forced himself to remain standing, knowing that if he stopped, he would be unable to rise again.

'This explains nothing.' Ballard hissed the words, the pain of his wound leaving him short of breath.

'Be quiet!' Jack snapped back. 'It explains everything. You

don't understand because you have not seen what life is like for people like us.'

'I do not need to see hell to understand the fire.'

Jack snorted his derision. 'You don't have a fucking clue what you are talking about.' He still held the revolver in his hand, and the weapon suddenly felt heavy. He tossed it on to Sarah's writing desk. He did not fear Sarah. He pitied her.

'I was eleven.' Sarah spoke quietly. 'My ma died.'

Jack had seen it. His mother's gin palace had had its fair share of whores. Many were young girls. He clasped his left hand around the wound to his arm, pressing his fingers into the torn flesh, trying to stem the flow of blood. The pain seared through him, but it helped to scour away the exhaustion and clear his mind.

'The colonel, Draper. He fell for you.'

Sarah nodded. 'He was a captain then.'

Ballard could not stay silent. 'Now that is a lie. Gentlemen do not take whores for their wives.'

Jack shook his head. 'It happens. I've seen it.'

Sarah was watching Jack closely. 'He loved me.'

'And he married you.'

Again she nodded.

'But someone else knew.' Jack felt his knees begin to buckle and he closed his eyes as he tried to summon some last remnant of strength. 'Someone knew you were a whore. They used it against you.' He spoke quickly, trying to understand it all before he collapsed.

'That man.' Sarah's words were like daggers. 'He had been with me before. Many times. He saw me in Bombay and he worked it out straight away.' She looked at Jack, her eyes pleading. 'I didn't have a choice. He would have ruined James. I couldn't do that to him.'

'You were saving yourself.' Ballard interrupted, his venom

naked. 'Do not attempt to pretend to have higher motives. You became a spy to save yourself.'

Sarah laughed. She fixed Ballard with a piercing stare. There was scorn on her face. Loathing. 'You think I'm the spy? You have no damn idea at all.'

Ballard did not take kindly to her reaction. He was hurting. 'You are a spy, and you will hang.'

The threat silenced her.

Ballard stood. He walked to the tent's entrance, stepping around Montfort's lifeless corpse.

'Watch her, Jack. I'll summon the guard. I will not hear any more. This is over.'

He walked out and into the darkness. It would not take him long to reach Shepheard's headquarters, where he would rouse the guard to secure the spy and keep her safe until she made her final journey to a cold and lonely scaffold.

Jack looked at Sarah. He could not find it within himself to hate her. They shared the silence, each lost in their own thoughts.

'Who is he?' Jack broke the spell. He poked the corpse with the toe of his boot, rocking the body that stared at the tent's ceiling with lifeless eyes.

Sarah smiled. It was thin, weary. She looked drained and exhausted, but life still sparkled in her eyes.

'Captain Sergei Dimitriovitch Sazonov.'

Jack threw back his head and barked a short laugh. 'A damn Russian?'

'You fools never once suspected anything.' Sarah shook her head. She could not share Jack's amusement, but she could tell him the truth. 'He came with me and not one of you questioned him, just because he spoke with the right accent and looked the damn part. It was so bloody easy.'

Jack shook with a potent mix of laughter and pain. He was

not the only impostor in the army. The idea fascinated him as much as it amused him.

'He was your link to the Persians?' he asked.

Sarah shook her head in denial. 'He was here to watch me.' She fixed Jack's eyes with her own. 'He was my jailer.'

Jack finally understood. Montfort was no guardian. He'd been here to make sure Sarah played the role she had been forced to take. If she had not done as she had been ordered, Jack had no doubt that Montfort would have killed her.

He thought about what she had said. Despite the agony of his wound, his mind was sharp enough.

'You're not the spy.' He spoke with certainty. It was all starting to make sense. She had been forced to act as she had, the presence of a Russian guardian proof that she was nothing more than a pawn. There had to be someone else. 'You were just playing a part.'

Sarah smiled. 'I always knew you were no ordinary soldier, Arthur.'

Jack looked at her. 'So who *is* the spy? Who is the man who knew you from before?'

Sarah held his stare. He recognised the fear in her eyes. He watched her gaze flicker over Montfort's corpse, then She looked back at him and he saw an unexpected sadness. Her jaw tightened as she made her decision.

'Fetherstone.'

'You let her go?' Ballard sat down as he contemplated Jack's astonishing confession. He had returned to the tent to find that Sarah Draper had disappeared. He hissed as he shook his head, whether at the pain of his wound or his subordinate's rash action Jack could not tell.

'She's not the one we are after.'

Jack picked up his revolver and thrust it back into its holster.

His actions were clumsy, his useless right arm hanging at his side. He felt the exhaustion swamp him. It was all he could do to stay on his feet.

'What?' Ballard's eyes flashed in anger. 'What the devil do you mean? Have you lost your senses? Has the fighting addled what little brains you possess?' He was incredulous.

'She was not important.' Jack's voice was cold.

'What the bloody hell would you know about it?' Ballard was raging now, his anger given full vent. 'You were here to do what I told you. You were my hired gun. My untraceable killer! I never told you to think.'

Jack stayed calm in the face of the storm. 'You once told me it was a job very few people could do. I believed you.'

'Then you were a damn fool. She would have hanged for her crimes. Perhaps you will take her place.'

Jack was too exhausted to care, even in the face of such a threat. 'You still need me.'

'What!' Ballard rose to his feet, his face twisted with pain and anger. 'I don't need you. Hired guns are ten-a-penny round here. You presume too damn much, Jack Lark.'

Jack smiled. 'Sit down. I'll have the guard summon the nearest surgeon. We both need him.'

'You damned viper.' Ballard snapped the angry retort before hissing in pain again. But he did as Jack suggested and sat back down heavily.

'That's better.' Jack nodded in approval. 'Now shut your muzzle and listen to what I have to say before we both bleed to death.'

He strode across the tent and picked up the pile of letters Sarah had been working on, turning to throw them clumsily on to Ballard's lap.

'Some light reading for when the surgeon is stitching you up. There will be nothing much of interest in them. Sarah *was* a spy. She passed on information, but she is not the one we were after.'

Ballard sank back on the travel cot. His anger was being driven out by the torment of his wound. 'Then who is?'

Jack faced his commanding officer. 'Fetherstone. Fetherstone is the spy.'

He let Ballard absorb the news. He was certain it would make sense. Ballard would understand, would be able to see how the naval officer's betrayal of his country fitted with everything that had happened. Fetherstone had fed them the information about the munshi. He had played them along the way and now he would be laughing at them as they rushed back to denounce a spy who was nothing more than a whore forced to do as she was told.

He had planned it all with meticulous care. Yet he had not calculated on the impact of an impostor.

Jack sat down and waited for the surgeon. He knew he would have one last task to perform. One job to do before he could move on to a new future.

For he was still the Devil's assassin, and he would have to kill a spy.

Chapter Forty-four

The alleyway stank. Without proper drainage, the townsfolk simply emptied their waste into the streets, which were left littered with the foul and the noxious, the noisome slicks just one of the pitfalls the unwary traveller faced in its barren streets.

Jack crouched in the shadows. He flexed his right hand, hissing at the painful spasm the motion sent searing up his arm. The surgeon had fixed him up, stitching together the tears in his flesh, but they had not had time to heal properly, the wounds still raw. His arm felt stiff and was prone to a dreadful cramp that rivalled the ache in his back, keeping him awake the previous night.

Not that he minded the lack of sleep. For he knew that if he closed his eyes, he would have to face the brutality of his nightmares. In his sleep, his carefully constructed mental barriers would break down and his mind would replay the battles he had fought. In the depths of the night he would see again the faces of the men he had killed, alongside the images of those he had lost.

He waited patiently in the dank alley. He could feel the

stitches that held his wound together pulling as he flexed his hand. He had been lucky. Sarah's pistol had lacked the power to kill him, even at such close range. If she had been armed with a modern revolver, Jack knew he would now be dead. He grimaced at the thought.

The British expeditionary force had made its way back to the main encampment outside Bushire. It had taken them two days, the exhausted redcoats struggling through the torrential rain that had barely stopped falling since the last gunshots of the battle had died away. It was a battered and bedraggled column that arrived back at the camp, but the redcoats marched with pride, their victory going a long way to dull the weariness. They had achieved much, and now they could recuperate and gather their strength ready for the next phase of the campaign.

But not all the men who had fought on the battlefield at Khoosh-Ab would be left to enjoy the short peace. For Jack had to complete his bitter task quickly and without delay now that the army had returned. The canker had to be rooted out and destroyed before it could do any more harm.

He picked at the wall of the house that backed on to the grim alley. The mud was soft and friable and he used a fingernail to prise away a tiny white shell that had been buried deep within it. He rolled the shell between his fingers, using it to unlock the muscles in his hand, releasing a little of the tension that he could not shake.

He heard footsteps and straightened up, dropping the shell to the ground and easing back into the gloom, hiding his profile in the darkness.

He watched as the figure carefully picked its way into the alley. The man he had summoned advanced cautiously, as if not trusting the shadows. It was exactly as Jack had planned.

'Sarah?'

Jack smiled. The man he had wanted to meet had taken the lure.

'Sarah, are you there?'

Jack heard the tetchy note in the hissed challenge. He closed his eyes and inhaled as deeply as his wounds would allow, summoning the strength he would need. Ballard had not forgiven him for letting Sarah Draper go free. He had allowed Jack to put his wild scheme into practice, giving his subordinate a final opportunity to seek redemption.

Jack stepped out of the shadows to stand in the meagre light that penetrated the gloom of the alleyway.

'Good evening, Commodore.'

The figure stopped abruptly. It was too dark for Jack to see the reaction on the creased and weather-beaten face, so he walked forward, revealing himself fully to the man who had been tricked into the meeting in the middle of the night.

'Expecting someone else?'

Fetherstone straightened up. 'Captain Fenris.'

The revolver was heavy in Jack's left hand. 'Sarah is not here. Your accomplice has fled the scene.'

The naval officer smiled. 'You tricked me into coming. And you come alone.' He sighed. 'That tells me you are here to kill me.'

Jack shook off the chill of the words. He had killed so many men, but never in cold blood. 'You are a spy. You knew the risks.' His voice was cold, emotionless. 'You know the penalty.'

Fetherstone laughed. 'Quite true, Jack.'

Jack started. 'How do you know my name?'

'It was in Ballard's papers. I rather suspect he left your identity in his documents as some kind of safeguard. Just in case you decided to do him in.' Fetherstone's eyes never once left Jack's face. He stared at him, watchful and calm. 'So now he unleashes his killer.' The naval officer shook his head, clearly affronted. 'Perhaps I underestimated him.'

'Perhaps you underestimated all of us.' Jack lifted the revolver.

Fetherstone saw the movement and straightened up; a final display of defiant courage. 'I think not.'

'A pity.' Jack felt the stirrings of anger. 'I think we could surprise you.'

Fetherstone laughed, his scorn revealed. 'You think the fact that you are a charlatan should surprise me. What a pathetic creature you are.'

'Better a fraud than a traitor.' Jack reacted to the scorn.

'You are a simple soul, Jack Lark. You cannot understand. You look at my actions and you see betrayal. Yet you know nothing. Nothing!' For the first time, Fetherstone's urbane charm cracked. 'Do not presume that a man like you can understand a man like me.'

'I understand a spy. I understand that men died as a result of your actions.'

Fetherstone shook his head. 'You understand nothing. What are the lives of a few soldiers? If they didn't die today, they would die tomorrow. They mean nothing.'

'They meant something to me.'

'How very touching, Jack. Is that what this is all about? Did I upset your fragile sensibilities? What an odd notion for a killer.' Fetherstone took a step closer to Jack, his face stretched with urgency as he tried to explain his actions. 'Can you truly not lift your gaze and see out of the gutter? You should try to think of a bigger world, one where the lives of a handful of redcoats mean little. Do you think Outram loses sleep over the men he lost? Do you think Wellington wept into his pillow thinking of the thousands who died carrying out his bloody orders?' The naval officer spoke with passion now. The revolver was forgotten. 'Great men cannot think of such things. They must do what they know to be right, and if there is a price to be paid, then so be it.'

'Is that what you are? A great man?' It was Jack's turn to be scornful.

'Perhaps. I don't expect you to understand. You have not seen the world as I have, or watched all those misbegotten fools who are allowed to govern and command when they couldn't even run a common whorehouse. We are a country that values the accident of birth over ability, and it is ruining us. These men fail us but are never held to account for their actions simply because they come from the right family. We are a nation of the blind. It is high time our eyes were opened.'

'And that is what you were doing? Opening our eyes?'

'We need to change, Jack.' Fetherstone spoke with intensity. 'Before it is too late. We need the best men to lead us, not just someone's bloody son and heir.'

'Men like you?' Jack's contempt was clear.

'Yes. Men like me. Men bold enough to challenge the status quo. Do you know how many times I have been passed over? How many times I have seen lesser men promoted? And why? Just because some damn admiral crooks his bloody finger, that's why. Merit means nothing in our world. Intelligence is sneered at. Ability is mocked. All that bloody matters is what family you come from.'

Jack heard the bitterness in Fetherstone's words. And he understood. He knew what it was to be denied a future by virtue of a low birth. Much of what Fetherstone was saying came close to Jack's own opinion of the world in which he served. But it was no excuse for betrayal. For Fetherstone was wrong. The lives of the men did matter. The redcoats might have marched with obedience, but they also marched with pride. They came from the lowest rungs of society, yet they were the ones prepared to fight and die for their country. For that they were owed so much more than their country deigned to give them. They did not deserve such scorn. They did not deserve death.

'You know you'll hang, don't you, Jack?' The commodore spoke more quickly now, a little of his sangfroid melting as he saw his death approaching in the barrel of Jack's unwavering gun. 'It's all in Ballard's papers. When you have done what he requires, you'll be hanged. He cannot allow you to live, do you really not see? It would be too messy. You would be a loose end. No intelligence officer likes loose ends.'

Jack narrowed his eyes. He ignored the words, focusing his attention on the feel of the trigger beneath his finger.

'Have you ever seen a man on the scaffold, Jack? I have. It's a terrible sight. Most piss themselves. Their final sorry act on this earth: to soil themselves to the catcalls of the crowd. Can you imagine what it feels like? The scratch of the rope as it twists round your neck. That final rush of terror as the floor drops away and you fall.'

Jack felt no emotion. He knew what he was and the future he faced. Fetherstone's words meant nothing.

'Then you kick. You cannot help it.' Fetherstone was speaking urgently now. 'You jerk and you thrash like a floundering fish as the last of your breath chokes in your throat. And then you die.'

He paused and looked at Jack, peering into the gloom to see if his words were having any effect.

'And then you die,' he repeated. 'Alone.' His voice rose in desperation.

Jack smiled. 'But not yet.'

He squeezed the trigger. The gun recoiled, the charge exploding under the hammer. The heavy bullet punched through Fetherstone's skull, ending his life in a shower of blood and bone. His body crumpled to the ground like a child's rag doll, arms and legs twisted, the life force snatched away.

Jack stared at the body for a long time. He kept his arm extended, aiming the revolver at the man he had been sent to kill, just in case he showed a final flicker of life.

But Fetherstone was dead. Jack had done his job. He had killed the spy.

'You can come out now.' He spoke into the shadows behind him.

Major Ballard, commander of the intelligence department, emerged from the darkness to stand at Jack's shoulder.

'That was a good shot.'

Jack grunted.

Ballard reached forward. His damaged arm was encased in a black silk sling and a thick bandage was wrapped around his midriff. His drawn features betrayed the pain of the twin wounds that he had received at the hand of Simon Montfort, yet still he managed to offer a thin-lipped smile. He clasped his free hand on to his subordinate's shoulder. 'It had to be done. I thank you.'

Jack said nothing. He shoved the revolver back into its holster and breathed out the lungful of air that he had been holding since he had fired the single, fatal shot.

'He was lying. I hope you know that.' Ballard patted Jack once before walking past him to stare at the corpse. 'I have no plans to have you killed.'

'He'd better have been lying. I'd come back and haunt you. I'd scare you shitless.'

Ballard chuckled softly. 'I'm going to miss you, Jack. Are you sure you won't reconsider? We have only won the first battle. The campaign is not yet done. We will have more work to do, you and I.'

Jack shook his head. 'No. I'm done.'

Ballard nodded. He looked down at the pathetic remains of the spymaster. 'Poor Fetherstone. I would never have believed that the old boy contained so much passion.' He sighed with what appeared to be genuine sadness. 'We will say he committed suicide. It is an ignoble end for a man like this.'

'Will anyone know the truth?'

Ballard furrowed his brow. 'You and I.' He paused, pondering the loose ends. 'Outram, certainly, and we should not forget Mrs Draper.' He shot Jack a disapproving glare but could not hold the expression for long. 'That is all. His secret will die with him. It's better that way.'

Jack nodded. He patted the heavy packet in the inside pocket of his hussar's dolman. It was his reward, the final legacy of his campaign. He might not have been awarded the medals he deserved, the public laurels presented to those officers who had fought with bravery. But he had earned something infinitely more precious. Ballard had made him the gift as recompense for all he had done. It was a reward worth so much more than any tawdry piece of tin.

He walked forward and offered his hand.

Ballard looked hard into his eyes. He slowly shook his head, as if unable to understand what he saw, before reaching forward and shaking Jack's hand.

'I rather think I will see you again, Jack Lark.' He smiled as he made his farewell.

Jack laughed. He felt the shackles of his imposition fall away. 'Not if I see you first.'

He nodded once and walked past his former commander. He had done what he had been ordered to do. And now he was free.

Epilogue

Jack stood on the quayside, looking warily at the city that awaited him. The fort loomed over the place just as he remembered, and if he tried hard, he could smell the olfactory horror that was the covered bazaar. It was his second visit to Bombay, and he had learnt his lesson. He would not waste any time there.

At least he would be in better surroundings than before. He waited patiently for the coach that would usher him into the serene and worldly comforts of the Hope Hall Family Hotel in Mazagon. Thanks to the valuables he had stolen all those weeks ago from Abdul at the Hotel Splendid, he could now afford to stay in comfort, far from the peril of midnight murderers.

For the first time, he would be able to register in his own name. Ballard's gift had been a set of freshly issued discharge papers. They vouched that the man carrying them had been allowed to leave the army honourably, freeing him from the ties of the Queen's service. Ballard had given Jack the one thing he had craved for so long.

He had given him back his name.

A fine carriage pulled up in a jangle of horse tackle and squeaking timbers. The door opened and a servant dressed in the fine livery of the Hope Hall hotel jumped from his perch at the rear and raced forward to lower the steps that would allow Jack to enter with dignity.

Jack stepped forward, but hesitated as he started up the steps. He remembered the last two occasions he had entered an unfamiliar carriage. He shivered at the memories. It was time to move on. He had to leave his past behind.

Jack snorted as he scanned the newspaper. The *Tehran Gazette* usually made for an interesting read, its news more current than even the most recently arrived *Times*. The paper's fanciful account of the Persian victory at Khoosh-Ab had made him laugh aloud. The description of the triumphant Persian forces pursuing a broken British army back to the coast read like an account from the distant past, the windy style presenting a clear picture of Persian valour and British cowardice. It was only as he read of the supposed destruction of several British squares that his laughter died, the memory of the slaughter at the real battle too fresh to be a matter for humour.

He read with sadness that the Persians claimed to have killed at least one thousand British soldiers. They also lauded the death of Major General Stalker. Jack had learnt of Stalker's death only three days previously. The man who had led the British to victory at Reshire, and then commanded the two divisions for most of the day at Khoosh-Ab, had killed himself, committing suicide shortly after Jack had left the army.

Jack could not begin to understand what could have driven Stalker to such an act at the moment of his greatest success. It was a sad end to a fine career. Despite everything Jack himself had endured, he had never considered the same solution for his own suffering. Even in his loneliest, darkest moments, he had not once thought of lifting his revolver to his head. He would never let himself give in.

He had experienced a different rush of emotion the following day when he had read that Commodore Fetherstone of the Indian navy had also killed himself. He could not help but wonder if anyone would suspect some skulduggery when they learned that two of the most senior British officers had killed themselves in such a short space of time after such a fabulous victory. Yet it was no longer his concern, and he forced the thoughts from his mind and sat back in his chair.

'Sahib, your carriage is ready.' A servant bowed low as he addressed the British officer, who stared into space, clearly lost in a different world.

Jack didn't hear the summons. His mind was replaying the moment when he had pulled the trigger and sent Fetherstone's corrupt soul to meet its maker. He saw the look in the spy-master's eyes as the trigger tightened under his finger, the last moments of the man's life etched into his soul.

'Sahib.'

The memory fled back into the recesses of his mind. He snapped the *Gazette* shut and tossed it to the floor, the only suitable resting place for a newspaper filled with such dross, then pulled himself to his feet, straightening his waistcoat as he stood up. It still felt awkward to be without a uniform, but at least he was no longer an impostor. The ticket on the Peninsular and Oriental steamer was made out in the name of one Jack Lark, Esquire. He had booked passage on the first ship out of Bombay, not wanting to risk staying a moment longer than was necessary in the city where he had lived as Arthur Fenris. The steamer was bound for Calcutta, where he would have to wait before he could board another P&O ship that would take him to Suez. From there he would travel overland to Cairo to pick up the last connection in his long journey. For Jack had decided it was time to return to the one place where he could be himself.

He was going home.

Historical Note

Perhaps the most astonishing fact about the campaign against the Shah of Persia is that even the British authorities seemed to forget about it so very quickly. Just fourteen years after the battle was fought, the Shah of Persia, Nasser al-Din Shah Qajar, was invited to visit Great Britain as a guest of Queen Victoria. During his visit he was appointed to the Order of the Garter, Britain's highest order of chivalry. Such was the fleeting nature of enemies in the days when the British Empire was at its height.

Outram's campaign was certainly a success. After the battle at Khoosh-Ab, he mounted an expedition further north, advancing up the Shatt al-Arab waterway before launching an attack on another Persian defensive position at Mohammerah. Despite the strength of the enemy position, Havelock's division captured it on 27 March with barely a casualty following a dreadfully effective naval bombardment. There was another skirmish on 1 April when the 64th Foot and the 78th Highlanders attacked a Persian force at Ahvaz, and then it was all over. The Shah asked for terms and within a year the Treaty of Paris was signed, ending further hostilities.

The treaty safeguarded the future of Herat and required the Shah to withdraw his troops. The British had fulfilled their objectives.

The Battle of Khoosh-Ab is largely ignored in the great histories of the time. Given that within months of the victory the Empire was thrown into complete disarray by the dreadful bloodletting that was the Indian Mutiny, this is hardly surprising. Yet at the time, it was John Bull's favourite type of military campaign. Not only did it provide a victorious demonstration of the power of Britain's army, but it was accomplished on a field of battle far from home and with a minimal cost in British lives.

The battle itself was largely as described in the novel. The British cavalry and the artillery did win the day without much help from the stoic British infantry. The efforts of the 3rd Bombay Light Cavalry were particularly striking. Their destruction of a battalion of trained infantrymen is one of the rare occasions when unsupported cavalry managed to best a fully formed square, and as such it is still lauded as one of the greatest feats of arms of its day.

However, as ever, the needs of the writer necessitated a few tweaks, for which I humbly apologise. Captain John Augustus Wood did lead the assault on the Dutch fort at Reshire, but he served in the ranks of the 20th Bombay Native Infantry and not in those of the 64th Foot. Captain Wood was awarded the Victoria Cross for his efforts, a decoration that was only just in its infancy but which conveyed, then as now, the extreme valour of the men to whom it was awarded.

More Victoria Crosses were won at Khoosh-Ab. The younger Moore did indeed leap into the Persian square, killing his horse and breaking his sword in the process. His brother, Ross, cut his way to his sibling's aid, but it was Lieutenant John Grant Malcolmson who fought at his side and offered

Moore a stirrup. Jack Lark stole Malcolmson's place, and for that I must again beg for forgiveness.

Major General Foster Stalker did commit suicide after the battle. There is something very wretched in the way this tragic event is mentioned in only a single, terse line in every history I have read of the campaign. It truly was a sad end for a man who had served his country so well in his long career.

Equally tragic was the suicide of Commander Richard Ethersey of the Indian navy just a few days later. Ethersey was very much the inspiration for Fetherstone, but there is absolutely no connection between the two. There was simply too much in the coincidence of the twin suicides for me to ignore, and I must quite rightly stand accused of stealing the history for my own ends.

The problem of spies dogging the expeditionary force was a genuine one. Major Ballard is based on the real head of the intelligence department, and the tale of his bold inspection of the Persian defences at Reshire is quite true. One of his roles was most certainly to root out the Persian spies who followed the army throughout the campaign. He was not without success, and the whole notion of the hunt for a spy was given life when I read of a Persian munshi who disappeared one night shortly before Khoosh-Ab. There is no evidence, however, that the Persian spies provided any great intelligence, and I fear I have made more of the situation than really occurred. The Persian commander retreated from Outram's rapid advance to Borãzjoon, but certainly there is nothing to indicate that this was the result of intelligence passed by any spy.

As might be expected for a battle and a campaign that have largely been forgotten, there are very few books that give more than a passing reference to it. I can, however, heartily recommend *Britain's Forgotten Wars*, by Ian Hernon. As ever, the Persian War is only given scant coverage, yet it is still a wonderful book for anyone looking to study the lesser-known battles of the British Empire. I would also highly recommend the grandly titled *Oriental Campaigns and European Furloughs*, by Colonel E. Maude. It never fails to excite me when I find a personal account of the period I am researching, and Colonel Maude is an enthusiastic writer who adds a wonderfully personal insight to the story.

Jack has now survived another campaign and has managed to secure the one thing he craves: his own name. With money in his pocket and a longing to see England, he is on his way home. But the British Empire is about to receive its greatest test, as the devil's wind blows through India, and Jack might not get his wish after all. For mutiny is in the air, and Jack Lark will surely have to fight for his country once again.

Acknowledgments

No book is ever the work of one person. To Dave Headley, my agent, I can only offer my most sincere thanks for his continued backing and for his tremendous support. Flora Rees, my editor, is owed a huge thank you for her tireless efforts to help me develop as a writer and for lifting my work to a quality it could never hope of reaching without her. The team at Headline help me enormously and I must thank Ben, Tom, and Darcy in particular for everything that they do. Most of all I thank my family. I could not do any of this without them.

Want to know where it all began for Jack Lark?

THE SCARLET THIEF

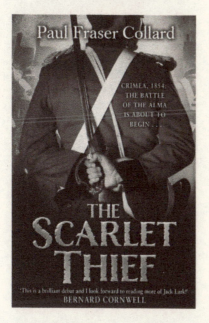

1854: The banks of the Alma River, Crimean Peninsula. The men of the King's Royal Fusiliers are in terrible trouble. Officer Jack Lark has to act immediately and decisively. His life and the success of the campaign depend on it. But does he have the mettle, the officer qualities that are the life blood of the British Army?

headline

You can also follow Jack Lark's adventures as

THE MAHARAJAH'S GENERAL

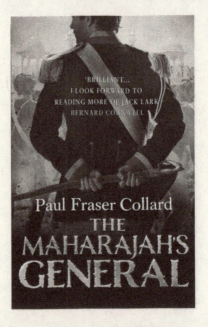

Jack Lark barely survived the Battle of the Alma. As the brutal fight raged, he discovered the true duty that came with the officer's commission he'd taken. He grasps a chance to prove himself a leader once more. Jack will travel to a new regiment in India, under a new name . . .

headline

And catch up with Jack as

THE LONE WARRIOR

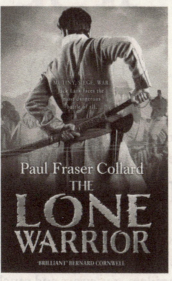

Bombay, 1857. India is simmering with discontent, and Jack Lark, honourably discharged from the British Army, aims to take the first ship back to England. But before he leaves, he cannot resist the adventure of helping a young woman escape imprisonment in a gaming house. He promises to escort Aamira home, but they arrive in Delhi just as the Indian Mutiny explodes.

As both sides commit horrific slaughter and the siege of Delhi begins, Jack realises that despite the danger he cannot stand by and watch. At heart, he is still a soldier . . .

headline